THE CHRISTENING

The Christening

DENISE NEUHAUS

faber and faber
LONDON · BOSTON

For my children, Max and Helene

First published in Great Britain in 1995
by Faber and Faber Limited
3 Queen Square London WC1N 3AU

Printed and bound in Great Britain by
Mackays of Chatham PLC, Chatham, Kent

A CIP record for this book
is available from the British Library
ISBN 0–571–17466–3

2 4 6 8 10 9 7 5 3 1

Acknowledgements

Thanks are due to the many people who helped me during the writing of this novel.

Margus Laidre, the Estonian ambassador to Sweden, provided a wealth of historical and personal information; Mats Stefansson of the Swedish diplomatic service discussed consular matters with me; Tove Nilsson helped with my children and answered persistent questions on a young woman's life in Sweden; Krista Lukki helped me through the frantic finish. As always, thanks to Louise Doughty for ruthless editing and moral support, and to Emma Platt for her determination to get it right.

I am grateful to Dr Olev Lugus, Director of the Institute of Economics at the Estonian Academy of Sciences, for enlightening conversations and material on Soviet and post-Soviet economics, and to Dr Aili Kelam, also at the Academy of Sciences, for important sociological background on Estonian education and family life.

Viktor Siilats at EVTV provided invaluable personal experience of the events leading to independence. For background on Soviet and Swedish journalism, Torgny Hinnemo at *Svenska Dagbladet* and Ulo Ignats of *Eesti Päävaleht* were very helpful.

Thanks to Andrei Zhgomov of Dvigatel and to Professor Lipmaa of the Lipmaa Institute for an eloquent historical overview. Riivo Sinijärv, the Estonian ambassador to Great Britain, and Lilika Sinijärv made many of my meetings in Estonia possible, and I thank them for their indispensable efforts.

I could not have written this novel without my husband, Henrik Neuhaus, who has translated and interpreted for me in two cultures and languages and acted as a literary critic, economics consultant and auditor of countless facts. My great thanks go also to our family: my sister-in-law, Anna Neuhaus, and my parents-in-law, Hinrek and Tiina Neuhaus, through whom I have learned about Estonian culture.

My very great thanks to our relations in Estonia: to Mai Taska for her powerful account of being deported to Kirov in the 1940s and to Jaak and Kai Innos for their many kindnesses; to Andres and Taime Nurmiste, who have become good friends and have provided me with considerable material, and to Ene Tomberg, who has done so much. My visits to Estonia, both as Estonian SSR and as the Republic, were made in difficult times; I will always be grateful to our friends for their generous hospitality.

I have used some of the names of my Estonian friends for characters in this novel, chosen for their suitability and ease of pronunciation, and not of course to imply any resemblance with my fictional characters. I have tried to use historical facts as accurately as possible; some events have been unavoidably altered in creating this work of fiction.

v

Family Tree
Jakobson

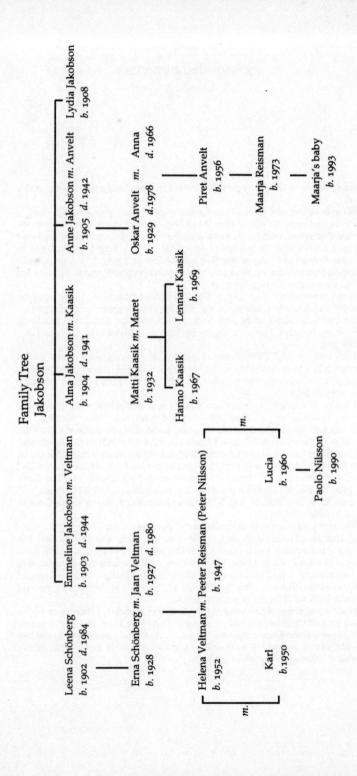

PART 1

October 1973

Ten months after her birth, Piret's daughter was christened in a secret ceremony at a derelict country church outside Tallinn. Piret was not invited.

Piret's second cousin Helena, who was twenty-one and married, had taken the baby to raise as her own. Helena had luxuriant blonde hair; clear green eyes; a beautiful, angular face. She had broad shoulders on which even shabby Soviet clothes hung like a model's. She had studied English and German. Her father was a doctor and her mother a lecturer.

Piret, on the other hand, was short, dark, unattractive. Her father worked in a factory and her mother was dead. She was seventeen; she was not married. Their very names summed up all that separated them: Helena sounded like a cool summer wind through the pine forest; Piret was the ugliest name in the Estonian language.

When she was five months pregnant, Piret wrote to her lover, asking him to come to see her. Piret sat on the lumpy brown sofa. Paavo sat on a chair, looking at Piret as though she were a problem in which he had no particular interest. He said, 'I suppose it's too late for an abortion?'

She shrugged and then nodded, although she did not know. She knew almost nothing about pregnancy; she had told no one until now.

Paavo stood up and put on his coat. 'Well, Piret, I wish you luck.'

She was not surprised when it was decided that Helena would have the baby. Erna and Jaan, Helena's parents, were used to deciding things for them. Piret's father shrugged his shoulders and said, 'It seems the best solution.'

Piret moved in with her Aunt Lydia, who lived in the country.

She spent the remaining four months of her pregnancy help-ing with chores and waiting to give birth. She felt as if her body belonged to someone else. Even when the baby moved inside, she felt like a cocoon, housing a parasitic being whose temporary shelter was her body. She was, from Maarja's con-ception, her foster mother.

Towards the end she was too large to do much work. She rose late and sat on the sofa, looking out at the wintry lake and the tall pines along the shore, sheltered patches of hardened snow, the shuttered summer cottages and abandoned gardens, the dark wooden piers impaling a fragile skin of ice.

She ate little; her stomach was compressed under the weight of the baby. She could not think about anything beyond the ordeal that awaited her. She could not imagine her body as her own again or what she would do when the baby was gone. She waited every day, quiet, frightened, ashamed. A pregnant woman was honoured unless she was an unmarried girl; then she was hidden away, an embarrassment to herself and her family.

Piret's mother had died when Piret was ten, of a cancer, two months after it was diagnosed. Towards the end Piret had not been allowed to see her. 'It is better,' her father told her. 'You will remember her as she wanted to be remembered.'

The funeral was held at Kaarli kirik. Afterwards Piret and her father went home. Her father took out the pots from under the gas stove. Piret peeled potatoes and her father fried them in a glistening black skillet. They chopped sausage and cucumber and put the cabbage on to boil. Afterwards he changed into his tattered blue dressing gown, and sat down on the sofa to drink quietly and decorously from a bottle of vodka lodged between his legs.

Her life did not change. She still took the tram every day to Viktor Kingiseppa School No 20. She bought potatoes and onions on the way home. She went through the board-ed doors of the house on Pärnu Street and up the stairs which smelled of cooking and piss.

She knew she would work in a factory after she finished

school. She had visited the paper factory where her father worked and seen reams of paper shooting through clamorous machines, wooden spools taller than a man, lines of women filling boxes with grey speckled sheets.

Piret remembered as a child her teachers talking of 'the radiant future', meaning that every citizen had a contribution to make, and that this would be given to each one, like a gift. Contribution meant work. She had always known this. She had been an Octoberist until she was ten: *only those who love to work are called Octoberists.*

Throughout her childhood Piret's family had talked about life before the war, before the Russians, before communism. Her parents wanted her to know that their life had been better, that the shops had been full of shoes and coffee, bolts of linen and cotton, fruit, meat, chocolate. Women had gone shopping downtown in hats and gloves, read fashion magazines from Germany and Sweden, had maids to clean their houses. Families brought in eggs and butter and vegetables from their country cottages and farms.

She had seen photographs of family picnics on Lake Peipsi: women and men in black swimming costumes, naked children playing on the rocks. Now the shores of the lake smelled like sewage and were lapped by grey foamy waves. The only people who swam in it were Russians, who did not know better.

Piret knew from school that her family's memories were of the days of bourgeois fascism. For the rest of her life she would think of ladies in hats and gloves taking the tram to the old town to shop as bourgeois fascism. She knew she must not tell anyone this.

She also understood that she must not tell her parents that she liked the blue serge uniform and taffeta hair bow she wore to school every day. She liked the Octoberists' 'socially useful activities', which meant decorating the school in December with pictures of Grandfather Frost and his elves.

She knew her parents would be horrified if they discovered that the word 'communism', which to them meant something evil, was to her shelter, peace. She knew she must never reveal

5

the profound calmness she felt upon hearing her teacher quote Lenin's hope for Soviet youth: 'The moral code of the builders of communism includes conscientious labour for the good of society, collectivism, moral purity, concern for children, and an uncompromising attitude to injustice and parasitism.' She loved the very words, their sound and shape: *uncompromising conscientious concern.*

She carried her crêpe-paper flowers and small red flag on May Day. She walked in her school's section of the October parade, holding her own card with one large letter which helped to form the slogan, Long Live the Estonian Communist Party. She understood that she must always hide from her family her wish to belong, her longing to find her contribution.

She tried to picture herself as an adult, alongside the other aproned women in her father's factory, her hair in a kerchief. She would be the best stacker of the lot. The foreman would notice her. She would invent a new method of production, working late into the night under the single bulb hanging over her father's kitchen table.

One day she would slip her plans to the foreman, who would look at the paper and glance at her with surprise and admiration. She would gaze back at him with the guileless eyes of genius. The plant manager would come personally and escort her to the office. He would sit her down and say, 'Young lady, your talents are being wasted.'

At school her class read Chekhov and Gogol and Tolstoy. They read excerpts from *War and Peace.* She wished she was like Natasha, who found happiness with Pierre despite her absent-mindedness and slovenly housekeeping. Piret knew she was not practical. Her potatoes were soggy and her darning clumsy. She could not make a bed properly. She could not eat soup without splattering her last clean blouse.

She longed to be conscientious, useful, talented. She knew she never would be, and yet she also knew she could never be like Natasha, who seemed to be a real woman, a wife who could believe in her husband's work without understanding it.

When she met Paavo, she understood immediately that he

6

was one of the useful ones, the ones with radiant futures. Paavo had a talent for the physical world; his mind was clear and objective. He understood electricity and combustion engines and oxidization and why electrons had orbits.

He was tall and thin, with spiky brown hair and a gaunt face. Piret loved his hard brown eyes, and the way he hesitated before speaking, the exactness of his words. He handled his bicycle with the same care he took with his books. He knew what he would be doing this year and the next, and in five years. He would not, Piret saw, make any mistakes.

Piret had only vague ideas, feelings she could not articulate. She thought she could do something, but she did not know what that might be. She went to bed with Paavo because he wanted to and because it was all she had to give.

It was Lydia who told Piret about the christening.

They were standing at the stove together, bottling cranberries. Piret could feel Lydia hesitate before speaking and glanced over. Piret could not remember a time when Lydia did not look old. Her nose was the texture of wrinkled fruit and her cheeks were a tangle of fine burgundy lines. Her hair was grizzled, almost colourless. Perhaps it had once been blonde.

Piret saw at once that what Lydia had to say was about the baby. She knew that expression well: she wanted to protect Piret, but she also wanted to hurt Helena.

Matti had told Lydia, in his ponderous, troubled way. Matti Kaasik was a soft bear of a man, all heart, enormous, with strong, clever hands. He could mend anything. He had helped Lydia lay the foundations for her house and dig the privy. He had built the pump that supplied the house with water from the lake.

Piret had gone down the road with a basket of jars to the co-operative, the *kolhoz*, to buy milk. Matti and Lydia were chopping wood; he stopped chopping, leaned on his axe and said, 'Helena's to come back with the baby.' He even told her the time and place: dusk, Jaani kirik, outside Tallinn.

Piret's body still bore the signs of childbirth. Her stomach

7

sagged and her nipples were large and brown; marbled purple scars radiated out from them. There were hours of pain, she remembered that more than anything. She remembered looking at Lydia in terror and appeal, reaching for Lydia's hands. The pain seemed to have a life of its own, as though coming from deep inside, pushing its way out in a desperate howl. She had fantasies that a monster would emerge from between her legs. It would come out and attack her; it would bite her breasts off.

Finally there was the cessation of pain and the baby was passing through. She felt the baby's head between her thighs and her body still inside. Jaan was gone and they were alone; Piret could hear Lydia's voice, but not understand her words.

Then Jaan came back, carrying a sheet. She closed her eyes and Lydia told her to push one more time. Jaan began to argue with Lydia and Piret pushed feebly as the baby slithered out. She felt Jaan's hands between her legs, wrapping the baby in the sheet; she heard the sound of metal. The baby began to wail.

Piret lay exhausted, unable to move. She wondered vaguely what would happen next. A door closed; the wailing grew more distant. Then came the jubilation, the false euphoria of the birth, followed by nothing, the crush of nothing. She heard the splashing of water, and Lydia began to wash her with a rough cloth.

A few weeks later Piret and Lydia heard the news. Jaan and Erna had obtained exit visas for themselves, Helena and her husband Peeter and, of course, Maarja. They were leaving Estonia. They were taking Maarja and emigrating to rich, free Sweden.

When Lydia finished speaking and Piret did not reply, she added brutally, 'Go if you want. It's your heartache.'

Piret was silent, stirring absently. Lydia had just come in with another basket of berries from the garden. She fell quiet and pretended to count the jars. Then she snorted. 'I can just hear her now, talking about it. A christening back home. Kodumaa.'

8

They both laughed. *Kodumaa* was the name of the Soviet Estonian cultural newspaper. It meant Homeland. It was full of articles nobody believed about Soviet technological superiority, the flowering of Estonian culture under communism, new housing developments, each flat with its own toilet and bath, the provision of modern sports facilities for Estonian athletes.

Lydia reached down for another piece of wood and pushed it into the stove. She had always disliked Helena. Helena was too emotional for Lydia's taste; her schoolgirl passions were earnest and indiscriminate; she lacked scepticism. She believed whatever she was told; she exhibited herself.

By the age of six, Helena had memorized the list of the virtues of collectivists: honesty, kindness, devotion to principle, steadfastness of character. At ten she became a Young Pioneer, her red tie a neat knot, her badge (Always Ready!) pinned alongside, fervently swearing *to love the Soviet motherland and to learn and struggle as the great Lenin bade her.*

Lydia said, 'If she loves the place so much, why doesn't she come back and live here? Life is better now. There is always sausage.'

Piret thought: The only reason you wouldn't leave is that you are old.

Lydia glanced sharply at her, as if reading her mind. She opened the back door to go out to the privy. 'You do what you want,' she said.

'I will.' Piret picked up the tongs, lifted a jar out of the boiling water, drained it and began to fill it with cranberries. Lydia delayed at the door, putting on her outdoor shoes, deciding at the last minute to shake out the doormat. She stepped outside, still holding the door. Then she walked down the path.

2

Helena stood inside the boat, watching the harbour as they glided closer to Estonian soil. Along the pier stood rusty cranes, all idle. The pier itself was of black, splintered wood, against which aged tugboats pitched. The dirty, foamy water splashed against the posts. Piles of coal were heaped against the shoreline and in the distance she could see relentless columns of smoke flowing from blackened stacks.

Beyond the gloom of the port the sun was rising and Helena could see the old town over the cranes: the steeples of St Olaf and St Nicholas; the tower of the Gothic town hall, Raekoda; the stone towers of the medieval city wall, Toompea. Except for the red and gold bulbs of the Russian Orthodox church and the occasional block of Soviet-built flats, the view was of an austere Nordic city, fortified by the solid houses of Protestant merchants.

As she drew closer, Helena felt all the strangeness of returning to a home which was not home, the betrayal of memory, the jolt of seeing that home was small, provincial and decaying. She thought of leaving Stockholm, gliding through the exquisite archipelago, with its tiny green islands, neatly moored sail-boats, iron red wooden cottages, and everywhere, on houses, boats, ferries, the bright blue and yellow flag. Sweden: clean, beautiful, safe.

She had walked around the enormous ship, sleek and white, with restaurants and bars; a dance floor and casino; a pool and sauna. The cabins were neat and trim and stocked with rolls of toilet paper, bottles of shampoo and small soaps. The sheets and pillow-cases were thick and starched stiff; the beds had been folded down and tied in place with buckled straps.

Then in Helsinki she boarded the *Georg Ots* to Tallinn, and immediately felt less sure of herself. The red hammer and sickle on the smoke-stack seemed more menacing than she remembered. It was, like all things Soviet, stark, worn, dirty.

She had distracted herself during the journey across the Gulf of Finland with the game of identifying passengers. She started with the young Swedish couples with backpacks, blond and confident, strolling about the deck. She observed their innocence with envy and dislike. She knew the type: they had decided against Inter-railing in Germany and France; they wanted an unusual, adventurous trip. They would spend a day or two in Tallinn and go on by train to Leningrad or Riga. They would be able to tell their friends they had been behind the Iron Curtain.

The Finns were easily distinguished from the Swedes by their more Eastern faces, their guarded manners. They did not annoy Helena as the Swedes did; they were not naïve. Like Estonians, they were originally steppe people and their language Fenno-Ugrian; they too had lived next to and fought the Bear for long enough to know that it was large and dangerous.

Inside the boat were small clusters of older, working-class Finns, intent on a weekend of cheap drinking. They gathered around the portholes on either side, guarding their clusters of plastic chairs. They smoked and sang drinking songs, clutching plastic bags filled with tax-free vodka, Finnish chocolates, American cigarettes.

Helena also saw privileged Soviets, returning from official trips. Both Russian and Estonian, and the odd Latvian, they looked nervous and greedy. They wore cheap shoes, thin brown overcoats; their plastic bags bulged with coffee, soap, sugar, butter, cigarettes.

Finally there were ones like her, cowed, skittish; the expatriates, the refugees, not yet Swedish, and still Soviet citizens. She would never be a Swede, but she would some day be Swedish, and own the black vinyl passport stamped with the three crown symbol: Sverige Pass.

From the gangway, she could hear a voice repeat in yet another language that photographs of the harbour and customs building were forbidden. She looked around discreetly; behind each gate stood an armed soldier in a grey uniform trimmed in red. Beyond, where luggage was inspected, more soldiers loitered, chatting now and again, their carbines slung over their shoulders. She saw at a glance that, except for one Mongolian face, they were all Russian.

She had been determined to have the baby christened in Estonia. Her parents and Peeter had tried to dissuade her. But she was adamant: Maarja was Estonian; theirs was an Estonian family. Did that mean nothing to them? Did they want to turn their backs on their homeland?

She tried to forget now about Peeter's glowering face; he had refused to take her to the harbour. Her mother had looked worried; her father grim and powerless. He knew he could not stop her.

Helena knew there was a risk. The Soviets were particularly hostile at the moment to Sweden and to the Baltic republics. The year before the Kremlin had refused a visa to the Swedish academician who was to deliver Solzhenitsyn's Nobel Prize. Soon afterwards a Lithuanian worker had immolated himself to protest at the Soviet occupation of his country. Demonstrations for independence followed, which were quickly suppressed.

Nevertheless she made up her mind to go. There was no reason they could concoct to detain her. The visas, and her story, were in order. But even so her hands trembled visibly as she shifted the baby on to her other shoulder and handed over the two dark-red CCCP passports.

The dark young Russian behind the window looked at the passports and then up at her resentfully. He opened her passport, glanced at it and announced, 'You have emigrated.'

She felt the blood drain from her face. Peeter and her parents had been right; this was madness. She wanted to turn and run back to the safety of the boat. She glanced around, half-expecting two suited men backed by soldiers to appear from behind the gate to escort her and Maarja away.

She looked back at the Russian. He was about twenty years

12

old. His skin was pale and tender. The black fur ear-flaps on his hat were pushed up. A red star sat pointedly at the front of the hat, over his forehead. The gold buttons on his jacket were stamped with stars. He seemed to be covered with stars. He looked up at her coldly.

She did not reply, but nodded slightly. He wrote something down as he flipped through the pages of the passport.

'For what reason have you returned?'

She did not dare speak Estonian. She said barely audibly, in her unpractised Russian, 'Family. To visit family.'

He frowned and wrote. 'Show me the baby.'

She turned and he glanced from the second passport's photograph to the sleeping child's face several times. Then he slammed his stamp down, tore off the perforated part of the visas and attached them to the landing cards. He tossed the passports on to the counter without looking up.

She pushed through the gate and queued at Customs. An official handed her the form, which was in Russian, Estonian and English. She was to write down all the jewellery, money, gold, gifts, guns, explosives, foodstuffs, airline tickets, cameras, film, electronics, microphones, batteries, stamps and publications she had brought with her.

She filled it out and passed on to another official, who read the form, opened her luggage, made a cursory search and waved her through. Throughout this Maarja slept, stirring only slightly when Helena shifted her in order to close her bags and place them on the rickety trolley she had been carefully guarding.

Helena pushed through the final gate and paused, scanning the crowd. How strange they looked to her now, after only a year. What was it that made Soviet Estonians look so poor, she wondered. She had never thought of herself as poor; that was Africa. Estonia was occupied, but it was Europe: industrialized and educated.

Now she understood that, despite these claims, her compatriots were indeed poor. The women's legs were bare and unshaven; two stood arm in arm, one in a pink floral skirt and

13

orange striped jacket, a dispute of curtain materials; the other wore a dull brown synthetic dress with large white ric-rac braid stitched along the hem. The men wore shapeless suits and nylon shirts; a few carried tattered plastic shopping bags.

They stood in groups, waiting for friends and family, the children holding small cornflower bouquets, the stems mashed into twists of tin foil. The children were slight and quiet, with the thin hair of the poorly nourished. The faces of the adults were stoic; they inspected Helena's dress and shoes with the same incredulity she had once felt towards visitors from that other wonderful, mysterious place: the West.

She had another moment of pure regret. She did not want to see this, the grey poverty, the grim faces. She wanted to flee quickly with her child back to Stockholm, where everyone was clean and healthy and babies were fat and their clothes were sky-blue and lemon-yellow and the shops were full of oranges, bacon and steak, sausages; electric food blenders and coffee-makers. She had wept the first time she went shopping, right in the middle of Åhléns.

She should not have come. She should have left all this behind for ever; this trip could only end badly. It was wrong to leave, only to return to see the misery she had left. She saw that she must turn her back on her old life in order to accept the new one. She could not live with her comfort and freedom if she felt others' need and deprivation constantly reproaching her.

But then Matti's face emerged from the crowd and she forced herself to smile and move towards him. He rushed forward, held out his arms and called, 'Helena!' He gathered her and the baby in his arms and she hugged him back, knowing that she now must go through with it. The visit would be over in a matter of days, she reminded herself; then she would return to Sweden.

3

Piret left the house at midday and walked the two kilometres to the bus stop, where she waited at the roadside for the dust-encrusted country bus. She sat next to a window for the hour-long journey, listening to the shriek of gears, watching the quiet landscape turn from farmland and forest into suburb and then into bustling city.

The outskirts of Tallinn were an odd combination of massive blocks of grey flats interspersed with pre-war neighbourhoods of small wooden bungalows with shuttered windows and fenced gardens on tree-lined streets. The houses were now peeling and their porches and shutters needed repairs, but in each garden vegetables grew in neat rows and laundry had been hung out to dry.

Piret had risen at six, revived the fire and, still in her dressing gown, collected the eggs, brought in wood, watered the vegetables. Then she went to the berry grove, netted to keep out birds. Above her, branches held up the net ceiling against the pink morning sky. Inside was sheltered, clean, quiet. She collected the last of the raspberries and let them fall from her hand gently into the bucket.

Lydia had built her house, with help from Matti, of timber she had chopped from a nearby wood and split and cured board by board. She had originally built one room; and cooked under a lean-to. In 1950 she had built the kitchen on and added a bedroom, sauna and balcony.

Piret dressed and then ate her breakfast on the balcony: the raspberries in fermented milk, tea, rye bread, cheese, cucumber. The lake was very still; steam rose gently upwards and the autumn air was brittle with the coming cold.

In the spring, near Lydia's pier and rowing boat, a colony of white water-lilies, large and nearly flat with pointed petals, would appear; at the opposite end of the lake, just visible from the balcony, would grow a nearly identical group of yellow water-lilies. Nobody knew why Lydia's were white and the opposite shore's yellow; it had always been that way.

Many of the houses bordering the lake were now party members' country cottages. Lydia had built her house long before the expanding city and better roads had made this lake so desirable. She was one of the first and one of the few year-round residents: reasons which made her difficult to evict.

Piret washed her breakfast dishes. Lydia awoke and went to wash. When Piret was ready to leave, she saw that Lydia had taken the boat out. Piret found her bag and left, closing the door gently behind her.

She got off at the bus station and went through the back streets, passing men and women walking to market with their baskets and plastic bags. She passed rows of dilapidated wooden houses and blocks of flats, two drunks arguing, a family of cats cleaning themselves languidly in the morning sun.

She came to Kaubamaja, Tallinn's main department store. She had stuffed in her handbag the two net shopping bags she always carried. Shopping was an arbitrary business, and Piret would never waste a trip to town without looking for light bulbs or toothpaste or socks or toilet paper or a bit of meat.

Kaubamaja was her first perfunctory stop, known for its large inventory of the inferior and unnecessary: Estonian folk costumes; machine-tooled leather key holders; nested Russian dolls, fat and rosy-cheeked; Russian classical records; plastic lace tablecloths; Soviet flags.

Piret quickly toured the three floors. She glanced in the glass cases in the jewellery section and saw that they were empty but for a few Lithuanian watches. She passed another case without stopping; it was filled with pins: CCCP rockets, red stars, heads of Lenin, Stalin, Brezhnev.

She briefly surveyed the women's clothing department, empty but for a few mink hats in a locked glass case, a half-dozen vinyl sandals in baby blue and a row of hospital-white polyester jackets with brown plastic buttons. On her way out she passed a partitioned section, fully stocked, selling military uniforms, shoes, belts and overcoats.

She went down the stairs and back out to the street. She walked along Lenin Avenue, past the theatre and Victory Square towards the old town, up the narrow stone streets to Raekoja plats.

Within two hours she had been through more than a dozen shops and had almost filled her two bags. A woman in a flower shop had sold her two greenish lemons and a small envelope of cinnamon imported from Armenian friends. She had bought a box of tea and a plastic bag of uncleaned raisins from Georgia at a greengrocer's, which had nothing else that day but a crate of onions and a few cabbages.

In a Russian store she found two candles, a box of matches and a roll of toilet paper. She had queued for thirty minutes at a street kiosk with men smelling of black tobacco and other women who had also seen the cans of Swedish deodorant alongside the magazines and cigarettes in the kiosk window. Flushed with success, she found a *kohvik* and treated herself to a sandwich of herring and black bread and sweet, hot tea.

Afterwards she stopped at the Raamatu kauplus near St Nicholas's and leaned against the counter, examining the books and posters. The two women attendants talked at one end. Piret tapped on the counter several times and one of the women plodded slowly towards her. Piret pointed to a copy of *Eesti Naine* – Estonian Woman; the woman wrote out the chit. Piret queued at the cash register and paid. Then she returned to the counter, waited again to catch the woman's attention and exchanged the receipt for the magazine.

She still had time and decided to walk to Toompea, the city's walled fortress, and then down to Kaarli kirik. Piret had not been to the church since her mother's funeral. It would be locked now; there were no services excepting the odd funeral or wedding, depending on the fluctuations of official policy. Piret wondered what her mother would have said about the baby. She had a vague feeling that her mother would not have allowed Helena to have the child, but this idea did not take hold and quickly evaporated.

Returning to the bus station, she could see the Viru Hotel, an enormous box of black and grey fronted by a black metallic canopy. Inside was a hard-currency shop which stocked meat, chocolate, Levis, toilet paper. Piret had never seen it: the only locals the doormen let in were Russian prostitutes.

Piret tried to imagine Maarja's face, which she had never seen; when she thought of the baby a miniature version of Helena always appeared in her mind.

But of course she herself had created Maarja, with Paavo. Maarja could not possibly look like Helena, Piret reminded herself. Perhaps she looked like Paavo. Piret hoped so; if she could give the child something, it would be the gift of looking like someone else.

Piret remembered Paavo's thin face above her, his eyes closed, his concentration, her loneliness at the thought of losing him. She had always known she would lose him. He was raw material, a boy who would go on to study, have a profession, marry an educated woman. Her own life Piret saw as formed, a stunted maturity; she was already decaying. She was not surprised at finding herself pregnant; she knew her life was effectively finished.

Paavo's parents' flat was at the top of six flights of dark stairwell. His father was a skilled worker, a tram mechanic, and as such had a better flat than even Helena's father; and of course better than her own: Piret's father was mere lumpen proletariat. He drank, was frequently absent with illness, and too lazy to better himself at night school. He was given the worst shifts and the lowest jobs.

Paavo's family had two bedrooms and a sitting room, kitchen and bathroom. Paavo's father had made kitchen cupboards and a small table that folded against the kitchen wall when it was not in use. He had rigged a shower in the bathroom out of some tubing and scrap metal. The wooden floors had been planed and painted; shelves by the front door held their shoes and boots.

Excepting Matti's, Piret had never seen a flat so meticulously ordered. Her father's mostly Russian neighbours lived in squalor: rusting pipes, decomposing wallpaper. She had always been told how filthy Russians were, but at Paavo's all she could think of was her own flat, the stack of blackened pots, the dripping kitchen tap, the lumps of hard green Russian soap coagulating on a shelf above, the bottles and papers stacked next to the sofa, the smell of unwashed clothes that she had lived with since her mother's death.

Paavo and his brother slept in the larger bedroom. They each had a bed covered with a brown bedspread, and each a desk and a bookshelf; Paavo's books were about physics and engineering. Piret met him at the flat after school; they would climb almost immediately into bed, under the covers, because it was always cold.

The bus came and Piret heaved herself up, gathered her packages and boarded. Once the bus left Tallinn, pine forest flanked the highway. From time to time she could see sand dunes littered with pine needles, and glimpses of the sea through the trees. The bus stopped every few kilometres at an unmarked brick shelter. They were passed by Ladas and Russian flat-bed trucks and once by a black party car, its blue light flashing importantly.

She knew of Jaani kirik, which was one of the oldest churches in the country. She saw it from the bus stop, off the main road, set at the end of an unpaved path and sheltered from view by a grove of neglected trees and an overgrown cemetery. Its paint was peeling and the steeple was damaged. Many of the window-panes were cracked and covered by latticed wire. It was well chosen for a secret christening.

It was nearly dusk and she wondered if she was too late. She trudged up the path with her bags, sweating, strands of hair falling in her face. The remaining light played tricks with the windows, making it difficult to see whether there was any activity inside, which was exactly why this time had been chosen. She put her bags down and tried the front doors: they were locked. She picked everything up again and walked around, through the cemetery, looking for another entrance.

She found a side door and pushed it open. An old lady sat at a desk, writing on what Piret could see was a hand-made christening certificate. The woman looked up in some alarm, until Piret spoke to her in Estonian. She pointed to the interior of the building and said, 'I am one of the family.'

The old lady replied, 'They have already begun,' and led her through the door that the priests had once used.

They stepped into near dark. Then she saw them at the altar, before a half-circle of frayed green cushions. The wooden frame that once held the arms of a congregation at communion was now gone.

Helena faced the priest, who stood above her at the altar in a smudged ivory alb. He held a frayed prayer book. He was a young, pudgy man, with white, bad skin. Matti and his wife Maret were behind her. Next to Helena, holding the baby, was an older woman, whom Piret immediately recognized from television as someone in the government.

Piret had two simultaneous thoughts. Why would this fat young man choose such a useless and dangerous hobby as the priesthood? And why would a politician, a well-known woman, so well connected, be at this christening? She was, it was obvious, Maarja's godmother.

The priest stopped speaking the moment Piret appeared. Helena turned. They all stared at her. For a few seconds nobody spoke. Piret watched Helena's shocked face slowly recover. Then Helena said, with an anxious smile, 'Piret, how nice of you to come.' Piret felt bile rise in her mouth.

'We would have asked you,' Helena went on, nervous and careful, 'only we did not know where you were.'

Piret grew hot with indignation at this lie and looked at Matti, who glanced around uncomfortably. She turned again to Helena. 'I wanted to see the baby.'

'Of course,' Helena said, like a gracious hostess soothing a drunken and recalcitrant guest. But the godmother was in no mood to humour Piret. She pulled the child closer to her, and Piret saw at once how she must look to them: they thought she

20

was dangerous. The strangeness of this idea stopped her for a moment. She had not wanted Maarja, had given her away without a second's hesitation, and yet she had never, once there was no longer the possibility of abortion, thought of hurting her.

Piret approached the godmother and Maarja, who was gazing around the church, curious, oblivious. Piret stared at her child for several minutes, she was so relieved by Maarja's beauty. Maarja looked nothing like her: she had Paavo's large eyes and angular cheekbones. At the top of her beautifully formed head was a crest of rich brown hair, thick and curly. Her skin was perfectly smooth; her face serene. For a moment Piret was completely absorbed by the sight of her child and an involuntary thought formed: *Please let her never be belittled or demeaned. Let her never be beaten down.*

She took a step closer to Maarja and the entire party tensed. She looked at the child again for a few seconds and then back at the others. She realized that if she pulled out a knife they would not be surprised. They thought she was capable of anything. She was at once appalled and curious to know what they saw in her: she had never thought of herself as having any power.

They were thinking that she wanted the child back. Even her father had believed she might want the child. He had tried to persuade her that giving the baby to Helena was the best decision. *The child will grow up with a mother and father,* her father had told her. *You should be glad. You should be grateful.*

She had not needed persuading. She had wanted to forget about Maarja. And yet here she was at the church. There were scars on her breasts and tears in her body that proved she had produced this child. She looked at Maarja and knew that she was hers; she could never relegate the memory of that winter night, the hours of pain, the sound of Maarja's diminishing cries, to a few scars; set her aside as an insignificant mistake.

And yet she still hoped that Maarja was not, after all, hers: a product of her own body and soul; although she had given birth to her, Piret hoped that this baby was created out of more

21

than the poor material that was herself, that this baby was somehow, after all, not made of her. This was why she had come: to see and believe that this child was not hers, that she did not have to feel anything, that the rage and pain that seemed to lodge in her was not, after all, anything.

She looked at Maarja again. Maarja Elisabet was Helena's choice. They had never asked Piret about the baby's name; and Piret never thought to ask for the privilege of naming her. The baby had never been hers, was no longer hers. Any feeling she had for her she saw now was a fantasy, a vestige of the pain of that night. All Piret had to give the baby was the hope that she would not be like her mother; this shabby wish, her own self-ish pain, the scars: Piret saw these as a poor claim to being a mother.

She stepped back. She willed this terrible longing away and assembled all her forces; and in seeking to fill her loss Piret found herself able to form one clear thought: Maarja was Helena's.

Piret's scars would fade, her body would return to normal. She would forget about the night of Lydia's hands, Jaan, the sound of metal, the brush of cotton sheeting between her legs; she would heal. She would dismiss from her mind the sight of Maarja's small head, the crest of wavy hair, the curve of her ears, her curious, large eyes. Piret took one last look at Helena's child, turned around and walked out.

4

Lydia waited for the sound of Piret's footsteps down the gravel path. She opened the door and saw Piret emerge from the dark, laden with her shopping. They looked at one another and Lydia stepped aside to let her in.

Piret stood inside the door, put her packages down and took off her shoes. Lydia hung up her coat and Piret brought the shopping into the house.

Lydia said, 'Show me what you have bought.'

They laid the things on the table and Piret told her where she had found each item. She handed Lydia the copy of *Eesti Naine* and Lydia poured her a glass of berry wine. Lydia had kept the soup hot on the stove, but Piret said that she was not hungry.

They sat down. Lydia glanced at the magazine and put it down on the table. Then she took an envelope from her apron pocket and handed it to Piret. Inside was an application form under the heading, Estonian SSR Ministry of Education.

Lydia said, 'I sent for it.'

Piret handed it back to Lydia, who continued, 'It's to study at night school.'

Piret shrugged. Lydia hesitated, and then added, 'You should do it. You may never get another chance.' She poured herself a glass of wine. 'There is nothing in your past against you and they will see that. You will get special treatment. Perhaps they will let you go to university. There's no reason why they shouldn't.'

Piret said, 'There's Maarja.'

'Nobody knows about Maarja.'

They drank the wine. It was Jaan's idea that Piret should go to Lydia's. Nobody outside the family saw Piret during the latter part of her pregnancy. She hardly showed until the fifth month, when she moved to the country. Then, as if waiting for a place of safety, her body ballooned as if suddenly diseased.

She remembered the day Jaan came to talk to her father. She had sat on a chair to one side, pregnant, listening to Jaan talk, watching her father nod dumbly. She was not consulted, but she did not resent it; she knew she would do whatever Jaan said. Her father was an unskilled worker; his cousin was a doctor. Everything was as clear as if it had all been decided long ago.

She remembered the only course in school on the topic, called the psychology of family life. The teacher had told them that only a socialist society can promote the harmonious development of the personality. There were lectures on the obligations to one's parents, grandparents and younger siblings. They were told that marriage was the 'highest level of development of the personality'. They were warned about 'looseness' as the infiltration of Western bourgeois licentiousness.

After Jaan's visit, Piret dropped out of school. She told her teachers she would look for work on a *kolhoz*. They were not surprised or disappointed: Piret was considered unexceptional, without particular gifts, the daughter of a drunk. There were always girls like her, girls who were absorbed into farms and factories, becoming machine-minders or tractor drivers. They sometimes married, more often did not, were frequent patients at the abortion clinic.

Lydia drank her wine and looked at her great-niece. Piret had tied her hair back and put on the apron she always wore at home, one of the millions manufactured without alteration since the 1950s, metallic blue with small white flowers. Lydia considered what Piret could do now. She knew Piret would never develop her cousin's beauty and charm. With her good manners, her energy and bossiness, her sweeping, undirected passions, Helena was made for men, marriage and children.

Piret had a bird's awkward face, pointed and small. With the kind of man she would get, she would work as much at home as at her job. Without a man, she would live like a beast, without a future, working in a factory, growing food on her allotment, washing and mending her ageing clothes at weekends, repairing the plumbing in her one-room flat.

Lydia saw the affair with Paavo as a brief aberration in Piret's life; Piret was as unlikely to drift from lover to lover as she was to marry. From Paavo's point of view, Piret had been a matter of convenience. Lydia had instantly recognized Paavo's type: serious, ambitious, inexperienced. Piret had presented herself; Paavo had not feared rejection. It happened often: girls without much to offer, boys on their way elsewhere. Paavo was an incidental event; if it had not been him, it would not have been anybody else.

Now, at seventeen, if Piret did not yet display the exuberance that attracted men, she probably never would develop it. She was quiet, plodding, stubborn. Piret would have to find another way, Lydia reflected, sipping her wine. It would not be Helena's. And she hoped it would not be her own: she knew the hardness of a life alone; she felt the years of work in her knees and back, her stiff fingers, as lined and dry as crumpled paper.

Even now, Lydia had little idea what Piret felt. She was always solitary, remote, self-possessed. Lydia recalled the two cousins in their childhood: Helena's emotional displays and Piret watching, observant, detached, inscrutable.

Lydia always knew that Helena's passion for communism was merely misplaced zeal. She also suspected that, for all her romanticism, Helena had a pragmatic core. Helena was like putty; she conformed, she chose what led to approval and acceptance. Lydia knew that Helena would outgrow her communist phase when someone directed her elsewhere.

And Helena did, as soon as she was old enough to understand the word *Siberia*, which was more than a place to most families, but an abbreviation, a code word for an entire catalogue of personal and historical experiences. Siberia was the proof of the power of words: riffraff bourgeoisie, fascist nationalists, capitalists, landlords, *kulaks*.

Once such words labelled families, there followed trains and then factories, mines, mills; barracks and unheated flats, partitioned by a curtain and shared with other families.

Jaan's parents were *kulaks*, rich peasants. Jaan's father died during the second major deportation; his mother Emmeline was shot by a Russian soldier at her farmhouse and Jaan himself was deported shortly afterwards. The farm was merged into Tallinn District Kolhoz No 11. The farmhouse was now used to store animal feed. The barn was filled with Russian-made tractors; the fields were tilled to exhaustion and the wood beyond had been plundered.

Discretion was never Helena's strong point. Most Estonian children absorbed a hatred of communists by some tacit, seeping process; Helena had to have it spelt out for her. Most children learned how to simulate compliance; Helena became as zealously anti-communist as she had once been a believer. She never learned to live with the duplicity that was an unremarkable part of daily life for others.

Her parents had learned to live in their society, overcoming their history to build a life, living the careful lies of the watched. They knew that all they could do was wait; their integrity lay in survival. But Helena shared her views with anyone who cared to listen: teachers, other students. By the time she was twelve, she was marked for a dismal future. She was not invited to join Komsomol after Young Pioneers; after secondary school she was not allowed to study medicine. She imagined her indiscretions were a measure of her integrity; she had merely made herself conspicuous. Her life became a closed file, suspect, determinate.

Lydia was not surprised by Jaan and Erna's decision to emigrate. She knew they would do anything for their daughter, and there was nothing for Helena in Estonia. Now Helena would have everything: the child, a husband, her parents, life in rich, clean Sweden, with a washing machine, central heating, food in the shops: a life where a woman was not a workhorse. It was all so perfect.

Lydia thought, *I will not let Piret get nothing.* She watched her great-niece, Anne's grandchild, the girl who had so little, and knew she would do everything to make sure Piret got one more chance.

Piret looked at the form. She had become accustomed to decisions being made for her and, like the others before, saw no reason not to go along with this one. She saw that she would have to make an appointment for an interview. She folded the form, put it in her pocket and said, rather indifferently, 'All right.'

5

The following day Helena sat on Matti's sofa, her knees pressed against the coffee table. She had put Maarja down for her mid-day sleep in the boys' room.

Matti's sons were at school. Helena was grateful for their absence; she did not know how she could bear two more people in the flat at the moment. She would never, she felt, be able to live like this again, the eternal presence of other people, the thin walls of the toilet. They were rats in a cage, keeping their voices down, putting things away, always having to think of others.

She was sleeping with Maarja in the boys' room; the boys slept on the sofa and floor in the living room. She would have been more comfortable at the Viru; as a tourist she was obliged to pay for her room whether she used it or not. But she could not refuse to stay with them; Matti Kaasik was her father's cousin.

Matti's wife Maret laid out lunch for them on the coffee table: pickled herring, boiled potatoes, cucumbers in sour milk, rye bread, blackcurrant juice. Maret tried to serve the expensive sausages and salmon Helena had brought from Sweden, but Helena persuaded her to keep them; she assured her that she only wanted to eat Estonian food.

She ate everything she was offered; to eat sparingly would be considered rude. She was in fact quite hungry. The past two days had taken more effort than she was used to.

She had forgotten that even the smallest tasks here took time and energy. At the harbour they had spent twenty minutes fitting the suitcases into the Lada. They left the port amid heavy traffic. Then Matti had seen an open petrol station and had queued to fill the tanks he kept in the boot.

At the flat Helena had unpacked, changed and fed Maarja;

they left for the church early. There they had been obliged to talk to a young and pompous priest. He had lectured her on keeping faith despite political realities. She half-listened, exasperated. Why else would she have come all this way if she had no faith in the Estonian church?

Then came that terrible scene with Piret. Helena had been terrified. How had she found out about it? She had come in wearing one of those shapeless farm dresses and her ancient black coat, shopping bags in each hand, panting, her dark hair wild and blown. She must have come all the way from Lydia's, if she was still living there. That would have involved two or three buses, a few hours' travel.

They had all stared at her as she moved towards Maarja. Then, without putting down her shopping or saying a further word, she had turned and left. She had come all that way and then left after a few minutes, without even touching her own baby. Why had she done it?

They had all discussed it after leaving the church, walking among the untended graves. Matti and Maret said nothing; Sylvia had never met Piret before, but was none the less convinced that Piret had come to hurt Maarja.

Helena did not want to believe it. Her own child? Sylvia had looked cynical. She had seen many irresponsible, even dangerous, mothers, in her work. A girl who had given up her baby could not be considered as having normal, maternal responses.

Sylvia worked in the Health Ministry. She had known Jaan since medical school and had helped him many times over in his career. Helena could not remember a time when Sylvia was not a family friend.

She had also helped Jaan to emigrate, providing the required letter that stated that his past work was immaterial to matters of national security. Helena had readily agreed when her father suggested she ask Sylvia to be Maarja's godmother. Sylvia had done so much for them. Besides, Sylvia already knew that Maarja was not Helena's child; she had helped Jaan to fabricate Maarja's birth certificate. The fewer who knew Maarja's origins the better.

29

Now, sitting in Matti's flat, Helena reflected on the past two days and the sights that had once been her life. She had watched, detached and slightly repelled, like a foreigner, the one or two shops below each block of flats, their interiors shielded by dusty, torn curtains. Sometimes the window displayed a few items: tins of sauerkraut, two or three spools of thread, a Russian-made iron. These, however, did not always indicate the actual contents of the store. Outside most shops Helena saw queues.

How could she have forgotten all this? She remembered arriving in Sweden and the astonishment she had felt at seeing the broad, gleaming windows of Swedish department stores, the seemingly endless supply of things to buy: make-up, clothing, shoes, scarfs and gloves, umbrellas, pots and pans, crystal and silver, furniture. The colours, the choice of sizes and shapes and styles confused her. She remembered staring at the careless faces and twisted limbs of mannequins dressed to go to the beach or on a picnic; the signs that appeared as regular as clockwork, *Rea*, one of the first Swedish words she learned: sale.

And now she remembered her shock at how expensive it had all been. Even bread, which was always available and never more than a few kopeks in Estonia, she had found expensive. Matti had paid for the petrol a fraction of the price it cost in Sweden.

After Maarja awoke, they decided to go for a walk in the old town. Maret had borrowed a strapless, rusty pushchair for Maarja. Helena had to keep the pushchair tilted on its back wheels to keep Maarja from tumbling out. The wheels clattered on the stone streets.

They bought some bread and Helena watched the girl's fingers dash across the abacus and heard the clicking of wood. She had not seen an abacus since she left. Maret put the bread in her net shopping bag.

The women on the street slowed their step and stared at Helena's shoes and handbag as they passed. They glanced at Maarja, who was so different from the thin Estonian children.

A group of Swedish tourists passed with their guide, and they too glanced at Helena and Maarja. The guide was explaining in English the history and current use of each building. 'The USSR puts great effort into the preservation of the local heritage of all Soviet peoples.' She went on to talk about the song festival and the parades with Estonian national costumes.

Helena felt her head grow hot with irritation: she wanted to interrupt and shake these gullible Swedes. Didn't they understand that every parade had a banner of Lenin at its head? She thought bitterly of the traditional song festival, the embroidered folk costumes, the dancing girls with rings of flowers around their heads, all tainted by the omnipresent hammer and sickle.

The guide did not mention these, nor the May Day parade, in which people were paid ten roubles to participate, the equivalent of two or three days' wages. In return, each was obliged to carry a Komsomol banner imprinted with the year's slogan: *Working Towards International Peace and Communism*, or *Long Live the Leninist Peace-loving Foreign Policy of the Soviet Peoples*.

Then, in the midst of her anger, Helena reminded herself that she was with her child, her Soviet child; she had to think always of Maarja's welfare now. She could not afford the luxury of her feelings. She forced herself to turn away and tried to concentrate on the charms of her home city. And it was lovely, she thought, seeing again the church steeples, a wrought-iron cock perched on a roof, a crowned, hissing serpent above a medieval chemist's, a weathered sunburst clock, the red-tiled roofs against the sky.

They stood on the Raekoja plats. Here, before the war, was the market place. Helena's mother Erna had told her about the stalls of fruit, vegetables, butter, eggs, meat and clothing. And how her mother, Helena's grandmother, would take her daughter shopping.

Helena thought of her grandmother, Leena, whom she would visit the next day, alone in her one-room flat. She did not want to see her loneliness; she did not want to hear of her small pension, her arguments with the butcher. Helena imagined presenting the woollen stockings and coffee she had brought and the old woman before her, silent, indifferent, forlorn.

But she wanted her grandmother to see Maarja. Family, Helena felt, was important. Her grandmother did not know that Maarja was adopted; she had been told Helena was pregnant a few months before the birth. Once the decision had been made, Helena, like Piret, went into hiding. She explained to her friends afterwards that she had been bedridden for fear of losing the baby.

Only the immediate family and Sylvia knew that Maarja was Piret's child. Helena was certain this was for the best. Her father had told her many orphaned children were adopted in the war and were never told. What purpose did it serve, to confuse a child?

Besides Maarja could only be disappointed by discovering anything about Piret. Who would want to know that her mother was the uneducated and unmarried daughter of an alcoholic worker?

But despite Maarja's parentage, Helena had not hesitated one moment when she understood there would be a child. Maarja was family, her second cousin's illegitimate baby; there was no question but that Maarja should remain in the family. And who else was responsible enough to raise her? Helena was a married woman; she and Peeter wanted children. And she had not yet fallen pregnant.

Maarja was hers now; she even imagined sometimes that she had given birth to her. There was no reason why she should not feel that way, she told herself; she loved Maarja as her own. She thought of the flight to Stockholm, and her Maarja, content in her lap.

She saw at once that Maarja was an easy baby. She slept anywhere and only cried when she was hungry or uncomfortable. Helena had touched Maarja's perfect face, her delicate, translucent ears, her minute, exquisite fingertips. She felt blessed, as though someone had given her an immense, honourable task:

32

the job of loving this child. Maarja would grow up as her own and Peeter's daughter, a free Estonian in Sweden.

Helena did not like Swedish people, but she loved Sweden. She loved the clean red buses that were always on time. She loved walking through PK-huset, up Hamngatan towards NK and into Gallerian. She adored NK; she even loved the name: Nordiska Kompaniet, the Company of the North.

They had been the object of much curiosity in the Estonian expatriate community; immigrants were few to Sweden. There had only been the occasional defector to the United States, and some Jews had been allowed to go to Israel.

It was a great shock to Helena that many expatriate Estonians were suspicious of them, as if they were spies. She and her family were treated with extreme reserve. Within weeks, she came to understand the difference between Soviets and expatriate Estonians. The Estonians in Sweden had fled during the war; they remembered and had taught their children to remember Estonia as if it had disappeared. Soviet Estonia was a different country. They believed that their refugee newspapers and cultural festivals and concerts were the only hope for their culture to survive the power of the USSR.

As for Swedes, Helena quickly discerned two dispositions. The socialists believed that the evils of communism were highly exaggerated by American propaganda. They went on marches against the war in Vietnam and believed the Baltic people were fascist and nationalistic. They would never challenge the Russian lies justifying their illegal occupation of the Baltic.

And there were anti-communists, who hated every thing and all things Soviet. Of course, people knew that the country had been invaded during the war. They understood that Estonians had fought against Russia. But they believed that all Soviets were now indoctrinated communists.

Nobody cared that the Baltic peoples were living under a cruel dictatorship. The West could never understand their anguish, the loss of their freedom and culture. Helena knew the tragedy of the Baltics was over.

Helena pushed Maarja behind Matti and Maret up Pikk jalg, lifted the pushchair through an enormous arch and walked on to the old city wall. Beyond a sea of red-tiled roofs they could see the *Georg Ots* docked in the harbour, the glittering Baltic Sea, cranes spiking the horizon. Closer to them were the fortress towers and the green copper spire of St Olaf's. To one side, in the distance, Helena could just make out row upon row of grey, rectangular blocks of flats fading into the horizon: Lasnamäe. Piercing the dense, brownish air, a stream of black smoke trickled from a factory stack. On top of the factory a monumental sign declared: *Our Creative Work Fulfilling the Goals of the Central Committee*.

The sign was old and weathered. Helena knew it had probably been there for years, and that she had probably stood in this very spot dozens of times in her life. And yet she had never noticed it, so effectively had she learned to ignore such intrusions. Now she read it over and over again, disbelieving. She turned away and waited for Matti and Maret to join her. She wanted to go home.

6

In Stockholm Erna lay on her bed, next to the telephone. Helena had said she would try to call, but neither of them knew whether this would be possible. Matti did not have a telephone, and even if Helena managed to find one international calls were difficult to make.

Erna waited; she did not have the energy to get up. Jaan had gone to the hospital, where he was an intern, a forty-five-year-old intern. He was studying to take his medical exams for the second time in his life. In another year he would be a doctor again. Erna worried that he was working too hard, that it was too much for a middle-aged man. It had been all much more difficult than they had ever imagined.

But they were not bitter; they were grateful. They had a four-room flat, with two toilets and a beautiful modern kitchen. They had been given Swedish lessons, money for furniture and food, jobs in their own professions.

They had been taken directly from the airport to a hostel in a suburb outside Stockholm. It was in a modern brick house on a quiet street, run by an old couple who took them upstairs to clean, plain rooms, showed them the shower and wrote down the times they served meals.

The following day a Swedish social worker, accompanied by a translator, came and told them they would be transferred to a refugee camp near Uppsala. She was a tall, thin woman, with dry blonde hair, like straw, and large glasses. She spoke in a loud, high voice, and moved her hands up and down as she spoke about what she called their 'rights'.

The camp was a converted school. They slept in what had once been a classroom, in military bunk beds. Down the hall was a room with a row of toilets and, facing the toilets, a communal shower. The social worker told them that a television and a cot for Maarja would arrive shortly.

Outside the window they could see a barbed-wire fence. There were no lamps, except a bulbous ceiling light. When night fell they turned it off to let Maarja sleep, and the four adults lay in the dark in silence.

Over the next few days they were interviewed by different people. One asked Peeter about his military service; another wanted to know if any of them had been in prison. Jaan had stared at the man and replied coldly, 'My wife and I were both deported to labour camps after the war.'

Their flat was not in the best part of Stockholm; it was north of town, in Rinkeby, in one of several huge buildings arranged around the underground station, interspersed with squares of sodden grass, crisscrossing pavements and small play-grounds. Its anonymous rows of windows reminded Erna of Siberia. She hoped that some day they could move into town.

Helena and Peeter and the baby had just moved into their own flat in a district in south Stockholm, Södermalm, with a two-year lease for 600 crowns a month. This was, they soon realized, a good price. But it was a great deal of money for them; the cost of flats in Sweden had been the family's biggest shock; in Estonia rent was a minute part of earnings.

Erna taught German part-time at the University of Stock-holm, attended her Swedish lessons, and helped Helena with the baby. But she was not busy enough; she found herself spending more and more of her free time in bed. The hours stretched out before her; there seemed so little to do. Now that Helena and Peeter were gone, the flat did not get very dirty and the shopping took hardly any time at all.

There were supermarkets at nearly every corner and under-ground station. And they had everything anybody could want: tomatoes and cucumbers, sacks of oranges, enormous wedges of cheese, metre-deep plastic-wrapped sausages in great refrigerated bins, dozens of kinds of soap, row upon row of shampoos, razors, disposable sanitary towels, toilet paper in different colours.

In the basement laundry room were four washing machines, a large sink and clothes line, two dryers, an ironing machine, an ironing board, a table and chairs, and several smooth, white metallic laundry baskets on wheels. Erna had never seen anything like it. At one end were a bucket and mop under a sign: *Who cleaned up after you?*

There was a system of signing your name on a chart next to the hours when you wanted to wash. In Estonia people would have erased your name and put up their own, taking with them the little stub of pencil that hung from a string; someone would have dismantled the machines and sold them, piece by piece.

Erna picked up a Swedish women's magazine, which was simple enough for her to read. She could not yet read the newspapers. Her Swedish teacher had encouraged her to read whatever publications she could manage, so she told herself this was her homework. But, in fact, she loved reading about the young king and Ingmar Bergman's romance with Liv Ullmann.

She loved the pictures of the English royal family. She read about Princess Anne's engagement and all she could find about Elizabeth Taylor's on–off romance with Richard Burton, and about the Swedish models and actresses who had gone to Hollywood. She knew all about the new short jackets designed by Christian Dior and the scandalous new film *Last Tango in Paris*. This was nothing like *Eesti Naine*, which offered sober articles on bottling fruit, dressmaking, the upbringing of children.

She had worked her entire life, harder than any Swedish woman could ever understand. She had a doctorate in German and now she lay in bed reading women's magazines, waiting for her daughter to call.

Erna imagined Helena in some shabby church; they were all shabby, except for the churches in the old town where the tourists went. They could have had a proper Estonian christening in Jakobs kyrka at Kungsträdgården downtown and gone to a restaurant afterwards. Only Matti and Maret and Sylvia were to be there, with no celebration afterwards. Of course it was nice that Matti could go, but he was hardly close family.

Erna suspected that Helena only remembered the good things. She remembered being a doctor's daughter and being respected. Here people did not care what her parents did; they were refugees and this marked them. Worse, they were Soviets, and distrusted because they were not dissidents. Erna and Jaan had left for Helena's sake, for Helena's children's sake; now their daughter was nostalgic, homesick. Erna thought: *She is twenty-two and she only thinks about the past.*

Erna had learned not to think about the past. She had returned from Siberia with her mother in 1950. She was twenty-two. Her father was dead. He had been a Baltic German, a chemist named Schönberg; he had been arrested as an enemy of the state; his crimes were having employed two assistants and renting out the flat above his shop. They did not know where he was buried. She had known suffering, the kind that history does not acknowledge, cannot tell about, because it is too personal and too common.

They had been deported in 1940; Erna was nearly twelve. She would never forget the knock on the door that day, the sight of a soldier's hat through the glass panes at the top of their front door. There were two of them; the older one said impassively, 'You have been deported. You may pack one suitcase each.' She stood between her parents, their arms around her.

At the port were hundreds of others. Her father was put on a different train. Erna and her mother sat with the other women and children on planks of wood, too frightened to talk. They left the port and Erna soon lost sight of her father's train. Through the hole in the floor of the car, they watched the endless rush of train tracks. They passed other trains of deportees even worse off than them, for they were all standing, packed tightly into the trucks like sheep.

The other women in the carriage shared food they had brought; soon there was nothing left to eat. A day later they stopped and were given salt fish and bread. A few days later they stopped again, somewhere near the Urals alongside another train of deported Estonians, and through the slots in the side of the carriage swapped a frenzy of questions and information: friends deported, businesses closed, whether there was still a government.

Erna and her mother understood then that the Red Army had forced in a puppet government, that thousands had been deported. Was there a single Estonian left? Was Estonia now Russian? People talked frantically. One girl on Erna's carriage saw her father on the other truck, and Erna remembered their fingers straining through the slots, trying to touch across an impossible distance; she remembered hating this unknown girl for being given the chance to say goodbye, for she had known that she would never see her own father again; she was certain that they would all die.

Then, a few days later, the train stopped again. They were unloaded and Erna saw that they were at a station, a small wooden platform alongside the tracks. Beyond were plains and forest; there was not a village or farmhouse in sight.

The soldiers prodded them with their rifles, and they were marched through the forest. When night fell they slept in a field, mothers and children together, their coats over them. On the second day one of the younger children died and Erna remembered the women persuading the mother to part with the body so that the soliders could bury him.

After another day they arrived at the camp, where they slept in huts on wooden plank beds; overhead were oil lamps hanging from the rafters. Erna's mother Leena was sent with other women to cut the branches from the trees the men had felled; the logs were floated down the river. Erna attended a three-room prefabricated school an hour's walk away in the local village. Estonian pupils were in the minority; most were Russian or Lithuanian. The local Siberians were the only ones who did not seem cowed; they were suspicious of the new foreigners, who, it was obvious, were criminals.

Later Leena was given a job in a brick factory and they were moved out of the camp to a seventh-floor flat in a new block in the village. They were given a box containing a bar of soap, a block of lard, a grey army blanket and a picture of Stalin.

39

There was no lift. They shared the three-room flat with two other families, each family to one room. The toilet was outside, behind the building; they cooked in a common room with the others on their floor.

At night Erna and Leena knitted by the light of small petrol lamps. They made caps and cardigans, which they traded to the local people for ration cards, eggs, honey and potatoes. Each week they reported to the NKVD office to sign their names in a large book.

After finishing school, Erna was given a job in a factory making circuit boards. She sat in a row of women, each in an apron, all attaching red and blue wires. They were from everywhere: Byelorussia, the Ukraine, Lithuania, Russia. A few were Jews. Some were old: survivors of the 1930s. A few, like Erna and her mother, would return home. And then their stories would disappear, because only the silent survived; those who talked nostalgically or complained were reported by one of the NKVD's many informers and arrested.

By the time Erna started working, posters had begun to appear in the village which said, *Come to Estonia: Good wages and a flat for all workers*. At about the same time, Erna and her mother were given an allotment, where they grew potatoes. They talked quietly at the allotment about whether they might one day be allowed to go home. 'They will let us', Erna said prophetically, 'when enough Russians have moved to Estonia.'

In the summer the village animals were let loose to roam in the fields and forest around the village. One evening they came home to find a Lithuanian woman sobbing next to her allotment; her cow had been killed by bears.

A particularly hard winter followed, and the villagers brought the animals into their houses and even into the flats. One of Erna's Russian neighbours complained that their pig kept them awake at night and chewed the edges of their blankets. Erna had been shocked; for ever she would think of Russians as people who lived with animals.

Upon her return Erna was permitted to attend university,

where she committed one of the few defiant acts of her life: she decided to study German in memory of her father.

She met Jaan at a Komsomol meeting. They saw immediately in each other the cautious look of the non-communist. They were both older students; they had known each other slightly at a private primary school before the war; they had both been deported.

They married quickly and almost immediately Erna became pregnant. It was itself a sort of political act: marriage and children. To create a normal life, to go on, was to defy Russification.

Slowly life settled into a post-war calm. The 1950s were a decade of building. The Estonia Theatre, which had been bombed, was rebuilt to the original neo-classical design. More flats became available and fewer families had to share. A few people got cars. Finally, Stalin died, and the weight of death and fear over the country lifted; censorship of the press, music and literature eased. The thaw had begun.

By the time Helena was in primary school, Erna and Jaan had, by Soviet standards, a decent life. They had a plumbed, two-room flat to themselves; they had good jobs. They did not have a telephone or car, but they lived in town and the tram stop was nearby.

Helena was their only worry. She was an emotional child, given to outbursts, indiscreet, obtuse at times. She married Peeter when she was twenty. 'He is the only man I know I will ever respect,' she declared to her parents. They consented, partly because they knew that to oppose her would make her even more stubborn; partly because, like many people who had lived through the war, they wanted to give their child everything they could.

Peeter was similar in character to Helena: highly strung, quick to jump to conclusions. Erna and Jaan both knew neither of them would survive in Soviet Estonia. They would make too many mistakes that would mark them for life. Only in the West would they be able to pull themselves up again.

They applied to emigrate. None of them were involved in

sensitive jobs. Peeter was a low-level translator of Russian, Swedish and Finnish. Helena had recently finished her degree in English at the Polytechnic.

Immediately Erna and Jaan were sacked from their jobs. Sylvia found Jaan work as a hospital orderly; Erna became a cleaner in a factory. Only Peeter was allowed to continue translating.

Then, a few months after they had applied for the visas, they found out about the baby. It was not difficult to persuade Piret's father to go along with the plan. Helena had been married for over a year and was not yet pregnant. She was desperate to have a baby. And here was a baby who was already part of their family.

They were all more or less convinced of the impracticality of Piret keeping the baby. She was always considered a dull, incompetent girl with little future. Besides, her father was a drunk and her mother was dead. And Jaan could never resist giving Helena what she wanted. Jaan always had a sentimental streak. He saw the baby as an opportunity to bring an Estonian soul into freedom.

Erna was not as concerned about freeing souls as she was about taking a child from its natural mother. She had only met Piret a few times, at Aunt Lydia's, where she and Jaan and Helena had occasionally spent weekends, helping Lydia in exchange for boxes of apples, potatoes, berries and vegetables. Jaan had wanted Helena to experience life in the country, as he had on the farm; to see food growing, to swim in the cold, clear lake.

Sometimes Piret and her parents also came out for fresh air, to work, to take back food to their small flat on Pärnu Street. Erna pitied Piret; Oskar was well-meaning, talkative, lazy. He obviously idolized Jaan. Piret's mother, Anna, spoke to Erna little, and did not hide her hostility. Her husband's ineptitude had embittered her; she resented their poverty and Jaan's and Erna's superior education and position. Erna was polite but did not force herself on Anna. She encouraged Helena to befriend Piret, but the girls were as different from one another as the parents. Not only their ages separated them; they could never be friends.

When she and Jaan understood there was to be a baby, Erna thought of her own pregnancy, her absolute and fierce love for Helena, and hesitated before agreeing to what amounted to expropriating this child. It had been done to them in the war, families separated, children taken. Erna thought: This poor girl has lost her mother, and now she will lose her child. But, in the face of Jaan's and Helena's determination, she had swallowed her doubts and gone along with the plan.

Now Erna lay on her bed and read about queens and kings and princesses, women in furs and paper dresses, plastic shoes and platform heels and see-through blouses. She understood now why people did not know, did not care, about her small country. Life here did not leave you time to think about the outside.

The Cold War was a good name, she thought. *It is as if we are frozen, in suspension. We live outside the events of the world.* Dramas came from earthquakes or droughts or wars. The difficulty of waiting ten years for a flat or telephone or finding sheets or towels or shoes were tedious to people who did not have such problems.

It was time for her too to forget about all that. She had more important things to worry about now. Helena would return from Estonia soon; she would have to find a job. Helena and Peeter would never be able to keep the flat if Helena did not work.

Erna was worried about Peeter. He spent his days perfecting his Swedish and trying to find freelance writing and translating work. They needed regular money, but he was not interested in getting a job.

Nor was he ever at home. She had called a few times since Helena had left, and he was always out. And Erna had noticed that the two of them seemed to be drifting apart since coming to Sweden. Helena concerned herself solely with the baby and Erna rarely saw Peeter touch his wife. He was angry with her for insisting on christening Maarja in Estonia, and

43

angry with Erna and Jaan for not stopping her.

Helena had never worked, but she did speak English and some German, and she was learning Swedish quickly. Erna herself would take care of Maarja when she wasn't teaching. The queue for a place in a day-care centre was quite long. Besides, she had so little to do; she would persuade Helena that this was the best solution.

Helena could not depend on Peeter; he was slipping away. He had that look about him: he was in love with the West. He was twenty-six; he wanted money and a position, but he also wanted to drink and go out. He hated everything Estonian now. Yet he was more Soviet than Western: he had the dreams but not the drive or the discipline that Swedes had.

As soon as Helena returned, Erna would talk to her. It was too late for her and Jaan to remake their lives; but she would make sure her daughter and the baby were safe.

7

Helena walked across the gangway into the Stockholm harbour building. She queued up with the other passengers
behind the glass booth, where an efficient, impersonal blonde
woman in a blue uniform stamped passports.

Doors opened on to the lobby, and Helena immediately saw
her mother waiting. 'Your father had to work,' Erna explained as
she took the baby and Helena pushed the trolley towards the lifts.

They walked to the taxi rank. A driver waved them to a
waiting Volvo. As they drove towards town, Helena relaxed.
She was home, driving on the clean streets of Stockholm,
watching the buildings and kiosks, unbroken street lights and
plexiglass bus shelters, Volvos and Saabs, the clear, smokeless
sky. She thought: *I live here.*

At Hötorget, streams of bag-laden shoppers queued for buses;
old ladies, carefully made up, wearing hats and carrying large
handbags marched purposefully down the street. She understood now that this was why she loved Sweden: the old here
did not look impoverished, hungry, weary, cold. They had a
kind of insolence, a presumption that they could expect certain
treatment which impressed her. In Estonia the old looked
frightened.

They arrived at the flat, paid the driver, went up in the lift.
Peeter was not at home, but Helena had not expected him to
be; he worked odd hours. She watched her mother go into the
kitchen to make coffee. Maarja had slept in the taxi, and now
woke and began to cry. Helena went into Maarja's room to
change her and called to Erna to heat a bottle.

Helena had noticed that her mother looked tense and worried; about the trip, she supposed. Erna had aged since they
had left Estonia. She was only forty-five, yet she looked old.

Her short brown hair had greyed; her face had become sunken, leaving prominent cheek-bones and diffident, weary eyes.

Helena thought: *in twenty years Maarja will be twenty-one and I will be middle-aged. Erna will be sixty-five, retired, old, dependent on me. My daughter will be an adult and I will have a new responsibility: my mother.*

Helena knew her father was unlikely to live twenty more years. Jaan had angina and was too arrogant to listen to anyone's advice to slow down. His career was effectively over, yet he worked obsessively as though he was a young doctor again. After his exams he could only hope for a position as a hospital ward doctor. It would be difficult for an older man, a refugee, to resume obstetrics.

Helena returned from the bedroom and sat at the kitchen table to give Maarja the bottle. Erna poured her a cup of coffee and sat down opposite her. 'You didn't have any problems?'

'Oh, Mother, of course not. You worry far too much.'

'Your father worried more than me.'

'How is he?'

Erna folded her hands in her lap. 'The same.'

'Well, it was fine,' Helena said heartily. 'It was lovely. Everybody was far too concerned about it. I wouldn't have done it if I had thought there would be any danger.'

'How was Sylvia?'

'She's fine, absolutely fine.' Helena was fairly sure that Sylvia would not tell Erna or Jaan about Piret's appearance. If Sylvia did tell Jaan, Helena knew that he would speak to her before telling Erna. Jaan always tried to spare Erna unnecessary worry.

'And Matti and Maret? And the boys?'

'The boys did not come. And Matti and Maret are well. And they send their thanks for the gifts.' Helena hesitated. 'It was dreadful, the flat, that awful toilet. Mother, the *smell*. I'd forgotten everything. It was so strange; I felt like a foreigner.'

Maarja finished the bottle and Helena gave her to Erna to hold. Erna hesitated before finally asking about her own mother. 'And Leena?'

'As well as can be expected. She seemed happy to see us.'
Helena knew that Erna was unlikely to believe this; Erna however said nothing. After the years in Siberia and the death of
Erna's father, Leena had made it clear that she considered her
daughter's emigration a betrayal. She believed they were leaving chiefly to rid themselves of the responsibility of an old
lady; yet she refused to consider going with them.

Helena felt suddenly quite exhausted. She watched her
mother shift Maarja to lie against one shoulder; Erna patted
the baby gently on her back.

Helena thought about Piret, her old black coat, her unkempt
hair, those terrible large eyes. She tried to imagine who Piret's
lover could be. Who would want Piret? She tried to imagine
her cousin in some man's bed, awkward and submissive.

Her own sexual history she thought of as special, untainted.
She knew this was hypocritical, but she could not shake off her
vision of Piret's affair as the rudest kind of copulation, ignorant and unthinking, two animals panting in secret. Helena
had only gone to bed with Peeter when she was sure she was
in love and marriage was taken for granted.

She had seen Peeter several times during her studies; their
affair began when they met accidentally on a tram. Peeter was
tall, broad-shouldered, fair. She liked his narrow hips, his
scarf, his loose tweed jacket. He was light-hearted; he laughed
easily, and she was tired of the seriousness and pessimism of
her family. Peeter seemed to her an independent thinker, a
rebel, a man who chafed against constraints. She thought it
criminal that such a man should not be free.

Helena now said, 'I wonder if you'd mind the baby while I
shower?'

'Helena – ' Erna stopped. 'Why don't you come over to dinner tonight? We can go now; bring your things and you can
shower there.'

'Oh, I don't know,' Helena said, rising. 'I suppose Peeter
will want dinner. Where is he, anyway? Do you know?'

'No.'

'What's the matter, Mother?'

'Oh, darling, I don't know. It's just that everything has been so difficult lately … '

'You think it was selfish of me to have gone. I've made you worry unnecessarily.'

'No, of course you must do what you think best.'

'Then what is it?'

Erna hesitated again. 'It's Peeter. I worry about him.'

'Why? This is what he's always wanted, to leave. He'll find a job.' Helena walked to the bedroom and returned holding a white bath towel and pink dressing gown. 'It's going to take time for all of us.'

Erna focused on the baby and did not answer; Helena left to shower.

Helena and Peeter had been married for nearly three years. Since coming to Sweden, they had begun to argue more and more. When Helena was with Peeter, he annoyed her; she found him naïve, evasive, glib. The man she had admired in Estonia for his optimism and independence she now found impractical and dreamy. She wanted to discuss their future; he told her she nagged. She cried; he placated her. They had both begun to tire of this routine.

But when she was away from her husband, Helena's marriage persisted in her imagination as unblemished as before they left; she thought of Peeter as she first saw him: talking on the tram, his patched tweed jacket falling open, his easy laugh. She had liked the fact that he was tall; she remembered looking up to see his eyes, and the way she felt when she imagined herself in his arms, his broad shoulders bending around her.

She knew now that Peeter was not all that clever; she knew the limits of her husband's aptitude and character. She considered journalism a good choice for him: he could write well and he was good at condensing certain kinds of information: events, facts, dates. But he was not an original or energetic thinker. He was quickly bored by any particular subject.

None the less, when she was away from him she thought of her marriage as something to be proud of, a good piece of work, like a well-made dress. She viewed her life as a compilation of her achievements; she was proud that there was no rumour that could touch her. The gossip of divorces, affairs, unemployment and debts among the Estonian expatriate community would never touch her. She imagined herself a mature woman, a wife and mother, the mistress of her life.

She came out of the shower, wrapped in two towels. Erna sat at the kitchen table, clipping something from the newspaper. Maarja sat on a blanket on the floor, whacking the air with a red measuring cup.

Erna handed the newspaper clipping to her. It advertised a programme to train for a career with the Scandinavian airline company, SAS. Helena saw immediately why her mother had noticed it: the advantages of a career with SAS were described as security, potential for advancement and special travelling rates. These were exactly the qualities her mother would look for. Helena saw that a training course was to begin shortly after Christmas.

Helena put it down irritably. 'Mother, will you please stop interfering? I will get a job when I want to. Maarja is too small for me to go to work. Don't you see? My baby will only be a baby for a little while longer. It's Peeter's responsibility to support us. We emigrated so that we could choose how to live. Why should I go to work?'

The week following Helena's return home, Piret took a tram to the Central Committee of the Estonian Communist Party on V.I. Lenin Avenue. Outside the modern office block was a statue of Lenin, his hands gesturing, his jacket open. Fixed to the plain rectangular base was a single star; underneath was his surname in large block letters.

Inside in the reception were three or four black vinyl sofas. On the wall were photographs of local party officials. A guard asked Piret her name and then directed her upstairs. She took the tiny lift to another floor and walked down the hall. Along the hall were more photographs, the members of the Central Committee in Moscow.

'Your father's cousin and his family emigrated,' said the

woman severely. She was a Russian, with bee-hived, bleached hair. Under her blouse her breasts pointed straight out like two cones, and Piret knew she was wearing a Soviet brassière. Russians rarely had relatives in the West and consequently hardly ever had good underwear, lipstick, leather shoes or blue jeans.

Piret kept her face blank and waited for a few seconds. She knew she must not over-react, it would not help her. 'I', she said quietly, 'have not emigrated.'

'You left school shortly before they left.'

Piret knew she was trying to connect these two events for some reason, and decided to disconnect them once and for all. She said, 'My parents were workers. I left school because I wanted to be a worker.'

She did not expect this to come across as well as it did. How could this woman interpret such a statement in any way other than mocking? Russians knew that no Estonian would ever be a believing communist. Estonians were known to Russians as ambitious, nationalistic, self-serving, bourgeois to the core.

Piret waited for the woman's sarcasm; she expected her to do anything except what she did. She smiled: as though Piret were a good student who had successfully recited a lesson. She closed her file. 'I will put forward your application.'

Piret left the building in a daze. She had never imagined that it would be so easy to lie, or that her lies would be so readily believed.

She took the tram back to the bus station. She found herself anxiously replaying the conversation with the Russian woman over and over again in her mind. She thought about her considered pause after the woman asked about Jaan's family emigrating; her calculated lie about wanting to be a worker; her careful, blank expression. She understood that she desperately wanted a chance to begin again.

She promised herself that if they let her study she would work hard. She would never forget her conviction that Maarja belonged to Helena and Peeter. She would think about the years ahead as clean and unformed. Perhaps she was stupid and clumsy, but she could work to overcome her defects.

She promised herself she would never stop to reflect bitterly. She would forget Paavo's face, intent and oblivious, above her own, his icy retreat when she told him she was pregnant: *I suppose it's too late for an abortion.* She would never pause to calculate Maarja's age, or wonder where she was at that moment, if she was happy, if she was crying, if other children were cruel to her.

She would never look back and wonder if she should have kept her. If she had kept her, Maarja would have grown to hate her. This Piret felt was certain. She would have hated Piret's ugliness, her own fatherlessness. She would hear of Helena living in wealth and freedom and hate Piret for keeping her from a beautiful mother who wanted her. She would find out. Helena would tell her: *I wanted to adopt you; I was educated and married and Piret was not. We had visas to emigrate. But your mother was too selfish to give you a better life.*

And so Piret stood at the bus station and decided to carve her child out of her heart for ever and start life anew.

By the end of January Piret was attending school every evening. She was the youngest of a mixed class of about forty students: ex-soldiers with army haircuts, factory girls in shop dresses, and coerced prostitutes, made up, in leather shoes and jackets, slouching listlessly at their desks.

The programme covered secondary school subjects: economic geography, political economy, social studies, literature, Russian, mathematics, the Soviet constitution, the history of the Estonian communist party.

Piret returned home on the bus each night to study, eat dinner, sleep. She could hear Lydia on the other side of the wall, stoking the fire and scraping vegetables. They usually ate in silence. After dinner Lydia would insist that Piret carry on studying; Piret would open her books, listening to Lydia heat water to wash dishes, bring in wood, empty the grate and cover the coals for the morning.

Piret discovered that she had a good memory. Her Russian improved dramatically; she wrote perfect exams, even in

Marxism, which the other students considered a joke. All of them in one way or another hated and ridiculed the political and economic theories of communism. The prostitutes wanted to go back to earning hard currency; the soldiers were bitter; the workers were in school in a desperate bid to escape from their factories.

They watched American television shows from Finland and listened to Voice of America. They believed they lived in a kind of prison. In private they talked about leaving.

But Piret never thought about all that and rarely watched television. To her the West was a place in a book. It was the place of capitalism: wealth, violence and decadence.

She suspected that life in America was not as perfect as her classmates believed. She knew American society was inequitable and run by criminal organizations. People did nothing except for money. The black people were oppressed. The Americans had fled from Saigon; the television carried pictures of American helicopters as they took off from the tops of buildings.

She had long ago tired of hearing about the days before communism. She thought of her parents; their sentimentality annoyed her. Life may have been good for all of you, she would have liked to tell them now, but what about the maids who cleaned your houses? What about the farm workers who ploughed the fields? Did they have a better life then, before communism? What about people like me? Would I have been given a chance at education?

But she did not believe everything she was taught. She was not like Helena. She memorized and filed her knowledge into mental compartments from which she extracted it for her examinations. She accepted nothing as the truth, but remembered everything she was supposed to say. She believed that she could develop and preserve a split self: parallel and separate.

Without a tremor of hesitation, she wrote for her history examination: 'In 1918 the bourgeois government applied severe measures to suppress the revolutionary movement, but the workers kept fighting under the leadership of the Estonian Communist Party. In 1938 revolutionary activity was revived. In 1940 the workers celebrated the re-establishment of Soviet power.'

She knew this was not true; she did not particularly care. Her parents' version was different, but then everyone else's probably was too. Her parents had told her how Jaan and Erna had been deported, that the Red Army had forcibly installed a communist government, that Jaan's mother had been shot and the farm collectivized. But these were individual stories, easily dismissed; nobody, Piret reasoned, knew the truth.

What Piret did know was that she wanted to succeed, to belong, to do what was required. She liked the simplicity of studying, of memorizing Russian verbs, the dates of wars, passages from Turgenev, Marxist terminology. She found peace in her books and she did not ask questions. Every student knew what happened to those who asked questions, as one boy in the group did. He asked the teacher why capitalism had not yet destroyed itself, as Marx had predicted, and why the proletariat in America had not yet risen up.

The boy was talked to. Not threatened, but simply asked: *What are your plans for the future? Do you appreciate the opportunity you have been given here?*

One day, towards the end of term, Piret's Russian teacher asked her the same question: 'What are your plans for the future?'

She looked at him, expressionless. She had perfected her ability to keep emotion out of her eyes. It was a very useful habit.

He went on. 'There are a number of places for exceptional students to continue on at the Polytechnic in the autumn. You have shown a certain aptitude for mathematics and economics. I suggest you think about engineering. It is a growing field and a good one for a woman.'

She knew already that she did not have to take this suggestion to heart. Neither he nor anybody else would tell her what to do. She already understood how things worked. She could attempt to do what she wanted, and if she made intelligent decisions she would be allowed to carry them out. The system was a benevolent but strict parent: the lightest of tethers until too much initiative or deviation was shown; then came the rod.

She had already decided she would not be an engineer, but she did not tell this Russian. She simply asked, 'What do I do?'

'Nothing,' he said, turning away. 'I will make sure it is taken care of.'

8

Piret registered at Tallinn Polytechnic on an unusually warm, sunny September day in 1974. President Nixon had recently resigned, and the Americans had a president they had never elected. The Watergate trials were in full swing.

Leonid Brezhnev was in his ninth year as general secretary; Kosygin was prime minister. Life was good: oil prices were high, new construction projects appeared regularly on the outskirts of Tallinn, there was more food in the shops, queues for cars and flats were shortening.

Piret took the bus into town from Lydia's with a sheath full of documents, then a tram to Mustamäe. The Polytechnic was a collection of red brick buildings, built in the 1960s, set on flat, cleared ground; to one side was a long grey block of student rooms. Surrounding the campus were pines, and through the small forest paved paths led to the tram and bus stops.

Piret walked into the college with girls in short skirts and high-heeled sandals, shoulder bags and long, straight hair. She saw boys in student caps, some carrying briefcases, some wearing goatees. She was one of them, a student now. Her life was beginning.

Inside was a large foyer where students were standing about in noisy, indeterminate groups. It seemed to her that everybody, except for her, knew what to do. She stood in a daze until a Russian girl directed her down a hall to an office.

She waited in a slowly advancing line until she faced an irritable woman behind a counter. Before the woman were binders full of typewritten sheets. She looked up Piret's name and told her that she had been enrolled in the engineering faculty.

Piret protested; she had not wanted engineering. She had

met girls preparing for engineering, grinding up numbers to build bridges and tunnels; she did not want to do that. She hated the idea of drawing heating systems, of being an educated plumber. She wanted to have a life of the mind.

The woman looked away, bored, and said she had to talk to the dean if she wanted to change faculties. Piret did not know how to do this; she did not even know who the dean was. She gave the woman an anguished look and said, 'But what shall I do?'

The woman looked at her and said, 'What faculty do you want to be in?'

'Economics.'

The woman crossed out the word engineering and wrote in economics.

'All right? Are you happy now?'

Piret stared at her and nodded. Surely this woman could not change her faculty like that? The woman tore off the bottom part of the form and handed it to her. 'Go and study economics.'

She was directed to another office, where there was some confusion since her name was not on the list. The woman administrator returned to Piret her slip of paper and said, 'I cannot register you if you are not on the list.'

Piret stood silently, afraid to admit that she was officially enrolled in engineering. She was about to turn away when a man walking by suddenly stopped before the woman's desk. His hair was grey and he wore wire-rimmed glasses and a very baggy, threadbare wool jacket. Piret thought he might be about fifty.

The woman fell still and glanced up at him respectfully, and Piret knew then he was somebody. She was afraid he was going to ask her to leave. Then she noticed that he smelled slightly. She detected cheap, black tobacco, unwashed clothing. She tried to keep her face perfectly blank.

The man looked at her and said in Estonian, 'What is the problem with this young lady?'

Piret blushed. She had never been called a young lady. She waited for the woman to explain, but the man was looking at her and she said tentatively, 'I want to study economics.'

'And why on earth do you want to do that?' he inquired aggressively.

She froze in terror. Why did she want to do that? She looked at this man and knew, then, that he was not a communist. He was somebody complex, neither one nor the other; he was somebody she wanted to know.

She took a breath and said, 'Because I want to understand the progress of history.'

He did not speak for a moment. What she had said could be taken in two ways. The Marxist interpretation of her phrase, the progress of history, was that capitalism was a historical development rather than an immutable manifestation of human nature. Humans were not predestined by their nature to be capitalist.

The other, subversive, interpretation was that communist Marxism-Leninism had corrupted and ruptured Estonian history.

He said, 'Register this young lady. If you have any problems, let me know.' He turned and left.

The woman enrolled her. She would attend five classes: introduction to political economy, theory and function of the state, planning and production, mathematical economics and Marxist-Leninist analysis.

'Who was that?' Piret asked hesitantly.

The woman did not look up. 'Professor Rozhansky.'

A Russian, thought Piret. A Russian who is fluent in Estonian?

'Not Russian,' said the woman, reading her mind. 'Ukrainian father, Estonian mother.' She handed Piret a sheet of paper. 'It's your lucky day. He doesn't like everybody.'

Piret returned home, exhausted by her day. Lydia looked through the books Piret had bought at the Raamatu kauplus.

'What are you studying?'

'Economics.'

'Why don't you learn something practical?' she asked. 'Like engineering?'

'I don't want to learn engineering.'

'Engineering is a good job for a woman.' Lydia picked up a book entitled *Principles of Economic Calculus in the Socialist Economy*. 'What is this?'

'Mathematical economics.'

Lydia flipped through the pages. 'It doesn't look very useful.'

'Nothing is useful without theory.'

She did not care about practical learning. She wanted to learn for its own sake, to cloister herself, to create a life of discipline and knowledge.

The other students who were to attend university had warned her against fields infected by communist doctrine, particularly history and economics. But she did not listen to them. She would find her own way. Marxism-Leninism was a separate compartment in her mind, like the Russian verbs she memorized. It was something she could do; she had discovered in herself a knack for theoretical subjects. It was true what everyone had always said of her: she was incompetent, clumsy. She felt capable only of working with problems which did not, strictly speaking, exist.

Lydia watched Piret unpack her books and paper and arrange everything neatly on the table. She knew that she had been right to encourage Piret to study; but now she worried. Piret was entering a minefield by choosing this subject. Lydia was not convinced that Piret had the sophistication to manage it.

She watched her great-niece open a textbook and begin to read. She was certain that Piret was sensible enough to know what to believe and what to ignore. But why had she chosen this? Lydia could not bring herself to talk about it. It was too late, she realized, thinking of the years of the silent, obstinate Piret; nobody had ever asked Piret what she thought. Piret was in another world now. All Lydia could do was peel the potatoes.

9

Peeter sat on the edge of the bed in his and Helena's bedroom in their flat in Södermalm. The bedroom, like the rest of the flat, was furnished with gifts, cast-offs, and sale items from Åhléns and Ikea. Their bed was unpainted pine; the bedspread was thin, quilted polyester in a salmon floral print. Helena's pine dressing table she had bought at an auction and repaired herself; Peeter could see a length of nail in the split between two panels. This sight made him more depressed than ever.

Helena stood a few feet away, bending slightly as if over her husband, with her arms folded in front of her. They had been speaking in loud, angry stage whispers; their voices had gradually become louder and then simultaneously fallen silent. Maarja, now nearly two years old, was asleep in her bedroom.

This argument ran along similar lines to their others. Peeter, Helena claimed, did not give a damn about anybody but himself. Helena, Peeter retaliated, was a possessive mother. Peeter was secretive and mean with money; Helena could not speak without hectoring Peeter.

Helena understood Peeter's complaints. She knew that they had once seen in one another some missing piece each yearned for. Helena had loved Peeter's sparkle; he had needed her solidity. Now they were disillusioned with the novelty of these qualities, and were angry at the childishness of their own desires.

She said quietly, 'You must see that you cannot expect me simply to sit back and say nothing while I work, run our home and take care of Maarja, while you waste your time doing God knows what. Where does your money go?'

'You don't know anything about journalism. This business is about contacts. I have to do a certain amount of socializing.'

'I am sure that whatever *this business* is about,' she replied sarcastically, 'it's about doing your work properly and on time.'

'Helena, you have no imagination or any sense of – ' He threw his hands up in despair. ' – of anything: of the way things work here. It's all to do with luck and meeting the right people. You don't keep your head down here. This isn't the goddamn USSR. You have to market yourself.'

They both saw they had yet again set out down the familiar road and fell silent. They could say nothing that would lead them elsewhere.

Helena knew he would leave soon and wished he would simply decide to do it: she would not tell him to go. She would not live with the responsibility, she told herself, although she knew what she really could not live with was the guilt and Peeter's eventual recriminations. She would do nothing to give him ammunition against her. She was perfectly capable of raising Maarja without Peeter – wasn't she virtually doing that already? – but she would not make it easy for him to go.

Peeter did not see the situation as clearly. He had a vague notion that he and Helena could not be reconciled, nor could they continue to live together as they were. But he could not take the first step towards separation. He could not imagine himself alone in Sweden, in some tiny flat, without his wife and child. Despite the dilapidated dressing table and floral bedspread, and despite his own desire to tear away from Helena's caution and pragmatism, he was not ready to make the break. He would be cast into bleakness where he would have to rely on himself, and nothing in his life had prepared him for that. Why should he be banished when, through no fault of his own, the situation had simply turned bad?

He had understood his fear when Helena had gone to Estonia to have Maarja christened. It was the first time he had been alone in Sweden. He had gone out on the first night, to a bar in Gamla Stan. He had cradled a single beer for an hour, frightened to spend another thirty crowns for a second. He had made himself miserable watching the couples at the tables and the groups of students standing around: they belonged. He did not know how to begin to belong.

The second night he had gone home with a Swedish girl. Later, he could not remember her name. She had dark blonde hair, possibly dyed, and a rather large nose. She was neither ugly nor beautiful. He knew that he had picked her because she did not intimidate him. She laughed at his accent and flattered him. She teased him that Swedes used to think Estonians were Nazis; now they were communists; and, anyway, weren't they really just Finns?

They went to her flat. There she removed her clothing without preamble and lay on the bed, her arms outstretched. He guessed her to be about twenty-seven or twenty-eight, which, for an Estonian, was far from young. Yet her body was lovely and cared for. Women in Estonia never looked like this. They married young and bore children young because, by the time they were thirty, they were old. Peeter already understood that a woman's life here was different. Although Helena worked a full week and did all the housework, she never had to wash clothes by hand, boil water for the dishes, spend her weekends preserving food. He had in fact justified his neglect of her in this way.

He now stared at the woman before him, mesmerized, and then said, 'You are so beautiful.'

She smiled and replied carelessly, 'Aerobics, darling,' pulled him on to the bed and began to undress him.

The lecture on Marxist-Leninist analysis was full when Piret entered. It was in a tiered room, a semi-circle of desks under fluorescent lights descending towards a tiny podium.

She noticed an unusually expectant atmosphere, unlike that in any of her other classes. Lectures on students' main subjects – mathematics, languages, sciences, literature – had an air of unflinching concentration; ideological lectures were attended perfunctorily, indifferent notes were taken, ironic glances were exchanged between friends, letters were written, newspapers read.

Rozhansky walked in moments after Piret was seated and a respectful hush spread across the room. Piret tried to imagine what his reputation must be to lead to such anticipation.

She waited, pen in hand, her paper ready. Rozhansky looked exactly as he had the day Piret had registered. He wore the same shapeless woollen jacket, the same baggy trousers. His hair was a motley grey, long at the top of his head, where he was balding; short at the sides. Strands of hair fell into his face from time to time. His wire-rimmed glasses sat crookedly on his nose. He looked bored and distracted.

He leaned on the lectern and began to speak to no one in particular, as though he were alone and talking to himself. There was no introduction. He simply began to talk about Marx's vision of social development. Occasionally he stopped and looked at his notes, but otherwise spoke as though he had given this lecture hundreds of times. It was dry and completely predictable. And yet seemingly every student wrote down his words with the utmost care, as though this unexceptional lecture were the most stimulating ever heard.

At the end of the class Rozhansky told them to write their first essay, to be handed in in two weeks' time. They were to choose a topic, subject to his approval. He wrote down his office number on the board and the hours he was available for discussion. Then he walked away.

As she left the lecture, Piret saw the Russian girl who had helped her at registration. Piret touched her arm and thanked her in Russian for her help. The girl gave Piret a startled look, surprised that an Estonian girl would speak to her in Russian. She shrugged and replied, 'Nitsevo.' *It doesn't matter.*

The following afternoon Piret went to Rozhansky's office and saw a younger man at the cluttered desk. He had very dark hair, nearly black and rather dirty. He wore a thin moustache and goatee and wire-rimmed glasses; he was about twenty-five.

'Yes?' He looked through her with a preoccupied expression and Piret saw how she appeared to him: another uninteresting student. She said, 'I've come to talk to Professor Rozhansky about our essay.' 'You can talk to me. I'm his assistant,' he replied. He glanced at her, then looked down again and continued to write. 'Well?' Piret looked at the head bent over the desk. She was disappointed, but went on, 'Well, I'm not sure what sort of essay – '

'You can write on historical materialism,' he interrupted irritably. 'It's the heart of everything, Marx's theory of social change.'

'Yes, I – '

'Concentrate on Marx's conception of the economic basis of society. Discuss the relations of production and system of property.' He looked up at her and tapped his fingers against his papers. She hesitated.

'Social development is dialectic,' he said impatiently. It was clear that he thought nothing of her, and could spare none of his valuable time.

'Discuss the stages of social development in relation to changes in production.' He picked up his pen and frowned. 'Is that clear?'

She did what he told her. She explained how the struggle between ruling classes and the workers was the stimulus behind the epochs of social development. After the feudal epoch came the modern bourgeois epoch; the final stage was the revolution of the proletariat, after which the means of production would be owned by all workers and a superior human society would emerge.

Professor Rozhansky gave her top marks. He wrote on the top of the page: 'Thorough and well written. Please see me.'

When she appeared at his office, he did not remember her. She stood before his desk as he sifted through papers, opened and closed drawers, took out his pen and then absentmindedly put it away again. 'And you are – ?'

She showed him her paper. 'Ah, yes, I see … May I see that again? Oh, yes, the methods of production … '

She had noticed the state of his office during her previous visit; it seemed now to have deteriorated even further. Books were stacked everywhere; papers poked out of files; filled ashtrays lay randomly about the room. On one wall was a copy of a painting of Lenin speaking on the eve of the Revolution; on the opposite wall, a portrait of Marx.

She put in hesitantly, 'It was your assistant who assigned me the topic ... '

'Ah, yes, Alexander. A fine student,' he added, trailing off, as he rummaged through a drawer. Then he seemed to recollect who Piret was and why he had asked her to see him. 'This doesn't seem to have stretched you far enough,' he told her. 'I want to see you do something more challenging next time.'

She realized that he was not as old as she had first thought. His worn appearance was no doubt due to his grey hair, his slight slouch, his incessant smoking. She noticed that his teeth were brownish, but his face surprisingly young and alert. From time to time he would look at her quickly and warily; then he would look away again. She thought of Alexander the week before at this same desk, and his steady, arrogant eyes, his transparent boredom.

They discussed possible topics, and Rozhansky lit one thick Russian cigarette after another, groping for crumpled blue packets of Kosmos which lay about the desk. Piret watched him light them, smoke them and then crush them into the ashtray, still smouldering. She tried to concentrate on their discussion, but the air became increasingly foul and she felt nauseated by the smell of the black tobacco. Her discomfort finally made her daring; she said, with the semblance of concern rather than reproach, 'Those cigarettes are terrible.'

He looked at the cigarette he was holding with some surprise, as though he had never noticed it before. He said, 'Oh, does it bother you?' She blushed slightly and nodded. He put the cigarette out. 'They are terrible. I don't like them at all, actually.' He tossed the nearest packet of cigarettes to one side of his cluttered desk. 'I remember you now. You were registering. You are the one who blushes.'

Piret felt submerged in pleasure: he knew who she was; she was somebody specific, distinct from the others. He returned her smile and then continued their discussion. She felt she could sit in this hard chair in front of Professor Rozhansky's desk for ever. He liked her; he had called her a 'young lady'; he thought she should try something more challenging.

They finally settled on Marx's analysis of competition in bourgeois economies as her next topic.

Leaving, she saw Rozhansky's assistant approach the office. 'Well,' he said, smiling, 'little Miss Anvelt; not bad for a first essay.'

She glanced at him and, murmuring something, walked quickly away. No man had ever looked at her like that: sarcastic, leering and yet admiring. *Predatory* was the word she thought of. She remembered his name now: Alexander. She tried to determine what he made her feel, and why, but she could not describe it; she only knew that she wanted never to be alone with him.

She went to the student cafeteria for lunch. She headed for the place she had staked out as her own, at the end of a long table. She was disappointed to see someone there, a girl. As she approached, she realized it was the Russian girl from Rozhansky's lecture. Piret touched the chair opposite and asked in Russian, 'May I join you?'

The girl nodded briefly and resumed eating. She was short, not attractive but with very bright, green eyes and olive skin. Piret sat down and told the girl her name.

'My name is Nadja Petravich Lykova,' she replied formally, in Russian. Piret saw that her teeth, like many Russians', were slightly crooked and bad with decay. The girl went on, 'I am studying English and French.' Nadja attended Rozhansky's lecture because Marxist-Leninist analysis was a requirement for all students. 'And because', she went on, 'his is supposed to be the best.

'But I for one', she continued, 'cannot see why. He is said to be so intelligent, but I found it dreadfully dull.'

Piret nodded and did not reply; she did not want to spoil her meeting with Rozhansky by gossiping about him.

They talked a bit about their studies and then Nadja told Piret she lived in Lasnamäe, where many Russians lived.

Again Piret did not reply; she had never been to Lasnamäe; it was a foreign place, a ghetto. Piret wondered why a Russian girl would be studying at an Estonian university, when Nadja suddenly said, 'But I am not Russian, not completely. I am Estonian.' Piret glanced up at her, and Nadja said, in Estonian, 'I read and write it, but I speak it poorly.'

Nadja's Estonian was accented, but not as poor as she claimed. Nadja gave a self-deprecating look and switched back to Russian. Her parents had been sent to Siberia in the early 1950s, she explained, among the last of Stalin's deportees. They had been accused of nationalist tendencies. Her father died in a camp shortly after she was born.

Her mother married a Russian who was from Estonia. 'One of the families who had been in Estonia since the days of the Tsar. He also wanted to return home. I believe he married my mother as a favour to her and to me. He was younger than my mother. I do not believe they were in love. But he was very kind to us.'

He had brought Nadja and her mother back to Estonia during the thaw; Nadja was ten. Her mother had died shortly after their return, and since then, Nadja had lived with her step-father and spoken Russian at home. 'But I hate Russia; I will never go back, even to study.'

Piret listened, taken aback by the girl's revelations. Nadja spoke impassively, as if reciting a story she had memorized. Piret saw that this was not an attempt at intimacy: she was merely relating facts which she clearly believed were as basic as her name; they would always separate her from others. The story was a highly worked version, shorn of its nightmarish details, scaled down to a minimum. It was a story she could live with.

Piret wanted to say, 'My mother is dead too.' But Nadja had not asked Piret about her family. And Piret thought: What would I say about her? She remembered so little now about her mother, which seemed shameful to admit. She remembered her mother's fair brown hair, the softness of her arms, the way she looked in the summer, on Lydia's rowing boat, her hand gliding across the water.

She remembered her mother dressing to go to Lydia's, collecting the baskets they would take with them on the bus, helping her father find his country clothes. She remembered being sent to collect berries and pick apples with Helena, and then bringing the buckets of fruit into the house, where her mother would be working silently in the kitchen.

She knew without being told that her mother never spoke to tädi Erna, although Helena's mother was kind; Piret was not afraid of her. Erna was short; Helena was like her father, tall and fair.

Piret's father would be outside, sitting and talking with Jaan, or drinking on the balcony, watching his cousin swim in the lake. Piret sometimes took the rowing boat out, pushing it away from the pier and jumping in as it rocked from side to side; Jaan would wave to her from another shore before diving in to resume his steady progress through the water.

Nadja said, 'But my father, my step-father, is very Estonian, in character.' She laughed. 'I mean, he works hard. He is a foreman.'

Piret did not want to discuss her own father. She did not want to think about the way he had sat at the kitchen table the last time she had visited him. She had watched him spin an empty vodka bottle in circles on the table top with one finger. He had refused to speak to her; she had asked him if he was angry that she was still at Lydia's. He would not answer.

She tried to change the subject: 'But why do you have a Russian name?'

Nadja said, 'My mother made Russian friends in Siberia. You know, it was not only Estonians who were sent to camps,' she added wryly. 'She named me after Nadezhda Mandelstam. The women in the factory taught each other poems and things. My mother memorized a letter written by Nadezhda Mandelstam to her husband when he was deported.' She stopped and bit into her sandwich. 'Because she was separated from my father. My real father.'

'Do you know it? The letter, I mean.'

'Oh, yes; my mother made me memorize it long before we left Siberia.' Nadja hesitated. 'Do you want to hear it?' she asked incredulously.

'Yes, please.'

Nadja took a breath, looked into the distance and recited:

'Life can last so long. How hard and long for each of us to die alone ... I could never tell you how much I love you. I cannot tell you even now. I who was such a wild and angry one and never learned to weep simple tears. Now I weep and weep and weep. It's me: Nadja. Where are you?'

Nadja stopped, expressionless, and then continued to eat. Piret, having nothing to say, opened the package Lydia had prepared that morning and took out her lunch.

10

Following Rozhansky's next lecture, Alexander followed Piret out of the lecture hall, saying, 'May I walk with you?'

She was surprised by his polite tone and glanced at him. She saw now that he was not tall, and that he was rather thin, like Paavo. She thought of Paavo's slender face, the way he cared for things, his innocence, his self-absorption.

Alexander had heavy, dark eyebrows which met over his nose; his mouth was set and he moved down the hall, next to her, with an air of certainty she had never seen in anyone, much less a student.

He went on imperially, 'My name is Alexander. Alexander Saar.'

'Yes,' she muttered, 'I know.'

He looked at her with an earnestness she found suspicious. She became annoyed: he wanted to tease her. Her irritation gave her courage. 'I am rather in a hurry.' She began to walk more quickly and he increased his pace as well.

He immediately changed tack and resumed his normal tone. 'A very diligent student, aren't you?' he inquired ironically.

She refused to answer and stared straight ahead, trying to disguise her apprehension.

'Ah, I see I have insulted you. Don't be so sensitive.'

Piret was walking quickly and he kept up, trotting slightly.

'That's the trouble with women; their minds are troubled by sensitivity.'

She had an inferior mind. She knew it; Rozhansky was being kind to her; this Alexander could see through her. She suddenly wanted him to tell her the truth, and despite herself she slowed her pace to listen to him.

'Not that you are particularly sensitive. You are simply a

woman. Don't look so stricken. Women are great forces in the revolutionary struggle,' he added derisively.

She did not answer or change her expression; it was a transparent attempt to test her, to probe. She distrusted his ironic tone; she was frightened of anybody who wanted to know what she thought.

After a moment he said, 'I'm sorry. You don't like being teased. I can't help it; I haven't seen such a first-rate mind in such an unlikely package in my entire life.'

She did not know what to say. He meant that she was ugly. Now she was angry again; why did this rude man think he could say anything he wanted to her? They had come out of the building. He had not noticed her annoyance. 'I have yet to meet a woman with a true understanding of the ideological – '

'I don't have to listen to this.' She turned to go.

'Please, wait. I didn't mean it that way, really I didn't. Please wait. I only meant – I only meant that – I like you.'

She stared at him for a moment and then turned and walked quickly away. She ran down the steps and across to the street. She jumped on the first tram she saw. She did not know where it was going; she would stay on it until she calmed down.

The tram started up and went down the boulevard. Piret watched the passing shops and houses without noticing her direction. She did not want this man and his aggressive flirtation. She was not flattered. She did not want sex or romance or this game he seemed to expect. She realized that she did not understand the manipulation, the inconsistency of men.

Paavo had wanted her to be more demanding, more intelligent, less willing to surrender herself to him. She had listened to his complaints about her, and when she did nothing to defend herself or try to change he was angry. She knew she ought to say something; he would wait impatiently while she tried to think of something to say, and then he would grow angry with her silence. She knew that he found her stupid.

She did not understand how men and women could love or trust one another when relations between them seemed to be a contest of wills. She could not be what they wanted; she had neither the energy or inclination to try. She had only enough stamina to concentrate on her studies.

She got off the tram and started to walk back to the bus station. When she got home, she took off her shoes and coat and sat down at the table. She opened her book and responded to Lydia's questions in monosyllables until Lydia left her alone.

She worked until dinner, and then again until Lydia was in bed. She undressed and climbed into the top bunk. She lay staring at the ceiling and listening to the wind across the lake, and eventually fell asleep.

The next morning was Saturday; Lydia asked Piret if she ought not to visit her father.

They were collecting fruit in the grove. 'You don't have to stay long; you need only say a few words. Try to be a bit kind. He has lost everything, you know.'

Piret knew what Lydia meant: that Oskar had never been given anything and Jaan had been given every advantage, every opportunity. Oskar had been first abandoned by his father, then orphaned by the death of his mother when he was thirteen. He had gone to live on his Aunt Emmeline's farm. His cousin Jaan was fifteen; he was sent to Tallinn every day to attend a private school, driven by one of the farmhands in a wagon. He wore a uniform, a blue suit with a felt hat, and carried his books in a leather satchel.

Emmeline decided not to educate Oskar and told him so shortly after he arrived. It was too costly and he was nearly the age of some of the farmhands. Besides it was 1943 and the war was on; food was becoming scarce.

Jaan did nothing to change his mother's mind, Lydia had told Piret. 'Emmeline adored Jaan. He could have changed everything for your father.'

Piret always shrugged at this; it was all a long time before she was born. She knew that her grandmother Anna – Oskar's mother – had been Lydia's favourite sister, and that of her nephews Lydia had loved Oskar the most.

But Piret did not want to imagine what her drunken father might have been had Emmeline been kinder, or had his parents not died; had he and Matti inherited the farm along with Jaan; had the Russians not come.

Thousands of farms were abandoned after the war, deportees' or refugees' farms, collectivized family farms; theirs was one of many. Piret had seen them, the low mounds in the fields, surrounded by groups of trees, clumps of shrubbery, the remnants of a stone foundation.

Piret went to see her father. He was sober and dressed. He had combed his hair. She glanced around and saw the newspapers stacked into a pile; he had thrown away the empty vodka bottles. He had cleaned the table in front of the sofa; she could see the streaks left by the cloth.

He stood before her, smiling. 'I have a new job. It's very important and very secret.' He named a factory which manufactured parts for nuclear reactors. Piret nodded.

'We have to put a card in a computer to go in,' he explained proudly. 'Only workers are allowed in. No one else.'

Piret listened to this without comment; her silence seemed to goad him on.

'It is so large that they must drive trucks from one end to another. And so important that it is all surrounded by barbed wire and guards and dogs.'

'What do you do there?' she inquired dispassionately.

'I am a lathe-minder,' he announced, watching for her reaction.

She did not question this, knowing that he was not qualified to operate a lathe; he probably assisted a lathe operator.

He looked a little disappointed at her lack of enthusiasm. 'I have started again. My life. I am beginning now. They told me – they told me I can have a chance again.' He looked at her and then said, 'Why are you so cold? What has happened to you?'

'Nothing has happened to me.'

'You never come here.'

'I'm busy. I have to study.'

'What are you studying?'

'Different things.'

'You're a communist. Lydia told me.'

Piret was furious; she had always relied on Lydia's confidence; she certainly never relied on her father's. Then it occurred to her that he had simply tried to think of something vile to say; it was a stab in the dark; Lydia was unlikely to have discussed Piret's studies with her father. 'I don't believe you. Lydia said no such thing.'

'Then why won't she tell me what you are doing, what you are studying?'

'Why don't you ask me? I am studying mathematics.'

He apologized. Then to her astonishment and revulsion, he broke down. He sat down on the lumpy brown sofa and put his head in his hands. He was lonely, he told her. He missed her. He missed how they used to cook together in the evenings, he missed her mother. He was all alone; why did she want to live at Lydia's and not in town? Why did she not want him any more? Why had she done this to him?

She did not reply; she could think of nothing to say. She could not say, 'Because you will always remind me of the past.'

Alexander apologized after the next lecture. She listened in silence, her head bowed in mortification.

'It's just that I'm not very – experienced with girls,' he went on in a rehearsed manner that Piret had come to recognize.

She looked up, her face still and composed. She felt her body recoil, but she forced herself to show nothing. She nodded at him and walked away. She would have to make an even greater effort to avoid him.

She thought that had she been another sort of girl, she might have liked him. He was Rozhansky's student; he was not unattractive. She had been quick to judge him; perhaps his impudence actually did cover awkwardness and inexperience.

Paavo's timidity had appealed to her. Now she saw that she had again drawn such a man. Alexander was arrogant, but he must lack confidence if he wanted Piret. He, like Paavo, probably believed he could not get a better girl, a tall, beautiful and intelligent girl like Helena. Piret could never imagine herself like Helena, laughing easily with a boy. She was weak.

Alexander was right about that. She was 'sensitive'. Her training had not yet made her objective enough.

Only when she could treat her own emotions with the same impartiality as she did her work would she feel at ease with men. That was, she believed, what successful women did: they controlled their emotions; they were not consumed by them. One day, she promised herself, she would have the ability to talk to a man without blushing, without faltering over every word. She would not care that she was ugly, short, dark. She would be an intellectual, a woman of ideas; she would have a mind people respected.

She congratulated herself on having eluded Alexander. She decided that she was privileged not to need a man. She was protected; she had rights. She was not a sexual machine like women in the West, trapped by the oppression of their bodies, enslaved by the family. She lived where women were respected. She remembered from her textbook the Bolshevik proposition that equal rights should be extended to women, non-Russians, atheists; that civil marriage should be valid and illegitimate children recognized. She lived in the land of justice and humanity.

She wrote another essay and Rozhansky asked her to his office again.

'You admit in your paper that there is much in Marx you do not understand.'

She sat on the edge of the chair. He now saw through her; he was disillusioned; he was about to tell her that she was far too stupid to have ever been admitted to the university. They would send her home and she would milk cows on a collective for the rest of her life.

'You understand the term "relations of production"?' he demanded.

'They are the relations between men engaged in co-operative production. They are determined by the methods of production and are thus independent of man's will,' she nearly whispered.

'And determine the number and nature of social classes.'

74

'Yes.'

'But?'

'Well – ' Piret felt herself trembling. 'Well, it's in the nature of the bourgeois epoch that the ruling classes will promote technology to extract greater profits from the workers. As technology becomes more complex, so should the class structure. At least,' she added apologetically, 'I think so.'

'You are correct.'

'But Marx also wrote that the number of classes should be simplified as we move towards social revolution. The workers should unite against the ruling class. And so greater profits actually contradict the idea of a united working class.' Piret stopped suddenly, aghast at this heresy.

Rozhansky did not seem disturbed. 'Um, yes. So it would appear. A small and yet vital point. For if there is no united working class, there can be no social revolution.'

Piret did not reply. She waited for him to decide where to take this idea. 'It would seem that there is much we could try to discover about Marx.'

By the end of term, she was spending an afternoon every two weeks or so in Rozhansky's office. Occasionally he asked her if they should walk to the cafeteria, or to the library. It was on these walks that he made his most ideologically subversive suggestions.

He asked her what would, after a workers' revolution, prevent the workers from enslaving the former ruling class? What if the workers organized to demand higher wages? She noticed that he never said anything that could damage himself. He never spoke against the Soviet system. Should anybody ask her, she could truthfully say that he only tested her knowledge of Marxism-Leninism.

This was not a theoretical concern. Solzhenitsyn had recently been deported. Dissident publications in the West put the number in labour camps in the tens of thousands. Piret knew that she must take as much care as Rozhansky.

She understood now why his lectures were packed; he committed the most dangerous of acts: he asked people to think for themselves, rather than merely memorize and regurgitate. Piret also realized that she had been chosen as his special pupil, as those eager students had hoped to be.

Christmas Eve arrived without snow. Lydia and Piret collected pine cones from the forest and hung red and blue paper chains about the house. They cooked for three days. They laid the table with meat in glossy aspic – *sült*, three kinds of herring, finely sliced black bread, potato salad and sauerkraut. They lit candles.

When Piret's father arrived, he was already drunk. He sat down at the table, took out a fresh bottle of vodka from his pocket, peeled off the metal top and began to drink. After ten or fifteen minutes, he moved to the sofa, lay down and went to sleep. Piret and Lydia ate dinner in silence.

Piret joined Komsomol in the New Year, after Rozhansky had hinted that she should do so. She knew she must protect herself. She would learn from him how to survive.

She told Nadja of her decision, who said, 'Why do you bother? Are you going to continue your studies?'

'Perhaps.' They were walking from the bus stop, through the newly fallen snow.

'Aren't you?'

'No.' Nadja fell silent, and Piret knew she was debating whether to explain her plans.

'What will you do?' Piret prompted.

Nadja looked at her. 'Leave.'

'Leave?'

'Don't you see? I have no future here. I am neither Russian nor Estonian. I can speak English now and I am learning French.'

'But how? Where will you go?'

'Oh, I don't know. Something will come up. America, maybe. I am too angry about everything to stay. You have something – you're a real Estonian, you aren't embittered like me. You can do something with your life here. I can't.'

They were silent, and then Nadja continued: 'Do you understand what I have lived through? I have seen what they can do to us. They are supposed to have given us dignity and security. But it's ridiculous, a sham. It's all about power.'

Piret shrugged. 'This is my country,' she replied impassively.

'For how long? For how many more generations will you speak Estonian? Estonians are a tiny tribe. How long were they independent? Once, for a few short years between the wars.'

'We have our culture. The Russians haven't conquered us yet.'

'Just wait.'

Piret did not reply.

'We live like schizophrenics,' Nadja went on bitterly, 'thinking one thing and saying another. People succeed here by pretending to believe something they despise. They have taken away our right to a conscience.'

Piret knew this was true. None the less, she resented Nadja's criticism; she knew she would never leave; she had to learn to live within the system that was her home; perhaps, she told herself, it would improve over time.

She replied obstinately, 'Who are "they"?'

'Oh, don't be coy, Piret. You know. The party. The government. You can't deny it. I remember the pictures in Siberia of Stalin and the tractors and the happy peasants. My father was tortured and shot. They are thugs.'

'That was Stalin,' Piret replied calmly. 'Anyway, the government has given us a lot the West doesn't have. We have rights, employment. You think you will have this in the West? You want to live where there is nothing but violence and exploitation?'

'I will live where I will be able to think for myself.'

'You are naïve,' Piret said mildly.

'And you are a typical Estonian: cold and unfeeling. You can live like a robot. I've never felt at home here. There is no warmth.'

Piret shrugged again. She knew Nadja was speaking from her own unhappiness, rather than from any logic. Perhaps this is the end of our friendship, thought Piret.

But it was not. They glided over their differences and continued to meet for lunch. They talked mostly about books or their studies; neither was interested in clothes and Piret watched little television. They saw each other occasionally on the weekends for a lecture or concert in town; Piret never went to Nadja's flat, and Nadja never visited Lydia's.

Piret's life continued throughout the year without incident. She attended her monthly Komsomol meetings regularly, studied, took exams, wrote essays. She lived beyond reproach. She never asserted her opinions, never revealed herself, never aligned herself. Even her friendship with Nadja was circumscribed. She never told Nadja about Maarja or the details of her family. Nadja did not know that Piret's mother was dead, or her father a drunk, or that her cousin had emigrated. Both let the subject of Nadja's plans drop from their conversations.

Spring came and Piret continued to see Rozhansky, always at his invitation and with discretion: as if by accident, or in connection with her studies. She did not talk about him with other students; she did nothing to give the impression that he was her mentor or she his disciple. She knew that although he was admired, he was also mistrusted for his independence. She knew the precariousness of an academic position, even one as respected as his. If Rozhansky fell from favour, she did not want to endanger her studies.

He had chosen her for her natural scepticism and because she, a girl, would not be conspicuous as a favoured student; she was a safe repository for his desire to talk. He was, she discovered, forty-three; younger than she had initially thought, but still over twenty years her senior. She had heard that he had been married and had a son who lived in Russia. He never spoke of this. Theirs was a safe friendship.

Her initial pleasure at having been chosen by him had been accompanied by fear of her own inadequacy. Now she worked to maintain his respect. She perfected the qualities he had chosen her for; her mind became the sharp edge of a knife: deducting, excluding, rigorous. They had, she felt, a friendship of the highest order, of two intellectuals who believed only in the pursuit of knowledge.

Piret knew from their discussions that there was no simple truth. But so much remained unanswered in her mind, tantalizing questions she could not ask directly. How did the West really work? She could not yet understand how, without a central planning committee, the haphazard decisions of millions of people coalesced to form a market economy. How did they decide how much to produce? She tried to imagine a group of American capitalists, smoking fat cigars around a table, giving orders to their underlings.

But she could not ask Professor Rozhansky. Their discussions were layered, opaque, sinuous. She had read some of his published papers and saw that they were as cautious and impenetrable as he himself. His writing was on the surface unobjectionable; between the lines Piret could see complexities she could not yet grasp.

She tried to compartmentalize her thoughts, attempting to keep one part untainted, fresh, inquiring. She tried to separate in her mind what she considered propaganda from what she considered serious economic analysis. But it was not clear how to pick through the maze. Her mind was formed every day by what she was told: that the Soviet revolution had advanced human society, that colonialism and racism were the foundations of capitalist society.

At the end of the year she was given a student room, her first privilege. She was told she could move in that autumn. This made her inordinately happy; she was part of something; she had been accepted.

Lydia could not object to Piret leaving; the journey to town took over an hour. Yet she knew she would miss Piret; she hid her distress behind her habitual grumpiness. Piret promised to return every weekend.

11

By the time Maarja was five, she was obsessed with clothes. She tried on Helena's old dresses and evaluated herself with a critical eye in front of the full-length mirror. She liked to hold her head at certain angles; she liked Helena's black chiffon evening wrap.

This alarmed Helena, who had never imagined a five-year-old could be entranced with her own image or could intuit the potential power of her beauty. Helena had become increasingly indifferent to her own potential since her divorce. Although only in her mid-twenties she had become a serious woman, warding off male interest with a forbidding manner, neglecting her hair and skin and weight. She watched her daughter grow and knew that her own life would now more or less follow a predictable path. Maarja's life held all the mystery and excitement now.

Helena had spent Maarja's first year striving to be an indulgent parent of infinite tolerance and patience. At first she had been optimistic and confident: there was nothing, she felt, that could stop her from being a perfect mother. Peeter's neglect had given her a gratifying antithesis to work against, which made it all the easier.

Whenever Maarja had been difficult and Helena felt her patience slipping, she remembered the tiny face on the plane to Sweden, the sleeping baby on her shoulder when they went back for the christening. It tore her heart: Maarja was dependent on her, alone, in need.

Then, after the divorce, Maarja seemed to change suddenly and become difficult; Helena could find no reason for it and was stricken with guilt. Maarja cried inconsolably, not wanting food, comfort, stimulation or sleep. There were times when

Helena was so tired, so completely exhausted, that she put her head down on the kitchen table and wept. One night, far past midnight, Helena left Maarja screaming in her cot and sat outside her front door in the hall, on the stairwell, and thought: I know now why mothers sometimes hurt their babies.

Her parents had moved from Rinkeby to Odenplan when Jaan had taken a job as a ward doctor in a nearby hospital. Odenplan was in town and much closer to Helena and Maarja, and Erna sometimes stayed overnight to give Helena a chance to sleep.

As Maarja approached her third birthday, she began to display her stubborn streak. She threw unwanted food on the floor and screamed when she was crossed. Although small, she was none the less strong. She could bring her weight down, arch her back and stretch out her legs until she was impossible to lift. Helena began to understand that a child could not, without violence, be forced to do anything.

Helena's efforts at perfection soon broke down completely in the face of her obstinate, wilful child. Maarja's lungs grew in power; she was capable of screaming at ear-splitting ranges for ten or fifteen minutes in the supermarket, in the underground, at church, whenever Helena had company.

It was when old ladies began to stop in shops to badger her with unsolicited advice that Helena decided something had to be done. She found that depriving Maarja of toys and sweets worked wonders on her daughter's behaviour. It was not at all the idea she had had of being a mother. She had imagined always being able to discuss differences with her daughter reasonably. She felt like a dictator.

Peeter came every second Sunday to take Maarja for a walk or to a museum. Neither Helena nor Peeter could say more than was necessary to one another, out of misery and guilt, and knowing that there was now nothing left to say.

Helena knew he was seeing other women. Peeter would now begin his life in Sweden: he was still young. Helena knew she should try to feel the same: she had a good job, for SAS; she was only twenty-six. But she had built her life on her marriage, and now she felt that she had lost what had made her special. She was now like millions of other women: a single mother with a job.

It was now the final year of Piret's undergraduate studies, a warm Saturday afternoon in April 1977. Nadja and Piret met at Raekoja plats to see an exhibition at the City Museum. Afterwards they walked through the old town, talking and stopping at an occasional shop.

Nadja said, 'I'm thinking of cutting my hair.'

Piret glanced at her and did not reply. She rarely thought about her own appearance. Lydia regularly trimmed Piret's shoulder-length hair, which she had worn tied back since her teenage years.

'Don't you ever want to change something about yourself?' Nadja asked.

Piret considered this. 'Not really.'

They passed a public lecture hall. They stopped to read the calendar of events for the month, which was a series of lectures sponsored by the Society of Knowledge: Social Problems of Divorce; Law and the Family; Socialist Development in Africa; Anthropological Findings of Pre-Soviet Steppe Peoples.

Several people were entering the building, and Piret and Nadja noticed that the day's lecture was about to begin on the subject of health education. 'It must be about sex,' said Nadja, laughing. 'Let's go in.'

They went in and found seats at the back. 'In case it's boring,' Nadja whispered. They sat down; then Piret looked up at the podium and froze with panic: she was looking at Maarja's godmother. Sylvia was sorting through some papers, apparently her notes for the lecture. Her dark hair was no longer in the traditional chignon she had worn at the christening, but was now short. Otherwise she was the same: the solid, regal bosom, the large, capable arms, her back straight and head high, her black glasses held by a chain around her neck.

Piret started to rise, but the rest of their row was filling up and Nadja gripped her arm. 'Where are you going? Let's at least see what it's about.'

Sylvia cleared her voice, peered down her nose through her glasses at the audience and introduced herself. She told them the name of the lecture: 'Health Education'. She scanned the audience like a school teacher searching for hints of sedition, and Piret slid down in her chair to obscure herself.

'I want to discuss', Sylvia began, 'a subject I feel is sadly neglected by our current state of health education: the topic of moral responsibility.'

Nadja glanced over at Piret and rolled her eyes. She did not notice Piret's discomfort.

'I am speaking of the responsibility of parents towards the children they bring into this world.' Sylvia's voice reprimanded every person in the room. 'We cannot deny that divorce is becoming a problem. We are seeing an increase in the number of single mothers raising children without the help of a husband.'

She continued her lecture, reciting statistical evidence. She spoke about the dangers of a lack of male role models, and the pressures on women to provide for their families while also fulfilling the father's role of discipline and authority.

Piret barely listened to this. She only thought about getting out as soon as possible. She disliked social issues, particularly when they were debated with statistics. Statistics, everybody knew, could buttress any argument.

'We are seeing children raised by bossy mothers and without fathers, creating confused sons without a strong sexual identity. And yet the rising generation is our hope for the future. The mother's upbringing of the child creates the structure of society and its values.

'What can be done about the next generation of our men? How can we persuade women to become more feminine? What is causing such a breakdown in marital stability?

'Women do not tolerate their husbands' weaknesses as they have in the past. How can women learn not be so exacting with their husbands? The masculinization of women is threatening an entire generation of Soviet men.'

The audience applauded and were then invited to write down questions or problems on slips of paper. These were collected and brought up to the podium. At this point Nadja wanted to leave, but Piret would not move for fear of drawing attention to herself.

Sylvia unfolded the first slip of paper and read aloud: 'Can this be the influence of Western values?' She took off her glasses and said, 'Of course the influence of Western decadence has to take some of the blame, but we must also look to ourselves, to our own men and women, in order to solve this problem.'

From the next slip of paper Sylvia read: 'Perhaps women are bored by their husbands. All men seem to want to do is drink with their friends.' She replied, 'If this is the case, then wives must educate their husbands to spend their free time more productively, on culture and on family activities.'

The questions continued for some time, and finally, to Piret's relief, people rose to leave.

Outside, Nadja said, 'You see? Society is rotten here. Women's life here is so difficult, it all results in their turning into men.'

'You think that women should all go back to being housewives, like in the West? To being a man's maid and prostitute?'

'I think women are tired of being cheap factory labour and doing all the housework and being responsible for everything. It's no wonder they're masculinized.'

'Capitalism', Piret said curtly, as if she were addressing her own audience, 'is by nature a patriarchical society. Women's relation to men is comparable to that of a vassal to his feudal lord.'

'Don't you understand that it is exactly the same here?'

'Of course it isn't. Don't be ridiculous. We have economic independence, the right to work, abortion, divorce, nurseries – '

'Women do not earn as much as men. And they are still their husband's domestic slaves. You heard her. Our men are lazy and boring and then they run off and leave their wives to raise the children.'

'You don't have to get married,' Piret pointed out.

'Of course I don't. But what if I want to? And what if I want to raise my children myself instead of being forced to work?'

'There is maternity leave.'

Nadja said crossly, 'There is maternity leave practically all over Europe. At least in the West you have the choice about whether to work or not.'

'Nadja,' Piret replied with forbearance, 'do you not understand that the entire Western economy is structured around men's wages? You have a choice whether to work or not depending on how much your husband makes. Women are assumed to live off their husband's wages; they are paid far less than a man for the same work. Men make more because they are assumed to own a woman, like owning a slave.'

'If you think women are paid equal wages here, you're wrong.'

'I know there are discrepancies. It is not the exceptions that count. The capitalist system is based on exploitation; the communist system is based on equality.'

'Piret, you live in a fantasy world, a world of theories. The exceptions are the point. You have to work whether you marry or not – '

'Everybody has to work. It is a right and a duty. Work is dignity.'

Nadja ignored her. 'You can't have children if your flat is too small or you don't have a flat and live with your parents; nobody makes enough money; and anyway there aren't enough flats.

'Besides, men never listen to all this official talk about helping with the housework. Do you remember when they decreased the working week for women from six days to five? It was so they could do their shopping and cleaning! You call that equality? You are some man's servant if you get married; you are alone if you do not. What kind of a choice is that?'

Piret sighed. Nadja said, 'Don't you see that the whole system is rubbish? It can't work for ever. Nobody has anything to work for.'

'You can work for an idea.'

'Perhaps you can. Most people want to work for themselves and their families. All we work for here is the right to have an abortion a year and no choice at all about where to live, what to read, where to travel.'

They walked on; they both knew not to discuss it further. It was not until they parted at the tram stop and waved briefly to one another that Piret realized that she had not once, throughout their entire discussion, thought of Maarja. The tram arrived and Piret boarded. A vision of Sylvia holding Maarja protectively against her appeared in Piret's mind, and she forced it away. She found a seat and quickly took a book out of her bag and began to read.

The following year, 1978, Piret turned twenty-three. She obtained her *Diplom*, printed in Russian and Estonian and bound like a book, its blue cover impressed with the hammer and sickle. She would now spend the next three years as *aspirantor*, on her post-graduate research. She would then, after her defence, become a *dotsent*, a doctoral candidate, and possibly an assistant professor.

She wanted to conduct research into the inefficiency of capitalist economics. The illusion of efficiency she considered to be the fundamental theoretical flaw of capitalist theory.

Sometimes she thought of the boy in her Marxism class years before who had asked the provocative question: Why had capitalism not yet destroyed itself as Marx had predicted? The teacher had turned red with annoyance; the entire class waited, paralysed with astonishment. The boy had continued to look at the teacher, who conspicuously made a note with her pen and then replied, quite coldly, 'It will.'

Of course it will, thought Piret: in theory. It had a pool of cheap, unrecognized workers: the poor, the blacks and women. And because prices only reflected the cost of capital and underpaid labour, the results were eroded living conditions for the workers, pollution and recurring economic crises.

Piret discussed her idea with Rozhansky, who suggested that she carry out the work at the Institute of Economics at the

Academy of Sciences. He knew a senior researcher there, a man called Vaikmaa, who was also a professor at the Polytechnic. They spent several afternoons discussing how to present her proposal; she would need approval by the Council of Sciences and funding from Gosplan, the state planning agency, or from the Ministry of Finance.

Rozhansky, however, seemed to approve of it; he pointed out that it would open to Piret a world of research and books and Western publications that many academics would never see; it might mean trips abroad. At the Academy research materials were freely available. No longer would Piret need a letter from her department head each time she wanted a book from the S-fond, the locked room in the basement of the Polytechnic library where each book had been marked with the hexagonal stamp of Glovlit, the state censor.

Rozhansky arranged an interview, and the following week Piret walked into the Academy, near Victory Square, and up three flights of smooth stone steps to the dark, quiet halls of the Institute of Economics.

Professor Vaikmaa led her to a small office furnished with a laminated, wood-effect desk stacked with papers, a single filing cabinet and two rickety wooden chairs. He asked Piret why she had chosen her topic.

'All theoretical questions under socialism have been elaborated,' she replied in the dry tone she had by now perfected to a fine point of effortlessness. Piret rarely discussed anything with other students or professors but economic theory. She never offered information about her private life, fearing she would encourage unwelcome questions. Nadja had graduated and now Piret usually lunched alone. The few who were aware that Piret and Rozhansky had a sort of relation knew it to be the dry, sexless friendship of two pedants.

Vaikmaa was a small man in his early sixties, with a moustache and goatee. He had the impassive frown and guarded eyes of the careful, of one who has survived. Piret wondered what he knew about Rozhansky and whether she could be of any use to this man. She sat quietly and they gazed at one another for a few seconds; they both knew they would get little information of any importance from one another, and this was how it should be: professional trust lay in safety and in reticence. He said, 'What do you mean?'

'The Soviet system is moving towards the ultimate goal of non-government.' She had rehearsed this statement. 'Our work is to attain production and consumption levels that bring our people the highest standards possible.

'All human problems can be resolved through Lenin's development of the Marxist framework,' she went on. 'Economic equality has created social equality. Any remaining theoretical questions therefore concern pre-socialist systems.

'I see in this research the possibility of targeting the breaking point of the capitalist economies. It is not only theoretically interesting, but it is a useful tool for future planning.'

'Yes, I see,' he said, writing something down. 'Yes, well, Miss Anvelt. I do see you are quite clear about your ideas.' He coughed and continued to write. 'I don't see why you shouldn't … I will submit this proposal to the Council with my full approval.'

She quickly discovered that this topic passionately interested her. No longer did she imagine round tables of suited capitalists chewing on fat cigars, deciding where their money would go. She knew now how capitalists controlled the government by manipulating the media and by bribery, how the stock market distributed capital in accordance with the profit mechanism.

Piret did not completely believe this simple picture, but she enjoyed it. She thought little now of what she believed; the part of her mind she once kept fresh and inquiring had calcified into a hard shell of indifference. Her work was a kind of game.

The year that Piret began her research academic journals began to print articles on a new topic: 'the elaboration of a contemporary model of socialism'. This was a euphemism for economic reform, which had surfaced under different aliases from time to time since the 1960s. Such work was always limited, usually focusing on increasing output. It would have been professionally and personally ruinous to question the fundamental workings of a centrally planned economy. This new research, however, seemed to verge exactly on this.

Piret knew as well as her colleagues that the economy was stagnating; output had fallen, quotas were unfilled. Statistics were either withheld or clearly doctored. Any economist could study the USSR's national accounts and see that the numbers simply did not add up. No economy can continue indefinitely with falling output and massive military and social expenditure: the money has to come from somewhere.

Piret wanted nothing to do with radical reform. Dogmatic Marxists were powerful in the Kremlin and would not tolerate any threat to Gosplan and central planning, to the massive system of privilege, job security and private arrangements that made the Soviet bureaucracy function. Piret instinctively avoided any subject that had political ramifications, that could draw attention to herself. She had worked too hard to lose it all now.

Professor Vaikmaa sometimes tried to draw her out. She had become known at the Institute as the dry stick, the robotic woman. He knew that she avoided any association with the 'elaboration of the contemporary socialist model'. He wondered if she knew something he did not.

Nadja came to Piret's room to say goodbye. She showed Piret her passport. Piret had never seen one; she took it and said involuntarily, 'It's red.'

Nadja laughed. 'Of course.' Piret, like all citizens, had a nearly identical document which was blue and acted as a domestic passport, a national identity card.

'Where are you going?' Piret asked, thinking of Vienna or New York.

'Oh,' Nadja said vaguely. 'I don't really know yet – I mean, eventually.'

'Eventually?'

'You know, perhaps America – eventually.'

'But where are you flying to?'

'Oh, it's just a temporary stop ... '

Piret looked at her, puzzled.

'Well, Tel Aviv, actually.'

'Tel Aviv!' Piret stared at her.

'Yes, well, it was the only place I could get in.'

They were both silent and then Nadja rose. 'Well, I suppose I shall go then.'

They hugged once, briefly. Then she was gone and Piret realized that she herself had not been the only one with a secret. Nadja too had kept something to herself: she was Jewish. Jewish immigration was not discussed in the papers, but rumour held that immigration had increased, fuelled and corroborated by the usual outbreak of anti-Zionist articles, including a few about Jews who had collaborated with the Nazis.

Piret had heard that many of the emigrants flown to Israel went on to the United States. What kind of people were they? They had turned their back on their country after everything it had done for them – they were, after all, mostly educated people. They applied for visas ostensibly for religious reasons, but in fact had lied in order to go to the United States to make money. Let Nadja join them, Piret thought. Let her see if life is better among the corrupt and the hypocritical; let her live off the sweat of the exploited.

The Institute allocated Piret two rooms in a grey concrete house nearby. She shared the house with three families; there was a rota for using the single kitchen and bath. She could hear children in the mornings, and one couple who quarrelled nearly every night, followed by frenzied sex. But she liked it; two rooms seemed luxurious after her tiny student room and, anyway, she was out much of the time.

A few months passed uneventfully. Piret worked hard and socialized little. She scoured the Institute library for materials: *The Economic History of Capitalist Countries, Capitalist Currency Systems, Financial Monopoly Formation in the United States*. Her English improved and she read, fascinated by their strange logic, Western textbooks: *Money and Banking, Microeconomics, International Economics.*

She sometimes missed Nadja and their difficult conversations. Nadja's combative opinions and grievances had been an exhilarating influence, Piret now realized. She was alone much of the time. She rarely went to the Polytechnic and saw Rozhansky less. She missed him, although their relationship was still, after five years, as professional and distant as ever.

During one of her explorations through the Institute library, she came across an article he had recently written and never mentioned to her. When she read it, she understood why. It was entitled, 'The Non-Capitalist Road to Intensive Economic Development'. It was ostensibly about developing a socialist economy in former Third World colonies.

Piret read: 'The overt use of force and armed territorial occupation have always underpinned the formation of colonies. Political coercion has been the main instrument to exploit oppressed people.

'Colonial bondage assured imperialist powers of markets, raw materials, military-strategic bases and reserves for manning armies. The colony is plundered of its raw materials; industries are developed to cater for the imperialist power; and the colony therefore loses the opportunity to develop its own resources.'

Piret saw at once that this was ideologically indisputable yet utterly subversive: he was not writing about the Third World; he was writing about Estonia and its exploitation as a conquered colony of Russia. Estonian land had been ravaged by mining; industrial production was mostly exported to other Soviet republics, and pre-war Estonian industries had vanished. Rozhansky would never have expected Piret to discuss the covert message of this article and so never mentioned it to her.

She had always known he was a nationalist, but she now found herself embarrassed and disturbed by his overt declaration. She shook these feelings off and put the article away. She had once found Rozhansky's papers opaque; it was now second nature to her to read for the hidden, for the implicit.

She thought briefly, fleetingly: If it is so clear to me, it must also be clear to many others.

Piret visited Lydia every second or third weekend; they never discussed Piret's work. Lydia did not understand it, and Piret needed the tranquil absorption of working at Lydia's as much as she needed her research.

One morning Piret came home late and found a letter from Lydia. She opened it and read that her father had been admitted to Kiirabi hospital in Mustamäe. Lydia had not been able to visit him yet as she herself was not well. She urged Piret to go; he was quite ill.

The following morning Piret took a tram to Kiirabi hospital, asked for his room and was directed to a ward. She passed down a hall and saw a row of elderly men, all unshaven, toothless, dozing or staring blankly before them. She hurried past them to the end of the ward, where two nurses were changing an empty bed.

They paused and looked up at her. She glanced around and did not see her father. Then she told them that she was looking for someone, a patient. She knew as soon as she spoke what they would tell her. She gave them his name: Oskar Anvelt.

They looked at her and then at one another. Yes, the elder nurse replied. She hesitated and then said that she was sorry: he had died that morning. She looked at Piret for a moment; when Piret did not react, she added that he had received no visitors; was she a relation? Could she help them with the name of the next of kin?

Piret did not answer. Her first thought was to deny all knowledge of her father. She wanted to reply, 'No, not a relation, only an acquaintance,' and walk away. But she resisted the temptation; it was impossible to avoid her duty as his daughter. She had become too rational for such an emotional impulse to form her actions. Somebody would have to tell Lydia, arrange the funeral, fill out forms, empty his flat.

She thought of her father's blue dressing gown, and the old black skillet he had used to fry potatoes. She thought of her mother's photograph album of her family at the picnics on

Lake Peipsi; and of the box of pictures of Emmeline's farm, of Jaan on the farm wagon, dressed for school. It occurred to Piret that she had never seen a photograph of her father on the farm; he was an orphan and farmhand, not worth the time and expense of a photograph. She knew she would have to go through all these pieces of her father's life deciding what to throw away, what to keep.

The two nurses stood over the bed, tucking the sheets in, looking at her. Piret tried to determine what she felt. She had not seen her father for nearly a year. That she had not seen him grow sick or die made his death all the more remote. She had been as little involved in his death as she had in her mother's. She knew there must have been a chain of events leading up to their deaths – the first signs, the worsening of symptoms, doctors' opinions, tests, the failing of one function after another. But she could not imagine the end of life.

She tried to believe that she would feel something later, that her response was normal: a delayed reaction. But she knew she would not. She would forget about her father as thoroughly as she had her mother.

All she seemed to feel was relief. This appalled and shamed her; she knew now that her heart had thickened into a mass of hardened tissue, comatose, yet alive. But she understood her relief: with her father dead, she would no longer be reminded of herself when she was young, confused, pregnant, stupid, clumsy. Unlike Lydia, her father had never accepted the new person she had become.

She was glad that he was gone. She had never trusted him; he was incapable of discretion; he had no self-respect; he did whatever he was told. It was better that he was dead; he knew she had had a child: the one flaw, the one weakness in the perfect structure that was now her life. It had been her one mistake, and he knew about it. Now, eight years after Maarja's christening, Piret was relieved that she would bury the corpse of her alcoholic father. 'Yes,' she said to the older nurse. 'I am the next of kin.'

12

Within a year Piret was made a junior researcher. It was autumn 1979 and she had already published two papers, 'Aid as Economic Imperialism', and 'Product Proliferation in American Monopoly Formation'.

Piret's specialty was pure theory; she had not lost her dislike of the concrete. The economics of assembly lines, *kolhoz* management, and mechanization she viewed as a marginally superior form of engineering.

Academic interest in the 'elaboration of a contemporary model of socialism' continued to grow, and Piret continued to avoid discussing it. She realized that any efforts to liberalize the Soviet economy would confront a basic incompatibility with a one-party dictatorship. Although she did not admit this openly to herself, she knew that her critique of capitalism was safer, more easily defended and more consistent. To open any discussion on socialist economic theory was a dangerous road.

She knew this because of Rozhansky. He had been thirty-seven and an assistant professor in 1968. He had realized from the first hint of the Prague Spring that he must avoid any association with the Czech reforms; and after the invasion, because of his caution, he was one of the few who did not lose his job. He did see several colleagues labelled 'covert Dubčeks' and sent to labour camps. He had paraphrased for Piret, with uncharacteristic specificity, the talk given to the faculty by a party functionary dispatched from Moscow to spread the official story.

The forces in favour of socialism, the man had said, had led to ideological sabotage and support for counter-revolutionary elements to engage in anti-Soviet provocation. The working people of Czechoslovakia, assisted by international efforts of the socialist countries, had resolutely ousted those conspirators trying to push Czechoslovakia off the socialist path. The brotherhood of socialism had saved the Czechoslovak peoples.

Piret and Rozhansky occasionally met at the Institute or at the Polytechnic; although they were now colleagues, they still used 'teie' with one another, the formal you. Piret considered her friendship with him crucial to her every professional decision. She was sure that she could neither survive nor develop without him. He had edited her papers; he had taught her the subtle art of evading the Glovlit censors, of the impregnable, yet evocative article.

She was grateful to him; she trusted him. She wished she could pierce a minute part of the wall he had built around himself; she wanted to believe that she too had grown in importance to him.

Their occasional and seemingly inconsequential chats were on general matters, during which he offered veiled opinions and aired his concerns for her career. They discussed her research and, sometimes, the 'elaboration of the socialist model'.

'I wonder what we shall see of this,' Rozhansky said one day in the light tone he often affected.

Piret wondered what he wanted to know and decided not to be drawn. She replied vaguely, 'I suppose some talk about bureaucratic constraints on production.' This was a safe answer: everybody knew that a major problem with quota fulfilment was the power of ministries, which were notorious for concealing and hoarding, fabricating statistics, inflating output.

'Yes, naturally. I was thinking also of theoretical possibilities.'

Piret waited to see where he would take this.

He went on casually, 'Constraints on production ... This is an interesting topic.'

'Of course,' Piret replied neutrally. 'Setting output quotas is the major concern of Gosplan.' She paused. 'But these are engineering problems. I mean, output is a mathematical problem: optimization under constraints. It's hardly a theoretical topic.'

'Um, yes ... Although such models do provide guidelines for resource allocation.'

Piret looked puzzled. 'Of course. Assuming the variables are realistic.'

'Yes, of course. Does the central planning model specify the method of resource allocation?'

The answer was no; they both knew it. Socialist theory was conspicuously lacking in economic theory. Lenin's ideas focused on the dissolution of the capitalist economy and on rapid industrialization. Central planning decisions were political; resources were heavily directed to industry and the military.

Rozhansky went on, 'Mathematically, if there is an increase in production by a reallocation of resources, is there not some mathematical value attached to such a reallocation?'

Piret did not answer, seeing now where the discussion was leading. Central planners were already using such mechanisms to set prices and quotas. They were among the world's best technicians in operations research, the very kind of mathematical analysis Rozhansky was discussing.

But Rozhansky was talking about more, a kind of internal market. The 'elaboration of the socialist model' was taking reform further than ever before. If anybody admitted that this was in effect becoming the foundation of Gosplan operations, it was tantamount to admitting that the entire Soviet economy had become a market economy. It meant that socialism was a failure.

This kind of work had to have support from Moscow. Nobody would take on such a topic without a clear directive. And there was no doubt in Piret's mind that this was exactly the kind of research that could land an academic in a political minefield. The Kremlin was a network of dissenting views.

Rozhansky paused; Piret remained silent. He was telling her that work on the 'elaboration of the socialist model' disguised the creation of a pseudo-capitalist system to try to restore the flagging Soviet economy. He was also telling her to stay clear of a bombshell.

Piret began to host visiting economists from Comecon and non-aligned countries. The following year she defended her thesis. She was now a *dotsent* and began her doctoral work. She was promoted to the position of researcher and advised that a post as assistant professor would be available in the autumn.

Shortly afterwards she was asked to host a group of Western academics. Before their arrival she reported to the Academy's Foreign Department, where a KGB officer gave her a five-page document to read and sign.

It stipulated that she could only meet her visitors in designated rooms at the Academy. She was not to meet them or conduct conversations outside such rooms or in restaurants, hotels, or her home. She was to give notice in writing when any individual visitor came to see her, where meetings would take place and for how long. A description of all meetings should afterwards be given to the Foreign Department in writing. Piret glanced through the document briefly and signed it.

When the group arrived, she gave her first speech in English. She introduced herself and began by saying, 'Soviet Estonia is a prosperous republic thanks to the industriousness of our people, who have been able to develop their abilities and talents under the finest facilities of the Soviet Socialist system. The Academy of Sciences conducts research to further this development.'

They had glanced at each other uncomfortably, unable to decide whether this was a joke, an elegant subversion, or serious. A few looked at her sceptically, their faces transmitting a clear message: Does she really believe this?

She observed their transparency with contempt. Her discipline and intellectual standards had made her the superior of these narrow, simple men, blinded by their own assumptions. That is the difference between us and the West, she thought. They are naïve; they cannot think for themselves.

She was in control of her mind. These men thought they knew the truth; they believed they lived free of propaganda; they had not learned to think critically. Piret lived the life of a sceptic. She lived a difficult life; her mind was constantly tested, attentive. She lived with lies and this made her serious and unflinching. She had survived and succeeded and

97

excelled; these men were soft and innocent.

Nadja had been right, of course. *We live like schizophrenics. They have taken away our right to a conscience.* Piret had resented Nadja's criticism, yet she knew the entire history of her country was a lie. She knew that the Estonian people had not rallied with neighbouring republics to throw off the yoke of the Tsar and unite to create the Soviet Union. She knew that history was simply the raw material of those in power.

Every day, on her way to the Institute, Piret passed a memorial to a Russian soldier before which a flame always burned; it said: To the Memory of the Liberators of Tallinn, 1944–5. Her parents had hated the memorial. Piret no longer even saw it.

She carried out her work with integrity. She enjoyed the elegance of her theoretical puzzles; they hurt no one. She had, after all, no political ambitions, no ideological conflicts. She recognized political realities, but nevertheless believed in the essential rightness of her work. Marxism-Leninism used economic laws for the good of society; capitalist theory worked to perpetuate the monopoly power of the owners of capital. This was axiomatic; Piret's vocation was to study this for its intellectual pleasure and for the security of respect and prestige it brought. She hurt no one, was responsible for no one but herself.

A few days after her visitors left, she awoke and went to her office as usual. She went through her letters and papers, preparing for the day's work. It was after about an hour that she found it. Later she could not remember where she had first seen it, whether it had been slipped in with the post or simply put on her desk.

She unfolded the paper and saw that it was a photocopy, which immediately gave her some alarm: very few people had access to photocopiers. It was a letter or a memo, or rather, part of a memo. There was no heading, no indication who wrote it, or to whom it was sent. It was either the second page of the original document or the top of the paper had not been photocopied.

She saw at once that she had been given something highly confidential and potentially very dangerous. It was some kind of discussion of the 'elaboration of the socialist model'; it said:

> Our country is operating under a system of beliefs which is itself rapidly eroding ... The formulation of a socialist economy is not even addressed in Marx and Engels's work ... What little discussion of socialist economy we find in Marx is itself vague or inaccurate ...

> We cannot completely blame our current stagnation on military expenditure brought about by the NATO threat. We must address the problems of low productivity, apathy towards work, alcoholism, cynicism towards quotas and indeed all official targets ...

> All analysis indicates that economic growth is virtually zero and that the costs of production exceed its value in nearly every sector. It is time that we question the very foundations of our economic system ...

As Piret read, her heart raced, and she felt something completely new and strange: her isolated life was now the focus of somebody who wanted to hurt her or involve her. She did not know why; she only knew that she had been sent something she should not have in her possession.

Her first instinct was to burn the document; it could easily lead to her dismissal or worse. The question was, why? What was she expected to do with it? It appeared to have been written by a high-level politician or economist. Or perhaps it represented somebody's notes and had never been sent. But why her? She was a woman, harmless, with no axe to grind, no desire to challenge the university or government. She had done everything to protect herself; now she was in possession of a document that had to be destroyed.

She looked around the room for matches; there were none. She folded the paper. She could not leave it in her office; she did not want to take it home. She put it in her pocket; then she took it out and put it in her bag. She would go shopping. She would shred it and drop the various bits in litter bins around the city.

She prepared to leave her office; her hands were shaking. She knew she must walk out without looking around to see if she were being watched; to do so would simply draw attention to herself. She wished she had some matches. She gathered her books and papers, and then somebody knocked at the door. She froze and stared at it without replying. The door opened slightly and Rozhansky put his head in.

He said hello and asked if he could come in for a moment. She nodded and he handed her a journal he had recently mentioned to her. She took it and laid it on the desk between them, next to her bag.

Normally she would have thanked him and asked if he had time for coffee, or he would have simply left. But she said nothing and an uncomfortable air quickly developed because such a pause was so uncharacteristic. He looked at her expectantly. 'Are you all right?'

She felt a tiny bubble of hysteria rising in her. She felt the photocopy in her bag on the desk between them, tiny and enormously explosive; she wondered in desperation how she could not tell him. They had known one another for years; he was her closest friend. She had learned to think and believe in herself because of him.

He took out a cigarette and held it without lighting it. He never smoked in her office. She watched him, wondering whether he had any matches. It was Boris who had given her a new life. She knew at that moment what she must have felt for a long time: that she loved him; that she could never hurt him. She must not compromise him; she must now face this alone and keep him from danger, in exchange for all he had done for her.

Yet she felt she must say something; it seemed suddenly important that if she were to be arrested, imprisoned, exiled, he should know how she felt. She faltered, 'Boris, I've never thanked you.'

Rozhansky looked at her, somewhat alarmed. She had never before used his first name.

'For everything you have done for me. You have – done so much. Thank you.'

He looked away, replying, 'It has only been pleasure for me to know you.' He put the cigarette in his pocket, picked up the journal again and turned a few pages uncertainly. 'Friends understand one another,' he added, as if to conclude the matter.

She moved around the desk, picking up her bag as if to go. Then she touched his arm. She said, switching to 'sina', the informal you, 'You must know that you mean much more to me than a friend.'

He hesitated. 'A friend is possibly the best one can hope to be,' he returned dryly.

She wanted to cry out what she could never tell him: that she could disappear tomorrow, that her life and position were now as uncertain as his colleagues' had been in 1968. She could not leave without telling him how she felt. 'There is no one who means more to me than you.'

He looked at her now. He too dropped 'teie' and switched to 'sina'. 'Piret, you cannot say these things. Understand that you are mistaking gratitude for something else. Your feelings cannot have developed distinct from everything else between us – our differences in age and position. I was your teacher. We know actually very little about one another.'

Her face drained, and she became cold and hard with embarrassment. 'I would be grateful if you would not analyse my feelings.'

'You must see that they are inseparable from how we have known one another. I could not accept your – regard without patronizing you in some respect.'

'And so people must not care for one another for fear that some imbalance of power or position will corrupt their relations? That is absurd. People are not so equal.'

He smiled. 'That, my dear student, is heresy.'

She did not smile.

He went on. 'Anyway, I am not talking about people.'

'Yes, I know.' He was talking about them, of course.

He went on reflectively, as if to himself, 'Some imbalance of power will corrupt ... Yes, that is precisely true ... '

She was angry now; she had seen him ruminate like this,

over intellectual puzzles; she wanted to shake him. 'I must go – now.'

He looked at her. 'Do you not see? It is not my power over you I am speaking of. You do not see that we cannot have a relation separate from our professional positions.'

She was beginning to panic now, so desperate was she to leave, to destroy the photocopy in her bag. She began to think that somebody might come in, see them together; yet he continued to stand, abstracted, analysing their feelings.

'Anything I do could affect you,' he went on, oblivious to her distress.

'I do not want or need your protection,' she returned, knowing this to be untrue. Please, please, go, she thought. She tried to calm herself; she did not want to poison everything; she wanted to stop the discussion before it went too far. She must leave, she must protect him. She shifted her bag and moved towards the door. 'Thank you for the journal.'

He too resumed his normal tone. 'Of course. Will you stop by next week?'

'I'll try. *Nägemist*.' She gave a little wave as he left. She waited a moment and then walked down the hall, reconstructing their conversation in her mind and now understanding how strenuously each had avoided using the one word that would have ruptured their friendship permanently.

How prudent we are, how wary, she thought. Love is the privilege of the undamaged.

PART 2

September 1984

13

Piret landed at Stockholm-Arlanda Airport on a Saturday afternoon. She had flown from Moscow to Helsinki and then caught a connecting flight to Stockholm; there were no foreign flights out of Tallinn.

She disembarked with the other passengers. At the end of the gangway automatic doors opened on to a spotlessly clean terminal. She followed suited men, couples, families with folded pushchairs towards the baggage reclaim.

The hall was lined with shops selling luxurious goods: smoked reindeer and elk, French and American cosmetics, carved wood, fine crystal, boxed chocolates, caviar. Piret had prepared herself to face extravagant, wasteful consumption on this, her first trip to the West; she had not realized how seductive it was.

She found herself mesmerized by the displays of rose and plum lipstick, the photographs of polished women with chiselled faces and brushed eyebrows, a rippled crystal vase holding two perfect white lilies. These feelings did not alarm her; she registered them with the alert and objective mind of a scientist. She understood now why people defected; these things made you feel as though you could not live without them.

The Aeroflot plane and its surly air hostess, the congealed tongue sandwich and weak tea, the dirty seats and tattered safety belts, had all seemed quite normal to her. Then she had boarded her connecting SAS flight and entered a different universe, as far from the Soviet Union as the pictures of America on television. Piret saw fresh, blue upholstery, smiling air hostesses, spotless white covers on the head rests, perfectly clean, unscuffed overhead luggage compartments. The passengers were stylishly dressed, perfectly groomed. The crew did not look cramped, bored, weak with hangovers.

She understood now in a direct, tangible way, that these people, passengers and crew, flew all over the world: Paris, Vienna, New York, London, Hong Kong. The women wore expensive jewellery and went to hairdressers; the men wore elegant suits and carried leather briefcases. Of course she had always known this; but seeing it suddenly made her feel small and unimportant and shabby, from another world that these people never thought about.

She was offered a cocktail, which she refused, staring at the hundreds of tiny bottles of liquor on the trolley, the silver bucket of ice, the bottles of tonic, juice and soda. She was given a wet towel, so hot she had to toss it from hand to hand. On her tray was shrimp salad topped with a lump of glistening orange caviar, a plate of five kinds of cold meat, cheeses, a pudding and foil-wrapped chocolates. The hostess brought hot bread rolls in a basket, covered by a white napkin.

Piret looked around at her fellow passengers, none of whom seemed surprised at this extravagance. Were they so used to this? Did they all think it usual to live like this? The majority of the world's population lived in poverty, and these people ate foil-wrapped chocolates and caviar and shrimp salad. These were the workings of the market.

The previous February Yuri Andropov had died after only fifteen months as general secretary. It was a victory for the old guard, the conservatives of the Brezhnev era, that the elderly Chernenko succeeded him.

Relations between the superpowers were strained. The USSR had decided not to attend the summer Olympics in Los Angeles, although denying the action was a boycott. It was the fifth year of the Soviet presence in Afghanistan; troop levels were at an all-time high. At the beginning of the year, Foreign Secretary Gromyko had attacked the United States at the Stockholm Conference on Confidence and Security; the conference was now deadlocked.

But the biggest news for Piret broke shortly before she left: a young Estonian couple, a party official and his wife, defected while in Stockholm. All Tallinn discussed it; Piret had feared that this would jeopardize her trip, but the visa was granted without a hitch.

At Arlanda a woman official in a blue uniform greeted Piret, flipped through her passport without comment, stamped it and buzzed her through the glass door, saying in English, 'Enjoy your stay.' The grey granite floor of the baggage-claim hall shone; there seemed to be hundreds of trolleys. People took them carelessly, without hurry.

She remembered boarding the Moscow flight from Tallinn Airport, its hard black chairs and single, clattering luggage carousel. She recalled the elaborate examination of her CCCP passport and Swedish visa by a sullen Russian. At the gate had been one shop selling Estonian and Russian vodka. Waiting with her were badly dressed Soviets carrying cheap vinyl shopping bags and Westerners who looked relieved to be going home.

Piret walked through the Green Lane while male and female customs officials stood around chatting, glancing at the passengers indifferently. Doors opened and a wave of activity hit her: music from the airport bar, coloured lights, people greeting and hugging one another, a congestion of trolleys, movement in various directions. Blue signs with white lettering in various languages directed her to Buses to Stockholm City, Taxis, Car Park. She felt suddenly frightened, unprotected.

She looked around and was relieved to see her name on a cardboard sign. Holding it was a dark, foreign man. He led her to a silver Volvo estate car and put her bag in. He opened the back door for her and said, in English, 'You go to where you live, no?'

She nodded. He had been told she did not speak Swedish. They drove away, on to a smooth motorway flanked by pines, towards Stockholm. Piret suddenly felt exhausted by the day and without warning fell asleep.

When she woke up, the man had stopped in front of a plain, modern, brick building. Outside was a small panel of numbers.

The man pressed in a code; the door buzzed; he pulled it open. She saw an expanse of stone floor, mirrors on either side of the foyer, fresh flowers in a vase on a small round table. A lift large enough to hold ten people waited. Piret had never seen a lift that would fit more than three or four. Inside the lift, next to the floor numbers, were imprinted braille numbers and mnemonic figures for children to remember their floor: a dog, an aeroplane, an elephant, an ice-cream cone.

He opened the door to the flat and Piret walked into a large white hall with a coat rack. She took her coat off as the man put her bag down and handed her the key. He motioned her to follow him. He led her into a white and stainless-steel kitchen. 'Kitchen,' he announced.

Down the hall, he switched on the light in a large bathroom. Walls of shiny white tiles appeared. Thick white towels hung from a polished metallic rack. He waved his hand: 'Bathroom.'

The bedroom window overlooked neo-classical architecture painted rust, lion-gold, pale sage; trees and bicycle paths, bridges over blue water dotted with jutting rocks. She heard the man behind her: 'Bedroom.' She turned and saw fitted wardrobes spanning one entire wall. He opened two of the tall doors and pointed to the hangers. 'Wardrobe.'

The living room alone was the size of a flat in Estonia. The man opened a wooden cabinet. 'Television.' She was afraid he would go on like this for some time, and so she thanked him profusely until he finally left.

As one of the Academy of Science's leading researchers, Piret had been invited to Stockholm for a two-week visit. She was to attend seminars, give talks and gather research ideas. She was now nearly thirty years old, far advanced in her doctoral research, and in addition to her post at the Institute an assistant professor at the Polytechnic.

The head of her division at the Institute had decided that it was important to improve the Institute's knowledge of economics research in capitalist countries. Piret knew her trip had the support of the Ministry of Foreign Affairs and of the KGB. Visits abroad and research on Western countries were always monitored closely.

Piret's had been a swift and conspicuous rise. She had moved from the shared house to her own two-room flat with kitchen and bath. It was nearly inconceivable that a single woman would have such a large flat to herself. She had a small washing machine in the kitchen and a new black Lada, which she drove to Lydia's on weekends. She had a passport.

Now Piret walked around this Swedish apartment, examining the immaculate appliances, the fluffy duvet across the bed, the sleek wooden floors and thick Persian rugs. She looked out of the window at large, shiny cars, swept streets, well-dressed children on bicycles and roller-skates, innumerable shops.

She turned from the window back to the quiet flat; the sheer feeling of space made her slightly anxious. Two families could have lived easily in this flat. She noticed that nowhere was left uncovered, unsealed, unpainted. The kitchen was a collection of perfect joins between cupboard, wall, tile, sink, floor. Every room was enveloped from any suspicion of pipes or wires or brick or structure. It all made her feel buffered from the outside world, as if she were floating in the sky in these rooms, sterile, endless, leading nowhere.

Her flat in Tallinn was in one of a dozen red-brick blocks on a cleared tract of land joined by gravel roads. There were no trees; nothing had been landscaped. Children played between the buildings on mounds of rocks, weeds, gravel, brick left by the road machines. Her living room was filled with books and dominated by a large table that served as her desk. Her kitchen had one cupboard, a sink, a small fridge, and a counter and stool, where she ate. On her balcony she kept a few potted plants.

Piret went to the bathroom. She took off her clothes and ran a bath. The bathtub was slippery, as if new. She washed quickly and got out, took one of the large towels. She looked inside the mirrored cabinet and found tissues, a jar of cotton balls and a can of air freshener. She touched nothing. On the back of the bathroom door was a fluffy white chenille dressing gown, which she left hanging. Wrapped in the towel, she went into the bedroom and unpacked her old dressing gown.

Boris Rozhansky and Piret were still friends; their relationship had continued the past few years in the same calm vein, with no more emotional declarations. She had grown to accept that her life would always be austere, limited. She found it appropriate that she should love someone with whom she was not intimately involved.

She had grown to understand Boris's reserve, the extreme caution he used in every aspect of his life. He had told her of his student days, when Stalin was still alive, and the required ideological coursework, scientific atheism and dialectical materialism; how his papers had been subject to inspection by a Komsomol official for subversive influence.

He told her about the economics research, which consisted of finding evidence to support selected quotations from party policy documents, and about the thaw under Khrushchev, when the lack of theoretical work in political economy was recognized. That was a time of high hope: amnesties of political prisoners, social reforms, better wages, improvements in education. After Brezhnev was elected, it all resumed: censorship, forced emigrations of dissidents, the purge of any academic or discipline that questioned the unity and cohesion of Soviet society.

Piret dried herself with the towel; she would never, she supposed, impose herself again on Boris. She looked at her body, a mature woman's body now. She had not been touched by a man since Paavo. She had heard news about Paavo; in such a small country it was impossible not to hear about people. He was married, as she had always known he would be, to a professional woman, an ophthalmologist; they had a son.

Piret did not want children. She did not want anybody to have claims on her time; she did not feel compelled to share her body. She knew her colleagues thought her a frigid intellectual; she did not care. Her happiness lay in her work, her complete absorption in her papers, her formulae, the books that lined the walls of her flat, her conversations with Boris.

She was at peace; even this trip to Stockholm had not disturbed her calm. So little did she feel about the past that she did not at once think of Maarja when she received the invitation. It was the day her passport and visa arrived that it suddenly occurred to her: she was going to Sweden, where Maarja lived. She could pass her own child on the street, and not recognize her. She would probably not even recognize Helena. Such an occurrence was statistically improbable, however, and the thought dissolved as effortlessly as it had come.

Barefoot, and still in her dressing gown, Piret sat in the living room and reviewed her schedule and duties for the coming two weeks: seminars, research, meetings, lunches, dinners. She glanced through her notes for her talks and made a list of research topics relevant to her own work.

She worked until six o'clock. Her contact at the embassy would be picking her up for dinner in an hour. He was not a minder: she was too successful, had too much at stake to be considered likely to defect. Minders were for athletes and ballet dancers. She was merely required to check in with him periodically.

She was also to compile for him a bibliography of statistical information on the Swedish financial markets, Central Bank policy and government proposals. She knew that this kind of information gathering was a type of spying, although the information itself was publicly available. Piret accepted that this was the price she paid for being here. She did not like the KGB; she disliked their obsessive conspiracy theories, their paranoia, their inexhaustible desire for information, but she knew that her behaviour here would be a crucial step in her professional advancement.

There was no reason to doubt her continued success. She had followed her every instinct and considered her every move; her position now was unimpeachable. She no longer even thought of the photocopy left in her office. Nothing had come of it. She mentioned it to nobody, continued to avoid any discussion of economic reform, and regularly scoured her office to dispose of any article or journal that could be used against her.

Since Brezhnev's death, poor grain harvests and falling productivity had increased talk of the 'elaboration of a contemporary model of socialism'. But Andropov's reforms had been very limited. Dissent was still quickly punished, although the crudeness of the labour camp had been replaced by the creative and more sophisticated use of psychiatric hospitals. There had even been a clinical diagnosis created for those with dissident views: paranoid reformist delusions.

At a quarter to seven Piret rose and put her papers away. She brushed her hair and tied it back. She dressed and put on the same brown coat she had worn for years, one of the two pairs of flat shoes she used for work. She wore no make-up.

She looked in the bedroom mirror and knew that there was no reason to feel alone or frightened. She would manage this trip successfully. She knew what her duties were, what her demeanour should be.

She looked exactly how she wanted to look: plain and dull. She cultivated her colourless exterior because she knew she had a rich interior life. She had a life of the mind. This was what she had always wanted. She had finally come to like herself. She knew who she was.

14

Maarja hated every single thing about her confirmation. It was to be the following day, Sunday, in an Estonian service, along with eight other Estonian boys and girls, all of whom were turkeys. Maarja decided she would rather be dead than attend. To make matters worse, her mother had insisted on making her dress. Every other girl would be wearing a dress from NK or Hennes.

She was Maarja only to Estonians. To Swedes she was Elisabet, her second name. She had used it since her first day at school when the other children teased her for having such a strange name and she had claimed that the teacher had mistaken her for someone else.

Maarja Elisabet was the name on her christening certificate from Jaani kirik. Her mother must have known from that moment that her life would be eternally divided between being Maarja, an Estonian, and Elisabet, a Swede.

She looked at the white dress on her mother's bed. It was made from a Burda pattern and she hated it. It had an empire waist and little puffy sleeves. It was short, above her knees, like a little girl's. This stupid dress was enough to make her want to be dead. But the last straw was that the confirmation party would be at home.

'Mamma!' Maarja groaned to Helena. 'Nobody does that. Everybody goes to a restaurant.'

'We don't. And we are not everybody. And don't call me Mamma. At home, you call me Ema.'

'Everybody who is Swedish goes to a restaurant.'

'You are not Swedish.'

She had been told a million times how she was born in Estonia and taken back to be christened in a secret ceremony.

Her mother, her onu Matti and tädi Maret, the priest and her godmother were the only ones there. Her mother made it sound as though she had single-handedly defied the KGB on a super-secret top mission.

She was special because she had been born in Estonia. Most Estonian families had come to Sweden during the war; the children had been born Swedish citizens. Many were perfectly Swedish, in fact. Some of the parents did not even speak Estonian at home.

'Why do other people speak Swedish at home?' Maarja had asked when she was five or six.

'They are Swedish.'

'Other Estonian people.'

'They are too lazy to keep up their language. They do not care about being Estonian.'

'I don't want to be Estonian. I want to be Swedish.' Helena's sharp look silenced her. Then Helena said simply, 'You are Estonian.'

She was Estonian. It was like being Jewish or foreign. She could deny it, but it would always show. She wished they spoke Swedish at home; she imagined that speaking the same language would unify her life: she would be the same person at home as she was in public. Her life would be simple, like other girls.

Swedish girls were blonde; Maarja was dark. Even her parents, who were blonde, didn't look Swedish. Her mother had high cheekbones and almond-shaped eyes. Swedish people looked Western, European. Swedish people played tennis and went skiing and drove to France in the summer in caravans. Swedish girls had boyfriends. Their parents had country houses on lakes.

They didn't have a country house and her mother would kill her if she had a boyfriend, particularly a Swedish boyfriend. 'You are not yet twelve years old,' her mother would say. 'Eleven-year-old girls do not have boyfriends.'

Maarja and Helena still lived in the two-bedroom flat in Södermalm. Helena made her wear woollen underwear in the winter, which Maarja took off under the stairwell before leaving for school. Her boots were thick and heavy and lined with fleece. Swedish girls wore trim, black leather boots to school. Swedish girls wore berets. Maarja's mother made her wear a knitted woollen cap which made her look like a farmer's wife.

They didn't have much money since her parents were divorced. Her father gave them money every month, but it wasn't a lot. He usually came every other weekend to take her somewhere. It was OK when she was smaller, but now it was a drag to spend every other Saturday or Sunday with him. On the other hand, her parents being divorced made her feel more Swedish. Lots of Swedish people's parents were divorced. Hardly any Estonians were.

But it was no good wanting to be Swedish. She had heard it a million times. Swedes were hypocritical and, worse, socialist. They had refused thousands of refugees after the war who then met their deaths in Siberia. They kowtowed to the Soviets; they did not understand the evils of socialism. They were one of the few Western states to have formally recognized the annexation of the Baltic countries.

'Then why did we come here?' she asked her mother once.

'Because they took us,' Helena replied curtly. Then she added, 'Because it was here or Canada. We wanted to live where there was an Estonian community. And Sweden came through first.'

Maarja tried to imagine herself as a Canadian. Canadian girls were probably much like Swedish girls. She wanted to be one of those careless girls with ratty jeans, long hair, a boombox, a punk leather jacket with safety pins through the sleeves.

Maybe she really was Swedish. Maybe her father was not her father, but another man, a Swede. She thought about this for a minute. Her real father would have had to be in Estonia since she was born in Estonia. And he would have had to be dark. There were not many dark Swedes.

Maybe she was adopted. She did not look really like either of her parents. 'You are a mixture,' her mother had told her. Maybe her mother was lying and her real mother was Swedish and her father was somebody dark. Her mother would have had to give her away from the shame of it. Perhaps her real father was somebody terribly important, like a diplomat or a politician from Italy or Spain, and they had had to hide her birth.

But what would a diplomat be doing in Estonia? It wasn't a country any more; all the diplomats were now in Russia. And you couldn't change things like passports, which listed her birthplace as Tallinn, Estonia. She had even seen her birth certificate, which said, Mother: Helena Linda Reisman, *née* Veltman. Father: Peeter Juhan Reisman.

Maarja undressed and tried on the confirmation dress. She went to her mother's room and stood before the triptych mirror on the pale wood dressing table. She rummaged through Helena's leather jewellery box, and tried to transform the dress with a few strings of beads. She saw her mother's sorority sash, with its colours of the Estonian national flag: the blue of the cornflower, white for innocence and black for the earth.

'It still flies at the Kennedy Centre in Washington,' her mother liked to remind her. 'We are an occupied country; our occupation is recognized not *de jure*, but *de facto*.' Maarja understood this to mean that it was illegal for the Russians to be there, but nobody would do anything about it.

Maarja thought of the church the following day. She would be confirmed in a Swedish church in an Estonian ceremony and would celebrate at home as Estonians did. They would have plenty to eat: sausage, stuffed *pirukas*, smoked fish, *sült*, potato salad, several kinds of cakes. One thing her mother was right about: Swedes never did give you enough to eat at parties. And she was always allowed to drink at parties; her Swedish friends weren't allowed to drink. She decided there were, after all, a few good things about being Estonian.

Anyway, there was no way out of it. She could wish for ever that she was different, that she was one person, one nationality. But she would still be what she was. But what was that? She knew she would always be two people.

She looked at herself: her dark hair, her Estonian eyes, her white confirmation dress, her mother's jewellery. She wanted to excise that part of her that she hated, that part that confused her, that was forced on her, that was not really her. She did not know what part this was, but as the question formed in her mind, she was aware that it was composed of Estonian rather than Swedish words: *Kes olen?*

15

The next day, Sunday morning, as Maarja prepared for her confirmation, Peeter was one of the first off the plane at Arlanda. He walked quickly down the gangway and the length of the terminal, and down the escalator. He was through passport control in minutes. He walked past the luggage carousels and through the green channel. He never carried more than his briefcase and garment bag.

In the twelve years since he had left Soviet Estonia Peeter had transformed himself from a frightened refugee into an international journalist. He flew around Europe regularly. He owned his own flat on a prestigious street in Stockholm. He had a Swedish girlfriend, Marie.

Peeter left the terminal building, got in a taxi and gave his newspaper's address. He took out his notebook and flipped through it. He thought, in Swedish: *The whole thing stinks to high heaven.* He could now think as easily as speak in all four of his languages: Estonian, Finnish, Swedish, Russian. In addition, his English and German were passable and he had picked up bits and pieces of Polish and Czech. He was on the Eastern European desk at the paper; his speciality was dissidents.

He had just returned from East Berlin. He had been given information that could, if true, be exactly the story he needed. He hadn't had anything really good in months and this was terrific. His contact had hinted that a few key Lutheran ministers, known for providing the backbone of anti-communist opposition, were in the pay of the Stasi. He had flown down to take a look around and come back with nothing reliable. The whole thing looked very suspicious, very unlikely. It looked like a Stasi leak.

He sat in the taxi, watching the dense green pines along the motorway; the massive warehouses, the Saab dealer and modern offices. It was nice to be home.

The story was tempting, and Peeter knew the paper wouldn't give a damn if the source wasn't clean, even if it came straight from the Stasi. *Morgon Bladet* was not known for its integrity. But Peeter didn't like the feeling of this one. And he couldn't get any reliable independent confirmation. It was too bad: it was just what he needed. *Too fucking bad.*

His contact had never been wrong before. He was, in fact, largely responsible for Peeter's success at the paper, Sweden's third largest. Almost all of Peeter's big stories had come from him, a man Peeter only knew as Mika. They had met once in Vienna; once in Helsinki; otherwise Mika rang him from phone boxes or left documents at predetermined places.

Mika claimed to be a disaffected East German party official who wanted the West to know the truth about the treatment of dissidents. He had contacts all over the Eastern bloc and travelled freely. Peeter usually pushed aside his suspicions about Mika; the more successful Peeter became, the less he wanted to think about the sources of Mika's information.

Despite his success, Peeter was dissatisfied with his career. *Morgon Bladet* had once seemed an unrealizable attainment; now Peeter saw that it was less than second-drawer; it was third-drawer, and this rankled. He was known for his Eastern European scoops, and if he had one more nice, juicy story he could make the move, maybe even to TV2. His dream was to be a news anchorman.

Peeter sometimes listened to himself, trying to detect any trace of Estonian accent, speaking in the bathroom mirror as he shaved, imagining himself reading the news on national television. He had a knack for languages and an ear for accents. People did not usually take him for a foreigner. And Marie told him his Swedish was indistinguishable from hers. But of course she would say that.

Now he wondered why the hell his contact had fed him this rubbish about the priests. The man had been setting him up, there was no question about it. Peeter realized that up to now he had been fed a string of clean, or at least, verifiable, information; now he was being drawn in for the bullshit. Well, he wasn't going to fall for this. The story might be good, but he would have to tell the foreign-desk head that it was a load of shit.

The taxi stopped in front of his building and the driver pushed the meter. Peeter paid and took a receipt. He got out, looking at his watch. He would check his desk for telexes and messages and then go straight over to the church. Today was Maarja's confirmation and he had promised to be there: his beautiful little girl, eleven years old.

Peeter had not thought of Maarja as his adopted child in years; he could hardly remember that first flight to Sweden, Helena beside him, both of them terrified and nervous, the tiny baby asleep, oblivious. Holding Maarja as a toddler had made him want to weep with the desire to protect, to provide, to hold her like a precious gift. She was the only reason why he had stayed with Helena as long as he did.

He had not felt like a father immediately. It had taken some months. He had not worried; he suspected it took most new fathers time. Men didn't look at babies and go soft inside. And Helena had been overly protective and critical. She had tried to keep Maarja all to herself, had criticized him when he held Maarja or tried to feed her.

He remembered his anger when Helena had returned to Estonia for Maarja to be christened, and that night with the Swedish girl from a bar in Gamla Stan.

'I want her christened in Estonia,' Helena had said for what seemed to him to be the hundredth time. She would not listen to his reasoned arguments: that it was dangerous, that they were still Soviet citizens, that she would upset her parents.

And what did it matter if Maarja were christened in Estonia? Nothing in Estonia mattered any more. It was a tiny country with no future. There were hardly more than a million of them: a little tribe; another minor tragedy. In three or four generations there would be no Estonia. They would all be speaking Russian; they would all be married to Russians. The damn place was half-Russian as it was.

Helena and her parents were obsessed with communists: what they were doing in Sweden, what they had done to Estonia. Helena's father prattled on for ever about that damn farm at every family dinner and how his mother had been shot and he himself deported to Siberia. All three of them were convinced that there were KGB spies on every corner, at every little Estonian tea party. Right, thought Peeter: bugs in the *pirukas*; KGB agents disguised as little old ladies cutting the cake.

Anyway, they didn't need to worry about the Russians creeping around at Estonian tea parties; the Russians made a point of making appearances, of carrying out their real business: intimidation. There had been another Russian submarine sighted in Karlskrona, where one had run aground two years before. Peeter considered the major good result from this sighting was the shift in Swedish public opinion. In the years after he had emigrated, polls showed that the majority of Swedes considered the USSR a 'friendly power'; now fewer than a quarter of all Swedes thought so. It was a damn good thing, Peeter thought. It was about time everybody woke up to what bastards the Russians were.

He and every other Estonian emigrant were all better off forgetting about Estonia and learning to be Swedish. The Swedes were the best in the world. They built the best cars and furniture, designed the best offices and houses. The language was simple and beautiful, unlike his ridiculous native tongue, with its stilted cases and absurd accent. Estonians sounded like a bunch of Finnish gypsies. And Swedes all spoke English; they weren't cut off from the rest of the world; they weren't clinging to the edge of Europe, trying to remind everybody they weren't Slavs. Yes, everything in Sweden was better: the cars, the herring, the vodka, the women.

The divorce was inevitable. It was terrible that they had adopted Maarja and then broken up, but it couldn't be helped. He had always known he would remain Maarja's father; he would always put her first. He had no interest in marrying again.

In fact the divorce unleashed in Peeter a man he had never known. Helena had been only the second woman he had slept with until their marriage. Within three months of separating from her he had slept with more than a dozen women.

Most he never saw again. He looked back on this time with some amazement: he had been simply unable to face his bed without a woman next to him. He remembered his raw, agonizing loneliness. He remembered his delight at the willingness of Swedish women to sleep with him. He remembered his surprise at their sexual sophistication, and their lack of reserve, their unashamed desire. He felt that Helena had never really wanted him.

A few women lasted more than the night, one or two for more than a week; he introduced none to Maarja. He imagined he and Helena would remain always single, their lives centred around their daughter.

Peeter walked up the steps into the empty building and took the lift. He had become more and more Swedish since his divorce. He still spoke Estonian with Maarja, but it had become a kind of private language, for a secret society of two. He had no family here and little contact with his relatives at home. His parents had died before he and Helena had emigrated; the only family he had left were some distant cousins. He had almost nothing to do with the expatriate Estonian community. He had to all intents become a Swede.

But what had he done? He stood in the lift and looked at himself in the mirror. Bloody hell. He was thirty-seven and he worked at fucking *Morgon Bladet*.

16

The Stockholm School of Economics was located in an imposing, 1920s columned building on Sveavägen. Inside the great wooden doors a granite staircase rose up to a glass wall overlooking an enclosed courtyard. Along the hallways were modern, immaculate offices and lecture halls. The floors were ash and the walls freshly painted; the chairs and desks were pale sanded beech.

Rows of computers filled the classrooms and offices, each animated with the blues, greens and reds of the newest financial software. It was a model of the Swedish mentality: the exterior architecture tastefully preserved, the interior modernized with the finest materials. Everything was clean, bright, new, equipped for the handicapped, thoughtfully organized.

Piret was given an office with an empty bookshelf, a lamp, two bright blue upholstered chairs for visitors and a bouncy swivel chair behind a desk.

It was Monday afternoon and she was preparing to give her first talk. She had arrived early and worked in the library, compiling the information her embassy contact had requested the evening before. Then she attended a morning lecture and had lunch in the basement cafeteria of the Student Union.

Her fellow academics had begun by speaking English and after ten minutes or so, reverted to Swedish, leaving her to eat in isolation. But Piret had not expected to be treated particularly well and took this with equanimity.

Now she sat at her desk, re-reading her notes, checking a few terms. She would speak on her recently published paper 'Obsolescence and the Pursuit of Profits', in which she had demonstrated how technological competition in the US computer industry led to inefficient investment.

She knew nobody here would be seriously interested; the Stockholm School of Economics was a bulwark of capitalism. No Marxism had ever penetrated these walls; students were taught finance and marketing: the economics of profit-making without the reality of social context.

Half an hour later Piret stood at the lectern facing about thirty postgraduate students and faculty. She glanced through her notes, looked up at her audience and continued: 'To sum up, efficiency in the capitalistic sense is an unrealizable ideal.

'Market economies can never be efficient. They can only ensure maximum profit to the owners of capital by minimizing workers' wages and running down resources. It is this mirage of efficiency that underpins all capitalist theory.'

A throat was cleared. She ignored it and continued to speak. 'The concept of efficiency – '

The throat was cleared again and she glanced up from her notes. From her morning lecture she had discovered, to her amazement, that students were permitted to speak at any time during a seminar.

She scanned the audience. Two professors listened politely. A few of the students were taking notes, but most were slouched in their chairs, watching her with a slightly amused, incredulous look. If a student in Tallinn had looked at her like that, she would have had him removed from the classroom.

The throat belonged to a boy of about twenty-five. He raised his pen slightly and jabbed the air, saying, 'You are saying that capitalist firms run down resources without investing?'

'In the pursuit of short-term profits, yes.'

'According to economic theory, those firms which do not invest to maintain their market position will ultimately go bankrupt.'

'Even capitalist economists agree that firms fail to invest in future production to stave off this inevitable bankruptcy.'

'So on the one hand you say they don't invest in order to

make profits; on the other, that they don't invest because they have to stay competitive.'

'That is not a contradiction.'

This was a point for Piret. She knew their theory better than they did.

The boy went on without acknowledging his defeat, 'You point out quite correctly that there is a human cost to goods allocation by the market. But according to economic theory human costs, or social costs, as we prefer to call them, should be factored into prices. If they are not, we have a case of market failure which should be corrected by government intervention.'

'My point exactly,' Piret returned coldly. 'You speak of market failure. I ask you if there are market successes.' A titter went through the audience, who were prodded out of their boredom by the possibility of a heated debate.

Piret went on quickly, 'The shortcomings of market efficiency run through every aspect of capitalist economic thought. Investment by a capitalist firm will always be undermined by the competitive pursuit of profits.'

'How so?' the boy gazed at her impertinently.

'Obsolescence,' Piret replied. She wanted to slap his face. 'Which I am sure you know is caused by improvements in productivity from technological advancement. Capitalists are forced to forgo investments they have made in order to improve their return on capital.'

She saw she would grow to hate them, these smug young Swedes. She was conscious of her shabby clothes, her unshaven legs, her worn shoes. These people never dressed up, yet they always looked fashionable. They wore clothes she had never seen: designer jeans, fine cotton trousers, linen shorts, brushed suede jackets, Italian leather sandals.

She took a breath and went on: 'Defence, education, the effect of manufacturing on the environment: all these capitalist economists call "market failure". What is left?'

She looked evenly at her tormentor. Every head in the room turned towards the boy.

He paused for a moment. 'How about the money markets?'

'Ah, yes,' she replied calmly. 'The market of money. The one thing in the West which works perfectly.' To her surprise, her audience now laughed out loud. The boy rolled his eyes, but could not think of a quick response.

She had won, but she was not pleased; she was furious and shocked. She had not meant to entertain them. She saw that they considered this a game and she had unwittingly joined in. Piret gathered up her papers, thanked her audience and walked out.

She left the school shortly afterwards and took the bus back to her flat. She watched the shops along the streets, the ice-cream kiosks, the ubiquitous announcement, *X-tra pris*. Everyone here was obsessed with money. Everywhere were people with carrier bags, designer labels, advertisements; slim models drank Coca-Cola, displayed lacy underwear, lay seductively across sports cars. Women, sex, money, cars, consumption: it was disgusting. These people had no spiritual life. It was all a beautiful façade covering a corrupt heart.

17

The following day, Tuesday, Piret heard a knock; the door to her office opened and a man appeared. He was clearly Swedish: tall and broad-shouldered, with large, healthy features.

'Ah, Miss Anvelt,' he said in English with a heavy Swedish accent. 'I attended your seminar yesterday.' He was smiling; his face had an innocence that Piret had come to recognize among Swedes. They all looked as though nothing bad had ever happened to them. 'Very good indeed.'

'My title is Professor.' Piret disliked compliments; she shuffled her papers, trying to look busy.

The man entered the room. 'Excuse me, then, Professor Anvelt. You are quite knowledgeable about the West.'

'It is my field.'

'I can see that. I'd like to know more. Can I take you out to lunch?'

'No thank you.'

'Surely you don't want to eat at the Student Union again with everybody speaking Swedish?'

'Have you been watching me?'

He looked surprised at the sharpness of her tone. 'I was there, yes.'

Piret realized how suspicious she sounded; she said, 'I'm sorry, I have a lunch appointment. My schedule is quite full. I'm meeting people every day – '

'I'm very sorry, Professor, but, you see, your lunch date is with me.'

She was silent a moment. She glanced down at the schedule the department secretary had photocopied for her. It said, Lunch: Professor Nilsson. Then she said, 'I'm actually quite busy today.'

'You have to eat.'

'I'll get a sandwich.'

He waited. Then: 'You are a good speaker.'

She looked at him. She did not know if Swedish women were impressed by flattery, but she was not. 'I am not interested in entertaining; I am interested in communicating ideas.'

'Well, you communicate them very well. I enjoyed the debate.'

'That was not the point of my presence. And, I cannot understand why you allow students to speak out uninvited in a classroom.'

'Because, Professor, we believe in the free communication of ideas.' His face had now lost its naïveté. He looked at her with interest.

'As long as they are fundamentally capitalist.'

'You were given your say.'

'For the entertainment of your faculty. I suppose you find this a game.'

'Don't tell me it's any different where you come from.'

Piret was silent. Then she said, 'I happen to believe in my work.'

'As I do.'

'Which is?'

'Industrial economics. Economics of the firm.'

'Oh,' Piret's face registered distaste at the idea of this man spending his time creating mathematical models driven by the maximization of profits.

He smiled. 'There are also firms in the Soviet Union.'

'Run by the state.'

'Run by a small group of managers and in their own interests, no doubt, just like managers in Sweden. Shouldn't we discuss this over lunch?'

Piret looked at her desk again, disinclined to admit the truth of this.

'I'm afraid not.'

He persisted. 'I'd like to hear about your work.'

'I explained my work in the seminar you attended.'

He changed tack. 'My dear Professor, are people really so

different? Do you believe that your economy runs without financial incentives? Without a black market? You are obviously an intelligent, successful young woman. There is so much we could discuss.'

She looked at him, now exasperated. Why was this man harassing her? 'Goodbye, Professor. I really have a great deal to do.' She looked pointedly at the door. She was furious. How dare he turn a professional meeting into a game?

Still he did not leave. 'Professor, I am sorry that you lack a sense of humour. I only came to show you that we are all delighted to have you with us.'

'Thank you for your hospitality.' She looked again through her papers.

'I also wanted to tell you that we would be pleased to maintain the contact we have established with Tallinn Polytechnic. We feel that there is a lot to be gained by opening up communication in research.'

'Perhaps we will,' she said vaguely, without looking up.

'Professor, you have a very good future ahead of you. Do you not see that we all have much to learn from one another?'

'I'm sorry, but what you are saying is nonsense. Our two systems are completely separate and will never mix.'

She had heard this before from visiting Swedes. They were too certain of the superiority of Swedish social democracy over socialism and capitalism. They considered their country beyond reproach, a perfectly honed blend of humane capitalism and social welfare. They did not see that theirs was merely a modification of the same brutal society created by European and American colonialists, that the welfare state pacified the poor in order to sustain class domination of wage workers by the bourgeoisie.

'You cannot claim to be ignorant of your present stagnation,' Professor Nilsson began, but then decided not to argue further with her. 'Professor Anvelt, I have no wish to antagonize you. All I am saying is that we hope to see you here again. That is, if you want to continue to visit. The department hopes that you do.'

'Thank you, Professor.' She again picked up her pen. He nodded and left. She wondered briefly what this man had really wanted and then went back to her work.

That afternoon she walked along Lake Mälaren, passed by joggers, bicycles, children on roller skates. She saw she was early for her appointment at the embassy and decided to continue to walk. She had explored downtown Stockholm on Sunday and now knew her way around. She walked up from the lake and past the offices of *Morgon Bladet*. With her map to help her, she crossed a long bridge over a wide span of blue water.

Centralen was a throng of people: young Swedes in jeans and unzipped jackets; old ladies with hats and gloves and warm coats; dark families, Turkish or Iranian, with beautiful children, their rich black hair in smooth plaits, their ears pierced with gold, strangely foreign in their Swedish clothing. Piret saw a poster for an American film about astronauts, the actors posing like cowboys, and advertisements for clothing and appliances at various shops.

Above the underground station was an enormous department store; she saw the large red letters: Åhléns. She wandered inside and looked at the directory, which was in five languages. She decided to tour the entire store systematically. She started at the basement and walked down the aisles of food: row upon row of fruit, fish, meat, canned goods. She looked at the price of each item with the objective curiosity of an anthropologist.

She went up each escalator, through cosmetics and scarfs, women's shoes, sportswear, lingerie. She saw women's silk underwear printed in zebra stripes and leopard spots. She saw one wall of various types of jogging shoes, racks of swimming costumes, women's tights of every possible colour. After a while, she felt her head begin to ache. Surely people could not buy all these things?

She left and walked towards Hötorget, and saw the blue concert house, Konserthuset, next to an outdoor market of flowers and fruit. She took an escalator below ground to an enormous collection of stalls: fishmongers, delicatessens, butchers, cheese-sellers. She made a quick tour, noting that it was expensive compared to Åhléns.

She returned to the street and walked towards Kungsträd-gården, past the large church across from the Opera House. Next to the church was Café Opera, where a patio covered by a marquee was filled with people drinking and eating.

On Sunday Piret had passed this same spot and seen people coming out of the church, girls in white dresses, men in suits taking photographs, women in hats: a wedding, she had at first thought. Then she saw that the girls were all carrying white prayerbooks; it was a confirmation. She had passed, noticing that the girls were all blonde, except for one or two dark ones.

The church was now quiet. Piret continued to walk. On her right was a harbour, moored sail-boats, restaurants on yachts, sightseeing boats for tourists. Across the water she saw the Strand Hotel. To her left were expensive shops in elegant stone buildings.

She looked into shop windows, and found herself struck by one shop in particular, with its windows full of simply designed furniture, upholstered in vivid colours, and pewter candlesticks, blown-glass vases and magnificent curtains, heavy and thick.

She stared at the curtains and then noticed matching place-mats and table napkins arranged in careful disarray on a glass table around the candlesticks. She stood perfectly still for a moment, looking at the fresh sky-blue, the pale green of a new petal, yellow as rich as beaten eggs, a sweep of cut wheat. As she stared, she felt a powerful and foreign sensation grip her, slow and unshakeable: envy, stronger than anything she had ever felt. She lived with so little and now she imagined the millions of people who considered it their right to live every day with these colours.

And she did not; she lived with the comfort that her life was pure and difficult. She did not go to places like Café Opera and drink from tall glasses under a marquee. She had the fineness of a mind that had learned to think with reserve, care, diligence. She had the passion of an interior life; Westerners had only the capacity for the frivolous.

She turned away, tired. She passed a kiosk and glanced at the newspapers, but could not quite decipher the headlines.

She reached the museum and made a brief tour. It was quite small and the art almost exclusively modern: Kandinsky, Klein, Duchamp. She looked at each picture carefully. She found them rather empty.

She decided to take a bus to the embassy; she was now quite far away. She read the bus stop schedules until she found one with her stop. She showed her ticket to the driver and he stamped it. A mother with a pram was boarding through the back door. She sat down in a seat alone.

After a few minutes she found herself eavesdropping on a conversation between a man and woman in front of her. It took her a moment to realize why she was listening: they were speaking Estonian. They were talking about a gift they were to buy for someone they would be visiting. Then she understood that they were brother and sister and discussing their mother's birthday.

She sat listening, unable to break her attention away. Their accents were just different enough from her own to sound foreign; an odd rhythm rather than an accent gave it away. They were Swedish, of course. As she listened, she heard words she had not heard in years; they were speaking their parents' language from forty years before, when their parents left; the dated language of the war refugee.

The sister got off at the next stop and the man was left alone. Piret could see his profile. He looked very Estonian, having the sculpted cheekbones and high-set, small eyes. After a while he got off too, and then Piret saw that she had missed her own stop and would have to walk back. It did not matter: the light was beautiful this time of evening and she enjoyed walking.

18

Piret pushed the buzzer at the black gates of the Soviet embassy on Gjörwellsgatan.

The receptionist, a man, spoke to her and she stated the details of her appointment. The gate buzzed open. She walked past the guard and the small consular section, and up the steps through the main entrance and foyer; the receptionist sat behind a glass window, in front of his microphone. He did not bother to look up as she passed.

Inside the waiting room were two leather sofas and two large tables. A few couriers lounged on the sofas waiting for visas. On the tables were Soviet publications in Swedish, Russian, Estonian and English. One was called *Soviet Manufacturing in the Technological Age*; another *Ethnic and Folkloric Customs of Soviet Peoples*. There was a stack of newspapers in the Baltic languages, including *Kodumaa*. The tourist brochures caught her eye: *Riga: The Jewel of the Baltic*; *The Exhibition of Estonian Economic Achievements*.

Piret stood and waited. She never read propaganda. She read newspapers with professional disinterest: *Pravda* and *Izvestia* as well as the Estonian papers, and took none of it seriously. She never listened to the Voice of America or the BBC and watched little Russian or Estonian television. She could never understand others' excitement over the rare appearance of a foreign, usually French or Italian, film, or why people would pay for an antenna to receive Finnish TV. All versions of the news she considered corrupt, the selective distortion of a minute part of the highly complex process of history.

Many times over the past decade Piret had faced what others might have considered to be important moral choices.

Invariably she chose the pragmatic path without a qualm or a moment of hesitation. In 1980, when elections were held on Estonian National Independence Day and many people risked losing their jobs by boycotting the elections, Piret voted.

When she was asked to be the secretary of the university section of Komsomol, she accepted without hesitation. She was neither zealous nor lax in her duties, but performed them exactly.

She had been a party member for several years. It had been quite simple. She had been recruited in her third year by a teacher and a fellow student. The party liked to have a good distribution of types and Piret was interesting: a student whose parents had been uneducated workers. It was an honour to be asked; she would never have been allowed to do research in market economies or go abroad if she were not a party member.

A Russian woman opened a door and said, in Russian, 'This way.'

Piret followed the woman through an office in which visa applications were stacked on two photocopying machines. Three or four Russians sat at desks, shuffling papers, obviously waiting for the afternoon to end.

Piret entered her contact's office, waited for him to wave his hand and then sat down. He continued to write for a moment. He was the economic attaché and the local KGB officer. He looked up at Piret and she handed him her report.

It stated her activities during the past two days, including where she ate lunch, with whom, what classes she had attended, what research papers she had obtained from the library, what technical journals she had read. She also handed over a thick binder of photocopied statistical information.

'Thank you,' said the Russian as he glanced through her report. 'You are very thorough.'

Piret took the compliment in silence. She was known for being organized, diligent, on time.

'What have you planned for tomorrow?'

'I have the usual classes and seminars. I will have lunch

with a lecturer who is a consultant to the Riksbank on monetary policy. On Wednesday I shall attend a lecture by an Englishman at the Hotel Diplomat on the English markets – something called the Big Bang. It has to do with allowing capitalists to extract greater profits from the stockmarket.'

'Fine. There is something else I want you to attend later this week.'

'Yes?'

'There will be an exhibition of Estonian costumes and handicraft at the Svensk Form gallery on Sturegatan on Friday at two o'clock. There will be coffee and food, that kind of thing. I would like you to go there.' The man hesitated, and then said, 'It will not be thought unusual for you to attend.'

This last sentence seemed to hover in the air between them. Distaste filled Piret's mouth. 'What are you asking me to do?' she asked coldly.

'Nothing. Nothing you could possibly object to.'

She waited in silence.

'You are to go in and look around at the exhibits. People will probably notice that you are not – one of them. They may stare at you. You are to ignore them and simply show interest in the costumes and such. Do not drink or eat anything.

'You will arrive at two-fifteen and stay exactly fifteen minutes. At two-thirty you will leave. As you leave, you will pass a table on which there are brochures. A girl will be sitting there in Estonian folkloric dress. Here is a photograph of her.'

He handed Piret a photograph of an eighteen- or twenty-year-old girl, blonde, clear Estonian features.

'You will say to her, in Estonian, "Thank you. It was a lovely exhibition." Then you will leave and report to me as usual.'

Piret was silent. She knew that this innocuous act was part of some greater intrigue. She also knew she might never find out the purpose of her role, whether it was as a messenger, a diversion, a warning, a signal. She would never know who in the crowd was watching her; who would be standing near the table overhearing her words.

She did not mind providing the KGB with information in

her field. It was simple to compile the information they required in the course of her own work and she understood its usefulness. This, on the other hand, was different. Now she was a tool, a minor puppet in some plan. She said carefully, 'Comrade, I have always performed my work with the greatest of care. I hope you agree that I am reliable and trustworthy.'

He looked at her with suspicion. The words, *But I am not a spy*, stuck in her mouth. Then she realized that this man was simply following orders and that he probably did not know what her presence and her words meant to whatever overall design this was. Her reluctance to follow his instructions would merely result in her immediate return home and a mark on her record. This probably had nothing to do with her. She was being used because she was here and convenient.

Then she thought of her visitor that morning. She had been given a message, perhaps unwittingly, by him. *Professor, you have a very good future ahead of you. We hope to see you here again. That is, if you want to continue to visit.* If she wanted to return, she must carry out her orders.

She returned his gaze. 'So I can assure you that I will complete your directive to my best ability.'

He did not smile as she rose, but only said, 'Thank you, Comrade.'

19

Helena had worked at the SAS ticket office on Sveavägen for over ten years now. She liked using her German and English and SAS was a good company: she would have a comfortable pension when she retired.

On Saturdays she went to the supermarket for Erna. Erna had stayed at the Odenplan flat after Jaan's death nearly four years before. It had been a heart attack; the stress of working as an orderly, studying, the exams, the internship as a junior doctor had all taken their toll.

He had become dreamy and nostalgic, talking about his youth and the farm, telling seven-year-old Maarja over and over again about the day the Russians came and shot his mother until both Erna and Helena were wild with boredom and irritation.

After shopping, Helena stayed to help Erna with her laundry and cleaning. Saturday evenings she and Maarja usually ate dinner at Erna's. Sundays Helena saved for her own housekeeping and for Maarja. When Maarja was younger they went to a museum, or to Skansen to see the elk and reindeer and walk in the woods and among the old Swedish houses. Lately, though, Maarja had resisted this routine. A girl of eleven did not always want to be with her mother.

Helena's life for the past eleven years had revolved around little more than this: work, shopping, housekeeping, her family. Helena's holidays consisted of taking Erna and Maarja where they might enjoy themselves: the German coast, Denmark, Gotland. They took boats and trains and did not go far; Erna did not like flying, or travelling too far from home. Much as Helena would have liked to see France or Italy, she did not allow these desires to surface. She had not once flown on an aeroplane since the beginning of her career.

Helena was restless. Sometimes she attributed this to Maarja's increasing independence. She had always known that Maarja's adolescence would not be easy; she had invested her entire life in her child. Perhaps it was living without sex for two years. Helena had had one brief affair then, the only one since her divorce in 1974: one affair in ten years.

The past few months she had been plagued by furious dreams about sex, usually with inappropriate men: the family doctor, who was old and short; or some unknown man who had pushed past her in the underground; or a clerk in the supermarket. She dreamed of the feeling of desire rather than of the act itself, of the intensity of some man's need for her; she could feel herself opening up to enclose his body, solid and primed.

She had been the silliest of girls, she knew that now. But since her divorce she had devoted herself completely to her parents, her daughter, her job. She felt now that she had compensated too much for her frivolous and melodramatic youth.

. She had monitored suspiciously her every emotion as a mother. She did not know how real mothers felt and she criticized in herself any ill temper, any impatience. She tried to be more perfect than any mother could be.

And even this desire for perfection made her worry: perhaps other mothers accepted their shortcomings. She was too frightened to ask them. The mothers at the Estonian nursery and later at Maarja's school seemed calm and authoritative and never looked as rattled as she felt. She felt as though her life was always on the verge of unravelling.

Maarja was a beautiful girl, not at all like Piret. She had Piret's dark hair, but she also had striking bones, deep brown eyes; she was not large-boned like Swedish girls, but slender, slightly exotic, almost delicate.

Helena worried that her daughter's beauty and her obsession with clothes promised a frivolous and promiscuous future, but was mollified by Maarja's very good schoolwork. Maarja was extremely determined and much brighter than

138

Helena or Peeter had ever expected her to be. They had, at the beginning, decided that Maarja might not do as well as their own child would have and that they must accept this. When they saw Maarja develop an inclination to study, they assumed she must take after her father, whoever he was.

It was shortly after Maarja's tenth birthday that they heard about Piret becoming a professor. News travelled via Matti and Maret in their occasional letters to Erna. Helena could hardly believe it: a professor at the Polytechnic. She received this news from Erna in stunned silence.

'A what?' she finally said.

'Yes,' said Erna. 'Extraordinary, isn't it?'

'But how? How did it happen?' Helena pictured Piret at the church, rumpled, unbrushed, weighed down with her shopping; Piret copulating with her lover; Piret in that filthy flat with her drunken father. She remembered Piret at Lydia's when they were children, hiding sulkily behind her mother, a strange and angry woman who never smiled, never spoke, except to give her daughter a bucket and push her out of the door to collect berries with Helena.

Piret had looked very much like her mother, although her mother was fairer. They were both thin and small and had the same sharp faces, piercing and hard. Helena remembered their postures were identical: round-shouldered, as though Piret had begun already to carry her mother's burdens. Helena remembered deliberately towering over Piret; she did not pity her cousin: she despised her for her poverty, her unlucky parents. She also avoided her, as though Piret's life might be contagious.

Erna continued to read Maret's letter and Helena was brought back to the present. Apparently Piret was a communist as well. That really shocked her: somebody in their family a communist.

'Well, a party member, at any rate,' said Erna. 'I expect she wouldn't have the job she does without it.'

Helena was disgusted. This news convinced her even more that the adoption had been the right decision. My God, she thought: a communist. She tried to picture Piret as one of those hard Russian women with hair like a helmet, strong and enormous, capable, bossy. But all she could think of was Piret's strange, desperate look at the christening and the bulging net shopping bags she had held in both hands. It was the first time she had seen her cousin in two or three years. They had not once met during the pregnancy: it was thought best to keep them apart.

Erna said, 'Don't be too hard on her, Helena. We don't know what life is like at home. We can't judge the people who live there.'

'Everybody has a choice,' said Helena in a hard voice.

'Not always,' her mother corrected her mildly.

Helena did not reply. She would never see Piret again anyway. They were separated by more than a mere sea; the communist East and the free West simply did not meet. Piret had her own life now; Helena had hers.

Or so she had always thought. Sometimes she thought she hadn't a life at all; she was the caretaker of her mother and daughter. But how could she complain? She had been given a child, she lived in a free country, she had a good job.

But Helena wanted more. Perhaps she had become too Swedish, too Western, too demanding to be content with her self-effacing life. She had changed over the years. She shaved her legs, dried her hair with a blow-dryer and round brush, wore patterned stockings. Her cupboards were filled with all the cleaning products she had once found mysterious and extravagant: different products for the toilet, the kitchen sink, the shower, the floors.

She tried different anti-ageing creams for her skin and sometimes splurged on expensive cosmetics from NK. She had discussions with her colleagues about the rights and wrongs of feminism. She read novels, watched television mini-series about ambitious businesswomen tamed by love, tried different recipes, thought about taking an aerobics class. She rode Maarja's bicycle along the bike path by Lake Mälaren. She saw the young, beautiful Swedish girls pass her on their way to their classes and jobs, and she understood that they hardly looked at her; she was now an older woman.

She tried to stay busy, although she knew in her heart that something was wrong. She could not pinpoint the problem. But whatever it was, the answer had been Gustav Bergman.

Gustav usually sent a courier round for his plane tickets. He worked for a Swedish bank and travelled often. Then, one day, he came in personally to collect his ticket. It was, Helena remembered, for Milan. Milan, she imagined, would from then on be their code word for the fortunate twist of fate that brought them together. She pictured them years from now, laughing together, saying, 'Thank God for Milan.'

He had shown very little interest in her that first time. He simply paid for his ticket and left. The second time he came in he explained that he usually had his hair cut on Kungsgatan and that this took him past the SAS office. The third time she knew he was not having his hair cut.

There was something confident about Swedish men, especially Gustav, as though nothing could ever damage them. He was a large man; the sight of his broad hands stirred up in her the same terrible, unprompted desire she had felt in her dreams.

The following week she began a new routine. She rose early and washed her hair, taking particular care in drying it. She began doing sit-ups. She started reading her mother's women's magazines, articles with titles like 'Colour Code Your Wardrobe' and 'Do You Intimidate Your Man?'

He moved slowly, agonizingly slowly. The third week he stopped by her office late and asked for a new Arlanda–Heathrow schedule. Then he asked her if he could walk her home. On the way they stopped at a café. He wanted to hear about her life; he was a good listener.

A few days later he rang and asked if she could have a drink with him after work. They met in the bar of the Grand Hotel. He seemed to be always on the verge of touching her. When they sat down, he held his hand just under her elbow, guiding her into the chair. She could feel the space between her body and his hand. He handed her the drinks menu and she felt the warmth of his fingers.

She thought, with some embarrassment, that she would burst if he did not touch her. When they left, he helped her with her coat and rested his hand for a few brief seconds on her back as he held the door. She stopped immediately, memorizing the sensation of Gustav's broad hand, the pressure of the fabric brushing her skin.

She got home and sat down in her coat, without taking off her shoes. She felt in complete despair. She thought: When he makes his move, how on earth will I manage to restrain myself?

He made his move on Wednesday. They had dinner at an Italian restaurant in Gamla Stan and walked down the narrow stone streets afterwards towards Strandvägen. The days were growing shorter, and the last light was now, at ten o'clock, nearly gone. White sail-boats sat docked against their piers, rocking gently. Across, towards the Strand Hotel, larger yachts, now restaurants, glittered in the black water.

For the past three weeks Helena had waited for what she knew now would happen. But instead of welcoming it she was terrified. Gustav pulled her closer to him as they walked, and she found that they were not yet used to one another and could not walk in step. She automatically thought: This is a bad sign.

Then, ridiculous, strange, juvenile fears began needling her and she felt tension line her face. She had not taken off her clothes in front of a man in two years. Two years. She could not remember how to kiss, how to touch a man. She was terrified what he might think of her body. She knew her breasts had begun to sag; her thighs reminded her of the texture of uncooked bread dough. I must stop thinking like this, she told herself.

Then, on the street, in the dark between two shops, he kissed her, and she realized at once that she did not have to do anything; she did not have to know how to do anything. Gustav knew. He kissed her hard so that their teeth struck slightly, but far from embarrassing her it seemed part of his craving for her.

He seemed to want her desperately. His hands were everywhere and she made a half-hearted attempt to push him away, not wanting him to stop, but merely to slow down and give her time to accept and enjoy him. He held her head between his large hands and kissed her hard, pulling her lip. He pushed her up against the cold stone wall, reached under her jacket, pulled her off her feet and leaned against her. He held her up, his body between her legs, the cold stones against her back, and she felt herself open up to him easily. She wished that he could push himself into her that very moment.

Three young boys crossed at the top of the street and whistled at them, and Gustav let her go. He took her hand and she followed him. They found his car and he unlocked the passenger side and opened the door for her. They drove to his flat.

Inside he took her through a small sitting room which immediately struck her as oddly impersonal; after a moment she realized why: it was furnished like a hotel room. On each wall was a framed abstract watercolour of the same terracotta and salmon as the fabric of the sofa and chairs. A drinks trolley of polished glass and metal sat to one side with two full and immaculate crystal decanters.

Gustav led her straight to his bedroom. She wanted a drink first, as she had sobered up slightly on the way, but he began removing her clothes immediately. She held his hand for a moment and said, 'Gustav, wait, just a bit more slowly.'

'Yes, yes,' he said indifferently. He removed his own clothes and pushed the sheets and duvet down to the foot of the bed.

Helena was now deadly sober. She removed her remaining clothes as though she were undressing at the doctor's. She looked at her body on the stark, white sheets, the duvet falling to the floor, the ceiling and bedside lamps glaring around them. Gustav lay next to her leaning on one elbow, running his hand to and fro across her body, stopping at each breast for a brief, clinical squeeze.

He pushed his hand down between her thighs and pushed

143

them open. 'I want to feel your cunt.' He began to kiss her again and she tried to relax. She closed her eyes; her legs against the sheet reminded her too much of the gynaecologist's.

He entered her from behind; she waited patiently until it was over. When he lay down again, she pulled a sheet over them. He buried his head in her neck and kissed her. 'Next time it will be better.'

She did not know what to say. She did not know if this failure was due to her own nervousness or his impatience. She had hoped for so much and this was a terrible disappointment. Her first sex in two years and she felt like taking a shower and going home.

She thought about her daughter and suddenly missed her terribly. Maarja was spending the night with her friend Kristina. They were probably sitting at the kitchen table doing homework, or washing their hair, or watching television.

She had stood in Jakobs kyrka on Sunday and watched her daughter before the altar in the beautiful white Burda dress she had made herself. The girls and boys had then poured out on to Kungsträdgården, holding their prayerbooks, for photographs. Helena and Maarja had gone back to the flat with Erna and their friends for the party. Her beautiful little girl. And, tonight, Helena had opened her legs to a man she had known for three weeks.

She sat up. 'I'm sorry, I must go. Maarja is waiting for me.' She rose and began to dress.

Gustav made a move to get out of bed.

'No, no. I'll take a taxi. Really.'

Gustav watched her. 'I'll call you.'

'Yes, all right.' She did not believe he would ever call her again after this disaster. Gustav, with his looks and position, must have had his choice of women. Why on earth would he ever want her?

Helena let herself out of the flat and took the lift down. What a stupid mistake. They should have waited longer, until they knew each other better. Oh God, why had she

144

done it? Well, it did not matter. It had simply been a mistake. It probably happened to millions of women. She would try to forget about him.

20

Peeter sat in his flat, looking through his notes from the East Berlin trip and wondering what he would say to Mika. Peeter had never refused to act on Mika's information before. He would simply tell him: Look, Mika, this just isn't good enough. I'm sorry, but I've axed it.

He had gone off to the church knowing he would have to explain to his desk head that the story was a crock of shit. They would have to shelve it; he couldn't get reliable confirmation. It hung over him; it had ruined Maarja's confirmation for him.

He had brought his camera, taken a few pictures outside the church and then hugged Maarja and left. She was disappointed that he did not go back for the party; he noticed Helena looked slightly relieved.

He wondered what was going on with Helena these days. She avoided him; when he saw her, she looked different, better. She was doing her hair differently and she had lost weight. He had watched her watching Maarja during the confirmation. Then it hit him. *A man*, he thought disgustedly, *she's got a bloody man.*

He had come home and called Marie, but she was not at home. She knew he was due back on Sunday. That was the thing about Swedish women; they were too independent.

He had wanted a permanent Swedish girlfriend after his years of sleeping around; he had thought of a desirable Swedish woman as the final symbol of his successful adaptation to his new country. And Marie was definitely desirable: a classic Nordic blonde, a successful stockbroker, an excellent skier and tennis player.

Now, perhaps because he was becoming more and more

Swedish, he wanted to cast his net wider. He had discovered other Swedish men also thought the women here were too practical, unromantic, even cold. They lacked the femininity, the softness, of Continental women. In fact, Peeter had recently met a new girl, a French girl. He had not yet slept with her; he had not yet decided what he wanted to do with Marie. He was watchful of his new, still-fragile Swedish self.

It was now Wednesday. Peeter had told his desk head about the Stasi story; his desk head was not pleased. 'You mean to tell me you spent a week out there and you've come back with nothing? Jesus fucking Christ, Peeter, which is it? Are those East German priests Stasi or not?'

The entire thing really irked Peeter. He had turned in some good stories. Now, after one disappointment, his desk head lay ready to pounce. He would have to come up with something else fast.

The telephone rang. Peeter picked it up expecting Marie, or even Mika. He heard an unfamiliar voice speaking Estonian. 'Peeter Reisman?'

'Yeah. That's me.'

'My name is Jaak Sepp. I bring you greetings from the homeland.'

Peeter sighed. 'Yeah?'

'I have just arrived on the boat. I have heard so much of you from mutual friends. It would be very nice to visit with you.'

Peeter hesitated. Another damn Estonian showing up out of the blue and wanting a free dinner. It happened occasionally, this kind of thing. Peeter was, apparently, something of a legend in Estonia. 'Yes, well, all right. When do you want to come round?'

'I can come now.'

Peeter could hear traffic over the line; the man was in a telephone box. He sighed again. 'Yes, all right, come over,' he said impatiently. 'We'll have a drink.' He gave the man his address; the man did not repeat it or even seem to write it down, as if he already knew it. Peeter was too annoyed to notice.

It was always the same. Somebody from the past, some visitor bringing a bottle of vodka and greetings from somebody he hadn't heard of in a million years. They were probably KGB, but who cared? He never told them anything and, anyway, it was a bit of a laugh. He liked the cat-and-mouse conversation, trying to figure out what they wanted.

He made a cursory effort to tidy up the flat. Then he took off his shirt, put on a pullover and made a drink. He looked in the fridge: nothing. Well, the man wasn't going to get dinner out of him. Peeter tried to determine if he felt hungry; he supposed they could go out for a pizza.

The bell rang and Peeter buzzed him in. Peeter stood at his front door, watching the lift come to life, descend and reappear with its passenger.

This one was exactly like the others. He wore a sad brown overcoat and held his plastic bag from the boat in both hands. He was all smiles, stumbling out of the lift anxiously. He took out a bottle of Soviet vodka; Peeter groaned inwardly. Why couldn't he have bought some Finnish or Swedish vodka on the boat? Not only was the Soviet stuff poisonously bad, but it had the tin-foil top that peeled off and could not be replaced; once the bottle was opened there was no reason not to empty it.

Peeter showed him in, taking the vodka. The man gazed around Peeter's sitting room in unaffected amazement. 'It is wonderful.'

Peeter shrugged to show that he was inured to life in the West. 'It's a flat.' He hung the man's coat up and waved him towards the sofa. He opened the vodka and poured them each a glass. They drank a toast before speaking.

'Your first trip over?' asked Peeter.

'Yes,' he replied, smiling excitedly. He had said his name was Jaak. They were all Jaak. John Smith. Sven Andersson. Hans Schmidt. What did it matter? Peeter poured more vodka.

'How was your trip?'

The man enthused about the boat, Stockholm, the shops, how clean the streets and underground were, how beautiful the buildings. It was all as usual. He went on to flatter Peeter about his successes and how important Peeter had become;

how everybody knew of him in Estonia. Peeter began to relax.

Finally, after the third vodka, Peeter remembered to ask, 'So, how are things back home?'

'Oh, very, very difficult now. We have so little. We struggle. Many people struggle. Especially the old.'

Peeter nodded. He had heard it all before. 'So, how did you find me?' Peeter enjoyed hearing the convoluted things these people came up with to explain their appearance. Why didn't they just admit his address was in the KGB files? Everybody knew the KGB kept tabs on expatriates.

'I bring greetings from one of your old friends from gymnasium.'

'Oh?' Peeter feigned interest. Most likely the old friend was some poor slob now working in a factory whom Peeter had never even met. They probably pulled a name randomly out of the school files. The KGB were sloppy; they often got their facts wrong.

'Yes. He tells me you were best friends. You wrote together on *Komsomolskaya Pravda*.' He was speaking of the communist youth daily.

Peeter looked at the man, who was still smiling and drinking. Peeter had never worked on *Komsomolskaya Pravda*.

'Where you learned journalism.'

Peeter looked at the man, who probably did not know that Peeter had never written a word of journalism in Estonia, but had learned it all in Sweden. He had been a translator before leaving. Clearly, though, this was a discussion about journalism, about his career. This had nothing to do with old friends.

'You wrote articles together,' the man prompted.

Peeter could not know, would maybe never know whether this man realized what he was about to say. It was perhaps the man's stupid smile that made Peeter suddenly feel quite sober, his neck grow cold and his armpits prickle.

'He is doing very well now. He is an important engineer. Mets. Paavo Mets.'

'Paavo Mets?' He had never heard the name before.

'You both attended Gogoli Keskkool No 21,' the man insisted.

149

'I see,' Peeter replied vaguely. 'Any particular year?'

'He knew your family quite well, he said.' The man was smiling, looking at Peeter hopefully.

'My family?'

'Yes, your cousin, I believe.' The man was smiling, repeating what he had been told to say. He had a slight look of panic in his eyes, as though anxious that he might have slightly confused his instructions.

Peeter had no cousins. He was the only child of two only children. His parents were dead; he could not even recall the names of his distant relations.

'My cousin,' he said tonelessly.

'Yes,' the man nodded eagerly. 'Your cousin. Piret. Piret Anvelt. He was great friends with your cousin Piret.' The man kept nodding, but sat back now and let out a great sigh. He had done what he had been asked to do. He looked at his glass and downed the rest of his vodka.

Peeter tried to keep his face blank. The man kept smiling, pleased with himself. He would now get the flat he wanted, or a university place for his eldest son, or a visa to visit relatives in Canada or whatever it was he had been promised.

Peeter looked down at his vodka. He had never heard the name Paavo Mets before. He could not, of course, know the name: Piret had never told him or Helena or her parents who Maarja's father was. But it was very obvious that somebody was telling him now.

21

On Friday Piret took a bus from her flat to the Stockholm School of Economics at her usual time. She attended a seminar and then worked in her office and in the library until lunch. She bought a sandwich, ate it in her office and at one forty-five walked to the underground station and took a train to Östermalmstorg.

At exactly two-fifteen she entered Svensk Form. She passed the reception table at which a dark girl sat, not the girl in the photograph. She glanced round briefly at the exhibits and began to stroll, keeping one eye on her watch.

The crowd consisted mostly of older people. A few girls in folkloric costume passed trays of *pirukas* stuffed with cabbage or meat. There were one or two young families, men and women with small children. They had Estonian features, but dressed and acted like Swedes. They looked reserved and slightly bored, as though embarrassed by the obsolete customs of their parents' dying generation.

She found herself sympathizing with the young ones, who were more or less her age. They were products of their environment, born and raised in Sweden, Swedish for all intents, but Soviet Estonians had the same look on their faces when confronted with their elders.

The older ones were pathetic, Piret thought, living in the past, in a dream world. They had fled to the West, found it degenerate and sought refuge in their homesickness, their small customs, their traditional food.

They had fled in a panic because of propaganda about communism. Now they were persuaded they lived in freedom; but of course their lives were as controlled as hers or any other Estonian's. They lived at the whim of government, the mercy of big business, advertising, the randomness of a competitive society.

Piret walked around. Each time she looked at her watch the minute hand seemed hardly to have moved. She tried to look a bit longer at the displays of costumes, textiles and silverwork; she had been now twice round the room. Then, quite suddenly, she saw her: Helena. Piret stared at her for a moment, disbelieving.

It was definitely Helena. She still held herself the way she always had, tall, striking, framed by those wide shoulders. She was changed, of course, had grown older, but yet it was unmistakably her. Her hair was still blonde, although, Piret saw, probably dyed. She was a little plumper, a little softer.

Piret willed herself to look away, but her shock had paralysed her. Then she saw that Helena was with a man, not Peeter. A fair man, in a business suit, clearly Swedish. Piret knew Helena was divorced; Lydia had found out from Matti. Piret watched, unable to break herself away from her curiosity and amazement; then Helena caught her eye and returned her gaze suspiciously. Piret watched as shock transformed Helena's face: she now recognized her cousin.

Piret knew at once that Helena would not speak to her and that she, Piret, could not approach Helena. What would she say? She could not possibly ask her about Maarja. Piret looked quickly away, thinking, *Oh God, Maarja*. She glanced around unwillingly; was Maarja here? She felt herself shake with fright at the thought; she desperately hoped not. She looked around; she wanted out, she had to leave immediately. For several minutes she completely forgot the reason for her presence here.

All these years she had successfully resisted thinking about Maarja and Helena. She had prided herself in excising any feeling she might have retained for her child. She had resisted the urge to count the years. Now it hit her, without even consciously calculating: Maarja was eleven.

She turned and stared at a mannequin wearing a red and blue costume, the white blouse with puffy sleeves, the embroidered bodice and silver medallion, long woven skirt and tall hat with streamers. She felt a flush envelop her neck. She gathered her thoughts and looked at her watch: five more minutes.

She kept her back to Helena and edged her way towards the exit. She had to get out as quickly as she could, but the dark girl, the wrong girl, was still at the reception table. She tried to calm herself, to look at the exhibits. But she could not concentrate, she could not stop looking round in panic.

The people around her glanced at her, sensing her sudden nervousness. She did not react and forcibly calmed herself until they returned to their paper plates of Estonian food, their small groups.

She stayed near the exit, waiting. She glanced around at the crowd discreetly, keeping her eyes away from the corner of the room, where Helena stood with the Swedish man. She looked at the sad, sentimental people around her; in fact, probably much like Helena: emotionally attached to some idea of Estonian culture. A tiny country: pathetic, really. Nationalistic, of course. And their children, their Westernized children, who cared nothing about the old country, who probably only cared about money, their clothes and flats and cars.

She looked at the front desk. The girl in the photograph was walking around the room. It was nearly time now. At two-thirty the girl would take her seat at the reception table.

And then, Piret thought, it will be my part. I will walk up to this girl and say something that costs me nothing. Why not? I have committed far more compromising actions before this.

And yet she hesitated. She had walked a straight and careful path for so long; now the aberrant thought suddenly took root: what she did could affect all these people. What she had been asked to say had something to do with these people, these expatriate refugees, who ate *pirukas* and went to craft exhibitions. The KGB considered these people a threat to Soviet security.

This was not a game. This was not a simple price to pay for the privilege of travelling abroad. She had wanted her life to be nothing but the pursuit of ideas. But her one vulnerable spot, Maarja, had been dredged up and used. She had given her child away; and now this fact was being used to further some plan. It could not be a coincidence that Helena was here. It must be part of the plan that Helena should see her. And, even if it were not, she was being used as a pawn to hurt real people, perhaps here in this room, her own family.

She thought: *I cannot do this*. She could gather information, numbers, articles, statistics, because it was a system she studied and wrote about. But these were people: frightened, nostalgic, romantic people. People who probably had wanted nothing more than to farm their land, run their shops, raise their children. Their lives had been ruptured.

She remembered her parents' stories of the Russians invading, the gunfire in the suburbs of Tallinn, hearing the news of the tanks moving north on the Tartu Road. Her mother had told her about that night; how she and her parents had fled from the south to a relative in Tallinn. They had stayed there as the Red Army marched in, eighteen people in a three-room flat. They had believed that they would be liberated by the Allies in a matter of days, weeks at the most.

Her parents could have been among the ones who fled. The difference between her and the people in front of her was that her parents had not had the money or contacts to get on a boat. She could easily be living here like these people, who lived in spacious flats decorated with green and blue and yellow fabrics, pewter candlesticks and glass vases. They bought birthday presents for their mothers and watched American films about astronauts and bought their fruit and vegetables at Åhléns.

And among these people was her daughter: she was now one of them. The daughter she had lost, had given away. Piret had been frightened then, had not known what to do. Her uncle Jaan and her father had made this decision, and she, because she was seventeen and thought of herself as incapable of motherhood, had agreed. She had thought of aborting Maarja, but she had not been given the chance to keep her. She had given Maarja away, but Maarja had also been taken from her.

Piret remembered the christening, standing in the church,

thinking of the scars on her breasts and abdomen, the terrible pain of the night of Maarja's birth. She remembered Helena's nervousness and fear; she had had power then and she had not known it: she was Maarja's mother.

She remembered her wish that Maarja would not look like her. Piret had been an inarticulate girl then, incomplete, unsure. Her own mother was dead; she had had no one on her side. Her wish had been the only thing she could give from a life she saw as without hope or future: Piret had wanted Maarja to be happy. She had wished that Maarja would never be demeaned, belittled, beaten down. Piret had gone to the christening to find a way to not love Maarja, a way to stop the pain of loving her own child.

Piret stood and looked around. Where was Maarja now? At home? Helena would go home after this exhibition, cook her dinner, talk to her as mothers talked to daughters. Maarja would never know about this; Helena, Piret knew, would never tell her.

Her daughter was eleven, somewhere in this city. Piret recalled herself as a child, ten years old, walking home from Kaarli kirik after her mother's funeral, watching her father fry potatoes in the black, oily pan. Her mother had died; she had never said goodbye to her angry, bitter mother. She had never said goodbye to her daughter; she had never wept for the loss of her child.

Unbidden, words came to Piret's mind: *I could never tell you how much I love you. I who was such a wild and angry one and never learned to weep simple tears ... It's me: Piret. Maarja, where are you?*

All her adult life she had learned how to think one thing and say another, how to live a life of duplicity, how to compartmentalize her mind into complex layers of truths, part-truths, lies, justifications. Now she saw how simple some decisions could be. Whatever this was about, whatever the reason that she had been brought here, perhaps to see Helena, Maarja was involved. Her child, now Helena's child, was part of a community which her government wanted to hurt.

155

In the midst of all these frenzied thoughts and emotions, Piret's own life took shape. Hers was no longer a life of ideas, of perfect invulnerability: it was now a life within her grasp.

She looked at her watch. The blonde girl was moving towards the table. It was time. Piret would have to go now. She had to say the words she had been instructed to say or walk out. She moved towards the door as the blonde took her seat at the table. Piret left without looking back.

22

Peeter woke up on Thursday morning with a hangover. He thought about his visitor and the name Paavo Mets. His headache and his fuzzy memory made him pause and go over the man's exact words again. *I bring you greetings from Paavo Mets ... friends of your cousin Piret Anvelt ...*

Peeter wondered: had he overreacted? Was Paavo Mets really Maarja's father? Why on earth would they have sent this stupid little man to tell him that they knew who Maarja's father was?

Peeter put these questions aside for the moment; perhaps it was something to do with Piret but not Maarja. Perhaps it had nothing to do with Piret at all. Why had the man said *your cousin, Piret Anvelt*? Why had he not said *your wife's cousin*? Why had he mentioned *Komsomolskaya Pravda*? It was all too confusing at the moment, and Peeter's head hurt far too much to try to piece the picture together.

He got out of bed and made coffee. It was nine o'clock; he drank his coffee quickly and went to dress. He did not want things with his desk head to get even worse.

The following evening, Friday, as he walked through the door the telephone rang. He picked it up as he took off his coat. 'Peeter, it's Helena.'

'Oh, hello.' Peeter thought: What the hell does she want now? She probably wanted to berate him about not attending the party. Helena usually rang him to nag him about Maarja.

'What are you doing at home? It's not even six. I thought you journalists worked every waking hour.'

'What do you want, Helena?' he replied irritably. This, he thought, was exactly why he had left: her sarcasm, her constant criticism. No doubt she was the first one in her own office every morning and the last one out.

Then her voice became anxious, 'Peeter, can we meet? Can I see you?'

Peeter was immediately suspicious; he remembered all too well the Helena who dramatized the most trivial events. 'Why?'

'Peeter, it's – '

Then he heard the genuine distress in her voice. 'Is Maarja all right?'

'Yes – '

'Look, I'm sorry I couldn't come to the party – '

'Peeter, I saw – Piret. She is in Stockholm.'

'What? What are you talking about?'

'She was at a gallery, at Svensk Form.'

'What? Piret is in Stockholm? Why?'

'I don't know why. There was an exhibition – ' Helena did not want to mention Gustav. She had always held out her fidelity to Peeter as proof that she had not been responsible for their divorce. She could not bring herself to admit to him that she had now faltered from being the perfect mother, the sacrificing daughter.

At the exhibition Helena had at first assumed the whole episode was a coincidence; she saw that her presence came as a complete surprise to Piret. After that initial shock she was then immediately consumed with fear; Piret had come to Stockholm to see Maarja, find her and talk to her, or even take her away.

Why else would Piret be in Stockholm but to see Maarja? Helena had always seen their lives as for ever severed; to see Piret in Sweden made Helena realize that the barrier between them was not impenetrable. In her panic Helena assumed the worst. Perhaps Piret had found a way to prove that Maarja's exit visa had been fraudulently obtained; after all, Maarja had never been legally adopted. Jaan and Sylvia had fabricated her birth certificate.

Then, as she left the exhibition, Helena began to doubt that the meeting had been a coincidence at all. Perhaps Piret's

158

performance had been planned. Perhaps she had the Soviet authorities on her side. Perhaps Piret knew Helena would be there. Perhaps they had been told. By Gustav. Perhaps Gustav had told someone.

Or she had been set up. Helena had left the building, this idea growing in force. Within minutes she was convinced of its truth. The whole thing had been planned. Either Gustav had been set up, or he had told someone they would be there, perhaps not in innocence. Gustav could be working for them. He had insisted on going; he had been used to take her there.

The thought developed in her mind; within seconds she saw the picture fit together; it explained everything: Gustav's sudden interest in her; his calculated charm; his reluctant, obligatory seduction. She had not listened to her inner voice, her instincts, which told her that this man did not want her; that his conversation was contrived and his every move calculated. She felt now drenched in humiliation; she was a vulnerable woman, no longer young, easily seduced, desperate for a man.

Gustav had insisted on taking her to the exhibition. When he had rung her at the SAS office on Thursday, his voice took her breath away; she could not speak for a moment.

'Are you there?'

'Yes, yes, of course. Hello.' She was conscious of her co-worker at the next desk busying herself, striving to not listen. She could not imagine why he had called her.

'I was wondering if you're doing anything tomorrow.' He knew of course that Friday was her short day. 'Are you doing anything in the afternoon?'

'No, nothing.' Of course not. What should she be doing? Did he expect her to have found another lover since the night before?

'There's an exhibition of Estonian costumes and things tomorrow at Svensk Form.'

'Oh, really?' She tried to hide her disappointment. Why would he want to do something like that? 'There are often those kinds of things.'

'Wouldn't you like to go?'

'Oh, Gustav, it's not what you think. It's a lot of little old ladies and tables of needlework and folk costumes. It's so – ' She stopped. She did not want to say, *pathetic*. 'It's not very interesting.'

'I had hoped you could tell me a bit about it. I'm afraid I know nothing about Estonia. I thought you'd introduce me to your culture. Let's go. It will tell me more about you.'

He wanted to know more about her. Still she hesitated. She imagined all the old ladies talking to her and the platters of homemade *pirukas*. She thought of them in bed, his indifferent touch, the bright lamp, the terrible white sheets at the foot of the bed. She felt confusion fill her mind; she could not think clearly.

'We'll have dinner afterwards – if you're free of course.' He spoke as he always had, as though the disaster had never happened.

'Yes,' she had said. 'I am.'

Peeter would be furious with her for having exposed Maarja to danger. But how could she have known? Gustav had appeared to be exactly what he seemed. But of course everybody had something to hide, something that could be used.

Helena realized now that Gustav was probably extremely easy to blackmail. She thought of the flat, which was clearly his *pied-à-terre*. Nobody lived in a flat that looked like a hotel room. Helena understood with sudden clarity that it was impossible that Gustav was not married. Gustav took women there. It was a classic KGB blackmail. An even more humiliating thought occurred: perhaps Gustav took men there.

Helena had left the exhibition shortly after Piret. Gustav had trailed after her; she noted his surprise at her distress, but as her theory developed she explained his surprise away. His instructions must have been simply to take her there; he had not known the purpose or the likely result.

He caught up with her on the street. She brushed his hand away and said viciously, 'Get away from me and never call me again.'

He followed her a few more steps; she was heading for the

160

underground. She turned around and nearly spat at him. 'Do you understand? Never, never call me again. If I ever see you again, I will spit in your face.

'I don't care why you did this or what they did to make you do it, just get away from me. For ever. For the rest of my life.' She stared at his stunned face for one frozen second and then turned and walked quickly towards Östermalmstorg station.

Now she said, 'It was an Estonian exhibition. I saw her. Oh, Peeter, what do you think she wants?'

Peeter said nothing. Helena had seen Piret; he had been sent greetings from Paavo Mets: Maarja's parents, Maarja's real parents. It was too much to be a coincidence. They knew who Maarja's real parents were. It was not clear what the implication of this message was, but what was clear was that Helena was being used to send the other half of it to Peeter. It was now very simple. Mika would be calling him again soon. And Peeter would have to do what he suggested.

He would not tell Helena any of this; there was no need to upset her further; it had nothing to do with her. It was only to do with him. 'Helena, listen to me, it's just a coincidence. I can tell you for sure that Piret probably had no idea you were there. How could she have?'

Because it was a set up, Helena wanted to say. It had to be; it all fitted. But she could not tell Peeter that she had slept with another man, much less one being used by the KGB. 'It was not a coincidence.'

'Helena, you are always too hysterical. How do you know? You and your mother were always convinced that something bad would happen to us here. You both want to pay for having emigrated. You both suffer from refugee guilt. You're like Jews. Because you got out, you are going to make yourselves pay with guilt.

'Anyway, how could Piret simply leave the country and go to Sweden to look for Maarja? She'd have to get a passport, an exit visa, foreign currency. It's just not that simple.'

'Perhaps she's had help. Maybe they found out Maarja was never adopted. Peeter, don't you see, if she's not adopted, she's not Swedish.' Helena voice was rising.·'Perhaps they are using her; or perhaps she is doing something for them in exchange for getting Maarja back. Peeter, don't forget, she's a communist.'

Peeter knew that Helena was right. He had received the other half of the message. Clearly Piret was involved in the plan; she was using her daughter to co-operate with the KGB. *That cold fucking bitch.* But he would never admit to Helena that what he had always called her paranoid fantasies were coming true.

Anyway, she would get hysterical and perhaps the entire thing would spin out of control. As it was, Peeter knew what they wanted was something from him. But what? Information? To print the Stasi story? Whatever it was, he did not want Helena involved. He would do whatever it was they wanted; he would make sure his little girl was safe.

He said, 'Oh, Helena, you are always the same. The KGB are hiding around every corner. Why should they give a shit about us? None of us are important.'

Helena hesitated. Peeter was right, in a way. Why should they care about a second-rate immigrant journalist, an SAS employee and their adopted eleven-year-old daughter?

'Well, why else would she be here?'

'You know she's at the Polytechnic now. Maybe she's on some kind of business or academic trip or something. People do travel you know. Especially party members. They're the ones who get passports. She's obviously in with the party machinery. She's a goddamn professor. It all adds up.'

'Yes, but I – ' Helena stopped herself. She was about to say: *But I was invited to go.* Was that a coincidence too? She was silent.

Peeter said, 'Why shouldn't she go to an Estonian exhibition?'

Why shouldn't she indeed, Helena thought, trying to convince herself. She thought it over. Maybe Gustav was now wondering why she had gone so wild. He had looked quite shocked.

Well, that did not matter: she could never see him again, even if he were not KGB. For one thing, she could never take such a chance. For another, she could never take back the words she had said. More importantly, she thought of the white sheets, her thighs, the bright bedside light: no, she could never see Gustav again.

Peeter said, 'Don't even think about it. Maarja is going nowhere. Piret can't do a damn thing and she probably doesn't want to.'

Oh God, she thought, let him be right.

'Why would she want an eleven-year-old girl who doesn't even know her? Piret knows Maarja is better off with us in Sweden. Piret's strange, but she isn't a complete idiot. She'd never want to transplant a child she hasn't raised back to a Third World totalitarian dictatorship where she'd be miserable. After all, Piret must have some maternal feelings: she gave Maarja up for her own good.'

'Yes.' Helena tried to believe this. Why else would a girl give up her baby? But she also thought of Sylvia's words at the christening: Piret had come to hurt Maarja; a girl who had given up her baby could not be expected to have normal maternal responses.

Peeter said, 'Anyway, Piret doesn't know that Maarja was never legally adopted. She was a child, for God's sake. She was seventeen. Nobody told her anything. She had no idea what was going on then. She was in a daze.'

'Yes, of course.' Jaan had said as much to Helena during the long weeks she had stayed in the flat, waiting for Maarja to be born. *She's fine physically, but she's withdrawn. She wants to get it over with. She's completely accepted that she will not keep the baby. Don't worry; it will be fine.*

Peeter went on, 'Who could have possibly told her that Maarja wasn't actually adopted? And please don't say the KGB, Helena. Why the hell should the KGB care about our adopting your cousin's baby? It simply has nothing to do with anything. I mean, God, Helena, these people are interested in industry and the military. Illegitimate babies are not in their line.'

Helena suddenly saw how absurd she was. 'Yes, I see what you mean.'

'Sorry, I don't mean to make you feel stupid. I understand your concern, I really do. I mean, if I had seen Piret, I'd be upset too.'

'Would you?' Helena was now quite anxious to believe him.

'Of course. It must have been a bit of a shock. But remember that Piret has probably tried to forget all this ever happened. My guess is that Piret is now one of those masculinized communist women who is obsessed with her career and her position in the party. She was probably as surprised as you were. She's probably back in her hotel drinking that shit Estonian vodka to ease the shock.'

'Yes,' Helena tried to laugh. 'I suppose she is.'

'You know, the kind that you can't close after it's opened so you drink the whole bottle?'

Helena laughed. Peeter still could make her laugh. 'I am sorry, Peeter. You can understand my panic.'

'Of course. Just don't worry,' said Peeter. 'Just forget about it.'

23

On Friday Maarja had come home from school and found a note from her mother. Maarja tossed it aside; why her mother went to those boring Estonian culture exhibitions was beyond her. Anyway, she was relieved; Friday was her mother's short day and they usually spent it arguing about Maarja doing more of the chores.

Maarja took out a slice of bread, smeared it with butter and squeezed on top a convoluted string of pink caviar from a tube. She carried it into the sitting room, turned on the television and sat cross-legged on the sofa, eating. She was not allowed to take food into the sitting room.

There was nothing on television and when she had finished the sandwich she decided to rummage through her mother's room. She had already found the new black underwear at the bottom of her mother's drawer the week before; this was her first opportunity since then to find more evidence of what she called in her mind *the boyfriend*.

Her mother was living on another planet if she thought that Maarja did not know about the boyfriend. The first inkling she got was when her mother started getting up early every morning and doing her hair and nails. Once Maarja caught her doing sit-ups. Then she found one of Erna's magazines under the bed. It was open at one of those stupid questionnaires: 'Do you know what kind of woman you are?' She wasn't stupid; it could only be a boyfriend.

She had just opened Helena's top drawer when she heard the front door open. She quickly closed the drawer and came out of the room, carefully nonchalant. Helena stood inside the door, her coat still on. Maarja said, 'Hello, Mother. How was it?'

Helena stared at her, and Maarja started to worry. 'What's wrong? I wasn't doing anything.'

Helena looked at her blankly and said, 'I have to make a phone call.' She stepped out of her shoes and came in, her coat still on. She walked past her daughter and into her bedroom. She sat down on her bed, picked up the phone and kicked the door closed with one foot.

Maarja could hear Helena in hushed conversation with her father. Maarja pushed the door open to ask if she could speak to him and Helena angrily waved her out of the room.

Maarja went to her room and sat down on her bed. What could her mother be so upset about that she would want to talk to her father? Could it be about the boyfriend? Could she be – here, Maarja stopped thinking. The words came painfully to her mind: could she be getting *married*?

It couldn't be. Maarja felt ill. That would be the worst thing that could ever happen. Her mother married to some man, in her bed every night. She couldn't even imagine it, it was so disgusting. Her mother and a man having sex. She had seen her mother a million times without clothes on: the wedge of stomach that squeezed out over her underwear, the puffy veins on the backs of her thighs, the way her toe-nails were turning hard and brittle. She'd seen her mother sitting on the sofa in her tatty pink dressing gown, cutting the dead skin off her feet while watching television.

Her suspicions about the boyfriend had been confirmed on Wednesday night, when she stayed over at Kristina's. Kristina's parents were out, a fact Maarja had not mentioned to Helena when she asked if she could stay over. She had behaved so well at the confirmation party, and had put up with so many boring old Estonian ladies, that her mother had agreed she deserved a night away from home. Helena had not asked for any details and had seemed quite pleased to have her go.

Kristina was Maarja's ideal: blonde, tall, beautiful. Her parents' flat was perfectly arranged. Each wall had a few carefully chosen pictures, hanging from the picture rail by thin gold wire instead of on a nail. Each table had one or two beautiful objects: a hand-blown glass vase or an empty silver dish. The furniture was richly upholstered; alongside the sofa was a set of small wood tables that nested one under the other, with thin, curved legs.

Maarja's flat was cluttered with junk: glasses filled with screws and pencils, old postcards. The tables were covered with newspapers, letters, photographs. Helena had kept every single picture Maarja had ever drawn or painted. Their sofa was of dark green brocade, thin from wear. The hall was lined with cheap painted wardrobes Helena had bought from Ikea, filled with clothes and bags and shoes nobody wore any more. In their hall cupboard were stacks of extra bath and tea towels and old winter coats. In Helena's room was her desk, a heap of paid and unpaid bills, chequebooks, lists, scraps of paper with telephone numbers.

Maarja knew what kind of friend she was to Kristina. Kristina had befriended her as a superior girl likes a grateful, inferior friend. Maarja was Kristina's lady-in-waiting. Maarja was unlikely to steal attention from Kristina. At the same time, Kristina enjoyed Maarja's company because she could exhort her to improve herself. Kristina dispensed helpful hints which she gathered from magazines, knowing they would alter nothing essential in Maarja. Maarja could never be transformed.

At about ten o'clock two boys, Johan and Mats, came over. They were both in love with Kristina. Kristina pretended that she had invited them over so that each girl would have a boy; neither girl believed this fiction.

They sat in the sitting room, Kristina on the sofa, the two boys on either side of her. Maarja sat opposite them on a chair.

Kristina had arranged her long hair over her shoulders. She crossed her hands in her lap, squeezing her maturing breasts slightly together. The two boys seemed unable to pull their eyes away from the view through Kristina's gaping blouse.

Kristina led the conversation for some time, bringing forth little grunts of agreement from the two boys. She let out a playful laugh and tossed her hair at their few, unintelligible comments.

After a while, it was obvious Maarja had been completely excluded from their circle, and Kristina said, 'You know Elisabet has another name, a secret name?' The boys did not respond. 'It's Maarja.'

The boys did not appear to hear; they were watching Kristina's breasts heave as she spoke.

'We'll call you Maarja from now on, then?' she teased. She had already discovered the trick of pretending to divert attention to another woman without in fact surrendering one particle of the spotlight.

'You can't; you're not Estonian,' Maarja replied hotly, annoyed that Kristina was using this personal knowledge to flirt.

'It must be weird, not being Swedish,' said Johan unpleasantly. He was a thin boy with glasses. He glanced at Maarja as though she were a chaperon or Kristina's kid sister.

Maarja was infuriated, but she would not defend her claim to be Swedish. She knew she could never amass enough evidence to convince these pure, blond boys. It would have been so nice to be able to say: I really am Swedish; my real mother was Swedish; I was adopted by these kind Estonian people after my real mother had to hide her passionate affair with an Italian count.

But she could not say this; it was not true and they would know. But Maarja had a flair for adapting to situations and for creating drama out of the story of her life. She said loftily, 'You would not understand what it means to be a refugee.'

'I would hate to be foreign,' replied Mats aggressively, to show he was not to be outdone by Johan.

'It's not her fault,' Kristina put in with patronizing indifference.

Then the telephone rang. Kristina answered it and handed it to Maarja, saying, surprised, 'It's your grandmother.'

Maarja took the phone and Erna said, 'Maarja, is your mother there?'

'No,' Maarja said with some surprise. 'Should she be?'

'That's all right, dear.' Maarja looked at the clock; it was eleven. Her mother rarely went out, but it was odd that her grandmother should sound so worried. Maarja said, 'I'm sure she'll be back shortly. How did you know I was here?'

'Oh,' Erna said absently, 'Kristina's mother mentioned the other day that you would be coming over.' Kristina's mother was the family dentist.

Maarja hung up, wondering if Kristina's mother had also mentioned that she and her husband would be out for the evening and if Erna would think fit to mention this to Helena. A thin layer of guilt and disquiet settled over Maarja, separating her from the others. The two boys were sitting closer to Kristina now; her blouse had come unbuttoned to the point between her breasts. 'What's up?' she asked with complete detachment.

'I don't know,' said Maarja. She looked at the three of them on the sofa, sitting with their drinks. They were blessed with the gift of knowing where they belonged and she hated them. Their absorption in one another and their hostility to her freed her to hate them.

She also felt compelled to demonstrate that she cared about her family, that she was not in the least affected by their opinion, that she had a life of important attachments that went beyond adolescent drinking and flirtation. Anyway, she wanted to leave. She dialled her grandmother's number: 'Vanaema, are you sure you dialled the right number?'

'Don't worry, Maarja. I'll try again in a few minutes. I'm sure she'll be back soon.'

'But where would she go? It's late.'

'I don't know.'

'Are you going over, I mean, to our flat?'

'Yes, dear, I've called a taxi. But I'll try her again before I leave, so really just go back to your friend.'

But Maarja was determined to go with her, and after some persuading, her grandmother gave in and agreed to pick her up. She left the room to brush her teeth and wash her hands;

she sprayed on some of Kristina's mother's perfume to hide the smell of alcohol.

She gathered her clothes from Kristina's bedroom and told the others she would take the lift down to the foyer to wait for the taxi. Kristina said with an effort, 'Oh, don't go now; the party's just begun.' But she did not rise from the sofa and Maarja left.

Erna did not notice the smell of perfume on Maarja; she was too worried. They let themselves into the flat and sat in the sitting room, watching the street and waiting. After an hour or so they both fell asleep, Maarja on the sofa and Erna on a chair.

They woke up at the same time, at the sound of Helena's key rattling in the lock. Maarja could sense her surprise at finding the door unlocked; she could hear the door open cautiously. Helena stood just inside and called out Maarja's name.

Erna called out, 'We're in here, Helena.'

Maarja's mother walked in. Her hair was brushed, but her clothes were wrinkled as if she had slept in them. They all stared at each other. Then Erna said, 'Maarja, go to your room and try to get some sleep.' Maarja knew then that something had happened that she was not supposed to know about, and she left the room.

She heard them go into the kitchen and make coffee. Their voices were quiet. She heard her grandmother say, 'It's not that I object; it's Maarja I am thinking about. Helena, you simply cannot give up being a mother because you are lonely.'

'Mother, I am thirty-three. I am not old. Do you understand that I have been – '

'Shh!'

A little while later Erna left. When Maarja woke the next day, her mother said, 'Your great-grandmother is very ill.'

'Oh.' She could not remember her great-grandmother. She was less than two weeks old when they came to Sweden.

'Well, that's why Vanaema called you.' She offered this as though it explained her own absence.

Maarja looked at her sceptically. Her mother refused to say anything more about it, but she kept looking at Maarja when she thought Maarja wasn't looking. She was wondering whether Maarja suspected.

Maarja knew all about it. The teacher had showed them with models, making an effort to be serious and matter of fact, while everybody in the classroom giggled. The whole thing made her want to puke.

The day after the exhibition was Saturday. Maarja woke late and went into the kitchen. Helena stood at the sink, making coffee and eating chocolate. She always knew her mother was upset when she started eating chocolate.

Soon afterwards Maarja heard her on the bedroom phone, talking to Erna.

'Don't you see, she was here, in Stockholm ... ' Helena spoke in an urgent whisper.

'How could it be a coincidence?' Her voice rose.

'Peeter said that I'm hysterical – ' This was in the bitter voice Maarja had learned to recognize when her mother talked about her father.

'Yes, I suppose it must be ...

'Of course I would like to go. I love Vanaema. Mother, I do want to take you ...

'Yes, of course I want Maarja to go. She's never been – I mean, since the christening ...

'No, no, I'm not ...

'No, I don't think that. Why would they? An old lady?

'Of course it's safe. We have Swedish passports, after all –

'Let's wait, Mother. Please. A few days, at least. This has all happened too suddenly. Perhaps she'll get better. Let's hope it's nothing serious.'

24

'They knew about Maarja. They found out,' said Lydia.

'Yes.' Piret drank her tea. It was mid-morning; they sat on Lydia's balcony. They had done the morning chores and stopped for a second breakfast of sour milk, fruit and tea.

Piret had been home for almost two weeks. She had been escorted directly from the airport to the KGB office on Bagari Street and interrogated. She had not lied when they asked her what had happened. She had said, 'I couldn't do it.'

They questioned her over and over. There was a man, Estonian, and a Russian woman. Piret sat on a hard chair in a small room. The man sat on the edge of a table in the corner. The Russian sat on a chair facing Piret, their knees close. The Russian moved her body to imitate Piret's posture; Piret felt as though she were looking into an metamorphosed image of herself.

The woman asked Piret why she had failed to lunch with the professor who came to her office. She asked who she had seen on her walk to Centralen and around Åhléns, why she had walked all the way to the museum, what she had seen on the way, why she had passed the church downtown, why she had stopped and looked at the people coming out of the church.

They shot questions at her seemingly at random, yet they never interrupted one another. They asked her why she had not gone into any of the shops on Strandvägen. Why had she taken a bus to the embassy from the museum? Why had she stayed on the bus and got off at a later stop? Who had she seen on the bus?

They tried to find a reason why a successful woman with everything to lose and everything to gain would not carry out the simplest of requests. Thus far she was able to answer everything truthfully. She was not surprised that she had been followed; she was only surprised that they had found her movements suspicious. She had thought of herself as completely trustworthy.

Then the questioning changed. They asked her about Nadja and why she had emigrated. Had she known Nadja was about to leave the country? Had she known Nadja was Jewish? Had she known that Nadja's father had been executed as a criminal? Had they spoken about Nadja's contacts with Zionist organizations in America?

They asked her about Rozhansky. Had he ever made subversive statements? Had he introduced her to any foreigners? Had he asked her to do any favours for him? Had he ever discussed with her counter-revolutionary activities against socialism?

After this the interrogators paused and looked at one another. Then the Russian said, 'Tell us about your contacts with nationalists.'

Piret stared back at her. 'Nationalists?'

They waited, and she said, 'I know nothing about nationalism.'

The woman said, 'None of you are innocent of nationalism. You all believe you have a nation. I shall tell you now, *Professor*, you are all nothing but peasants.'

Piret did not reply. Her silence seemed to enrage the Russian; she went on, 'You would be nothing without us: nothing. You think you are a nation when you are nothing but an insignificant tribe, serfs under whoever has owned you. None of you knew the meaning of dignity before the Soviet Union set you free.'

Piret remained silent and the Russian resumed speaking after a moment. Her voice was brittle with hostility: Who had she seen at the exhibition? It was Piret's only lie, and she lied because she knew she could make it plausible and remember it: she had seen nobody she knew.

Who had she seen? She spoke calmly: old ladies and young

173

girls in Estonian costume, a few families with small children. She had not carried out her instructions, she explained for the hundredth time, simply because she was not a spy. She was a scientist, a researcher. She loved her country, she would do anything for her country, but she could not spy. She was not trained to do it; she was incapable of carrying out orders that had nothing to do with her work.

The Russian nearly spat with anger, 'You think scientists are above patriotism? You think you have a special privilege exempting you from your obligations?'

Piret stuck to her story. After a while the Russian left the room. The Estonian said gently, 'You must tell us all you know. It will go easier for you if you do.'

Piret looked at him briefly and said nothing.

When the Russian returned, she said abruptly, for maximum impact, 'Did you know that your child is living in Sweden?'

Piret was expecting this, and knew there was no way out of it. She was prepared. 'Yes.'

'And did you see somebody there who reminded you of your daughter?'

'Yes.'

'Who?'

'The girl at the reception. The dark one. The one at the table when I arrived.' Piret tried to make her voice choke. 'She was too old, of course, but she looked as if – her appearance was such that she could have been my daughter.'

This seemed to satisfy the woman. She wrote something down. 'How would you describe this reaction?'

'As an irrational, emotional reaction.'

She lost her flat, job and car. Her published papers were removed from the library. Her name was struck from the university register and her status as a doctoral candidate was invalidated. The books in her office at the Institute and at her flat were confiscated as university property. Her passport was withdrawn.

'If you are thinking of emigrating,' her interrogator told her

174

before she was released, 'you are dreaming. You have shown how ungrateful you are for all the opportunities you have been given. You have thrown away your education. You were rubbish before; you are rubbish again. You are a parasite, an expensive, selfish parasite. You will never work in a university again; you will be lucky to clean toilets.'

She packed her suitcase with what clothes she could. They did not give her very much time. She was forbidden to take her papers, or any books or pictures. She walked to the tram and took a bus to Lydia's. She had nowhere else to go.

They drank their tea. 'Well, of course. At first I thought I was just a messenger, a tiny pawn in one of their games. My instructions were so simple that I naturally thought it was a signal of some kind. But clearly it had something to do with Helena. And Maarja. It was not by chance that I was used.'

Lydia listened without speaking, stirring jam into her tea.

'They must have fixed it so that Helena would be there. That wouldn't be too difficult. I remember her face still. She was frightened.'

'She recognized you.'

'Instantly. Well, almost at once. It was her worst fear come true. The implicit threat would be, of course, that I was there to find Maarja.'

'But why? Why would they want you to see her? Or her to see you? What do you or Helena or Maarja have that could be so important?'

'I don't know. What would Helena do after seeing me? The answer lies there. That is the way they work; they create circumstances under which people will react in ways that suit them. You know Helena as well as I do. What do you think she'd do?'

'Panic. She was always impulsive.'

'And then?'

'Panic and – I don't know. Call Peeter?'

'They're divorced.'

'I know.'

Piret reflected for a moment. 'She was with a man; I thought he was Swedish, but I could be wrong. Perhaps he persuaded her to go there; perhaps he then suggested that she do whatever it was they wanted her to do.'

She went on, 'It must be something to do with Peeter: he works for a newspaper. Perhaps this man suggested that she tell Peeter about me. It would be just one more piece in the puzzle.'

'And Maarja would be the stake.' Lydia paused and then pointed out, 'Why use Helena to send a message to Peeter? Why not contact Peeter directly? Unless Helena was in on it.'

'Yes, I suppose that's possible. I'm sure Helena would sabotage Peeter to protect Maarja. A mother would do that, wouldn't she? To keep her child.' Piret thought: *I do not know the answer to this question. Yet I sabotaged myself to protect Maarja.*

Lydia was thinking: *But Maarja is not her child.* Instead she said, 'But, again, why Peeter?'

'I don't know. Information about something he was working on? Would he have access to confidential information?'

After a moment Lydia said, 'I wonder how they found out about Maarja.'

'Oh, Jaan, maybe … Maybe he left notes somewhere. Maybe the doctor who certified Helena's pregnancy, or whoever signed the birth certificate. Everybody can be got to.'

'Umm, maybe.' Lydia's tone was reluctant.

Piret did not reply, realizing that she did not know who had signed Maarja's falsified birth certificate, or certified Helena's invented pregnancy. She had never asked. Surely it could not have been Jaan; that would have been too risky. Piret wondered if Lydia knew.

She looked at Lydia, uncertain whether she really wanted to ask, whether she wanted to know. Lydia glanced at her and then rose to clear the table. Neither spoke. Piret watched Lydia walk away with a tray of dishes and knew what they were both thinking: *Sylvia.*

Piret woke up the next morning. She chopped wood and gathered eggs, weeded the vegetables and collected fruit. She and Lydia cooked lunch and talked about bottling for the winter. They discussed repairs to the roof.

The next day she took a bus to the cemetery, Metsakalmistu, and found her parents' graves side by side. She swept and washed the gravestones. She had brought with her a glass jar and flowers. She queued at the water pump behind several old women.

When she got back, she took the rowing boat out to fish. It was dusk. She pushed away from the tiny pier with her oar, through the weeds and flat green lily leaves. After a few metres the boat was in clear water and she took a worm from her bucket and speared it on to the hook. She cast her line out.

The sun was low in an orange and lilac sky. She was surrounded by the calm, dark water, sitting in the gently rolling boat, holding a fishing rod, watching the dark houses on the shore. She reflected impassively on all she had lost: her child, her mother and father, her position and career, her credentials, her home and car.

Yet these all seemed unrelated to her at the moment. She felt now the loss of something else she could not name: perhaps, she thought, it was her certainty, her footing in the world, something more than security or job or family.

She remembered a childhood rhyme from a textbook, which she and her classmates had memorized and recited for a school presentation to parents. It was accompanied by a picture of Lenin as a child, along with a story of Lenin's schooldays and how he helped the other, less gifted, children in their studies:

Üks pilt on meie seinal (The picture on our wall)
Kui kallis on mul see (How dear it is to me)
Seal Lenin suurel Oktoobril (There Lenin on the great October)
Kõneleb rahvale (Speaking to the people)

She had been excommunicated, but she was still the same person, and this was her loss. She could never transform her life and education, all that had formed her. She had lost her position in a world in which duplicity was the backbone and only legal currency. She could no more change herself than she could her language. She would be for the rest of her life what she was now. She thought: *I am truly damaged.*

The following day she took a bus into town to shop. She walked around the streets of the old town. She wondered if someone was watching her. She wondered why they were leaving her alone. Perhaps, she thought, they think they have done enough to me.

She saw a poster in the Raamatu kauplus where she had once bought her schoolbooks: next year would be the fortieth anniversary of the German surrender to Soviet troops in Berlin. The motto for the year would be, the poster said, 'Salute, Victory! Let the march "Salute, Victory" become the march of memory.' She thought of all the Komsomol students who would paint in giant letters across a banner, 'Salute, Victory!'

She went home. The lake was busy with people fishing, with swimmers, with children on the beach. It was hot. She sat on the lawn under a tree, looking out.

After a while she walked to the orchard and pushed aside the net. The sky above was blue and dazzling; inside the shelter of the fruit trees cooled her. Birds flew over, searching for berries. Piret thought, *I should be happy. I should feel free. I made the first free decision of my life. But all she felt was alone.*

In Stockholm the weeks passed uneventfully. While Piret worked at Lydia's, Peeter returned to the newspaper and Helena to her office. Oddly, nothing happened. Helena did not hear from Gustav. Peeter's desk head dropped the subject of the East German priests. Mika did not contact him. Life went on as normal.

Both of them tried to put the incident with Piret out of their minds. Peeter tried to forget about Jaak Sepp and Paavo Mets, although he knew that even if Piret's appearance could be explained away as coincidence, Jaak Sepp's could not. Both Helena and Peeter expected something to happen; nothing did.

Peeter took the precaution of seeing a lawyer, who told him

it was highly unlikely that a child of twelve who had been living in Sweden her entire life would be expatriated to the USSR. The lawyer urged him to settle Maarja's position by applying for citizenship, but Peeter demurred. He was frightened of stirring up trouble when it was just beginning to die down.

He wanted to call Helena and talk to her, tell her to keep a close watch on Maarja, even to keep her out of school. But he did not; he did not want to upset her and alarm either of them.

He began to think he had imagined the entire thing. He could not see why he should warrant the KGB's interest. It was true that he had been leaked information in the past that had come from dubious sources, but he had always verified it elsewhere. He was not a dupe. He began to believe that Jaak Sepp's words were a garbled or misdirected message.

A month later something happened that seemed to close the matter. It was Saturday morning; Maarja was still asleep. Helena had risen and made coffee. She went to the front door and scooped up a pile of post. She noticed a magazine covered in plain brown paper. She tore off the paper; the magazine was called *Estonian Culture*.

She saw at once that it was Soviet, the cheap paper gave it away. She opened the front cover and read: published in Tallinn, Estonia, USSR.

She took her other letters to the kitchen table and opened the bin to throw the magazine away: it was just propaganda. Estonian expatriates often received propaganda through the post, sent by Soviet Estonian organizations ostensibly created to promote friendship with Estonians abroad.

These kinds of magazine usually contained articles revealing the 'inside facts' on expatriate Estonian organizations and their secret meetings, their attempts to promote anti-Soviet influence in overseas governments. They revealed how refugees stole gold after the war, or how they had collaborated with the Nazis.

Nobody knew whether such stories were true or even partially true. The KGB had enormous archives, files on millions of

179

people created from documentation appropriated in the Eastern Bloc after the war. Any information coming from the KGB was likely to be doctored to suit their particular purposes.

And although Estonians were no more innocent of anti-Semitism than other Europeans, they had reason to be sceptical of Nazi collaboration stories. For one thing, the Jewish community in Estonia was far smaller than that in Latvia and Lithuania. And most of the Estonian Jews had gone by the time the German forces arrived; they had been deported to Siberia under Stalin.

As Helena tossed the magazine into the bin, she saw a note slip out. She retrieved it and read, 'I am sorry if I upset you. It was a terrible coincidence. I will not bother you again.'

She took the brown paper wrapping from the bin and looked at it again. The magazine had been sent direct from the publisher in Tallinn.

She went immediately into her bedroom and called Peeter, waking him. He listened in silence and then told her he would be there within the hour.

By the time he arrived, Maarja was up and eating breakfast. As soon as she had finished, Helena told her to go and shower. Maarja stared at her parents resentfully and left, dragging her towel on the floor.

Peeter looked at the magazine, note and wrapping, and said, 'Well, that's that. You see, Helena, it was a coincidence.'

'But how did she get a note into this magazine? How do we know it really is from her?'

'She could hardly send you a letter directly, could she? If it were confiscated, there would be questions. She obviously doesn't want to compromise us or Maarja or herself.'

Helena watched him. He was clearly relieved. He was almost smiling. He flicked through the magazine and added, 'Anyway, she's an academic. She's got contacts. She probably knows these people.'

Helena looked doubtful.

'Come on, Helena,' Peeter said. 'Relax. All these party people are linked; they all owe one another; it's a network of favours.'

Have you forgotten everything? She's in the system; this is exactly the kind of method she'd use to get a message to us.'

Helena thought: *That is what makes me suspicious. It's exactly what they think would fool us.* Was she paranoid, as Peeter had so often accused her of being?

Peeter went on, 'This is just what we needed to know. The whole thing was a terrible coincidence. Piret doesn't want to contact us any more than we want to see her. Let's put this behind us.'

25

In mid-November Helena's grandmother Leena died. Erna received a telegram from a neighbour who was her mother's only friend.

Erna called Helena, who hung up the telephone and told Maarja to pack; they were going to Estonia.

Maarja hardly got to take any clothes. Her suitcase was filled with instant coffee, tea, biscuits, sugar, two pairs of Levis, spices, raisins, cooking chocolate, toilet paper, a wool scarf, socks, stockings and underwear.

When she complained, her mother said, 'We have to take all this. We can't mail things any more; they are taxing people now on gifts.'

'Oh,' said Maarja, not understanding.

Her mother looked at her. 'Whatever we send they will have to pay for, do you see? If we send coffee for twenty Swedish crowns, they will have to pay five or ten roubles when they get the package.' She sighed and continued to pack. 'Maarja, five roubles is a day's salary for Matti.'

'Oh.' Maarja thought about this for a minute. 'Why are they doing that?'

'Because they are Russians!' Helena said impatiently. After a minute she said in a quieter voice, 'It's because of those defectors.'

They walked from the boat through immigration without a single problem. Maarja trailed behind her mother and grandmother, staring at the Russian guards. They left the terminal building and a dirty lime-green Lada pulled up. The man grunted at them and Helena nodded.

Maarja looked shocked. 'You mean we're getting into that?'

Helena turned on her angrily, 'Shh!' She pulled the suitcases towards the car; the man helped her fit them into the tiny boot.

The boot would not close; the man tied it down with a length of cord.

They set off and Maarja noticed that her door would not close properly. Helena said in Estonian, 'The Viru Hotel, please.' Maarja giggled and Helena glared at her. 'What is the matter with you?'

Maarja said in Swedish, 'I've never heard you speak to a taxi driver in Estonian before.' Helena sighed with annoyance and Erna glanced from the front seat back at her granddaughter with a look that said: Don't give your mother a hard time.

They checked in and went to their room. Outside the lift was an old woman at a desk with a telephone. 'Who's she?' Maarja asked in Estonian.

Helena pulled her by the arm down the hall towards their room. 'Please, Maarja, please just shut up. She's called a lady-bird. She's there to listen in on us.' Maarja stared at her mother, saying nothing.

They unpacked. They washed and changed their clothes and then took a tram to the funeral home where Leena's body lay waiting. She had died quietly in the night of a heart attack. She was over eighty and had a history of angina.

The funeral was simple and followed the state ritual. Helena did not care how her grandmother's death was observed: she had come for Erna's sake only. She was not sorry that her grandmother was dead; her grandmother had been unhappy, engrossed in her memories of Siberia, her bitterness over her daughter and granddaughter leaving. Helena now only thought about the living: herself, Maarja. She thought about returning home to the safety of Sweden.

After the funeral Helena and Erna and Maarja left with Matti and Maret and their two sons, Hanno and Lennart, now teenagers. They all returned to Matti's and had lunch; the three women then took the tram back to the hotel.

Leaving the tram, they passed an enormous building of grey stone under construction. Helena asked a woman passer-by what it was and was told it was to be the new library. 'But it will never be finished now,' said the woman after a pause. 'The government is cutting back on everything.' She shrugged and walked on.

Across the street from the library was Kaarli kirik. Helena thought of Piret's mother's funeral there. She had been nearly fourteen at the time; Piret must have been ten. Piret's mother had died quite suddenly, Helena remembered vaguely. She recalled feeling nothing about Piret's mother; she remembered Piret's blank face.

Helena had always thought Piret rather stupid. Now she saw that Piret's secrecy, her muteness, her detachment probably disposed her well to being a Marxist academic. She could imagine Piret absorbed in books and papers, spending years of her life poring over some obscure ideological problem, never saying what she thought, never compromising herself.

Helena wondered where Piret was now; she thought about the note. For the first time since seeing her, Helena wondered whether Piret had suffered, whether Piret had grieved as a result of giving up her child.

They walked down the boulevard towards the Viru. Helena wanted to return to the hotel, but Maarja insisted on seeing the city. After some discussion, they decided to walk to the old town.

Maarja seemed fascinated by everything she saw. She read the street and shop signs out loud to her mother, so delighted was she to see that they were in Estonian. She was amazed that people on the street spoke Estonian. 'I can't believe it, Mother; it's incredible,' she kept repeating, a bit loudly.

'Shh,' Helena hissed at her. 'You forget people can understand you.'

They ate at a restaurant called Du Nord, which was so dark inside they could hardly see the tables. There was one dish available: a cutlet with potatoes and cucumber.

When the food arrived, Maarja made a face and said, 'Mother, these potatoes taste like chlorine.'

It was on their return to the hotel that the trouble began. They asked for their key, which was not at the desk. The clerk grunted indifferently and accused them of not having depositing it before going out. It was, he lectured them, the hotel's rule that the room key must be left at the front desk when leaving the hotel.

Helena argued with him for a few minutes, and then they all sat down in the lobby not knowing what to do. Finally Maarja said, 'Well, why don't we just go up? I mean you could have left it in the door, Mother.'

'I most certainly did not,' replied Helena.

Maarja knew this was true. Still, she prodded: 'Let's go up.'

Maarja followed her mother and grandmother down the dark hall from the lift. They passed the ladybird, who smirked at them. The key was in the door and the door was ajar. Helena pushed it open. Both she and Erna were quiet, obviously frightened. Helena told Maarja to stand outside.

The room seemed at first untouched. Then Helena saw the cigarette smouldering in the ashtray. She pushed open the bathroom door and switched on the light. The black plastic toilet seat was up; in the toilet bowl was urine. Helena went in, flushed the toilet and lowered the seat.

When she stepped outside, Erna was holding the ashtray. Helena took it from her, stubbed out the cigarette, emptied the ashtray and placed it in the bureau drawer. 'Come in, Maarja,' she called. 'It's nothing, darling, nothing at all. You were perfectly right; I must have left the key in the door.'

When Maarja came in Erna was lying down on the bed, her eyes closed. She looked on the verge of tears. Maarja said, 'What's wrong with Vanaema?'

'Oh, Maarja, let her rest. It's the funeral and everything.'

Maarja and Helena took off their shoes and drank some Swedish mineral water they had brought from the boat. Helena took out her map and read it with unusual absorption.

When Maarja proposed that they take a walk that afternoon to see where her grandparents had once lived, her mother snapped at her. Maarja stalked off to the bathroom in a huff.

185

When she returned, she could see that her mother had been crying.

The next day they were to check out of the hotel and be at the harbour by four o'clock. The boat left at six.

When they went downstairs with their bags, the same clerk looked at them as if he had never seen them before. No, he said, he did not have their passports. No, he did not remember them. Well, if they had checked in, they were supposed to leave their passports at the desk and it wasn't his problem if they hadn't done that.

Now Erna looked as if she would faint and Helena was completely ashen. But Maarja was outraged. 'What do you mean you don't have them? What is this? We were in this hotel. You can't steal our passports.'

The clerk glanced at her briefly as though he had heard these objections countless times before. Then he turned away.

Erna, Helena and Maarja stood at the counter, forming a huddle around their bags. 'But what now?' Helena almost wailed. Then she turned back to the desk. 'Please,' she called, 'can you give us our key back? We have to go back to our room until we can sort this out.'

He looked at her contemptuously. 'The hotel is full.'

The Swedish embassy was located in Moscow; the nearest Swedish consulate was in Leningrad. They picked up their bags and found the lobby telephone.

Helena was put through to someone in the Leningrad office who listened to her story and then told her that dual citizens had to abide by Soviet law. Soviets who had emigrated must arrange to terminate their Soviet citizenship if they did not want to be considered duals. If their passports had been confiscated, all the Swedish embassy could do was pass on a message to a relative. The consul could make inquiries as to what charges would be brought, but since they were not in custody he did not know what he could do.

186

Helena hung up. They sat down on the sofa in the waiting area. Maarja stared at her mother, waiting for her to decide where they would go, what they would do. Erna stared into the mid-distance, as though unconcerned, waiting, expecting something to happen.

'Mother, stop that!' Helena finally said. 'You look like you're waiting to be put on a train to Siberia.'

Erna shrugged.

'What do we do now, Mother?' Maarja asked.

'I don't know,' Helena said. 'I have to think.' Where could they go? Why was this happening? She knew a few people in Estonia, none of whom she wanted to call on. She did not want to cause trouble for Matti and Maret; Hanno and Lennart were in school; Hanno was waiting to be offered a place at university. Peeter's remaining family were only distantly related; she had never met them.

Then she had an idea: Sylvia, Maarja's godmother. She had no idea whether Sylvia was still at the same office, or even the same flat after so many years. Helena had sent Christmas cards with a photograph of Maarja over the years, but since Jaan's death she had let this lapse.

Sylvia's home phone number did not answer, but her office did. Helena said, 'Sylvia, it's Helena Reisman. Helena Veltman. Maarja's mother.' For a moment she thought they had been disconnected.

Then Sylvia said, too casually, 'Hello Helena. How nice to hear from you. Where are you?'

'I'm – I'm here, for a funeral.' Helena was so upset that she did not register Sylvia's strange tone of voice.

'And how is Maarja?' Sylvia asked with brisk indifference.

'Sylvia, oh Sylvia, I don't know how to begin. We're in trouble, some kind of – '

'I'm sorry Helena, but the line is rather bad, and I can't hear you. I'd love to see you, but I'm terribly busy at this time. Perhaps on your next trip over – '

'Sylvia, don't hang up! Please listen to me. They've confiscated our passports – '

'No Helena, you listen to me. I cannot help you. I cannot get involved in this.'

Helena was confused and distressed, but she immediately sensed the menace in Sylvia's words. She felt a headache form as she tried to incorporate this into all that had happened: Piret's appearance in Stockholm, the affair with Gustav, the note in the magazine, her grandmother's death. Her mind was a cloud of unexplained motives, the random mixed with the calculated, the innocent with the intentional; and now Sylvia was saying to her that she could not get involved in this. In what? 'Why not?'

'I cannot do anything about this now.'

'What do you mean?'

'It is simply nothing to do with me.' Sylvia hung up.

Helena sat down. Erna looked at her, but Helena refused to meet her eyes. Helena went to the hotel reception and stood for a moment. A woman came up and asked her what she wanted. Helena shook her head without replying and then began to cry. The woman hesitated and then said she was sorry, but all she could suggest was that they go to the police station and try to 'resolve their situation'.

They picked up their bags and went out to the street. They stopped while Helena counted her roubles, and then Erna and Maarja followed her towards the taxi rank. Helena had not yet decided where they would go. She simply knew she had to get out of that oppressive hotel, but she was not going to walk about with all their bags.

A Lada flashed its lights at her and she lifted her hand tentatively. When it pulled up, she saw that it was not a taxi but a plain, unmarked car. The Russian inside looked calmly at her and said, 'I suggest you go back to the hotel.'

'No thank you,' Helena retorted briskly and tried to wave down a taxi.

'Please do as I ask; you have nowhere else to go. There will be more boats. You may be able to change your tickets.'

Maarja, who did not speak Russian, glanced from her mother to her grandmother and back. Erna watched Helena in silence. Helena hesitated. The man spoke again, a little more kindly. He said, 'There will be a room waiting for you shortly. Please do not make me arrest you for soliciting.'

Helena stared at him. Then he got out of the Lada. Erna, Helena and Maarja stood rooted to the pavement. He raised his eyebrows and gestured towards the hotel. 'May I help you with your bags?'

26

Peeter received two messages that day. The first was a telex from the Swedish embassy in Moscow. They had been notified by the consulate in Leningrad that a party of three women – Helena Linda Reisman, née Veltman, Maarja Elisabet Reisman and Erna Veltman, née Schönberg – had had their passports confiscated by the Soviet authorities. No charges had yet been brought.

The three women were dual Swedish-Soviet citizens, and the embassy regretted that in this case there was little they could do but pass a message to the family, which was Peeter Reisman.

The other message was from Jaak Sepp, the man who had visited Peeter at his flat. He called, he said, to say goodbye as he was now returning home. He had, he told Peeter, in the course of his visit, attended some gatherings in the expatriate community in Stockholm. These he had enjoyed as they gave him an opportunity to pass messages of good will from relatives and friends in the homeland.

Yeah, I'll bet, thought Peeter.

The man went on: he had also attended a few meetings of the organization Estonian Scholarship Fraternity. This was a professional and student organization loosely based on pre-war Estonian university fraternities.

The man told Peter he had obtained some documents which would interest Peeter. He had a few hours before his boat if Peeter wanted to meet him.

'And what do these documents relate to?' Peeter asked wearily.

'I think it is better if you see that for yourself.'

Peeter lost his patience. His daughter was being held

somewhere in the Soviet Union and this ridiculous little man wanted to play spy games. If he had something he wanted to leak, Peeter wished he would simply do it and get on the goddamn boat. They had him where they wanted. *Let's just fucking do it.*

'Look, you just tell me what it is. Tell me what your fucking message is and I'll fucking do it. But don't play games with me.'

'I think you would be interested in knowing that a number of prominent members of the exile community have a history that your paper might find interesting.'

'What kind of history?'

'As I said, I think it is better if you – '

'What kind of fucking history?'

'From the war.'

'So fucking what?'

'Of wartime activities.'

Peeter sighed. The Russians loved bringing up the war. It wasn't the German priests' story, after all. That must have been to test how easy he would be. This was what they really had in mind.

'Of Nazi activities. And not just sympathizers. Active participants. You may find it is the public's right to be informed about such – '

'Oh, shut up.' Peeter sighed. So this was where it was all leading. Here he was, finally at the end of the story.

He spoke into the phone again and took some notes. Then he hung up. He threw down his pen. Oh, yes, he thought, of course, the timing is perfect: an international committee had recently been formed to discuss Russian war crimes against the Baltic; in addition, various Baltic and Jewish organizations in America had announced plans for a conference on Baltic Jewish culture. It was of course in Soviet interests to disrupt any such activities. The release of information about real or alleged or exaggerated Nazi activity among Balts was always carefully timed to distract the media or discredit anti-Soviet coverage. Peeter should have seen this coming all along.

He left the building for his meeting with the man. He would be given documents from KGB archives, implicating certain people in wartime fascist activities. There might be letters confirming these actions, written by survivors who could not be traced; or perhaps by prisoners of war, now pensioners in the USSR. Perhaps some of the documents would be genuine; Peeter did not know or care. All he knew was that he was about to do something he had thought he would never do, which was deliberately publish anti-Estonian disinformation provided by the KGB.

Later that afternoon he would walk into his editor's office. He would have to make it sound convincing. And he would have to make sure it was in *Morgon Bladet* in the next forty-eight hours. He would do his best. He wanted Maarja out of wherever they were holding her as soon as possible.

As Peeter walked into his editor's office, Piret was walking up the steps to the office of the KGB on Bagari Street. She had received a letter a few days before which told her to report.

Piret was not surprised. She was unemployed, which was a crime. It did not matter that she kept busy, had a place to live, was not a burden. She had to have a job. They would find her one; if she did not want it, she could be threatened with prison.

As she walked up the steps, a man leaving the building caught her eye. She watched him for a moment. Yes, she thought: Paavo. Still tall and angular, he had gained weight. She wondered what he knew, if anything, about what had happened.

She watched him a moment. He stopped. She looked directly at him. He said involuntarily, as though to himself 'Piret.'

'Hello, Paavo.'

The look of shock faded; he seemed to gather himself. He nodded and made to move away.

'Paavo – .' She put her hand out.

'Get away from me.' He suddenly became indignant. 'I have no idea who you are.'

She watched him walk away. Then she understood she had been meant to see him and he had been meant to see her. They were both to know that they were controlled. And that nothing in their lives was exempt.

How did they know it was Paavo? Sylvia was somehow involved, Piret was certain, but Piret had not told Sylvia who Maarja's father was. If she knew, it must have been Jaan who had told her; Lydia would not have. But how did Jaan know? Piret searched her memory, but came up with no sure answers: Lydia knew of Paavo, of course, but now Piret could not be certain who else did.

At any rate, once they had identified Paavo, they would have then contacted him to obtain more information. Paavo had been told the result of her actions, heard of her downfall. He had a child now, she knew, a job. Of course he would tell them anything. He had too much to lose.

She thought of Paavo's closed eyes above her face, of feeling that her life was formed, completed; he was leaving her behind. And now again she watched as Paavo walked away from her.

She entered the building and told the receptionist of her appointment. She was sent up to an office where a few people stood awkwardly, avoiding one another's eyes. Two women, one young and one old, sat behind a counter, shuffling paper. Eventually a woman came out and looked at Piret. Piret followed the woman to the office. She saw, behind the desk, her Russian interrogator. Piret sat down and the door behind her closed.

The woman said, 'Well, Miss Anvelt, I understand you have returned to your aunt's place.'

'Yes.'

'Have you thought about what has happened? The loss of everything you worked for?'

Piret was silent. She knew the woman did not expect an answer.

The woman picked up a piece of paper. She glanced at it and put it down again. 'You have demonstrated your parasitism.

You are now unemployed. What do you plan to do?'

'I am not sure what I can do.'

'You know of course that your aunt's lease on state property – ' The woman looked at another sheet of paper. ' – is subject to short-hold regulations?'

Piret did not answer. She knew they could do anything they wanted. They could evict Lydia, put Piret herself in a labour camp or in prison. She thought it unlikely; she suspected that the woman wanted something else. She should have known that they would not leave her alone. This was the preamble, the build up; intimidation was usually mere groundwork. Piret knew how the KGB worked.

First they set the scene; then they offered the deal. This made the deal seem easy, after explaining what they could and would do. They wanted you to feel grateful. They wanted you to thank them for not doing what they had the power to do.

'You have a chance to repair some of the damage you have done to yourself and to your socialist motherland by your actions.'

Piret was silent. She waited.

The woman waited too, for just a moment. Then she said, 'I have a transcript of our last discussion.' The woman opened a file and laid it on the table. On top was a typewritten sheet which she removed and handed to Piret. Underneath were three Swedish passports.

Piret saw the passports; she glanced at the typewritten sheet and saw at once that the transcription of the conversation had been reconstructed to appear as a confession. She had suspected she would be asked to sign something. She did not care now. Her life was over.

'You may read it.' The woman laid a pen between them.

Piret shrugged and read it. It was not until the second page that she understood what was going to happen. It was the section on Rozhansky that she stopped at and began to read intently.

In front of her she felt the woman notice the change; the woman picked up one of the passports and flipped through it.

Piret read. The confession stated that Rozhansky had attempted to corrupt her. He had attempted to seduce her. He had encouraged her to believe in counter-revolutionary Western bourgeois ideology.

He had introduced her to a secret plan to overthrow socialism under the guise of an academic ruse called 'the elaboration of a contemporary model of socialism', which was a fraudulent term disguising a plan created by nationalists and intellectuals to implant capitalist spies into the Ministry for Central Planning, Gosplan. Their aim was to spread ideological pluralism and split the monolithic unity of the party.

A copy of a memo detailing the plan had been discovered in Piret's office. She had been seen passing messages from Rozhansky to expatriate nationalist contacts in Stockholm.

Piret looked up at the woman. They had found perhaps the one thing that she would resist doing for them. They knew that for Rozhansky she would probably go to prison rather than hurt him.

Then the woman opened one of the passports with studied carelessness. It was Maarja's. Piret understood quite clearly: her journey had now come to an end. She had been tested in Stockholm and she had passed: she had shown them that she would not hurt Maarja.

Her instructions at the exhibition in Stockholm had not been a message or signal involving some plan. She had not been used because she was there and convenient. There was no plan. The meeting between herself and Helena had been created to test her willingness to sacrifice herself for her daughter.

It was Rozhansky they were after. She was his closest colleague; she was the one they needed to bring him down; she was his only vulnerable point. Nobody else had anything on Boris. And they needed evidence. These were not the days of Stalin, after all; these were not the days of a pure, arbitrary, lawless despot. There were courts, committees, bureaucrats; these people wanted complete files; judges wanted evidence; these days everybody covered themselves with the pretence of legality.

If they had simply demanded that she betray Rozhansky by signing a concocted confession, she would have refused. Even if threatened with the loss of her job or the loss of Lydia's home, she might still have refused. She was an unknown quantity. She was secretive and prudent, as difficult as Boris to penetrate. Boris himself had taught her. They had to find a way to ensure she would not refuse.

And they had. They had found the one thing in her life for which she would throw everything away. She would never risk any harm to Maarja. She would never be responsible for taking Maarja away from her home or her mother.

Piret looked up and saw the Russian before her, flipping through Maarja's passport. She understood that this story, this undertaking, had taken time and planning. It had been going on for some time, perhaps years. When did it first start? When she was a student? When she first met Boris? When the 'contemporary socialist model' was in academic fashion? Or simply when she had been invited to Stockholm?

Piret knew she might never know. Not that it mattered. They had her, and Boris, where they wanted. And now, of course, they had Maarja, somewhere in the country. Probably frightened; perhaps separated from Helena, held somewhere under duress. An eleven-year-old girl. Piret's daughter. Piret reached for the paper and picked up the pen.

PART 3

May 1992

27

Maarja knew from the moment she met Anton that she could never love him. She would be grateful to him, even like and enjoy him. But he would never arouse in her the kind of desire she knew she wanted to feel.

Anton was large and stocky. His hair was cut too short, his face was too broad. He wore small round glasses like Trotsky's. His clothes were all wrong; his jeans were too new, their indigo fresh from the factory; they were rigid instead of faded, loose instead of tight. She knew she could never fall in love with someone whose buttocks protruded like two ripe plums.

They met at a party at Kristina's flat. Maarja had not seen Kristina since graduating from high school. Kristina had gone on to study at Handelshögskolan, the Stockholm School of Economics; Maarja went to the University of Stockholm.

Maarja saw Kristina one day at NK, at the cosmetics counter, where she worked on Saturdays. Maarja saw her walk through NK's broad doors. It was still cool in Stockholm and Kristina wore brown leather trousers, a long tweed man's jacket and a white silk shirt as long as the jacket, double breasted with a large collar. She smoothed her slightly blown hair, which was still pure Nordic blonde and then looked up, right into Maarja's eyes. They could not avoid one another.

Maarja recalled that night at Kristina's, the two adolescent boys flanking her friend, gazing at her unbuttoned blouse. She remembered talking to her grandmother on the telephone, calling the taxi, waiting outside alone, hating the three of them.

When she returned from Estonia, Maarja had desperately wanted to recount to Kristina how she had been stranded in the USSR without a passport. Her mother had warned her not to tell anybody; Maarja decided this meant anybody except her best friend. In any case Kristina was uninterested, and Maarja hung up the phone deciding not to call her again; she fervently wished Kristina would get pregnant and ruin her life, burn out early, look old and worn before she was twenty-five.

Now Maarja tried to smile. Kristina, it was obvious, had not burned out in the slightest. She approached the counter, completely at ease. Her skin and make-up were perfect; her nails were slender and long and polished very pale rose. She was carrying an expensive leather bag, which she casually mentioned she had bought in London the week before at a shop called Mulberry's.

'Off Bond Street,' she explained. 'All the Swedes shop at Burberry's on Regent Street, so I avoid it like the plague.'

Maarja smiled knowingly, as though she too strenuously avoided the Swedish tourists in London.

'Come round on Wednesday night if you're not doing anything. It's just some people from the school.' Kristina gave Maarja her address, which Maarja recognized immediately as a street in Östermalm, the best part of Stockholm. Kristina could never afford a flat in such a neighbourhood without her parents' help, and Maarja felt a sliver of envy pierce her heart, as sharp as shrapnel.

Kristina removed a chequebook and a thin gold pen from the Mulberry bag and added, 'About nine or ten.'

Maarja forced herself to emulate Kristina's nonchalance. 'Sure, why not?'

Kristina smiled and pointed at the Lancôme display. 'I might as well take a lipstick while I'm here.' She held out her perfectly manicured fingers in front of Maarja's face. 'Do you have anything to match this?'

Maarja dressed in tight jeans and an emerald green silk shirt. She put her hair up in a twist. It made her, she felt, look distinctive, difficult to categorize. She knew Kristina would be recognized as Swedish anywhere in the world. Maarja looked in the mirror and told herself she could be Italian, German, French.

She took a bus to Östermalm. On the bus shelter was an advertisement showing a sensual black model wearing silk underwear. She was pleased to see that the models this year were dark and exotic, not the traditional Swedish blondes. The advertisement said in English: 'What the au pair will be wearing this summer.'

Maarja did not want to be an au pair, but she did not yet know what she wanted to be. She was not worried; she felt her life was perfect. She had a student flat, which she loved even if it was not in Östermalm: a studio with a bathroom, a kitchen the size of a closet and a tiny balcony. She had painted the walls of the studio sky blue and the woodwork pale salmon. She had bought wooden bookshelves from Ikea and two posters: a Matisse nude and Monet's water lilies. Her flat made her feel European, Bohemian, young and free.

She had got the job at NK because of her English and German. She arrived every Saturday and made herself up with the samples. The other girls loved working at the cosmetics counter because they got free make-up. She liked it because her counter was at the entrance to the store and she could meet as many people as possible. She imagined that people must walk by, look at her and think: *Why is that intelligent-looking girl working at a cosmetics counter?* She wanted to explain to passers-by that she was only doing it for the money.

She rode her bicycle everywhere, from her studio on Valhallavägen to the university, and into town to her job. Stockholm came alive in the spring. The water glittered; the sunlight was warm and yellow and only began to fade close to midnight.

She was in her first year of studying history. She had written her high school *specialarbete* on the history of Estonia up to its incorporation into the USSR. She loved the early stories of her country and knew by heart the first words describing Tallinn, written by an Arabian geographer in 1154: 'A town in Astlanda is Koluvan. It is small and resembles a stronghold.'

The moment she read about the Finno-Ugarian tribes that came across the steppe 2,500 years before Christ, splitting into groups who would become Hungarians, Finns, Estonians, Lapps, she knew she had found her topic. She understood that she had always wanted to know where she came from. She wrote about the German and Danish conquests, the Reformation and the Swedish era in 1629, the conquest by Russia in 1710, the rise of nationalism in the nineteenth century. Her teacher gave her top marks.

Maarja's mother had wanted her to study something practical. This had made her even more determined to follow her interest in history. She was tired of her mother's caution, her frugal life, her concern over her pension.

Towards the end of Maarja's final year at school the collapse of the USSR seemed inevitable. Then came the attempted *coup* against Gorbachev. Maarja went to Helena's flat to watch Boris Yeltsin and the Russian Parliament under siege. They saw Russian tanks driving on the streets of Tallinn towards the television tower; then finally they watched a relieved and exhausted Gorbachev disembark from his plane after days in detention and the Russian tanks leaving Estonia.

Their country was again a free republic and in the headlines of newspapers all over the world: 'Baltic Republics Declare Independence'. A month later, as Maarja started her first classes at the University of Stockholm, the Republic of Estonia became a member of the United Nations.

Her life, like that of her country, lay before her, full of interesting possibilities. Her mother was now married to a man named Karl, who was solid, reliable and sweet, but who Maarja felt was rather dull. It was because of Karl that her mother agreed to let her move into her small studio. Well, if her mother was happy, fine. But she wanted more. And she would get it, she knew.

Maarja was buzzed into Kristina's building and took the lift up. Her knock pushed open the door of the flat. She stepped in. In the middle of the tiny foyer was an immaculate oriental rug. It looked as if nobody had wiped winter boots on it in its life.

Maarja hung her coat alongside the others on an English bentwood coat rack. Maarja's studio did not have a foyer. Inside her front door was precisely what every other Estonian had: a clear plastic mat, over which was a brown jute door mat. To the wall Maarja had attached a white metal rail punctuated with plastic knobs.

Kristina's flat was perfect. The kitchen was a square of new, lacquered cabinets; on the shelf above the round white sink was a basket of lemons. In the sitting room vases of fresh flowers sat on small round tables, which were covered with the same blue and yellow fabric as the curtains and the small pillows Kristina had tossed carefully into the corners of the sofa.

The room was crowded; Maarja saw immediately that she knew nobody except Kristina. At least three or four tall blond boys stood in a circle around Kristina, holding their glasses and trying to keep her attention. Kristina waved at her and whispered something to a boy next to her. With obvious reluctance he fetched Maarja a drink and then returned to his place next to Kristina.

When dark, solitary Anton struck up a conversation, Maarja summed up his fresh face, new blue jeans and Trotsky glasses and thought: *Some things never change.*

Maarja smiled at him guardedly and responded to his questions in short, accurate sentences.

After a moment he said, 'I thought at first you were not Swedish.'

This pleased her. She said, 'I'm not; I'm Estonian.'

'Ah,' he nodded. She waited for his comments on the break up of the USSR; everybody had an opinion about it, whether Sweden should have recognized the Baltic countries sooner, whether the United States would be forthcoming with aid, whether a military dictatorship in Russia was inevitable.

A Swedish boy standing nearby said, 'I expect the honeymoon will be over soon, once the nationalists take over.'

Maarja was furious. She had seen the pictures of the Estonian Parliament, barricaded by granite blocks and surrounded by unarmed civilians, huddled around fires, ready to stand before Russian tanks. The last winter had been one of the most severe in years. What did this provocative Swedish boy know about people who were willing to defend their country with their lives?

Maarja was about to object when Anton said mildly, 'Nationalism is often the only way to survive under occupation.'

'And an excuse to exterminate everybody you don't like. Like the Balts did in the war.'

'You must be thinking of Lithuania,' Anton replied calmly. 'There were no mass exterminations in Estonia.'

'It's early days yet. What will happen to all those Russians living in Estonia? Has anybody thought about them?'

'I don't know what will happen. But I do know that Estonians have never had pogroms.'

The Swedish boy looked away and Anton turned back to Maarja. She had watched this exchange in silence, impressed. She looked at Anton gratefully, as though he had saved her from a thug. Then, to her astonishment, he said in Estonian, 'I too am Estonian.'

Maarja thought: *How odd. All these years I was ashamed to speak it. I was ashamed of being foreign.* Now she replied, not caring who overheard, proud to speak Estonian.

Anton was impressed by her decision to study history; most girls, he said, would not choose something so 'unuseful'. He said this ironically, as though the only subjects worthwhile were those without any practical application.

Maarja looked at him and knew he understood her and liked her; but she felt only disappointment. She had seen Kristina glance approvingly at them, clearly thinking it appropriate that Maarja should attract the least interesting and oddest man at her party.

Anton ran a publishing press, he told her: he published one of the small expatriate Estonian newspapers and books and political tracts. Did she want to come and see his office? He told her the address.

Maarja saw Kristina glance again at them, and out of spite and pride agreed to meet him for lunch the following day.

His office was a room behind a recently opened travel agency specializing in Baltic travel. She walked in and saw racks of brochures and an obviously Estonian girl behind a desk. Maarja greeted her in Estonian, and the girl directed her down a short hall to a back room.

There Anton sat, behind a desk heaped with papers, a computer and a printer. Books were everywhere: on shelves, on the floor, on the window-sill.

Anton showed her one of the tracts. It was called *The Truth about Soviet Health Care*.

She glanced at it reluctantly. She had seen this kind of expatriate propaganda many times and it depressed her. It was so obvious; it was exactly like Soviet propaganda. How tired she was of hearing about the oppression of the Baltics, the evils of communism. She handed it back to him without comment.

'I'm obsolete,' he told her gleefully. 'I've got to move on to more important matters: rebuilding our country.'

Our country. Yes, she thought, it is our country. She had always thought of herself as an ethnic oddity, another refugee, protesting, ignored, intractable. But now she belonged to an independent country. Her country.

He went on, 'We will once again be part of Europe.'

'Yes, I suppose so,' Maarja said reflectively. Anton was smiling at her. And, despite his innocence, his fanaticism, his enthusiasm, she found that she liked him.

28

It was Anton who made Maarja begin to think about going to Estonia to see the farm. She and Anton had seen each other three or four times by then: for lunches, drinks at Café Opera and once at Jazzpub in Gamla Stan.

She never gave him any sign that she would like him to be more than a friend. The few times that Anton moved too close, or his tone became overly familiar, Maarja gave him a surprised, alarmed look and he retreated. Maarja had the feeling that he was biding his time, waiting for her to get used to him, for her feelings to develop. She did not have the heart to tell him that they never would.

But she liked going out with him. He was completely unaffected; he was like no Swedish boy she had known. His enthusiasms were spontaneous and he had an innocent confidence that she had never seen before. Most of the boys she had met before Anton were conscious of their appearance, anxious to impress. Anton cared little about what he looked like; his only affectation were his Trotsky glasses, which slid down his nose and which he pushed up from time to time.

His greatest asset was his insatiable interest in Maarja. He seemed to want to know everything about her studies, her plans, her family. He was overcome with excitement to discover that she had been born in Estonia.

'But that's so unusual,' he enthused. 'You're a real Estonian. You could apply for a passport.'

'A passport?' The idea appealed to her; she had understood that she was once Soviet, but it had never occurred to her that she might now be an Estonian citizen.

'You could vote,' Anton went on.

'If I'm old enough,' Maarja said. She had no idea what the

names of the political parties even were in Estonia, much less what issues Estonians would be voting on.

Anton's questions made Maarja realize how little she knew of her family or background in Estonia. She told Anton what she knew: that her mother's father had grown up on a farm, which had been collectivized under Stalin. 'I don't know much about it. I remember my grandfather used to talk about it a lot. He drove my mother crazy talking about that farm.'

'Where is it?' Anton asked.

'I don't know. All I know is that my grandfather's mother was shot on it; she was a patriot. She killed Russians, I think. Well, at least, she helped the partisans, the Forest Brothers.'

Anton was clearly riveted by this information, and Maarja tried to recall everything else she knew about her family and the farm. 'I believe my mother spent weekends there when she was a child.'

'That's impossible,' Anton pointed out. 'If it was collectivized under Stalin, your mother was not yet even born.'

Maarja shrugged. 'Oh well, maybe it was somewhere else in the country she went to. Some other farm.' She stopped to think. 'We have some cousins; I met them when I was eleven. Remember? I told you, when we went to Estonia for my great-grandmother's funeral. They live in Tallinn, though, not in the country.'

'Where did you stay when you were there?'

'The Viru Hotel. I'll never forget it.' Maarja briefly recounted the story of the missing room key and confiscated passports.

Anton was beside himself with excitement. 'You mean the KGB held you? They took your passports?'

Maarja was startled by this reaction. 'Well, it wasn't really like that. We just sat in a hotel room for three days. I mean, we weren't interrogated or anything. Nobody spoke to us.'

'But why? Were you traded for somebody?'

'No, no, I don't know.' Maarja was slightly annoyed that she could explain so little of the incident. Her mother had not wanted to discuss it, and after some weeks Maarja had ceased to bring it up. Anton's fascination exasperated her further. It was so trivial and he wanted her to make it into an international incident. 'I don't know why. Nothing happened.'

'I've got something to show you,' Anton said one day. He handed Maarja a notice published by the Estonian government explaining the procedures for reclaiming land confiscated under the communist regime.

Maarja looked up. 'What does this mean?'

'Don't you see? You can claim your farm back.'

Maarja looked at the paper doubtfully. 'I can?'

'Well, your family anyway. Your mother or your grandmother.'

Maarja shook her head and handed the notice back to him. 'My mother has a fit whenever anybody talks about that farm. She hates it. She hates talking about Estonia. She says she'll never go back even if it is free. It was that last trip, when they kept us there. She's never got over it.'

Anton paused, pressed the paper into her hand, and said, 'Non-residents aren't subject to a filing deadline. You have all the time in the world to change her mind.'

Maarja finished her exams; she would now spend the summer working full time at NK. She contemplated this in despair; she did not have the money to travel, and anyway would not be able to continue her studies if she did not work the entire summer. She would end up like her mother, she thought angrily: hard-working, self-denying. She would never have the money to go inter-railing around France and Italy and Greece, or touring America.

Her mother had stifled her, Maarja saw that now. Her mother had created a life in which Maarja was doomed to be unhappy. She was not allowed to become Swedish; and she was cut off from her Estonian background. Her mother did not want to talk about their life in Estonia, or the farm, or the incident in the hotel. Maarja had been condemned to a life of isolation.

Her mother would probably have been very happy to know that she now had a friend like Anton. Another expatriate was the kind of man her mother would want her to marry. They would continue to live like outsiders and raise their children to be as confused and separate and odd as they themselves were. But Maarja was not going to let that happen. She took out Anton's newspaper notice from her desk. Now that she had the opportunity to discover who she was, she was not going to let her mother stop her.

A few days later she sat at Helena's kitchen table. She had decided first to persuade her mother to visit Estonia again. She did not want to mention the farm too quickly. 'But Mother, it's different now,' she said for the second or third time. 'We can come and go whenever we want.'

Helena did not turn around. She was chopping vegetables for soup. 'Speak for yourself.' Hearing Maarja talk about Estonia made Helena's stomach churn. She had sworn never to go to Estonia again.

'It was your home, Mother. How can you say you never want to go there again?' Maarja watched her mother's back, looking for a sign that she might soften. 'It was your country and Vanaema's country. What about your heritage? What about the land the communists took?'

'I don't want to hear about that farm.'

'But it's yours. It was Vanaisa's. We could go there and look at it. Maybe we could get it back. We could even live there if we wanted to.'

'Live on a farm,' Helena said acidly. 'You think we are going to go to Estonia to live on a farm?'

'All right then, but we could turn it into a summer cottage or something.' Maarja automatically looked to Karl for support. Helena and Karl had been married for nearly two years. He was the Swedish product of Estonian parents; his Estonian was poor. Of all the cases, Helena and Maarja liked to joke, Karl had nearly mastered the nominative.

He did, however, understand Estonian. And so Helena and Maarja spoke Estonian and Karl spoke Swedish. He usually took Maarja's side in disagreements. While this exasperated Helena, it also pleased her.

Karl sat across the kitchen table from Maarja. He had listened

209

to the conversation in silence, drinking his coffee. He said, 'Perhaps we should wait until things calm down a bit.'

Maarja did not know how old Karl was; she thought he must be about forty. He was not her idea of an attractive man; he was short, slightly overweight and balding on the back of his head. But she liked him and she knew he made her mother happy. When Helena was overwrought, Karl could calm her simply by touching her hand. Maarja had never seen him lose his temper. She could torment him or tease him; when she was rude or disagreeable, he would smile and tell her she was far too clever and beautiful to say such terrible things. This usually shamed her into an apologetic silence.

Maarja said, 'Oh, Karl, don't be such a wimp. Let's go. It's our farm. Why shouldn't we have it?'

'Maarja, stop it,' Helena finally turned around, exasperated. 'Don't you see? It's probably worthless. The whole country is bankrupt; the communists ruined everything. Who knows whether the house is even standing?'

'Well, we can go and look.'

'No.'

'I will.'

'Fine. All right, fine. You go ahead and do that.'

'Well, I don't have any money.'

'Don't look at me.'

Maarja glanced at Karl, who did not meet her eyes.

'Come on, Mother, what's the harm in going over and looking at it?'

'Go and look if you want. Do you really think they are going to hand all that land back? Do you know how many farms were collectivized? Thousands. *Thousands.* What will they do with the people living on those farms? Don't you see? It's not that simple.'

Helena turned her back on her daughter and returned to her chopping: the subject, as far as she was concerned, was closed. She remembered all too well the three days they had been stranded in the Viru Hotel; it came back to her frequently and with excruciating clarity.

She, Erna and Maarja had returned to the hotel with their bags and been handed a key the moment they approached the desk. They took the lift up, put their bags on the floor and sat down to wait. They did not know how long the wait would be or what they were waiting for.

After an hour or so, somebody knocked and a porter appeared with a tray of food. They ate the food and afterwards put the tray outside their door. After it got dark, Helena decided they had better unpack their night things.

The following morning they woke and again they were brought food. Helena knew not to leave the hotel; in fact they did not want to. Erna sat on one of the hard brown chairs and watched the telephone; Maarja took a shower, lay on one of the beds and read. Helena sat by the window, looking down on the trams and cars and buses.

They waited all day and again all evening. Again they slept. When the telephone did ring the following morning, they all jumped. Helena picked it up.

A woman's voice said, 'This is the Intourist office. Please pick up your tickets for the ferry to Stockholm at the terminal building in the harbour.' Helena listened for a few more seconds, but the woman had hung up.

They took their bags downstairs and checked out of the hotel. The clerk, the same clerk, handed them their passports with no show of irony, or even of recognition.

Helena walked out of the hotel with her mother and daughter behind her. Her hands were shaking. A taxi pulled up. Helena bent over and said, 'Can you take us to the harbour?'

He grunted, not moving from behind his steering wheel. They lifted their bags into the boot themselves. As soon as they were in the car, he drove off.

They sat through the journey in silence. When they had arrived and unloaded the car, the man looked at Helena's money and then grunted again, put the car into gear and drove off.

They walked carefully up the gangway into the terminal. They checked in and boarded. They went directly to their cabin.

They sat on their bunks and stared at one another. Finally, Maarja said, 'Mum, can we go to the restaurant?'

Helena looked at her daughter. Then she sighed and her face, which had been hard with tension the past forty-eight hours, felt as though it would collapse. She closed her eyes and could feel what must have been thousands of tiny lines ease and her face return to normal. She had never felt so exhausted in her life.

She tried to understand that their life was now again what it had been. The nightmare was over. She felt as though they had lived through arrest, torture, escape. She could not believe that they could walk into a restaurant and sit down and eat with dozens of other people, as if nothing had happened. She could not believe that she would ever walk the streets again without the KGB following her in a dirty Russian car, or telling her when she could return to her own home, or showing her in their small, cruel ways that she lived with her daughter only because they allowed it, and for the moment it suited their purposes.

She opened her eyes. Her daughter was hungry. Her eleven-year-old Swedish daughter, who knew nothing of fear, wanted to eat. She said, 'Yes, let's go to the restaurant.'

They took a taxi home from the harbour. Helena thought she would weep at the sight of peaceful, busy, heedless Stockholm. She and Maarja dropped Erna off at the flat in Odenplan and then continued on to their own flat. The telephone was ringing when Helena unlocked the door. She ran to pick it up. It was Peeter. 'You are all all right?' He sounded relieved.

'Yes.'

'And Maarja?'

'Yes. Peeter, what is going on?'

'I got a message that your passports had been confiscated. That you had been arrested.'

'I wouldn't call it arrested. We were confined to our hotel.'

'They didn't do anything to you?'

'No, no. Peeter, I am tired. Please just tell me what is going on so that I can sit down and put my feet up.'

'I have no idea. I told you, I got this message.'

'Don't tell me you know nothing about this. It's something to do with – ' Helena lowered her voice, 'with Piret, isn't it? What is it, Peeter? What happened?'

'I don't know what happened. Do yourself a favour, Helena, just forget about it.'

They unpacked and Helena made lunch. Maarja watched television while Helena washed the dishes. Later that night, as they prepared for bed, Maarja came into her mother's bedroom, and said, 'Mum, we were in big trouble, weren't we?'

Helena was removing her make-up. 'Yes, for a bit. Well, I think so, anyway.'

'But why? Why did they keep us there?'

'Because, darling, they are Russians. Because they are communists. They can do anything they want to us. We are Soviets; we will never be free.'

The next morning Helena went to the corner kiosk to buy some milk and a newspaper. It was then, seeing the front-page story in *Morgon Bladet*, that she understood. She read the headline, 'Nazi Collaborators Hiding in Sweden', and the by-line: Peeter Reisman.

Helena skimmed the article. Information obtained by *Morgon Bladet* implicated several exiled Balts, Estonian and Latvian, in war crimes, and included considerable evidence of the torture and murder of Jewish Baltic citizens. At least ten people living in Sweden between the ages of sixty and seventy were involved; evidence indicated that many more had entered the country after the war under false pretences. Several had held official positions under the German occupation, including in the police force.

Helena understood now that she, Maarja and Erna had been kept to blackmail Peeter; he had done what they asked; he had done it for Maarja, and perhaps also for her.

Helena returned to the flat and sat down on the sofa. She wanted to weep for Peeter. She knew that he loved Maarja; now he had ruined his life to save her. He so loved his little girl, and she had never really given him credit for that. She was suddenly very, very sorry. She held the paper, looked at his name at the top of the article and thought: *Poor, poor Peeter. His career is over. He will never live this down.*

Helena met Karl two years later, when Maarja was fourteen and she herself thirty-five.

She had not wanted a lover, nor to marry again. What was the point? She felt too old to have children. She had a teenage daughter who would probably hate her mother getting married. And she had made a disaster of her love life up to now; how could she trust herself to make another choice?

Her life was more or less a series of disappointments, a failed marriage and mediocre career partially redeemed by her devotion to her mother and her child. She had never had a chance to have another child, her own child. After she and Peeter emigrated, she had not wanted him and sex between them had virtually ceased. She had absorbed herself completely in Maarja; she had transferred her love and passion to the baby and neglected Peeter, his hopes and problems, his worries about his work. She had nagged him and had never listened.

Then came all those years of living alone, of helping her parents and thinking only of her daughter. Men had asked her out, but she always found a way to put them off. She told them she was busy or that she could not leave Maarja. She knew that these were excuses; she knew that she was frightened of men, of sex, of trying to suit her life to another man, who might not love her little daughter. Helena pictured herself in bed with a man and Maarja toddling into her bedroom, her look of shock and surprise and her own shame and embarrassment.

Karl won Helena by attrition. He would simply appear at her office to take her out to lunch; she found it difficult to refuse such an overt request. He would drop by her flat with the Sunday papers, a stack of magazines for Maarja and a bag of fresh, soft cinnamon buns.

He came by the flat one day, explaining he had three tickets for *Carmen*, and Maarja screeched at Helena when she tried to

214

refuse; Maarja had never been to the opera house before; she had always wanted to see *Carmen*. She jumped up and down and waved her arms. Karl stood at the door, smiling, and Helena sighed and said, 'Oh, all right.'

Afterwards he took them to Café Opera and told Maarja to order anything she wanted. When Helena tried to object, Karl looked at her and smiled indulgently, and Helena resumed examining her menu.

He took them to the country in his old Saab and let Maarja drive, despite her mother's protests. He borrowed a friend's boat, took them sailing and let Maarja take the tiller. It was two months before he even tried to kiss Helena.

The first time they slept together, Maarja was at a girlfriend's overnight. Helena woke at six and roused Karl. 'You have to go now.'

He sat up in alarm. 'What? Why? What's happened?'

'You have to go. Now. Before Maarja comes back. Come on, get up.' She pulled at him.

Karl fell back on to the bed, pulling Helena with him. He laughed. 'Helena, it's six o'clock on a Saturday morning. Do you know any teenager who is going to get up at six to come home to catch her mother in bed with a man?'

Soon after, Karl asked Helena if she would consider having another baby. Helena had never told him that Maarja was not her biological child. She hesitated and then said, careful not to lie, 'No more children. It is too late; I am too old.'

When he asked her to marry him, she again told him she would not have more children. 'Do not marry me if you want a baby.'

'You are only thirty-six,' he pointed out.

'Thirty-seven.' She did not want to tell him that Maarja was not hers; she did not want to tell him her real fear: she was frightened of trying and failing. She was frightened of wanting a baby and then having to reconcile herself to her age, her infertility, her wasted years.

She had raised a child, yet had not ever had a baby. She loved Maarja as her own, but she envied the women who had pushed an infant out of their bodies, bloody and screaming. She had never created a new life and she felt her body was an aged child's, sterile and empty and innocent of what all mature women should know.

As her wedding to Karl approached, she found herself clinging to Maarja in what she knew was an unhealthy way. She did not want her to go out with her friends; she interrogated her at the end of every day.

She wanted to give Maarja the freedom to grow up, but inside, Helena knew she wanted to hold her close for ever. She felt the ache of every lost day. She thought nostalgically of Maarja's first words and even remembered her tantrums with painful tenderness; she felt the terrible knowledge that her child would one day be grown and gone and she would never again know the certainty and joy of having Maarja near.

She had agreed to marry Karl even though she imagined them growing old together, two lonely people. Maarja would be gone and Helena would continue working towards a day when she lived like her mother: shopping, cooking, collecting her pension, waiting for her child to visit. She would be an empty shell of a woman, having done nothing of any value.

Maarja registered her mother's moodiness without sympathy. She chafed under Helena's questions, her reminiscences, her occasional tearful goodbyes. Maarja grew increasingly irritable.

Finally one day she called Karl. She had never called him before and he was clearly delighted. She said, 'Karl, could you come over and talk some sense into my mother?'

Karl laughed. 'What do you mean?'

'I think you should speed up the wedding,' Maarja said. The last thing she wanted was her mother breaking up with Karl; Maarja knew that Karl was critical to the loosening of her mother's anxious hold. Without him, Helena might never let her do anything or go anywhere. 'You'd better come over today. She's getting cold feet and she's taking it out on me.'

29

Maarja knew she would never get any money out of her mother and so decided to call her father.

Peeter answered the telephone, 'Nilsson.'

'Hi, it's me.'

Peeter Reisman was now Peter Nilsson, forty-five years old and a TV2 anchorman. He covered domestic issues: government, the economy, crime. Every night Maarja's father read the news out on national television. If her friends asked her if she watched her father on television, she always replied, 'Why should I? I've seen him my whole life.'

Peeter had transformed himself into a Swede after becoming *persona non grata* in the Estonian community, among whom his story was still discussed. Some thought he had knowingly printed the article about Baltic Nazis; some thought he had been an unwitting pawn.

Other Swedish papers had picked up the story shortly after its appearance. One paper learned from *Morgon Bladet* that one of its sources of information was a periodical called *People's Watch*; it was pointed out that this was a Soviet publication, edited by the head of Estonian counter-intelligence under a pseudonym. Another discovered that several people named in Peeter's article had been dead for several years. A week later another paper reported that two of the named suspects had sued *Morgon Bladet* for slander.

Peeter left *Morgon Bladet* shortly afterwards. He worked for a tabloid for a year and then left to write freelance features for various magazines under his new name. By the time he joined TV2 he had managed to cast off the gossip. Journalists, Peeter discovered gratefully, had short memories. Some of his colleagues at TV2 did not even know he was not Swedish.

'Hello, darling,' Peeter said neutrally, waiting to find out what Maarja wanted. She tended to call him when she needed money. 'What's up?'

'Nothing, Dad, do you always suspect me of having a reason to call you? I just wanted to know how you are. How's Paolo?' Paolo was Peeter's two-year-old son by his Italian wife, Lucia.

'Fine. A terrorist. It's his job to be a terrorist.'

'Dad, I want some money.'

'I thought as much. Why?'

'I want to go to Estonia. I want to go to the farm. I found out that you can claim the property the communists took. Mummy doesn't want anything to do with it.'

'Maarja, that farm is not ours.'

'Why not? It was our family's.'

'No, darling. Look, nobody knows what's going to happen, and anyway people living there will claim it. We are refugees; we have no claim. We don't live there. We're Swedish citizens now.'

'Why should somebody there get it when it's ours?'

'People live there, or farm it now – '

'But it doesn't matter. I found out about it. We can file a claim for restitution.'

'Well, there are other people who will claim it, relatives – '

'Who? Just Matti and Maret and their sons. They won't want it.'

'Perhaps they will.'

'Well, we can share it.'

'No, Maarja. No.'

'Well, I want to go anyway. I want to see what it's like now; it's all different. It's independent. We're free Estonians.'

Peeter sighed. 'Maarja, darling, I almost always give you what you want. Just listen to me. Your future is here; you've got a job and your studies. Those are too important for you to go running around Estonia. Concentrate on your education and stop worrying about Estonia. It's a mess right now. There's a lot of crime. Russians are shooting at people. There

218

are still soldiers there. It's dangerous. Just forget about it, honey. Believe me, it's nothing but trouble.'

Maarja did not want to run the risk of getting the same reaction from Karl. 'Please, Karl, please; I'll tell you later. Please don't make me tell you now.'

Karl wondered whether she was pregnant. 'I really think you ought to talk to your mother about this.'

Maarja pouted. 'I can't; I just can't. Don't you see? Oh please, Karl, I've never asked you for anything. Just give it to me for my next birthday. I won't ask you for anything then.'

He groaned. 'Maarja, don't you see? I just can't do this. I simply cannot give you this much money without telling your mother. It's the same as a lie.'

'Will you give it to me if I tell you?'

'Probably.'

Maarja frowned. 'All right, then, I'll tell you. I have to go somewhere. It's a trip.'

'You're going to Estonia.'

'Yes.'

'No. I am not giving you the money.'

'Karl!' She was indignant. 'You lied.'

'No, I didn't.'

Maarja felt like stamping her feet, but she knew she would get nothing out of him by doing so and controlled herself. She said, her voice consciously wavering, 'Oh, Karl, Mother never lets me do anything. I've never gone anywhere alone, and I never will. Don't you see, I don't make enough money ... ' She threw her arms around him and cried, 'I want to see where I come from, don't you understand? And Mother will never take me there.'

When he wrote out the cheque, he said, 'Just don't let anything happen.'

'I won't. Oh Karl, thanks a million.' She hugged him. 'I'll be back in three days. Thank you thank you thank you. You don't know how much this means to me. I have a feeling this trip is going to change my whole life.'

'Yes, well, let's hope not.' Karl hugged Maarja back. He could hardly resist giving Maarja what she wanted and she seemed to want this so very much. He hoped that Helena would not throw a fit when she found out; she would know eventually. But he had always wanted to be a father and to indulge Maarja gave him such great pleasure.

30

Maarja's memories of her last trip to Estonia were mostly of her mother's and grandmother's anxiety. As she walked off the deck of the *Nord Estonia* down the gangway into the harbour memories began to flood back. The harbour building was of course the same; the differences, however, were striking. The soldiers had gone. The customs officials were now young Estonian men and women in blue jackets with the national emblem on the sleeve. She smiled at the man at passport control; she knew she had come home.

It was summer now and the harbour was bright, not as depressing as she remembered that November years before. Outside Estonians greeted their visitors with hugs and flowers; Maarja imagined that their happiness was all the greater now that they met on free Estonian soil.

She hailed a taxi. They were still Ladas, dirty, rattling, driven by surly drivers. The taxi left her outside the Viru Hotel. Inside signs directed her to a disco and a restaurant on the top floor 'with stunning views of the city of Tallinn'.

Maarja checked in and went up to her room. The hotel had not been redecorated; the walls were still brown and the lift directions still in Russian. She came out of the lift; where the ladybird had once sat at her desk a square of carpet had been nailed down and cut wires protruded from the walls.

Maarja dropped her bag and washed her hands in the bathroom. On the toilet seat was a square of paper, on which was printed in English: 'For the sake of your cleanliness.' On the back of the room door was a sign offering advice to tourists: *'Not to exchange currency with the crazy rates of the exchangers. Telephone calls need patience. Keep your hair on. Not to go walking in dark alleys with commodities like video.'*

At first everything delighted her: the Pärnu Street cinema offering a double feature of *Back to the Future III* and *Licence to Kill*, and the rows of flower sellers. Then she noticed a few old women holding out dirty, tattered clothing. She walked down towards the old town. She passed fountains she remembered from that previous trip; they now lay still.

She reached Raekoja plats. There was an Indian restaurant and an ice-cream parlour. A horse-drawn carriage stood waiting for customers.

She made her way to Toompea and Parliament. There were still the enormous granite blocks meant to deter Russian tanks and at the entrance to Toompea was a sign: the symbol of a tank, crossed by a red line. This sight touched Maarja more than she expected.

She walked slowly among the winding streets of the old town. Traditional nested Russian dolls were still on sale; alongside Maarja also saw a doll of Gorbachev, inside which was a smaller doll of Brezhnev holding a still smaller one of Stalin, and finally a tiny doll of Lenin. She passed peep shows and nightclubs, video clubs offering screenings of American films, newly opened street cafés, a pizza parlour with two tiny tables.

Everything was strange and small, the attempt to become normal almost pathetic; yet her feeling of having come home strengthened with every step.

She went to a bar at the top of Pikk Street. Like most Estonian cafés, it was dark inside; at one end was a woman behind a counter selling sandwiches of black bread and pink sausage, *pirukas*, weak coffee in brown ceramic mugs. The tables were black lacquered wood, surrounded by short bar stools. It was the opposite of a Swedish *konditori*, which was light and clean and displayed rows of uniformly baked cinnamon buns beneath colourless glass; a place where people did not linger, where conversations were transient and inconsequential.

Two young men sat at a nearby table, talking quietly. Maarja wondered if they were students and what the hopes and fears of the young must now be. She wanted to join them, to follow them in their everyday lives, to understand the great upheaval they must feel; they – and she – were the generation that was living through history.

She took out her map and decided she would take a tram somewhere away from the tourists: Lasnamäe, perhaps, which she knew was predominantly Russian, or Mustamäe, where the Polytechnic was, where her parents and her grandmother had studied.

Then a voice said in English, 'Are you looking for something?'

She looked up at the two young men. They watched her with polite curiosity. She said in Estonian, 'I was just studying the map.'

The same boy spoke again, 'Are you from Canada?' He had a round, friendly face, large black glasses.

'Sweden. My parents are Estonian.'

He introduced himself as Jüri, and his friend as Mihkel. She told them her name and they briefly exchanged information about one another. She had been to Estonia once, when she was young, she told them; she was a student at the University of Stockholm; Mihkel was a student at the Polytechnic and Jüri was at Tartu University.

Jüri began to question her on her impressions of Tallinn, what she had seen, where she planned to go. She glanced for a moment at Mihkel, who was turned slightly away, but nevertheless watched her intently. Through the dark, she saw the honed edges of his cheekbones, fine and solid like polished marble. He would never be mistaken for a Swede. His hair was thick and dark blond; he sat away from the table, as if waiting for something. He was waiting, she decided, to see her reaction to himself and Jüri. He reminded her of a package; she felt the sudden urge to open him.

Jüri began to speak more loudly, trying to recapture her attention, and she forced her gaze back to him. Mihkel did not move.

Jüri was explaining that he was pro-Western, but doubtful

that Estonia would ever catch up with the rest of Europe. 'Our economy is destroyed. What's worse, we are ruined by Soviet habits. Nobody here knows how to work hard.' He was not much older than Maarja, but she could see his cynicism. 'We are as corrupted as the generation after the terror. We have been debilitated by communism. It will take generations to become normal again.'

Maarja had never heard such ideas debated; the situation had seemed simple to her: once Estonia was free everything would work out. After all, they had been waiting all these years for their freedom.

She turned to Mihkel for his opinion. He said, quietly, 'The West will do nothing but corrupt us. They have never done anything for us. They abandoned us in the war to the communists.'

She continued to look at him and she thought: *I know now what it means to want a man.*

Later, Mihkel told her his country made a pastime of bickering. 'Do you know how many political parties we have?' he asked rhetorically.

Maarja shook her head, dazed. He told her that his country, their country, was poised between the poles of Russian orthodoxy and Western consumerism. At least under communism they had had the advantage of having to fight for their identity. Under capitalism their identity would be squandered, sold at a profit, and nobody would care until it was too late. The mine would be empty; the well dry.

They were at a disco which was so dark that Maarja could hardly see the people standing around them; outside the building was a sign that said *Dance Bar*. It had recently opened, and was exactly what she had wanted to see, to experience: a new, free, Western Estonia. On the stage was a band: three men in hats, sunglasses and matching black tee-shirts on which were printed the English words 'Nice Trio'. They shook their long hair into their faces as they sang; Maarja could barely make out the lyrics.

The other young men and women danced or stood in groups, holding beers. Maarja wondered whether any of them had thought about their future path with the seriousness that Mihkel felt. Certainly her mother had never thought about it. All her mother and father had ever taught her was that communism was evil. To them the situation was simple.

They ordered drinks; Mihkel said, 'So, tell me, do you feel Swedish or Estonian?'

'I am both.' She felt strange; for the first time in her life her two sides had come together, parallel and equal. 'My parents left when I was a baby.'

'And what do they think about everything now?'

Maarja said carefully, 'They are very Swedish now. I don't think they understand what it's like here.'

'You mean they have become corrupted and materialistic.'

Maarja was angry at this, but did not reply.

'And what do you think?' he asked, looking into her eyes.

'I think it is very complicated.' She wondered what her mother would think of him. Her mother mistrusted Estonians; she, like Jüri, thought that they had been corrupted by communism.

Mihkel said, 'I think *you* are very complicated.' Maarja did not answer. She was complicated; and here was somebody who understood her complexity.

As they danced, Mihkel let his hands move slowly along her shoulders, arms, waist. He exerted the slightest, tantalizing pressure with his body from time to time. Maarja had never felt anything like this in her life. Certainly, she had never felt it with Anton.

She had never slept with a boy. She had experienced the odd fumble and grope: once at summer camp in a boy's tent; at a party in high school in the girl's parents' bedroom; the night of her graduation from high school; one drunken party at university.

She had been more curious about sex than interested; she did not understand her own physical desire when all it resulted in was a bit of unpleasant grabbing and wet, amateurish kissing.

She had seen films of what she considered real sex: *Body Heat*, *Pretty Woman*; French and Italian films. She imagined that real sex would be far removed from the clinical descriptions she had been taught in school; she would meet someone whose passion so overwhelmed him that she would be swept away with reciprocal desire.

At midnight they walked to Mihkel's flat, which he shared with his brother. His parents were now living in the house of his father's childhood in Maarjamäe. It had been confiscated in the 1930s; they had recently reclaimed it and were now restoring it. They had left their sons the two-room flat Maarja now entered.

Mihkel showed her around proudly; it was unheard of for two Estonian boys to live in their own flat. Maarja followed him in a blur, hardly able to speak; she realized that she was very drunk.

He pulled her down on to the sofa and began to kiss her. He said, into her ear, 'Tell me what Swedish girls like.' This confused her and, as she tried to think of something to say, he took her hand and led her to one of the single beds in the bedroom. As he pushed her on to the bed, Maarja realized that she had no desire at all to sleep with him. This was not the boy whose passion would ignite hers. But she was already here and she had no idea how to extract herself from a situation in which she seemed already to have committed herself. She was too young to allow herself to act badly; it worried her more to admit that she was frightened and unsophisticated and too drunk to make a reasoned decision rather than simply to go ahead and have sex.

He entered her quickly and clumsily; she lay beneath him, rigid and frightened. Shortly afterwards they both fell into a drunken sleep.

In the morning she woke before he did. She went to the toilet, which smelled of leaky plumbing and bad drainage. It was so tiny that her knees pressed against the door when she sat down. She washed herself in the adjoining bathroom in a bathtub that was so dirty she squatted and splashed the cold water over her body. She dressed quickly; Mihkel still slept.

As she gathered her things and prepared to leave, he heard her and appeared in the doorway, wearing his dressing gown. He asked her how long she was planning to stay. His tone was casual and friendly.

Maarja looked at him and understood that this boy cared nothing for her at all. She explained that she had several things she needed to do over the next few days; he could leave a message for her at the Viru if he wanted to contact her. She left the flat.

She was more embarrassed than upset by the experience. She understood that they had been brought together by nothing more than sheer chance. She told herself that she was relieved she had finally done it. When the next man came along, the real man with the passion, she would not be embarrassed by her long-standing virginity, but could welcome him with the sophistication of an experienced woman.

31

Maarja sat on Matti's sofa, her knees pressed against the same coffee table that Helena's had twenty years before. She drank her coffee and talked with Hanno.

She had rung Matti's flat from the Viru. Neither Matti nor Maret was at home. Hanno had answered the telephone; Maarja had tried to explain who she was, but Hanno interrupted her, 'Of course I know who you are, Maarja.' He insisted that she come over immediately.

Hanno was now an engineer, working for a construction company. Maarja had heard about Matti and Maret and their two sons all her life and she remembered them from her great-grandmother Leena's funeral. She had heard many times how Matti and her grandfather Jaan had grown up together on the family farm, how Matti had gone to a neighbouring farm and narrowly escaped deportation with Jaan.

But she realized now that she had never thought much about these people at all. She had grown so tired of hearing her grandfather go on about how his mother died fighting Russians that she had simply stopped listening.

Now she understood that she was much more real to Hanno than Hanno had ever been to her, that she meant something of value to him because she was family. She felt suddenly sheltered by her mother and father and grandparents; she felt grateful and special. She wanted Hanno to understand that she now was glad he was her family.

Hanno was explaining that he was lucky to have a job. His company was working on several projects: a hotel built by a Swedish consortium, a block of flats for the employees of a Finnish company, an embassy.

Hanno shrugged when Maarja brought up the farm. 'Who

228

knows what will happen? All they do in the government is argue.'

'But it's ours, your family's and mine.'

'I don't know about that. My father would not have inherited it, you know.'

'Why not?'

'It would not have gone to my grandmother, my father's mother.'

'What do you mean?'

'Emmeline, the eldest daughter, got the farm. Your grandfather's mother. She died after the war. She was a patriot. A Russian shot her.'

'Yes, I know. So the farm would be Jaan's.'

'Yes. It's your mother's, tädi Helena's, now.'

'So it's mine.' Maarja nearly clapped her hands in delight. 'But why? Why did Emmeline get the farm?'

'I don't know really. My father told me Emmeline was the only one who could farm it. But I know that's not true, because tädi Lydia has a little place. Not a farm, but she could have – '

'Who's tädi Lydia?'

Hanno stopped, embarrassed, and said reluctantly, 'The youngest Jakobson daughter. Emmeline's youngest sister.'

'I've never heard of her. I've heard Mother talk about Emmeline, of course. And about Matti's mother Alma. Your grandmother.'

'Yes.'

'But not Lydia.'

'No, I suppose you wouldn't have. I guess I shouldn't have mentioned her.'

'Why not?'

'Your parents never liked her much. Your grandparents too. I'm not supposed to tell you this. My father asked me not to. Please don't mention it to him. It just slipped out.'

'So there were Lydia, Emmeline and Alma on the farm.'

'And Anne. Anne Anvelt.'

'What? Who's that?'

'The fourth sister. She's dead, too. Only Lydia's alive.'

'Is she? Where does she live?'

'Near a lake, outside town. We still visit her sometimes. She's old. She must be over eighty now.'

'All alone?'

Hanno hesitated. He never knew the details about Piret, but he did know, without having been told, there was some matter involving her which was best not discussed. He said confusedly, 'Well, yes, in a way, I suppose. I mean, there are neighbours.'

Maarja was oblivious. 'Can you tell me where it is?'

'No, I don't know. I'm not sure I want to discuss this with you.'

'Why not? She's my relative isn't she?' Maarja thought for a moment. 'She must be my great-great-aunt. God. She must be ancient.'

'Yes … I don't think you should go there. Anyway I don't know how to get there. And I'd rather you didn't discuss this with my father.'

'Perhaps I will.'

'Maarja, I'm asking you not to.'

'Well, then, why don't you take me there? If she's the only relative we've got left in Estonia on Mother's side, I mean besides your family, I'd like to meet her. Can you call her?'

'She doesn't have a phone.'

'Can we drive there?'

'No, my parents have the car.'

'Well, is there a bus?'

'Well, yes, but it's not very convenient.'

'Oh, come on, Hanno, don't be so stubborn. I won't tell Matti.'

'Maarja, I don't think this is a very good idea. I think you should talk to your mother first.'

'Oh, come on, it'll be fun. What's the harm?'

'No, nothing I guess; Lydia's OK, actually. If I ask her not to mention it, she won't.'

Maarja saw the house from the road. It was tiny, a cluster of timber nailed together with a ramshackle balcony on top.

There was a privy to one side, an enormous vegetable garden and an orchard covered with netting. The land sloped down towards a shimmering lake. Alongside the pier, a rowing boat was tethered and a bit further out, among the reeds, enormous water-lilies, white with yellow centres and pointed petals, perched on flat, green leaves.

As she and Hanno walked down the path, Maarja thought she saw the old lady's face in the window. A few minutes later, the woman appeared at the doorstep, watching them suspiciously.

Maarja glanced at Hanno and saw an embarrassed look spread across his features.

The old woman opened the door silently and let them into the tiny, spotlessly clean house. She waited until they had taken their coats and shoes off and then greeted them formally; they all shook hands.

Hanno said, 'This is Maarja.'

The old woman nodded at her without surprise; apparently she knew who she was, although Maarja could not understand how. Perhaps Matti had shown his aunt photographs of her. Had the woman seen her as a baby before they went to Sweden? Had tädi Lydia seen her christened? No, Maarja remembered: her mother had told her only Matti, Maret, the priest and her godmother Sylvia had been there. Maarja could not remember ever meeting her godmother. She had a vague recollection that her mother had called her a few times, but that was all.

Lydia went to the kitchen without asking them if they wanted something to eat. Maarja knew to wait for her to prepare food; Estonians always fed guests immediately, and before any conversation. It would be considered highly unusual and rude to visit somebody without having a meal, regardless of the time of day.

They watched Lydia revive the fire in the stove, boil water for tea, remove various items from the larder. She told them to sit down. She laid a tablecloth out and put down pickled cucumbers, rye bread, a minute pat of butter, preserved plums, smoked fish, sliced tomatoes, all neatly arranged in small glass dishes.

They ate in near silence. Lydia asked Hanno about his parents and brother; Hanno gave her brief, polite answers. He was clearly embarrassed that he had allowed Maarja to bully him into coming.

Maarja spoke occasionally; Lydia looked at her each time, guardedly but not unkindly, and nodded without answering.

Finally Maarja gathered her nerve and said, 'May I call you tädi Lydia?'

'Please,' the woman said formally. Maarja knew to continue using 'teie', the formal you. 'You are my mother's great-aunt?'

The old woman paused and then said, 'Yes, I am.'

Maarja was relieved that some kind of conversation had begun. 'Did you know my mother when she was young?'

'Yes.'

'Did she come to visit you here?'

The old woman nodded again.

Maarja looked around. 'So this place is part of my mother's childhood.'

Nobody replied.

'What kind of girl was she?'

Hanno touched Maarja under the table and shook his head slightly when she glanced at him. She gave him an annoyed look, but fell quiet. They finished the meal in silence.

Lydia cleared the table and offered to show them her garden. They put their shoes on at the door. Lydia handed them their coats and Maarja understood that they were expected to leave directly afterwards.

She followed Lydia and Hanno out of the house. Hanno was right: this had not been a good idea. This old woman must really dislike her mother, or perhaps it was her grandparents whom she disliked. How could they have quarrelled this badly? It must have happened ages ago, before they emigrated. But why was the old lady so angry with her? She had done nothing. They had so little family; why on earth shouldn't they acknowledge one another? Especially now that

Estonia was free and they could travel and visit.

Hanno and Maarja walked around Lydia's land and looked at the meticulous rows of vegetables, the netted orchard, the lake. Lydia had brought with her a battered plastic bag printed with the words Tallinna Kaubamaja; she began to fill it with fruit, but Hanno stopped her.

He said, flushing and mortified, 'I really would rather my parents did not know I had come.' Maarja understood that Hanno considered any lie to his parents an injury to them and discredit to himself; she was embarrassed to think of her cavalier attitude towards her own parents and towards Karl. She shared Hanno's embarrassment: she had forced him to lie and to ask Lydia to lie, and Maarja knew she would regret this.

Lydia nodded to Hanno and walked them to the top of the road. The light had grown dim, and across a field Maarja could see a wagon piled with green hay, drawn by a donkey, moving very slowly.

They stood for a moment. Lydia embraced Hanno and told him that he looked well. She held Maarja by the shoulders and looked at her for a few seconds. Maarja returned the old woman's gaze, but could not interpret the look in her eyes. Lydia let her fingers touch Maarja's cheek briefly.

They crossed the road. About half a kilometre away, in the other direction, a woman carrying two baskets walked towards them. Lydia turned to Hanno and Maarja. She said, 'You must go now.' She pressed her palms towards them, as if to urge them down the road. 'Go. It is two kilometres and the bus will come soon.' Then she stood, rooted to the ground, watching as they turned and walked away.

32

It was now nearly November. Stockholm was no longer beautiful; as winter approached, the shortening days and icy rain made the city grey, dull, miserable.

Maarja was sure that it was exams that were making her so ill. She looked terrible and felt worse. She could not remember the last time she was this depressed. Her stomach ached, she could not eat, all she wanted to do was sleep. She had skipped classes and stayed in her room, trying to study, but she could not concentrate.

Her mother had not seen her in two weeks, although they had spoken on the telephone. Helena had wanted her to come over, but Maarja had put her off with various excuses. Maarja was better at embellishing than at outright lying, and she was afraid she might admit that she had been to Estonia under her mother's questioning. Besides, she knew Karl was waiting to give her a chance to tell her mother herself and she wanted to put this off for as long as possible.

She had returned on the boat without incident. She had gone directly home. She was glad that she had taken the trip; it had made her understand that there was a complexity to her family and her country that she had never appreciated.

It had been, she told herself, a maturing experience. She understood that Mihkel had slept with her partly because she had made herself available; partly because she was foreign, to his mind, Swedish. She understood that some boys found foreign girls particularly attractive, and of course the only foreign girls most Estonian boys were likely to meet were Russian. She felt embarrassed, but relieved that she was no longer a virgin. She would forget about Mihkel; on her next trip over she would be more circumspect in her behaviour.

After her meeting with Lydia, she and Hanno had spent a strained hour on the bus, speaking little. She saw that she, a nineteen-year-old girl, could not simply stroll into a foreign country and reclaim her family's land. She understood that Hanno's parents were probably following the debate over restitution of confiscated land quite closely. She had learned that she knew very little of her family's history nor of their present relations. She also saw that she should not and could not interfere.

Her mother rang her again and Maarja could put her off no longer. She agreed to come for lunch the following day, Saturday, after Helena told her Karl would be out the entire day.

When Maarja walked in, Helena immediately said, 'What on earth is wrong with you? You look awful.' Helena peered at her. 'Are you getting enough sleep?'

Erna was there, sitting on the sofa, dressed to go shopping: hat, gloves, handbag. Maarja kissed her, 'Hello, Vanaema.'

Erna looked at her and said nothing.

Helena turned away, saying, 'I'll start lunch. And I've made some saffron buns. Your favourite.'

'Don't bother, Mama, I'm not hungry. I'll just have tea.'

Helena walked into the kitchen, saying, 'Don't be silly. Of course you're hungry. You're a student.'

Maarja sat down. She suddenly felt very tired.

Maarja and Erna were silent for a few minutes. They could hear Helena in the kitchen, taking out china.

Maarja said, 'Have you been shopping?'

'I was on my way. I just stopped in to see you.'

The kettle began to whistle. Erna said quietly, 'What's the matter, Maarja?'

'Oh nothing, studying.'

'Feeling all right?'

'Just a bit – ' Maarja shrugged. 'Maybe it's the flu.'

Her grandmother looked at her and said, 'Maarja, are you pregnant?' Maarja's head shot up. She stared at her grandmother in terror. Then she glanced towards the kitchen; she could hear

Helena stacking cups on a tray, running water, opening and closing cupboards. Maarja looked back at Erna.

'My dear child, it does happen. You look pregnant to me.'

'I do?' Maarja was completely terrified. Someone could just look at you and know you were pregnant?

Erna smiled. 'I have seen many pregnant women in my time. You forget your grandfather was an obstetrician.'

Maarja stared at her and knew that her grandmother was right. 'I can't be.'

'Before you alarm your mother, I suggest you go to a doctor. I won't say anything until – and unless – you want me to.'

Maarja stood up. She looked at her grandmother: it was true. It couldn't be true, but it was. She had known something was wrong all this time. The knowledge had lain in her mind, restless, growing, waiting for her. And now she had to face it. Oh God, she thought, oh God. She couldn't let her mother see her: it showed; her grandmother knew immediately. Her grandmother could see it. Everyone would be able to tell just by looking at her.

She had to leave now, immediately. What would her mother say? She would have to have an abortion. Oh God. No, it couldn't be true. You couldn't get pregnant with a boy you did not know after one night. She had been a *virgin*. It didn't happen like this.

'I've got to go,' Maarja said quickly. She gathered her things, talking to herself involuntarily, 'Oh God, oh God.' She called out as she headed down the hall, 'Mother, I'm going. I've got to go. I forgot something – '

Helena came running into the room. 'What? Where are you going?' She looked down the hall at her daughter opening the door, pulling her coat on.

'I've got to go. I'm sorry. I just forgot I have to do something. I'll call you later.' Maarja slammed the door behind her.

She walked out of the building and to the underground. She got on a train, feeling the weight of her body drag on her like extra baggage. How could she have been this stupid?

Her mother would kill her. She would have to have an

abortion. She would have to have a test, just to be sure. They had counsellors at the youth clinic. She could talk to somebody. Nobody would know. She could have it done and not tell anyone. She would tell her grandmother that she had been mistaken.

No, she couldn't. She couldn't lie to her mother and grandmother. She thought of Hanno; oh God, he would never disgrace his parents or lie to them. She had done it now; either she had to lie and hate herself for lying or confess to her mother and face her shock and disappointment. God, oh God.

Maybe her grandmother was wrong. She couldn't see into Maarja's body, could she? Just because Jaan had been an obstetrician did not make Erna telepathic. She would have to have a test. Maybe she did have the flu. She must not get worked up before she knew for certain.

But Maarja knew as she sat on the train that her grandmother was right. There was a living thing in her body and it would grow and take over and make her stomach and breasts enormous. It was there and she had to do something before it consumed her. Maarja was frightened.

She got off the train and walked home. She punched in the code and pushed the door to the building open. She took the lift up to her room and went inside. She sat down on her bed. She stared at her blue walls and salmon woodwork. On her little desk were some notebooks, an open textbook and some pens. She stared at them as though they had nothing to do with her now. There was a microscopic baby inside her and it was growing. She needed help. She knew she did not know what to do; it was impossible for her even to think.

She lay down on her bed and cried. She either had to kill a baby, get rid of this baby and lie about it, or tell the truth and shock her mother, or have a baby and ruin her life. Her mother would die, absolutely die. Her mother had never done anything wrong or shameful in her life, Maarja was certain. Her mother was perfect, self-sacrificing. Her mother had never slept with anybody but Maarja's father and Karl and they probably didn't even do it much.

She couldn't have a baby. She was not yet twenty; she was a student. She had a job at NK, a student flat, a bicycle. She was young. She rode around Stockholm, free, her whole life ahead of her. This could not happen.

It was not a baby. It was a small mass of cells. It was an operation they did every day to lots of girls. It was not yet a baby. It would be like a late period. Lots of them miscarried anyway. It would only be a baby if she did not do anything.

She thought: I don't even know his surname. I don't remember the name of the street where he lives. I don't even know what his parents do. And she cried even more. Her mother would die of shame. Then she remembered: she had got the money from Karl. Her mother would kill Karl. She would never forgive him for having done this. Maarja would be responsible for the break up of her mother's marriage, her mother's one happiness. Every thought that came to her seemed to confirm her stupidity, her impulsiveness, her utter disgrace, her lack of regard for herself and her family.

After a while she sat up. She knew a counsellor was not the person she wanted to talk to. She picked up the telephone and after one ring, as though expressly waiting for this very call, Erna, still in her shopping clothes, picked up the telephone.

33

'There was no one else?'

'No.' Maarja blushed. 'Only him, only that night.'

'You didn't see him again?'

Maarja felt dark shame cover her. She had slept with a boy for no reason at all. She had just slept with him. She imagined her grandmother during the war, passion, death, bombs, families torn apart, couples in love. Those people simply did not go to bed with a boy they had met at a disco called Dance Bar.

Maarja sat in her grandmother's sitting room. Erna's flat was an old person's; it had not been redecorated since Maarja could remember. The bathtub was worn with use and the kitchen cupboards were from the 1970s, of dull blue Formica. Maarja looked around at the pictures of forests and vases of flowers on her grandmother's walls, at the frayed armrests of her chairs. The dark bookshelves were filled with Jaan's medical textbooks; everywhere were pictures of Helena, Peeter, Jaan, Erna and Maarja. Maarja's entire life was documented on Erna's shelves: as a baby, throughout her childhood, at her confirmation, her graduation from high school.

Maarja felt that her life had no substance, no significance; she was inconsequential; she had simply had sex with a boy, any boy, for no particular reason. She knew her grandmother could see her, legs apart, the nondescript boy panting over her, propelling himself into her body. A boy she would probably never see again. 'No.'

'I see.'

Maarja began to cry. 'I am so stupid.'

Erna patted her on the shoulder. 'No more stupid than many girls. Don't cry, darling. I only asked because if you didn't know him, well, he doesn't matter.'

Maarja looked up and immediately stopped crying. She had never imagined her grandmother so calm, so practical about something so shameful. Why wasn't she angry? Why wasn't she lecturing her?

Erna thought for a moment. Then she got up to pour more coffee. 'What else did you do in Estonia?'

Maarja shrugged. What did it matter? 'I just walked around. I had this idea of going to see the farm.'

'Yes, I thought you might. Why didn't you?'

'Because – ' Maarja stopped. She did not want to hurt her grandmother or make her angry. Getting pregnant suddenly seemed less serious than her visit to Lydia. She knew she had overstepped some specific but undefined boundary by going where she ought not to have gone. She knew she could uncover some story about her family if she told Erna about her visit; she did not know if she wanted to hear it.

'I don't know. It was too far.'

'Did you visit anybody?'

Maarja looked up and saw that Erna already knew about Lydia. 'Did Matti call you?'

'Yes. You shouldn't have persuaded Hanno to take you to Lydia's. You put Hanno in an embarrassing position. Matti was very upset with him.'

'Oh. I'm sorry.'

'Your mother would not be happy to know you went there.'

'I know. Hanno told me.'

'The history in that family is full of bitterness. They all hate each other because of that wretched farm.'

'Yes. Hanno told me that too. Because Emmeline inherited it.'

'Yes.'

'Why did she get it and nobody else?'

'Oh, it's a long story ... Emmeline was a difficult mother-in-law, Maarja. She would not have liked any woman who married her son, and so my view is not very reliable. Your grandfather was her darling boy.

'But the reason she got it over the other sisters was that she

240

married a boy on an adjoining farm and her father wanted old Jakobson to see the two farms united.'

'Oh.'

'And most of that land was not even the Jakobson's until the 1920 land reform. Anyway, it wasn't just the farm. They all hated Emmeline because she was quite cruel and arrogant. She did not approve of any of her sisters and made their lives miserable.

'Because she had the farm, you see, she could say anything she wanted to them or criticize them. That's why Lydia left. She refused to live there any longer. She would have been Emmeline's servant, really, not having any claim. The family story was that Lydia walked out one night with only the clothes on her back and said she would never return. And she didn't.

'Anne and Alma got married, not terribly well, either. But I suppose it was partly Emmeline's fault. They married to get away. And, of course, they had no dowry and so they both married workers.'

As Erna spoke, Maarja listened, absorbed and distracted. Alma, Matti's mother, died in childbirth along with the baby when Matti was about ten. He was sent to live on the farm and Emmeline took to him: he was an easy child, worked hard, didn't ask for much, and wasn't jealous of Jaan. He was useful. He could fix radios and shoe horses and repair fences.

'Emmeline helped the Forest Brothers, the *metsavennad*, with food and she hid ammunition for them. She was very brave and she was not afraid of dying. But she was not kind and Lydia always resented her for the way she treated her sisters.'

'So Lydia must not have liked Vanaisa either,' Maarja said.

'No. For being Emmeline's son and also because he was so favoured over the others.'

Maarja did not notice Erna's hesitation. 'And she hates me because I'm Vanaisa's granddaughter?' she demanded incredulously.

'Of course she doesn't hate you.'

'She didn't seem very happy to see me.'

Erna was silent.

Maarja's mind returned to her immediate problem. 'Oh, Vanaema, what shall I do?'

'My dear child, I have seen this happen many times, and it is wrong to do what your parents, your lover or your grandparents want if that is not what you want. If you have a child, it will be yours for ever and you will never be free again. Do you understand what I am saying? You will never be free again. A child ... a child must come first, always. Do you see?

'If you don't have this child, you will have to live with that decision and I cannot tell you if you will regret it. You may not. You do not know how you will feel in ten years about aborting a baby. You may feel that it was for the best.'

'I don't know what I want,' Maarja cried. 'I just don't know. It feels like a growth, like something taking over my body.'

'I know,' said her grandmother. 'But you cannot know now, at this moment, whether you want it or not. Your body is playing tricks with you. You need some time. Many women do not want babies that they then love with all their hearts. Many women are terribly disappointed by their baby's birth. Not all mothers love their children.'

Maarja rose. 'I suppose I'll go home now. I'd like to sleep.'

'Sleep here, Maarja.' Maarja sat rooted to her chair and Erna rose to make up the extra bed, the bed where Maarja had always slept when she stayed with her grandparents. She lay down and began to cry again, for she was no longer a little girl.

When Maarja woke it was dinnertime. As they ate, Erna told Maarja, 'You are still a child, and you have much to do before having a child of your own. If you have this baby, it will be difficult if you ever marry.'

'I'll never get married,' Maarja said obstinately.

'Perhaps not. But I also know that when I was young girls were often forced by their parents to have abortions or give up their babies. And to have a child is your right, Maarja, if you want it. To tell a girl that she cannot keep her baby simply because she is young and unmarried is wrong. A baby is a

242

wonderful thing. This baby might seem like a catastrophe right now; it could turn out to be a blessing. You are not a child, after all: you are nineteen; you are a woman.

'I remember getting pregnant with your mother and thinking that it was the most important act of my life. We had lived through so much death in Siberia and life is important.

'When I returned with my mother from Siberia, everywhere were Russians. They had all the flats. They spoke Russian on the trams and in the shops. I went into a shop and spoke Estonian and they shouted at me and refused to serve me, even after I switched to Russian. It was terrible, as though I had come back and we had never existed. We were unwanted, foreigners, in our own home.

'There were still people being taken at night and then disappearing. Life – Estonian life – meant something more than just one individual baby. Having a baby was a kind of statement that life would go on, that our culture would go on, that we would not perish. You must see that we had a completely different perspective.'

Maarja was eating, her head bent over her plate. It did not matter now whether her culture went on. She had no culture. She was neither Swedish nor Estonian. The father of this baby did not love her or even know her. Having a baby in Erna's day seemed romantic and brave; right now, having a baby seemed a complete disaster.

'Your mother – ' Erna stopped, and Maarja glanced up. 'Yes?'

'Your mother would know what I mean. I think you should tell her. Your mother gave up a great deal for you. She would know what I mean by a child coming first.'

Maarja turned glum and continued to eat. The last thing she wanted to hear was how perfect her mother was. 'Mother would kill me.'

'Maarja, don't be ridiculous; your mother would do anything for you.'

Maarja let out an impatient breath. 'Yes, because she is perfect. She's never done anything wrong.'

'Of course she has done wrong things.'

'Name one.'

Erna sighed. 'Oh Maarja, you are so young. You will understand later what I mean.'

'Oh, now I am so young. A few minutes ago I was a woman and old enough to have a baby.'

Erna was silent.

'Well?' Maarja demanded.

'You are in no shape to discuss anything like this. You need time, you need to calm down.'

'I am a woman and pregnant, and now you refuse to tell me something I ought to know about my own mother. I'm certainly not going to tell her if you don't tell me what you are talking about.' Maarja thought a moment, and added, 'And I don't see why I should have bothered telling you in the first place. You treat me like a child.'

Erna took a breath. 'Maarja, I will tell you why Lydia acted so strangely to you.'

Maarja glanced up at Erna, surprised at her sudden change of tone.

Erna knew she had no right to say what she wanted to say; no more than Maarja had to impose herself on Lydia; or Helena and Peeter had when they lied to Maarja about her origins; or any of them had when they took Maarja from Piret.

Erna saw her granddaughter in front of her, pregnant, her miserable, angry, innocent face, on the verge of knowing the truth, still living in a lie. Whether it was for her to decide or not, Erna felt that the time had come to admit the mistakes they had all made; the time had come to put what remained of their home and their family in some kind of order. 'Maarja, Helena is not your mother.'

Maarja stopped eating. 'What are you talking about?'

'Lydia lives with a niece, Piret. She must have been out when you were there. No doubt Lydia was trying to get you to leave before Piret returned. Which was why you thought she did not like you.'

Maarja stared at her grandmother. 'No one else was there.'

'Piret is a cousin of Helena's; they are second cousins. She is Anne's granddaughter. Do you see? Anne's son's daughter. Helena's and Piret's grandmothers were sisters.

'She was a young girl when she had you. She went to live with Lydia when she was pregnant. We – Jaan and I – thought it was for the best, what we did.'

Maarja sat staring at Erna, saying nothing.

'I don't know if what we did was right. She was younger than you are now, seventeen. We thought we were doing the right thing.

'Piret has suffered a great deal. We don't know everything that has happened to her, but we do know that she has had a very hard life. I suspect that Piret has suffered more than any of us, including your mother, knows.'

'Are you telling me that Mummy and Daddy adopted me?'

'Piret is your mother, Maarja. I don't know who your father is. She never told us.'

Maarja did not speak. She dropped her fork and it clattered on her plate. Then she stood up, looking around at the objects and photographs in her grandmother's flat as though she had never seen them before.

'Sit down, Maarja, you look like you will faint.' Erna paused and then said, 'Piret was seventeen and unmarried. Listen to me, Maarja, try to understand. We had applied for visas. Your grandfather thought – I suppose we both thought it was the best solution for everybody.'

PART 4

June 1992

Piret found Lydia collapsed and only dimly conscious at the bottom of the steps, outside the sauna. Laundry was scattered around, blown across to the vegetable garden and the orchard and down to the lake. It was late evening.

Piret carried her to the house and laid her on the sofa. Lydia looked up, dazed, as Piret took her outer clothing off. She had of course seen Lydia unclothed many times, but Lydia's body now startled her. Piret saw the brittle bones and slackening flesh of an old woman, a small white skull under sparse, grizzled grey hair.

She covered Lydia with a blanket, then went into the kitchen and stoked the fire to boil water for tea. She thought: *Lydia is old.* For her Lydia had always been old; it had never occurred to Piret that age could incapacitate Lydia.

Piret brought out the tea; Lydia had recovered slightly and was able to sit up. Piret held the cup and helped her take small sips. She said, 'I can walk down to the *kauplus* and call the doctor.' Lydia glared at her and Piret fell silent.

Piret thought: We can no longer live here. They were far from doctors and hospitals, and two kilometres' from the *kauplus*. Besides, it was too much work for them now. They could get rid of the chickens, but there would still be the vegetables and the orchard to tend, wood to be chopped, the house to keep up.

She spent several days trying to decide how to broach the subject of getting a flat in town. She compiled her arguments, and was about to speak when Lydia suddenly said, 'You should do something with that farm and you know it.'

Piret was silenced, her words cut down before her. Lydia had a talent for the conspicuous and logical; Piret knew she was no match for her. Piret remembered arriving at her house twenty years ago, pregnant, holding her mother's tattered suitcase. Lydia knew she was coming, of course. Jaan had explained the plan to her. Lydia looked at Piret and said, 'Was this your idea or did they think it up and then tell you afterwards?'

Piret knew she would bring up the farm; it was impossible that she had not seen the announcements about property restitution in the paper.

'It belongs to us,' she said pointedly, the way she spoke when she thought Piret was ignoring her. 'It's ours. It was confiscated.'

Piret shrugged her shoulders. 'It was never mine.' She knew what the farm would look like, although she had never seen it: fields, great pieces of rusty farm machinery, decrepit barns used for storage. Collectives looked much the same everywhere.

Piret added, 'Besides, everything else.' *Everything else* meant, as Lydia knew, that Piret had been a party member, a Marxist economist.

'You defied the regime. You lost everything. That will make you look good.'

'I don't want to "look good".'

'Why not? Everybody else does.'

'I just don't care.'

'You never believed that nonsense anyway.'

Piret had never discussed with Lydia what she believed. 'Why don't you put in a claim if you want to?' she replied.

'I am too old.'

'So am I,' Piret retorted.

'No you're not. You could do something with it. It's better than letting it go to whoever wants it,' Lydia said irritably. 'Better than some communist.'

The third or fourth time Lydia brought up the farm, Piret finally said, mystified, 'Lydia, what is it with you?'

She grunted gloomily. 'Well, it ought to go to you. Oskar would have – '

'Please, do you have to bring up Oskar?' Piret completed the sentence in her mind: *Oskar would have inherited his share if Emmeline had acted decently.*

Lydia said nothing.

Then Piret said, 'Lydia, why do you want the farm? Tell me, please.'

'It's ours.'

'It's because you don't want Helena to get it, isn't it?' Lydia made an exasperated sound and looked away.

'You think she'll make a claim, don't you?'

'She might.'

'Why shouldn't she? After all, it would have been Jaan's.'

'Why the hell should she get it? They left. They didn't want to live here. It's not their country any longer.'

Piret shook her head. 'Lydia, that doesn't matter. If it's legally Helena's, your feelings don't enter into it. Anyway, whether I get it or Helena gets it, Maarja will inherit it.'

'I know that,' she returned obstinately.

Piret smiled and said, 'You don't want to see it go down through the family as Jaan's.'

'Well, why shouldn't I feel that way? You've suffered; you gave up Maarja, you lost your job and your flat. What has Helena done to deserve it?'

Raise Maarja, Piret answered silently.

'And what if Helena doesn't claim it?' Lydia went on. 'It was our farm. You have a responsibility to keep that farm in the family.'

'Perhaps Matti will claim it.'

'Oskar had as much of a claim as Matti.' Lydia was jabbing her finger at Piret now, the beginning of a tirade. 'Besides, you're the one who's doing something for the country. You're probably the only person here who knows anything about the way things ought to work.'

She was talking about Piret's job. After nearly eight years, Piret had her job back.

That afternoon, in 1984, Piret had come home after signing the statement against Boris Rozhansky. It was very warm for September. She went inside the house; she could not bear the heat of the sun after what she had done.

She could have refused to sign. She did not know if they would have forced Lydia to move or prevented Maarja from returning to Sweden. She did not know what the Swedish government would or could have done to help. But she had known that she had no other choice but to sign. There are some acts which are too simple to bear analysis. She did not contact Boris: he would know soon enough. Nothing mattered at that moment. It did not matter to her if she were alive or dead.

Piret found a job in the next village, about three kilometres down the road, as a cleaner in a *lastekodu,* a home for mentally handicapped children.

The home was once the eighteenth-century manor house of a Baltic German family. It was completely white, spread out before a forecourt, with turrets on either side and massive arched wooden doors: a miniature castle. It was completely enclosed by the surrounding forest; the only way in was up a tree-lined gravel drive.

The director's name was Anna Jakobson; like Piret, she was short and dark. Piret followed her up dark stairs, feeling like the woman's shadow. Anna Jakobson sat down at her desk and indicated a chair for Piret. Piret sat and then positioned her eyes at a point between the woman's face and chest, to avoid any suggestion of presumption. She needed a job and she knew that this woman did not have to give her one. The woman gazed at her for a moment, asked her a few questions, and then told her that she 'would do'.

They went back down the stairs and into a kitchen. Enormous tin soup pots hung from the wall; in the corner was an ancient black stove and a stack of split wood. In the centre of the room were small tables and chairs of chipped, speckled red Formica. Anna introduced Piret to the staff supervisor, who, she said, would explain to her the duties.

Piret turned to face a woman who looked exactly like a witch. She had frizzy brown hair streaked with grey, which stuck out intractably from her head. Out of her enormous nostrils sprouted coarse black hairs; her hands were prodigious, strong. She was tiny and yet terrifying. When she opened her mouth to speak, Piret saw that she was missing some teeth.

The witch looked suspiciously out of one eye; the other eye roamed about. She indicated that Piret should follow her. She showed her where the rags were kept for cleaning. There was a rusty bath where the children were bathed once a week. On one shelf were a dozen or so very old and scratched children's potties. The children were trained to use these four times a day, the witch explained, showing Piret the outdoor privy where she was to empty them.

On another shelf were the nappies: rags of various colours and patterns which looked to Piret no different from those used for cleaning. The witch took one down and showed her how they were cut in a triangle and how to fold them. Then she took down the wash tubs for the children's laundry from the wall and the washboard alongside.

She spoke with a rural, uneducated accent. Piret tried to say as little as possible. The witch kept glancing at her and finally asked her where she came from. Piret told her the name of Lydia's village. She nodded, satisfied for the moment.

Piret did not mind the work. She did not think while she worked. The witch followed her around for the first week, checking that she had cleaned properly. Piret knew that the woman sensed that she was city-bred and educated, and looked for the telltale signs of carelessness. But Lydia had trained her too well.

At night Piret massaged into her hands anything she could find that would soften them. Her knuckles grew large, red, cracked. Her cuticles were ripped and dry; her nails peeled off in layers. Her back ached and when she went to bed she slept the sleep of the dead.

They spent the autumn cooking and preserving fruit, making pickles and wine and sauerkraut and fruit juice, splitting wood for the winter. When the weather turned cold, they stayed in and sewed and watched television.

Piret was neither happy nor unhappy; she was hardly alive. Nothing pleased her, not the beauty of their jars of tomatoes

253

and plums, or the frozen lake, or peaceful evenings on the sofa, mending clothes. But she was, at least, content. She walked to the *kauplus*, where she occasionally found meat. In the morning she passed the shorn, quiet fields, for everything had been harvested by then. Snow began to fall, and she was grateful for its temporary camouflage, as peaceful as a shroud.

She did not watch the news. She did not read newspapers or books. If the news came on, she switched the channel or turned it off. Lydia did not object. They talked about what they would do the following day, the weekend. They planned their Christmas, the quiet dinner of two women living together without luxury, need or dissent.

The following spring, 1985, they knew that Chernenko had died because the radio played a constant stream of sonorous Russian music. Mikhail Gorbachev was promoted to general secretary. Lydia watched the news, pronouncing and complaining. Piret paid little attention.

She spoke little to the other women in the home. When she arrived she would hang up her coat, put on her apron, change into her work shoes. The children would be having breakfast as she swept and washed the floors of the rooms where they slept. She could hear them in the kitchen shrieking, and the staff gently cajoling and admonishing. She would make up the tiny iron beds, fold the grey blankets and set against each small pillow the child's stuffed bear or cat, their only personal possessions.

Next she would do the babies' room: two dozen painted white cots in rows, at the end of which was a changing table. By then the babies would have been fed and dressed. In the winter they were wrapped up and put in a giant cot kept in the conservatory. In the summer they were put outside on blankets spread on the lawn or veranda.

After she had cleaned the children's rooms she washed the breakfast dishes. Every morning they were fed porridge. She scrubbed the giant tin soup pot the witch used; caked porridge peeled off in sticky grey slabs. She washed the painted metal bowls and large spoons, and wiped the tiny chairs and tables.

From the kitchen she could hear the children being led to the potties, which she would empty and wash after the children had been taken to the day room.

Summer came and the children's routine became less rigid; they ran indoors and out at will, and were taken in small groups for walks in the woods to pick blueberries. Piret found herself unable to avoid them.

The children liked her as they did the other staff. They had no reserve, no suspicions. They would throw themselves at anyone remotely kind; their affections were indiscriminate, desperate. When a child threw itself at Piret, her hands responded, but without emotion. The children did not care. They only wanted the touch of another, the feel of human warmth.

The witch was far less fierce than her appearance and the children were not afraid of her. She occasionally called on Piret to help her with a child. The first time Piret picked up a baby, she felt revulsion and fear. The child, wrapped up tightly to be laid on a blanket outside, stared out with detached idiocy, happy to be held. After a moment, the smell of urine and sweat rose and Piret drew back. She handed the baby to the witch and returned to her cleaning.

Over the summer, despite her efforts to isolate herself, Piret heard snatches of news. Gorbachev talked about 'restructuring peoples' psychology', although he also spoke about the dangers of capitalism and the superiority of socialism. He spoke of the Brezhnev and Andropov years as the 'pre-crisis situation', an admission that Soviet economic problems were longstanding. Piret understood immediately that he was fighting to save a rapidly sinking economy in the face of Kremlin conservatives.

The war between liberal reformists and conservative Marxists had come into the open, but Piret did not care; her life had ended the previous autumn, on the day she flew back from Stockholm. This was the political debate that had ruined her career, threatened her child and ruined the life of the only man who had cared for her. She wondered where Boris was now, whether he hated her. She watched the news with the detachment of a patient dying of an illness for which a preventative vaccine has just been discovered.

On New Year's Eve Lydia watched Gorbachev's address on television. Piret sat beside her, sewing, glancing up indifferently from time to time. As Gorbachev summed up his speech, Piret rose to put her sewing away and inadvertently caught his last sentence: 'The departing year will remain in our memory as a year of strenuous labour, of hope, and of bold plans for the future.'

35

Piret did not think about the future; she had no reason to believe that she and Lydia would do anything but go on as they were, untouched by the world. The passing of seasons, the growing and preserving of vegetables, the constant cleaning of what would immediately become soiled seemed to Piret a gradual, unremarkable meandering towards death. She did not welcome or fear the end of her life; she was comforted by the monotonous and the familiar. Time passed neither quickly nor slowly.

One cold February morning that winter, 1986, Piret and Lydia heard on the radio that the Swedish prime minister had been shot leaving a cinema. Piret knew that Maarja had returned safely to Sweden, because Matti and Maret had received a Christmas card the year before from Helena. Thinking of Maarja, Piret felt bitterness grip her heart. She did not feel heroic or self-sacrificing, only angry for the insignificance and anonymity of her loss.

She had been working at the *lastekodu* for over a year. She had grown used to the work; she was stronger and less easily tired. But she also felt that her body had aged and that she was, at thirty-one, no longer young. The other women, all from the country, were not much older, and one was even a grandmother.

She had grown used to the smell of the children, the stale, faecal smell of the unloved and poorly fed, the abnormal, the misbegotten. It was impossible to keep them any cleaner without a washing machine and with only one bathtub.

Even their breath was sharp and sickly, but there was little they could do: their diet was limited and there were no toothbrushes.

Some of the older children went away in the spring, transferred to homes where they would be taught basic literacy and, later, some limited skill. They were replaced by more babies and toddlers, abandoned or given up by parents without the money, time or will to raise a mentally defective child.

There was one little girl whom Piret had grown to like who went away that year, Mai. She was only mildly retarded; she lacked the telltale round head and eyes. She had thick, dark hair, cut in a circle around her face. She clung to Piret whenever she saw her and had to be pried away for Piret to continue her work.

Piret had no idea why the child liked her. She would sit Mai on her lap, the little girl's legs bouncing, her head tunnelling into Piret's body. Piret thought sometimes about that tiny mistake inside her, that one critical chromosome wrong. Mai was not an easy child: she had sufficient understanding of her condition to feel frustrated and she had amazing fits of anger. Piret knew by then what her life would be: desire without delight or achievement, sexual promiscuity, deadening, repetitious work, the dim knowledge that she was an unwanted mistake.

A woman from the ministry came to take Mai and the others to their new home. Piret stood with the witch and other staff, the two teachers, and the Director, Anna Jakobson, to see them off. Piret kissed Mai on the cheek and then closed her heart so that she would not weep. There was nothing she or anybody could do for this child.

Mai herself did not fully understand that she would never see Piret again; she waved happily, for she could not ever remember going anywhere away from the home and understood only that this was some sort of adventure. They drove away, and Piret turned and walked with the others back to the house.

The first sign that Piret's life, and the lives of everybody around her, would change so incredibly, came from Anna Jakobson. She asked Piret if she would rather work with the children instead of as a cleaner. Piret had been in close contact with the children for nearly two years already, she pointed out; they knew her.

It was summer then and they all knew about the hundreds, perhaps thousands, of children who were suffering from radioactive poisoning. They knew from foreign radio broadcasts and had seen the pictures on Finnish television: the thin, small faces, the tiny bald heads.

They also heard of the soldiers and doctors who had been taken to the site without protective clothing and would now die. Piret thought bitterly of her own people: the young conscripted men far from home and the doctors sent from their families, who would suffer for something that had nothing to do with them. What Piret did not know was that she was not alone, and that the bitterness of all the other people who heard these rumours was accruing and would grow.

Gorbachev made vague admissions of damage on television. What nobody knew was whether the wind had blown towards them and Poland and Sweden, or away, towards Russia. They did not know if the food and milk was poisonous. They ate and drank anyway, and fed what they had to the children. Piret thought of all the mothers – Estonian, Ukranian, Lithuanian, Polish – who were doing the same thing. They had no choice.

The children were easy work compared with cleaning. Piret's constant backache diminished; her hands began to heal.

Anna worked in her office in the mornings; after lunch she would tour the children's rooms and speak to the staff. She described to Piret the sheltered workshops where some of the less severely retarded would work later, sewing or packing or assembling simple parts. Piret listened, remembering her dream of being a stacker in her father's paper factory, thinking of Mai at fourteen or fifteen sewing in a factory with other retarded women.

Piret asked Anna why they must be employed by special factories and why they could not work in a regular factory; Anna looked surprised at the question.

'We do not believe in integrating them into society,' she explained. Anna was a 'defectologist'. 'A collective of those with similar abilities is the best environment. The education of the disabled depends as much on the social learning environment as on innate abilities.'

Piret listened, thinking of her youthful belief that she could create a separate self, impartial, independent. She knew that Anna was not a communist; and that Anna was a dedicated professional, truly concerned about the welfare of these children. She would never have considered her views politically motivated. Yet Piret knew at that moment that there was no discipline, no belief, left untouched by Marxism, and that Anna was as infected as she herself had been.

Anna went on, impervious, 'We believe that the higher mental functions develop through the quality of social interaction. Normal people would not understand and might act cruelly towards the weak and vulnerable.'

Piret soon developed the impersonal, professional kindness of the other women. They changed the babies when they were wet or dirty from sodden triangular rags into clean, rough ones. Under their clothes their skin was always red and broken and unevenly coloured.

They supervised the older ones and threw balls with them, or took them on short walks. The days passed, filled with the simple, tedious tasks of everyday maintenance. She was the perfect person for the job; she performed her duties and expected nothing in return.

The year passed, and sometime before winter Anna told them that milk would be rationed from then on: children under two would be allotted one half litre per week. Older children would receive nothing.

As the winter progressed their allocation of milk fell even more and most other food began to be rationed. They only received supplies of potatoes and cabbage without disruption. Piret saw how little children could live on, having nothing to compare with deprivation.

She and the other staff brought in something from their own

gardens and cellars every week or so to add to their diet: a few jars of last year's apples, a cauliflower for the soup. But no one owned a cow and the *kolhoz* had now turned into a co-operative, setting its own prices. They could not afford milk.

The following spring Anna asked Piret to her office. She told her that visitors would arrive the following week: a delegation from the Swedish government; they were touring Estonian children's' homes. Anna asked Piret if she would translate as she did not speak English.

Piret understood then that Anna knew that she spoke English, knew something of her background. She did not perhaps know the details, but Piret saw then that Anna had probably taken a personal risk by hiring her. Piret replied that she would be happy to help Anna in any way.

Anna went on to explain that she was now free to hire whom she pleased, and that she had long needed an assistant; she asked Piret if she would like the job.

Piret stared at her. She never learned the source of Anna's kindness; or discovered what brought about her decision to make Piret such an offer. She did not want to question her; she told her she would be very pleased. *Perestroika* had come into Piret's life.

They stood outside the house to welcome the delegation. A grey Volvo estate with diplomatic plates turned into the drive. Piret realized that the last time she had seen a Volvo was in 1984, in Stockholm.

Three women and a man got out of the car. One of the women was heavily made up; Anna later told Piret that she was a Swedish television actress.

Piret translated dutifully everything said to her into Estonian and translated Anna's words into English. The actress's English was rather poor, but she insisted on speaking more than the others.

They took the delegation around and showed them the single bath, the outdoor privies, the children's rooms and the kitchen. Anna told them what they needed: food, toilets and bathtubs, blankets, clothing and shoes, toys, bandages, antibiotics, powdered milk, educational materials – crayons, paper, scissors, glue.

The women all listened to this; the young man took notes. The actress kept breaking into Piret's translations. She told her how brave and dedicated they all were and how difficult it must be under these circumstances. Piret did not translate this.

She did not mind that the woman was patronizing, that her façade of concern was probably born out of boredom, and would become the material for interviews with Swedish magazines. Perhaps, Piret told herself, the woman was in her heart genuine, or had some motive, had a mentally retarded child herself or knew someone with one. Piret imagined her telling herself that she wanted 'to do something'.

But Piret knew that the actress had no idea what their life was like. There was not one woman in the home who chose the tedious, thankless job of feeding and cleaning several dozen mentally deficient children merely out of the desire to help. Their work lacked even the pride and dignity of the two teachers' positions. It was the work of women whose only alternatives were factory or farm work.

But this woman had chosen to come, to try to give something useful. Piret saw that she would help make possible a bathtub and toilets, and she was grateful to her. And, because of this woman and her delegation, she thought of Maarja for the first time without pain or without trying to persuade herself that she did not feel terrible loss and regret. She thought simply: *I hope she is happy; I hope she is safe.*

Slowly Piret's life became like others'. She began to read the newspapers as voraciously as everybody else; she stopped turning off the television when the news came on. As Anna's assistant, she began to hear gossip; every day she talked to various government offices and heard of the sporadic, yet recurring incidents: a demonstration in Riga to commemorate the anniversary of the Stalinist deportations; a proposal of economic autonomy by a group of Estonian politicians; a small, unreported demonstration in Tallinn, broken up by the police.

Then, shortly after the visit from the Swedish delegation,

came the event that everybody watched on television: through wet spring snow the Soviet flag was lowered from the top of one of the city wall towers, Tall Hermann, and the Estonian National flag was raised. The national anthem was sung, but there were few smiles. It was, the crowd knew, a dangerous act.

Everybody knew that this could begin a chain of events whose only conclusion would be the upsurge of nationalist feeling and, ultimately, the discredit of Soviet rule: once the truth of the Baltic countries' forced annexation was openly acknowledged there would be no turning back. Anything could happen: Soviet tanks, martial law, deaths.

Piret thought about Helena's parents and about her father hiding with Jaan in the forest, hearing the shot that killed Emmeline. She thought of her old indifference, her childish, reckless belief that history was mere opinion, the material of the victorious.

She thought of the demonstrators in Riga and Tallinn, some of whom had been injured. She knew that they were afraid; yet they still did this. These people risked losing their jobs and homes and tarnishing their children's futures and getting arrested. She knew that they would not be on the streets saying that their country was illegally occupied if they believed this was an aberration. They believed in the future; they believed in revolution.

Two months later Piret took a bus into Tallinn and a tram to Toompea on an errand to the ministry. Afterwards she walked around the old town and down to Raekoda plats. A few hundred people had gathered to listen to an outdoor concert in the square.

She stopped to listen and then saw a group of boys, students, perhaps two or three dozen, in student caps and carrying national flags. They poured on to the square, singing and chanting 'Freedom, freedom'.

Piret was frightened, but could not move; the crowd squeezed around her and then began to move, quickening into life. She was swept along towards the students, shoulder to shoulder with people she did not know, about to act as one.

Then everything began to happen quickly. They moved out of the square and on to the streets of the old town in a great stream, following the students. Piret could see the flags far ahead, held above the heads of the crowd. People began passing among themselves the message, 'Go to the stadium. Go to the stadium.'

As soon as she disentangled herself from the crowd, she made her way to a stop and boarded a tram, but it soon stopped when a small crowd waved the driver down with Estonian flags. The driver let the passengers off, who immediately went in the direction of the outdoor stadium, where the song festivals were held.

When Piret got home more than an hour later she turned on the television. The cameras had been taken to the stadium and already hundreds of thousands of people had gathered there. The audience stretched beyond the camera's reach; it seemed as if the entire city was there. On the stage was a well-known pop singer; everywhere were flags.

Piret and Lydia watched, hardly believing that this could happen so quickly; that so many people, holding the illegal national flags they had kept hidden at home and which once could have led to arrest, were now in one place, standing and singing national songs in a massive, spontaneous demonstration.

They sat in front of the television, unable to move. A few people in the crowd began to dance. The camera scanned the faces of old and young, amazed, hopeful faces. Two or three had tears in their eyes.

They watched all evening until they went to bed. In the morning, when they awoke, it was still going on. They watched the television as they ate breakfast; finally Piret had to leave for the day.

When she got home Lydia was sitting in front of the television, still watching. They crowd had grown. Piret could not believe it was still going on. *They will not be able to stop this, she thought. This is something even tanks cannot stop.*

She and Lydia went to bed, expecting anything in the

264

morning: martial law, declarations from Moscow, war. What did happen was not what they expected: it was still going on.

It went on for four days.

Letters and articles began to appear in the newspapers exposing the brutal truths of Stalin's rule. One about the 'doctors' plot' caught Piret's eye, a conspiracy concocted by Stalin at the end of his life against a group of Jewish doctors. They were accused of conspiring to kill Stalin at 'the behest of international Zionism'. This had followed other campaigns against 'rootless cosmopolitans', the Stalinist code word for Jew.

Piret thought about Nadja. Her father had been deported in the early 1950s, she remembered. Either he or Nadja's mother must have been Jewish, she now realized. *Oh Nadja*, she thought. *Forgive me for what I thought about you. I hope you have found happiness, wherever you are.*

Piret had felt numb for three years; now it was impossible not to feel, not to live in a kind of fervour. The possibility of war or revolution changes the texture of the air, the way bus drivers and clerks speak; normal life becomes subordinate to each day's political events. Piret, like everybody else, woke up with a hunger for news. The radio and television became an extension of her life; she needed it as she needed food and drink, no, even more. She would have given up food to know the answer to the question everybody asked every day: What is happening?

People – Estonians, Latvians, Lithuanians, Russians – did things once considered unthinkable. There were protests against Moscow's plans to establish new phosphorus mines. Nobody was arrested. There was talk of economic autonomy, of independence within a federation; nobody said, or knew, what this meant.

Gorbachev spoke of the effect on generations of living by a rule book. Piret knew what he meant: the Soviets were a people without initiative; the USSR was a country of waste and carelessness. And she knew that she was one of the old generation he spoke of; she was one of the ones that had to die before life could be renewed.

Hundreds of photographs of the national flag flying above Tall Hermann began to appear; postcards and posters of the scene were sold in bookshops and Lydia and Piret pinned one above the sofa. Students wore tee-shirts printed with the flag and the words 'Freedom for Estonia'.

Piret went into town and saw a young man on the street openly selling illegal passport covers. They were made to fit over the CCCP domestic and international passports. Imprinted on them were the words *Eesti Kodaniku Pass*: Passport, Citizen of Estonia.

About this time Piret saw an article in the newspaper about women. She was halfway through it before she realized how profoundly it disturbed her and thought to look at the author's name; it was Sylvia, Maarja's godmother.

It was, Sylvia had written, time that the truth of the condition of women under the Soviet government was revealed.

She wrote that women were disproportionately represented in dangerous industries and on night shifts throughout the USSR, despite laws against such work. Women were the majority of unskilled workers. There were virtually no women managers and no women in high-ranking party positions. Pregnant women and women on maternity leave were routinely sacked and had no defence or right of appeal.

Women's education was neglected. There were no cultural histories of women's lives and achievements. There was no contraception available; abortions approached the number of live births. Women performed three times more housework than men. Their health and their children suffered: infant mortality was above that in many Third World countries.

Women had been routinely exploited by men and were sick of it. Who could blame them for initiating the majority of divorces? Sylvia wrote, 'It is clear that the communist regime has broken down all stability in the family. Our living conditions are a direct result of the economic system we live under, creating the pressure that leads to marital and parental conflict, a low birth rate and alcoholism.'

Piret thought of the day she and Nadja saw Sylvia at the

266

public lecture hall. *The mother's upbringing of the child creates the structure of society and its values. How can we persuade women to become more feminine? The masculinization of women is threatening an entire generation of Soviet men.*

Sylvia had reversed herself and in good time. Women were once to blame for the country's ills; now she was using women's grievances to position herself as a nationalist. Sylvia was preparing for what everybody knew by then must come: independence.

The posters were everywhere, on buses and trams, in shops. Radio, television and newspapers invited all Estonians to participate, told them where to telephone for information: coaches would be arranged to the countryside, directions given to those sections of the highway where people were most needed. Lydia and Piret took a coach to Rapla, south of Tallinn.

It was 23 August 1989: the fiftieth anniversary of the Molotov–Ribbentrop Pact, in which Stalin and Hitler had agreed to the illegal occupation of Estonia, Latvia and Lithuania by the USSR.

For over fifteen minutes a human chain stretched unbroken for nearly 400 miles, from Vilnius to Riga to Tallinn. Piret and Lydia stood holding hands with neighbours and strangers, all of whom had come out to demand their freedom. For as far as they could see cars and coaches were parked alongside the road, and people, everywhere people, some singing 'Mu Isamaa', My Native Land, some listening to car radios broadcasting speeches from Parliament, some chanting 'Freedom, freedom, freedom'.

Piret held Lydia's hand on her left and the hand of a woman she had never seen before on her right. Television cameras swept by in cars and above in helicopters, and this time, unlike some previous demonstrations, faces were not hidden, people were not frightened. They stood in the summer air, on the open roads, arms stretched, hands clasped, their faces savouring the feeling of relief, of the power of their sheer presence: *We are here in our thousands and we will not go away.*

That evening Piret and Lydia saw the footage on television

267

of the thousands upon thousands of Baltic citizens holding hands, carrying flags, burning effigies of the Molotov-Ribbentrop document; it seemed as if three entire countries had stopped, as if hundreds of thousands of people could finally speak their minds: For ye shall know the truth and the truth shall set you free.

The unified passion of unarmed civilians was still a poor opponent for Soviet tanks, which attacked the television tower in Vilnus the following spring. Fourteen Lithuanians were killed, including an old woman who stood in the path of a tank and refused to move. The tank rolled over her without a pause.

Soon after granite blocks were brought to Toompea to surround and protect the Parliament building. Estonians waited for the worst, knowing that the Red Army could and would invade, as it had in Lithuania.

It was seven years since Piret had returned from Sweden to be interrogated, lose her job and flat, and go back to Lydia's. She remembered standing in the Svensk Form gallery in Stockholm, surrounded by expatriate Estonians, and seeing how little actually separated her from them. She remembered thinking of her mother's family fleeing the invading Red Army; of the thousands of refugees, frightened of communism, of losing their rights, their land, their lives; of the thousands, like Jaan and Erna, who did not flee, and who, because they were Estonian, were sent to Siberia.

And now she understood what it meant to want freedom, and to wake every day knowing it could be taken away at any moment, and that very probably nobody would do anything about it.

36

By Christmas of the following year, 1991, Piret had not seen
rice or flour for two months. The children at the *lastekodu* had
not had meat since the previous summer. Heating, electricity
and water supplies were erratic.

It took all of the staff – Anna, Piret, the witch, the teachers
and the cleaner – to cope with the children. Every day they
dressed them well, expecting the worst. They could not bathe
them as frequently as before, and had to ration clothing. The
smell became even worse, and finally they all took turns to
bring water from a nearby stream and collect wood to heat it.

Government agencies were being reorganized; Russians
were leaving the country, shredding and seizing documents.
Telephones went unanswered; nobody knew who was in
charge; supplies did not reach their destination. If it had not
been for the shipments organized by the Swedish delegation,
the children would have lived for two or three months on
boiled potatoes. This was independence.

The year had begun with exhilaration. A general referen-
dum resulted in an overwhelming majority in favour of independence, supported by Boris Yeltsin; in August the Estonian
Parliament officially confirmed that Estonia was no longer
part of the USSR.

Then came the crisis. Five hours after the parliamentary vote
Soviet tanks entered Tallinn, as they had fifty years before,
and drove along the city's streets to the television tower.

Within seven minutes the Russian soldiers had taken the
first twenty floors of the tower. The woman broadcasting
stopped speaking for a moment and then calmly announced to
her viewers, 'They are coming. I can hear Russians outside. I
will be cut – ' and the signal went dead.

But four men had barricaded themselves on to the twenty-first floor and continued to broadcast on one frequency, which everybody tuned into. Crowds gathered around the television tower and politicians arrived to negotiate. Military occupation and the reinstatement of a Russian dictatorship seemed imminent. But by the next day, it was over. The *coup* in Moscow had failed and Estonia was a free country.

It is difficult to believe in democracy and freedom when each day is the summation of dozens of minor yet exhausting struggles, when every waking hour is spent working to feed and keep warm and dry small children who are always hungry, dirty and cold. Each day Piret came home more and more depressed. Their supplies were low, and she could not take what little Lydia and she had to the *lastekodu*; there would not have been enough to distribute evenly.

One February evening she came home and Lydia handed her an official letter from the Institute of Economics at the Academy of Sciences. The letter informed her that she had been reinstated as a doctoral candidate and her academic papers would be recovered and placed in the library once more.

She read it, shook her head and handed it to Lydia. Every day she worked with three dozen children who had little more than potatoes to eat, no medicines, insufficient clothing and no hot water. She could not believe that anybody could bother with an obscure Marxist economist who once wrote about the illusion of efficiency in market economies.

Lydia read the letter and said, 'But they want to see you.'

Piret took it from her and looked again. The new director of the Institute had written by hand at the bottom that he would very much like to meet her and hoped she could visit him: perhaps the following week?

She went more out of curiosity than desire. And because Anna told her that she looked exhausted and needed a day away from the home.

She walked through cold drizzle from the bus station along

the familiar route past the market in the direction of the Estonia Theatre. Victory Square had been renamed Freedom Square and Lenin Avenue was now Reval Avenue. The Central Committee of the Estonian Communist Party was now an office building. The forecourt in front was empty; Lenin had been bound and lifted, laid on the bed of a truck and taken away.

Piret reached the Academy and walked up the same worn stone steps and down the dark halls of the Institute, remembering the day that Boris came to see her, the cigarette he had held, her bag lying between them and the photocopied document which had for ever separated them.

Piret knocked on a door and was shown into the office of a man so young and energetic that she felt like a relic. Even his handshake made her feel tired and old. She noticed that the central heating was functioning, but barely. She did not take her coat off.

'I am so pleased to meet you,' he said enthusiastically as they sat down. She nodded, wondering briefly if he had a perverse interest in minor figures from obsolete disciplines.

'I hope you are pleased with the restitution of your academic work, Professor Anvelt.'

She was startled at being addressed by her title and did not reply. Her career was over; the act was a token, for which she supposed she was to feel grateful. She did not care much, but decided to accept it graciously. 'It was very kind of you.'

'Kind, perhaps. Let me ask you quite simply: how would you feel about returning?'

She looked at him. 'Returning? To what?'

'Here. As a researcher.'

'Researching what?' Did they want a Marxist economist? She wondered if this young man had confused her with someone else.

The man smiled a little. Then he took out a folder of papers. 'Professor, let me show you a few interesting figures.'

He began handing her charts. 'Initial figures indicate that industrial production in our country has fallen by nearly forty

271

per cent since independence was first declared. Real disposable income has fallen by nearly forty per cent. The consumer price index has increased by over two hundred and fifty per cent. The average monthly wage is sixty dollars, less than half the wage level in Poland.'

She took the charts without comment. She looked at one: two simple lines, output and prices, forming a cross: the first dramatically falling, the second dramatically rising. She knew this one simple picture, two lines, hid a wealth of suffering: old people without heat, children without milk, meat once a month. She already knew this: she had seen it every day.

'Do you understand what I am telling you?'

She wanted to throw the charts in his face. 'Of course I do.'

'Do you not see that our country has to be completely rebuilt? That all new legislation has to be drafted? Property reform, currency and investment regulation? That we need every single person who can contribute?'

She was annoyed. Did this young man think she had been on a different planet these past years? 'Contribute? Do you think I have not been contributing?'

The young man paused. 'Professor Anvelt, our country has suffered severe shock on many levels. Every economic structure of the planned economy has collapsed. New market-based structures must be developed. We need economists.'

She shook her head. 'All these things are just theory to me. I studied capitalism and market economics, but I know nothing about them. Those models had nothing to do with reality. What I did was completely useless. I might be able to talk to you about income and expenditure, but it's all just so much abstraction. And, anyway, I can't remember it now; I've done hardly anything for the past seven years but grow vegetables and scrub floors and take care of mentally retarded children. I can't remember.'

'Yes, but you can remember. You were trained; you can begin again, work again, think again. You are not old; you are only thirty-six.' He took out a file and laid it on the desk. It was marked 'retired'. She was reminded of her KGB interrogator

272

and the file containing the three Swedish passports.

'I am not useful to you. I don't have the first idea what I could do.' She pointed at the file. 'See for yourself. All I knew was Marxism.'

'You were the leading specialist on market economics.'

'I can't involve myself in economics again; I don't have anything to contribute.'

'Please do not make me insult you by repeating the obvious. We cannot hope to compete on foreign markets without rebuilding our industry. We need to develop sectors which have some hope of competing on world markets. We need the help of people who understand competitive economics.'

She looked at the young man. He knew nothing about her life, about chopping firewood, taking care of her ageing great-aunt, wiping faeces and urine off children who would never mature beyond their existing level, whose only feelings were the instinctive need for human contact. She said, 'Listen to your statistics: prices rising, wages falling, production declining. I know what these things mean; I know what it means to live on far less than sixty dollars. I don't care about productivity and competitive sectors. Don't you see? I don't want to get involved in helping a new breed of capitalists make money.'

'Professor, you *are* involved. This is our country, and we are fewer than two million. Everybody counts. Are you going to sit back and complain or are you going to help create an economic system that will change the way we live? If you believe in something, this is your chance to have some influence.'

She paused. She did not know what she believed in, but this young man had offered her a job and she did not know what she felt. She did not know if she could leave Anna and the children, and yet she thought of the books in her flat and office. She remembered the years of study, her contented absorption in her work, her discussions with Boris.

'I don't know.'

'Think about it. You can come back and talk to me again. Is there anything I can do for you in the meantime?'

'Yes,' she replied. 'Can you tell me where Professor

273

Rozhansky is now? Has he returned to the university?'

'Ah.' He folded his hands and looked down. 'Professor Rozhansky.'

'What has happened?'

He took a breath. 'He is not well. Perhaps you would like to visit him?' The young man looked through a file and then wrote an address down. 'I'm sure he would appreciate seeing you.'

The following Sunday she rose and started the fire in the stove. She cooked some porridge for Lydia and left it on the stove. Then she walked to the bus stop, and from the bus station took a tram to Lasnamäe.

The tram left town along a highway bounded by rocky slopes and heaps of gravel encrusted with blackened snow. They passed a large *kauplus* perched on a hill, an enormous windowless box with a sign, *Leningradi-pood*: the Leningrad store.

Dozens of buildings appeared in rapid succession, mostly grey, with red or yellow balconies and broken, boarded doors. Outside were grey telephone booths, mostly vandalized. Piret saw a playground furnished only with a rusty yellow frame which once held swings. People walked on the pavement, bundled up, their heads down.

Piret got off the bus and began to walk. She found his building, another grey block of flats, each one with a rusty metal balcony of peeling red paint. The temperature was below freezing, but laundry hung outside many of the flats.

The lift did not work and she walked up the five flights of stairs to the flat. She knocked several times before she heard him move about.

He opened the door and stared at her. He was unshaven; she had woken him.

'I am sorry, Boris, but you have no telephone.'

He stared at her and said, 'Piret.' Then he opened the door. She stepped in. He passed his hand ineffectually over his face and through his hair. He looked older, thinner, confused. He wore an overcoat and dirty trousers. She looked away, embarrassed, and then saw the overwhelming clutter around

274

the flat; she instantly recognized the home of an unhappy, solitary male.

He cleared a chair for her to sit and went to make tea. She heard him fill the kettle and take out tea cups. She looked around and saw empty vodka bottles behind the sofa, a stack of newspapers on a chair, unwashed clothing in a corner, overflowing ashtrays, rubbish in plastic bags, a plate and fork solidified with the previous evening's meal.

When he returned, he told her he did not have a job. He would have to apply for citizenship; the criteria had not yet been established. He had been born in the Ukraine of a Russian father; his mother had been born of Estonian parents living in Russia. He did not know whether he would qualify.

He poured the tea and shrugged. He had been in Narva until a few months previously, where he had been sent to work as a clerk in a Russian library. Narva was almost completely Russian and was agitating to secede from Estonia and join Russia; upon independence he had returned to Tallinn hoping to find a job.

He began to talk incoherently about the government, about Russia and the CIS, about nuclear missiles in the Ukraine, about the Crimea. Piret sat and drank her tea, listening to him without comment.

After a while he began to make more sense. He told her about working in the Narva library. He was assigned to the history section. He told her he liked reading about Stalin. 'A great man, you know, Piret, a man with a vision ... ' He told her how he had obtained the key to the S-fond, the safe in the basement where restricted books were kept. He laughed, 'I was supposed to be there to stay out of trouble, but all I did was read subversive books.' He recited:

'The stars of death shone upon us
And innocent Russia writhed
Beneath the blood-stained jackboots
And the wheels of Black Marias ... '

She watched him as he fell silent. He looked up and said,

275

'The KGB agent who interrogated me has started a "business security" firm.' He laughed again; his voice was high and nervous. 'I saw his picture in an advertisement in the paper. "Specialists in all aspects of surveillance and protection. Guns and ammo provided."'

She tried to remain calm; her calm was a talisman that would save them.

'What will you do now?'

'I don't know. I am old, old, old.'

'You will not return to your work?'

'Even if they asked me back, what would it be like? If I, who am more or less Russian, say anything heretical?'

'You are not Russian.'

'Ah, but I have a Russian name; I was born outside Estonia.'

'You don't know what the situation is. I don't know either. We could find out. I could find out for you.'

'I know fanatics well enough.' He paused and said, 'My son –'

Piret was startled by this, the first mention of Boris's son.

'He is here, working. But he never learned Estonian very well, although now he is trying … ' Piret waited, unsure what she could say. Boris continued, 'He studied in Moscow, you know, and worked there for a few years, at a ministry.

'Now, he is – caught, I suppose. He is not Estonian, or Russian. His mother, you see, was Russian … It is very difficult for him here … The citizenship problem, you see; there will be a language test.'

Piret was silent and after a moment Boris said, 'They've asked you back?'

'Yes.'

'And?'

'Well, it was unexpected. I don't know what I think about it yet. They seem to think I can contribute something.' They were again silent.

Boris said, 'Piret, you look tired.'

She looked at him, startled. 'Yes, I suppose I am.'

'Do you want to go back?'

'I don't know; it is probably too late for me. Anyway, I don't

276

know what I believe. I know that I will never again see economics as I once did, as a theoretical game. I suppose I have become a cynic.'

'You mustn't say that. It's the new heresy. The market will solve our every problem.'

She smiled wryly, thinking of the children at the *lastekodu*, and whether the market would solve their every problem. 'Perhaps there is a balance to be found.'

'What is this? The rigorous intellectual admits the imperfections of her models? The leap of faith into the anarchy of life?' His tone was sarcastic; he was an injured animal.

Piret leaned towards her former teacher, the man she had once loved so much that there was only one person she would not hurt to save him. 'Boris, don't be bitter. We are too old to quarrel.' She hesitated, and then said what she had come to say. 'Please forgive me. I – ' She who had never wept now could hardly speak for fear of tears.

'There is nothing to forgive. You must believe that I have never despised *you* for what happened.' He hesitated. 'You could not have prevented it. It started very early.'

She looked at him. She knew what *very early* meant: it meant before she knew him. She had always known that he was watched, mistrusted. And then Piret understood; her memory returned and she could not believe that what had once seemed opaque was in fact so simple. It had started when she took Boris's Marxism class. 'It was Alexander.' *Ah, Alexander, a fine student ...*

Boris raised his eyebrows and did not reply. She knew it was true. 'He watched you. He was waiting for somebody like me to come along.'

She wondered now if she could have prevented what she had done to Boris. She had known in her heart the truth about Alexander. Each time he looked at her, she had felt before her a dangerous man. Could she have humoured him? Could she have persuaded him that she knew nothing of Boris? She could not have known that Alexander was an informer; she was too young and naïve. And Boris had not warned her outright; he was far too cautious. He had urged her to protect herself and she had left herself vulnerable.

But Boris had encouraged her; he had solicited her friendship and she was always careful to see him only at his invitation. She understood now that Boris, whom she had betrayed, had spent these years with the guilt of his own actions. He had brought her into his dangerous, observed life; Boris considered that *he* had betrayed *her*; it was she who had been harmed and he had done it.

She felt the tears in her eyes again; she had no idea what to say. With so much damage and pain between them, she could think of nothing to do. She sat, her hands folded in her lap, Boris's knees across from hers, his large hands pressed flat together.

She waited until her tears receded and she was calm enough to speak. She was frightened of losing him again, of saying the wrong thing, of creating more damage. She said, 'Boris, let me help you. Let me be your friend again.'

37

Lydia recovered from her fall. She was bruised and frightened, but had not broken any bones. Piret waited for her to heal; they both avoided the subject of the farm. Piret, however, wanted to persuade Lydia that they should buy a flat as soon as possible. Prices were for the moment low and she knew that this was unlikely to last.

She decided to go into town to look at flats, and afterwards boarded a tram to Kaarli kirik. The church was closed, but she saw that the National Library across the street had opened. She walked over and stepped inside.

A party of schoolchildren milled about in the foyer. She looked up at the high walls of brick, cold and large, heard the children's voices rising and echoing. She went through and took a small lift up to the second floor, where the economics books were kept.

On open shelves were books once kept in the S-fond, books which would have been confiscated if held by someone unauthorized, which could even have led to arrest. She wandered about the shelves and touched them, picking up a few and leafing through.

At the back was an old textbook on political economy. She picked it up and opened it at a chapter entitled, 'The Transition to Socialism'. She read, 'In the transition period in the USSR nationalization was effected in the form of total and coercive confiscation of the basic means of production, made necessary by the bourgeoisie's counter-revolutionary sabotage against Soviet power.'

She had never seen such a bald admission; then she wondered if she had simply never noticed such statements before. Perhaps she had been as blind as the Western economists she had once so despised.

She thought about the farm. The problem of the farm would not go away, she knew; it was her family's, and Lydia would pester her to do something. She could not imagine herself as a small landowner; the tainted label she had learned came indelibly to mind: *kulak*. She would wait until Lydia was well.

She wrote to the Institute and accepted a research post, beginning in September.

In the meantime she had been asked to write a report for a government ministry. It was a survey of the Estonian economy, information for foreign investors. It would, the director told her, give her a chance to 'ease into things'.

She wrote about the highly educated labour force, the low rate of unemployment, the country's natural resources, the price reforms. She knew it might be years before any of this changed anything, before it resulted in jobs, investment, houses and flats and cars. But she also knew that she would do her best.

She received a letter from Nadja, postmarked Chicago, addressed to the university and forwarded to Lydia's. Nadja wrote:

'I have thought of you over the years and have wondered how you are, whether you continued your studies. I have of course followed all the events at home and wonder what it's like to be living through it. So here I am, writing to you, hoping you will write back, and tell me what your life is like now.

'Here it is very hot in the summer and very cold in the winter, like Russia, and not at all like Estonia.

'I teach French and Russian to students in a secondary school, ages fifteen to eighteen. I find them rather stupid. They know almost no history. They have read very few of the great writers. They appear to have no sense of right or wrong. Everything is relative. Except America, which is always right, and Arabs, who are always evil. It reminds me of the "evil empire". Remember?

'I also find my students lazy and ill-mannered. They watch television every day and do not do their work. They are assigned far less work than you or I did at their age. There is an English teacher here who assigns her students essays on television films instead of on books! American society could use more discipline.

'Remember when we saw that lecture about masculinized Soviet women? We had an argument about Soviet and Western women. Well, it's completely different here from what I expected.

'American women talk about feminism all the time, but not about the things that matter. They talk about whether you can take a boy into your flat (they have their own flats!!!) and kiss him and whether this is an invitation to sex.

'And they have something called a glass ceiling, which means that women can't become managers, and they talk about how terrible this is. I find this very funny, because they don't even begin to talk about the basic things. They don't have maternity leave and they have to pay for their children's nursery.

'Now I shall stop complaining and tell you about the other things. The shopping is amazing. You can buy anything at any time. You can buy food in the middle of the night! They have machines outside shops where you can take money from the bank, any time, day or night. People have two or three cars and some Americans own airplanes! There is a wonderful store called Marshall Field, which is twice the size of Tallinna Kaubamaja and is packed with clothes and make-up and shoes, all the time.

'I have my own house and a vegetable garden the size of our entire flat in Lasnamäe. And I have a washing machine. The bad part about all the things you can buy here is that it is so easy to borrow money that you can easily go into debt.

'And the poor. It's just like the propaganda they showed us at home. It's terrible. People die of cold (like in Siberia). Some of the blacks live like the worst kind of Russians in Estonia, in filth, with no self-respect at all.

'Now I shall tell you my real news. I am getting married, to an American. He is not like other Americans, he has lived abroad and is quite sophisticated. He was a journalist for an American newspaper in London. He is now trying to learn Russian. I never laugh at him when he is trying to speak.

'I do not think I will ever come back. My step-father writes to me sometimes. I want him to come here to live. He says he does not want to start again, but I will try to persuade him.

'I hope you are well and that you will one day visit me in America. The land of the free, like you now! By the time you come I will be an American. I have applied for citizenship.

'I send you my love.'

She signed her name 'Nadia'.

Piret visited Boris's flat in Lasnamäe every third or fourth day, despite his protests. She emptied the ashtrays and threw out the vodka bottles. She washed his clothes and scrubbed the floors.

'You are not a maid,' he growled. 'Let me rot in my own rubbish. I will do things in my own time.'

Piret ignored him and continued to work. She cleaned with all her heart, for her dead father, whom she had never helped, who had cleared away the vodka bottles and newspapers and wiped the table with a dirty rag to win her back. And she cleaned for Boris and herself, who both needed absolution to begin again.

When he protested too much, she did not explain herself but merely replied, 'I am good at this; I have learned how to clean.'

In the spring he came to visit her. They sat on the back steps of the house after dinner; Lydia had insisted on washing up herself.

The last light glittered across the lake and on the tall pines on the opposite shore. They each held a glass of berry wine. As they drank, the shadows across the trees deepened and the temperature fell slightly. Piret thought of fetching a cardigan, but did not move.

They drank the wine. Boris had eaten little at dinner. The day's stubble on his face was grey. The top of his head was almost bald; above his forehead grew a persistent patch of wispy long hairs which he pushed back from time to time.

Piret looked at his hands and his chin, which had begun to sag a bit. She had never seen his body, nor had he hers, but she felt that she knew every inch of him. She knew his arms and the way he held a pen; she knew what made his eyes become animated. She knew his voice and how he tapped the fingers of one hand against the back of the other to ward off the desire for a cigarette.

The last light died quickly and night fell over them like a blanket of ash. Piret could not make out the boundary between the lake and the shore. The fruit grove was a black thicket. She picked up the empty glasses, rose and went into the house. After a moment Boris followed her in and thanked Lydia for dinner before he left.

Over the summer Boris and Piret began to talk again. They did not talk about the past, about what had happened. Piret did not know how to tell him about Maarja. It was economics, of course, that started the process of healing: their language.

They talked about the IMF and about Russia. They pretended to argue about policies, politicians, the future of Europe. They read newspapers and discussed the day's events. They began to be happy.

One day Boris said, 'Piret, you always had a taste for the fanatical.'

She hesitated and then affected to be offended. 'I had a taste for the elegance and simplicity of theory.'

Boris smiled. 'Theory is always fanatical. You did not like the unpredictability of real life.'

Piret considered the unpredictability of her own life, the small acts that had reverberated so decisively; these were too whimsical to fit into a historical process: Paavo, Maarja. She said, 'And you did?'

'Of course. I always knew the system would break down. I suspected I would not live to see it do so.'

'Why were you so certain?'

'Oh, the cost of controlling so many people. People will not tolerate economic deprivation and dictatorship willingly. It takes a police state.'

Piret was silent, knowing he was right. She and every other working Soviet citizen had accepted the bargain they were offered – social and job security in exchange for limited freedom and basic living standards – because they had no choice. Piret remembered her airy dismissal of Nadia's complaints: *that was Stalin*. She had not wanted to see how they still lived in the shadow of Stalin's terror.

'And, of course, this constant question of reform. They knew they could not finance the military without it. But they did not see that liberalizing the economy could never coexist with political control.'

Piret remembered having once said, 'Our systems are completely separate and will never mix.' Yet she had assumed the country would simply muddle along, loosening up here and there. She never thought it would collapse. Boris's age gave him perspective; he could see the ebb and flow of history. 'What did you think would replace it?'

He shrugged. 'Capitalism. What else? But I am not surprised that there is so much resistance to a market economy. People are steeped in the idea that capitalism is equated with indifference to human frailty.'

'And they are right,' Piret pointed out with a hint of her former self-assurance. 'The free market works against individual rights.'

'Yes, yes.' He waved his hand impatiently, and Piret smiled at this, a brief glimpse of the old Boris. 'But without a free market there can be no freedom.'

'Ah, but how free? This is the question we must decide.'

'We? You and I are scientists, Piret. Economics is only a tool to analyse choices; there are no answers when it comes to social policy. That is politics.' He waved his hand again, dismissively, and Piret felt that something had turned for them: they could argue again; they would recover.

She went on, calm, emphatic: 'No, Boris. Economic theory is run through with value judgements, with assumptions about what is worth keeping and what isn't. And it is about power, about the struggle between those who have and those who do not.'

But Piret was wrong; Boris sighed and fell silent, as if he could not bear any disagreement between them. Piret saw that they needed more time. He said, a bit sadly, 'You are a philosopher, Piret. I will always be a simple economist.'

November was rainy and grey. Piret had found a flat, which they could have in January. Lydia was not pleased, but she had agreed to move. Piret had begun teaching one class: welfare economics, at the Polytechnic. 'Until you are feeling on your feet again,' the department head said. She was grateful for the free time; she had much to do before moving, and also spent one or two days each week helping at the *lastekodu*. What time she had left she spent reading economics papers.

On Saturday the rain let up and Lydia went down the road to buy milk. Piret took some laundry down to the sauna. She had bought the washing machine with her first wages from the university. Both women adored this machine. The first time they used it they sat in the sauna dressing room for an entire wash cycle, watching the clothes swish back and forth through the glass porthole.

Piret took the wet laundry out, hung it on the line strung across the three sauna rooms, and put in another load.

She came up to the house and took her shoes off, wondering what she should cook for lunch. She saw a girl walk down the path. Piret wondered vaguely what she was doing. Perhaps she was lost or looking for the village. Then Piret saw that she was foreign; her coat was expensive and she was carrying a large canvas and leather bag. Piret stood at the door, watching her. The girl approached and put her bag down. Piret nodded and said, 'Hello.'

She was Piret's height, with a thin, angular face, and large brown eyes. Piret felt an uncomfortable prickling at the back of her neck. Instinctively she stepped back into the house and put her hand on the door. The girl said in Estonian, 'My name is Maarja Reisman.'

Piret felt complete, pure, absolute panic. She stared at the girl, speechless. Maarja stepped forward and put out her hand to prevent Piret from closing the door. 'Are you Piret Anvelt?'

Piret wanted to deny who she was; she saw in an instant that what little peace she had made for herself was now about to evaporate. She was frightened. She blurted out, 'You cannot come here.'

Maarja held the door, and did not move away. 'Please. I have come all the way from Stockholm.'

Piret paused, looking at her, terrified at the thought of what Helena might think. 'Does your mother know you're here?'

Maarja looked shaken now, confused by Piret's reaction. Her face was lined with anxiety, and she pleaded, 'No. Please let me in. Please. I'm pregnant.'

38

Helena arrived two days later.

They sat around the table in Lydia's tiny house, quiet and polite. They had eaten a meal and now drank coffee. Piret could feel Lydia looking at her as she watched this beautiful unhappy girl, her daughter.

Piret glanced at Helena, who drank her coffee in silence. She was obviously anxious, but remained calm; Helena, Piret saw, was an experienced parent. She remembered her cousin as a girl, and then thought of the fear and shock on her face that day at the exhibition in Stockholm. *Poor Helena*, Piret thought now; she had lived through so much fear for Maarja, and now this.

Helena and Piret exchanged brief summaries of their present lives and polite questions about their respective jobs and then fell silent. Maarja had not dared to look at Helena throughout the meal.

Finally Helena said, 'Maarja, I think it's best if we go home tomorrow. We have to decide what you will do.' Maarja nodded and Helena continued, 'Piret, this must have been a terrible shock for you. I'm sorry.'

She did not reply, and Maarja said defiantly, 'Mother, please don't apologize on my behalf; I am not sorry that I came.' Piret looked at Maarja, startled by this show of confidence.

Helena was annoyed. 'Well, then; why did you come?'

Maarja said, 'I had to, don't you understand? I had to. You don't understand.'

'No, *you* don't understand. It's a very long and complicated story.'

'I know. Vanaema told me everything.'

Helena's face was tight. 'Yes, I realize that.'

Piret said, 'Helena – '

Helena said, 'Piret, please, just answer one question: did you know I would be there, at that exhibition?'

'No, Helena, of course not.'

She sighed. 'I'm sorry then that I asked you. I did not think so. Well, I did at first, I admit. But later, I heard what happened to you, losing your job and everything, I knew you couldn't have done it deliberately. I was rather stupid. I'm sorry.'

Piret said, 'We have all done and thought things we wish we hadn't.'

Helena said, 'How did they find out about Maarja?'

Neither Lydia nor Piret spoke and Helena prompted, 'Well? Do you know?'

Piret hesitated. 'I don't know.'

Helena said, 'Was it Sylvia?'

'Sylvia?' Maarja looked confused. Then her face cleared as she remembered: her godmother. She looked at Helena and then at Piret, who said to Maarja, 'She's a minister in the new government.'

Helena said, 'My mother thought it was Sylvia. We'd always known that she was a party member. But my father trusted her. I'm afraid he was very naïve. We should have been more careful of Sylvia. We never thought she would betray us.'

Piret asked, 'How do you know?'

'Well, I'm not completely certain. But we called her, when we were in Estonia, when they took our passports away. She kept saying, "This has nothing to do with me." She wouldn't help us.

'Perhaps the whole thing was set up from the start,' Helena continued. 'Why else did we wait all that time after we applied to emigrate, and then as soon as Maarja was born we got the visas?'

'You got them', Lydia said suddenly, 'because Erna's father was a German.' Helena and Piret both looked at Lydia. She went on, 'He had a German passport; Erna was a German citizen.'

Lydia paused. 'Well, it was more complicated than that.

They didn't have to let Helena and Peeter go. It is true that they got the visas shortly after Maarja was born.'

Maarja looked confused, 'But why then did they let my parents go as well?'

Piret said vaguely, 'To have people abroad with some vulnerability perhaps – it comes in handy.' She did not quite believe this; it was too implausible.

'How could they possibly know that we would be useful?' Maarja persisted.

Helena warmed to Piret's theory: 'They probably didn't. But it was their business to keep tabs on people, to have educated people abroad who could be used for various purposes. Probably it was only when they wanted Peeter to plant that story that they decided to use Piret.'

'And Sylvia was a part of that from the beginning?' Maarja said.

Piret said, 'Don't be too quick to judge her; we have all made compromises.'

Helena looked slightly shocked at Piret's generosity. Piret had, after all, refused to collaborate with the KGB. Helena did not know, of course, about her denunciation of Boris, and Piret did not want to tell her. Helena thought that Peeter's article was the entire story and Piret saw no reason to explain to her that it was a mere extra to them; it simply fitted neatly into a larger plan. She did not want to demean Peeter's actions in her eyes; he had acted, as they all had, to save Maarja.

Only Maarja asked about her father. Helena had not dared to bring up the subject.

Piret said, 'I can give you his name if you like. I do not want to see him; it is your choice whether you do.'

'Is there any reason why I shouldn't?'

Piret said simply, 'I want no contact with him.'

Maarja thought for a moment. 'Well, I guess I can think about it. I have enough new relatives for the moment.'

Lydia rose to clear the table and Piret went to help her, leaving Helena and Maarja alone. Piret thought: *Will any of us dare to ask Maarja about the father of her baby?* She would not. She could hear nothing from the kitchen, and when she returned, Helena and Maarja still sat in silence.

Helena said, 'Piret, I am sorry.'

Piret knew that Helena meant she was sorry for everything; Piret did not know what to say in return. A heavy silence settled between them. Then Helena said, 'Maarja, are you sure you want to have this baby?'

Maarja looked at her. 'I think so. I'm not completely sure.'

Tears rose in Helena's eyes as she watched Maarja's face.

'Oh, Mama, what shall I do?'

Helena said, 'I can't tell you. I – oh Maarja, what we did was wrong, to take you from Piret. I wanted you so badly, but it was wrong. I thought it was the right thing, but you see Piret had nothing and we had everything. We thought we could do whatever we wanted.

'I can't tell you now what to do. I will help you if you have this baby, but I will be heartbroken to see you saddled so young with a child. Oh Maarja, you will understand one day what it means to want everything for your child. I wanted you to study and travel.' She began to cry. 'Now you will have a baby and your life will be over.'

Then Helena wiped her face and said, 'I don't know if that is true. Your life may be better because of the baby. Maarja, this is your baby. I always wanted a baby and perhaps part of me aches that you are pregnant. I cannot tell you what to do. I cannot.'

Maarja also began to cry. 'I am so stupid.'

Her mother reached over and touched her daughter's hand: 'No, no darling.'

'Yes, I am. I don't know why I did it. I was, I don't know, I wanted to – ' Maarja stopped.

'I did many stupid things as a girl, Maarja,' Helena said calmly. 'This is not the worst thing you could have done. It's a very normal thing, it's not even a bad thing. We have all done things much, much worse than having a baby. We have all made mistakes.'

That, of course, was one thing they all knew.

Epilogue 1993

We drive up the unpaved road Lydia has not seen in nearly forty-five years. Lydia says, 'The hen house has gone.'

We turn at the top of the road towards the house. I stop the car. I would not know about the hen house, of course. I see a house, well built, two storeys, neither large nor small. Beyond is a ramshackle barn inside which I can see dilapidated farm machinery. Out in a field I see a workhorse grazing.

Lydia is looking at the barn. 'The foundations are seventeenth century.'

Across a small meadow are rows of vegetables and a hut for tools. Just beyond is a barbed-wire fence and then fields.

'How far does it go?' I ask Lydia.

'See the line of trees?' She points. 'That is where the stream turns. Beyond is another field about the size of this one here. I suppose it's over a hundred hectares. Big enough to support a family.'

She stops. 'We used to play in the forest.' She points to the porch on the side of the house. 'That's where Oskar found Emmeline, shot dead. She had been giving food to the Forest Brothers.'

We open the door; the house is nearly empty, scattered with sacks of feed. Lydia shows me the room she slept in, her sisters' rooms, her parents' room. We see the kitchen, which still has its wood-burning stove, but the chimney has collapsed. She shows me a larder, where my father slept in the winter. In the summer he slept in the barn.

One of the questions of our family's story has been answered: it was Oskar, my father, who told the KGB of Maarja's parentage. My father, who had been made to sleep in a barn and was never educated beyond the age of twelve, who drank and worked as little as possible, was interrogated and offered a better job, a chance at starting life anew.

I know because I obtained his file and mine from the KGB archives in the building on Bagari Street, where I was interrogated. I do not know the circumstances of the interrogation, but I can deduce from the transcript that they flattered him, probably encouraged him with vodka, told him he had never had a chance in life, that he deserved better:

Q: Did your cousin tell you he was planning to emigrate?

A: Well, no.

Q: You did not want to go with them?

A: No. They wouldn't want me anyway.

Q: Now why is that?

No reply.

Q: He never thought much of you, your cousin the doctor. He had everything, didn't he? He did whatever he wanted; he told you what to do. He never asked what you thought, did he?

No reply.

Q: And his daughter, she got whatever she wanted didn't she? Not like your daughter.

A: It's all right now.

Q: It's all right?

A: She's come out all right.

Q: After what happened?

A: You know about it then.

Q: Why else would your daughter leave school and move to your aunt's house?

A: It was Jaan's idea. He delivered her.

292

Q: And did he decide what to do with her?

A: He wanted Helena to have her.

Q: No one asked you or the father?

A: The father. The father, he disappeared. Screwed her and disappeared.

Q: Such people should be disciplined. Your daughter was quite young.

A: What does it matter now?

Q: It would be a shame to let such a matter stand in the way of your advancement. I can imagine your name on the Book of Honours. Last year the workers chosen for the Book were awarded vouchers towards a car.

A: I don't remember. Just some boy. Paavo, maybe. I don't remember his surname. It was a long time ago. Piret never told me much. He went to her school, maybe. His father was a tram mechanic, something like that. I remember that.

There is only one other fragment of my father's life I should add. When I showed Lydia the transcripts, she told me the story of Jaan's deportation after Emmeline's death; he was fifteen and my father was thirteen.

Jaan heard the shot that killed his mother and persuaded Oskar to remain hidden. Then he came out from the forest and gave himself up, hoping to divert them, to give my father a chance. And, my father was never found, never deported. Perhaps this explains something of Oskar's miserable life, of his terrible self-loathing and guilt, of his relationship with his cousin Jaan and, perhaps, of Jaan's attempt on that day in the forest to compensate Oskar for what Emmeline had made him suffer.

The story of these two cousins is over now; they are dead. I have decided to think about it no longer. We – Helena, Matti and I – have filed a joint claim on the farm, although we have not decided what to do with it. Hanno and Lennart, Matti's sons, do not want to leave Tallinn; I cannot run a farm, work and look after Lydia. Helena and Karl certainly do not intend to leave Sweden. And, of course, Maarja will be living in Stockholm with a baby to take care of. What seems important at the moment is to decide together, as a family. We will probably lease the fields out, and come to a decision about the house and forest later.

Helena and I will become grandmothers in May. I do not know what it feels like to be a mother; I will instead learn what it feels like to be a grandmother. I wonder if I will love this child without the terrible, corrupt reserve I have spent my life acquiring; the idea slightly frightens me.

Boris comes to visit often now that Lydia and I have moved. Lydia complains that she feels cooped up, although the flat is larger than the old house. She does the shopping and cooking while I am at the Institute. She takes her baskets and walks down the boulevard, just like a country woman. People look at her. She refuses to take the tram. She says she needs her exercise.

My feelings for Boris are still dominated by my old reverence and admiration; as he pointed out, our relationship will never be equal. But I am also on occasion impertinent. I see him with perspective now: a man whose definition of intellectual discipline means defiance of the official line, whatever that may be, a man who believes in science, in a random order, in conflict. He consigns social imbalances to a category of exceptions which can be cured with money.

He is also, something I never saw before, a man who needs someone to care for him. I expect he and I will always be together, in our own awkward, stoic way. It is a strange way to love someone; but it is our way.

I have bought a colour television, which Lydia and I love as ardently as the washing machine. We even watch it during dinner. Boris comes in the evening. He sits on the sofa, I sit next to him and Lydia has her own armchair. One night, after Lydia had gone to bed, I rose to bring us each a glass of wine. We were watching *Gone with the Wind*, from a Helsinki channel.

When I returned I sat down again, but close to him. Our

shoulders touched. I remember looking at him as he watched the television. I could sense his tension from my proximity, but I did not move. I looked at him watching the film. His skin is very white. He is old, but his skin is still quite smooth.

I brought my legs up and lay my head on his shoulder and continued to watch the television. After a while he patted me on my knee, awkwardly. I took his hand and held it. He tried to take it away, but I held on. After a while he gave up.

Boris has returned to the Polytechnic, now renamed the University of Tallinn. He was not welcomed back by all. Russians are feared and hated, and although Boris is not Russian and is in fact an Estonian citizen, he is not Estonian enough for some. What will happen I cannot know, of course. The Russians have been part of our history for a long time. Will we find a way to live as tiny neighbours to this vast and unstable country? I am a cynic; I know that our continued independence will depend on the whims and interests of the powerful.

Maarja is still working. She has taken leave of absence from the university. She knows that Helena and I and Erna will do what we can to help her continue to study. We all know that a woman without education will live in hardship, without hope or dignity.

Helena has written to me twice. She told me about Maarja's friend Anton, who may or may not be the father of her baby; Maarja has not told Helena and Helena has not asked. Helena thinks he is in love with her but Maarja has kept him at a distance. She told Helena that she doesn't want to make any decisions about her life until she has had the baby.

Helena wrote, 'But I do hope she doesn't wait too long. I feel that I kept love out of my life for too many years.' I am glad for Helena that she now has her Karl and that they are happy. For the first time in my life I can say that I am fond of my cousin.

What can I do to help Maarja, my daughter? I have my job and my education; I have the flat. So I have a home for Maarja and her baby to visit if she wants. Will she want this baby to feel Estonian, to know us? I think so.

I think of Nadia sometimes in America. Nadezhda means hope. *I could never tell you how much I love you. I who was such a wild and angry one and never learned to weep simple tears – now I weep and weep and weep.*

I weep for how much we have all lost, and for what my country has suffered. We have been all damaged. Some things will never heal.

Nadia will only return for visits. I try to picture her, with her job teaching American teenagers and her American home. I try to imagine her furniture and appliances, a man who looks like the cowboys and astronauts on cinema posters, and I know that I cannot understand her new life.

Maarja will never live here. She is too Swedish, too used to another way. As I am too used to my way and Helena to hers; we will never leave our homes.

But perhaps we can be a family. Neither Helena nor I chose what we did. Our lives, and Maarja's, were decided by Helena's father. The damage that was done to us as women can never be undone.

I pray, as I did twenty years ago, that Maarja and her child will never be demeaned or belittled. I hope that she and her baby will never be used as cheap labour or reproductive fodder. I hope that Maarja will always be able to speak, will never be silent and obedient.

After the baby is born, Maarja will return to christen her baby at Jaani kirik, where she herself was christened. This was her choice.

We will all be there: Helena and Karl and Erna; Peeter and his wife Lucia and their son Paolo; Matti and Maret and Hanno and Lennart; Boris and his son Andres, Lydia and me, Maarja's mother.

Afterwards we will go to Matti's, where we will have *pirukas*, *sült*, black bread, smoked herring, potatoes, a ham, vodka and berry wine. It will be a traditional Estonian christening.